The Future King

ROBYN SCHNEIDER

VIKING

VIKING
An imprint of Penguin Random House LLC, New York

First published in the United States of America by Viking,
an imprint of Penguin Random House LLC, 2023

Visit us online at penguinrandomhouse.com.

Library of Congress Cataloging-in-Publication Data is available.

Printed in the USA

ISBN 9780593351055 (hardcover)

ISBN 9780593528921 (international edition)

1st Printing

LSCH

Design by Opal Roengchai
Text set in Garamond MT Std

For every reader searching for pieces of themselves in books.
I hope you find what you're looking for in this one.

Prologue

Morgana le Fay staggered onto the shore of an unfamiliar world, her boots sinking into bone-colored sand. Moments ago, she had been falling, not just in darkness, but in nothingness itself. And now she was here, in Anwen, the world beyond the stones. A world of endless possibility.

She'd thought traveling through the stones would be like walking through a doorway, something you *did*. But it felt more like the doorway had walked through *her*. Dark spots danced in her vision, and she braced her hand against a stone column, fighting back a wave of dizziness. When the world stopped spinning, she looked around.

She was at the edge of a forest, on a strip of narrow sand jutting into a dark and restless sea. A pale stone arch, identical to the one she had traveled through, stood tall and still, no longer swirling with the magic that had brought her here.

The night sky was salted with hundreds of stars, all in strange new constellations, but the stars were nothing compared to the forest. It hummed and vibrated with life—and with magic. She could practically taste it in the air, tart and sweet on her tongue, like winter cherries.

Ivory trees with black leaves stood tall and primordial, their branches beckoning. The leaves covered the forest floor in deep piles, as though it was autumn here, even though it had been summer back in London.

Her hands were still stained with Arthur's blood. Only minutes had passed since their fight beneath St. Paul's. Somewhere in another world, the prince of Camelot was dying. Or perhaps already dead.

She wiped her palms against her skirts, the damp sand sucking at her boots as she made her way toward the forest. Her breath came in clouds against the night air, and she shivered from the cold. "*Hætu,*" she demanded, envisioning the warmth that would cover her like a coat, but no magic rose up to meet the command.

Why isn't it working?

When her naive half brother had pressed Excalibur to her throat, she'd thought she was through. But he had hesitated, and she had seized the moment for herself.

Where he was weakness, she was strength. All she had needed was a dagger and some nerve, and she had gotten exactly what she wanted.

Anwen was real. Everything she'd dreamed of as a young girl at the convent, after she'd stopped dreaming her mother would come back for her, lay at her feet for the taking.

"*Calor,*" she insisted, a variation on the same warming spell. But the power to shield herself from the icy winds was nowhere to be found.

All around her, Anwen pulsed with magic, yet her own lay dormant. She tried again, and again, calling for a flame, a spark, a pebble to change into flint, but nothing happened.

No matter how many ways she summoned it, her magic wouldn't come.

Chapter 1

Emry Merlin hurried through the dark London streets, cursing her good-for-nothing brother. Of course he'd pick a night like this to cause trouble. What had started as a tentative drizzle was now an enthusiastic downpour, and Emry shivered beneath her wet cloak as she squelched her way down the Strand.

Half an hour ago, she'd been lying in bed reading a novel about love-crossed pirates. Then a castle guard had knocked on her door, concerned that Emmett still hadn't returned from the tavern.

"I think somethin's wrong," Tristan had told her. "He had this tortured look, like he was goin' off to do something reckless. But reckless shouldn't take four hours."

"No, it shouldn't." Emry had lowered her book and considered the young, frowning guard with a sigh. "Do you know which tavern?"

"He said he was headed to the Tipsy Merchant."

She knew it, but only by reputation. The tavern was a haunt of the city's rougher types: petty criminals, laborers spoiling for a fight, and the occasional guard when they had coin to lose, and when they didn't, but couldn't help gambling anyway.

"I'm going after him."

Tristan had blanched. "By yourself?"

"I'm a wizard."

"But you're also a lady, and it 'ent safe, down that way, late at night."

Emry had assured him that she'd take precautions. *And I have*, she thought. Under her sodden cloak, she wore a boy's tunic and hose. Her dark hair, which fell just below her chin these days, was tucked beneath a hat. It was a hasty disguise, and one that wouldn't hold up on close inspection, but still. It was better than traipsing through the city—not to mention the mud—in skirts.

As she walked, she considered creative ways to torment her brother if it turned out nothing was actually the matter. Death by a thousand parchment cuts was currently winning. Honestly, there was mud inside her boots.

Emry drew her cloak tighter around her shoulders as a gust of cold air cut through the wet fabric. Between the late hour and the rain, London's streets were empty. The merchants' shops were boarded up for the night, and not even the vendors were out with their carts and wares.

Even though she'd lived at the castle as herself for more than a month now, there hadn't been many opportunities to venture beyond its walls. The city still felt new to her, a living thing full of dangerous turns and secrets tucked into the shadows. But dangerous and secret were two things that had never intimidated her, and she wasn't going to let them start now.

Especially since Tristan had called her a *lady*. She wasn't anything like the fashionable court ladies in their low-cut gowns who made pleasant conversation about the weather. But that's what she got for being the sole female apprentice at Castle Camelot, training to be the prince's own court wizard.

Meanwhile, Emmett had settled in easily, strutting the corridors in his courtier's finest, nodding hello to every lad his age, and not bothering to magic away the telltale ladies' perfume that often clung to his jacket.

He had never needed to pretend to be anyone other than who he was—the great wizard Merlin's son and rightful heir. It was his unshakable confidence that so often led him to trouble. And it was Emry who so often got him out of it.

Yet she was the one the king had placed on probation.

Her cheeks burned with resentment when she thought about it. How King Uther had summoned her to his apartments two days after she and Arthur had nearly died at the hands of Morgana le Fay. The king's icy glare as he'd accused her of encouraging Arthur to seek out life-threatening danger. "Since you share your father's talent for magic, you may remain an apprentice, for now," the king had allowed, his eyes dark with malice. "But give me a reason, and you're gone."

She had gritted her teeth and mumbled that she understood, even though what she really understood was that she still hadn't proven herself, despite everything she'd done.

"Remember your place, girl," Uther had warned as she sank into a curtsey. "And stay the hell away from my son."

So, she'd avoided Arthur in the corridors, pretending she didn't see his hurt and confusion when she accidentally met his gaze across the Great Hall. Pretending it didn't hurt her as well. Because she would do anything to keep studying magic.

And that included marching halfway across London to either rescue or drill some sense into her foolish brother. If Emmett got himself dismissed from his apprenticeship, she worried the king would send her away, too. There was no way King Uther would commit to the next court wizard being a woman.

The Tipsy Merchant was down by the docks, in a rough-and-tumble part of the city where the half-timbered houses were pressed so tightly together and tilted so precariously forward with their oversize upper stories that the slender streets resembled tunnels.

The tavern's roof was in desperate need of thatch, and the windowless exterior was more wattle-and-daub than wood. She paused on the front steps, cracking the tension from her neck as she gathered her magic and pushed back her hood.

Extergio.

The unspoken spell released with an elegant snap. Emry held back a grin as her formerly sodden cloak flowed warm and dry from her shoulders, and the mud melted from her boots.

Much better. She took a steadying breath and pushed open the door.

It was a low-ceilinged place, noisy and dim, with cloaked patrons hunched over their cups and their dice and their business. She'd been right about the roof needing repairs. A couple of ceramic pots had been placed under the worst leaks, and rainwater dripped into—ugh, she really hoped those weren't *used* chamber pots.

She edged past one with distaste. The tavern stank of sweat and damp wool and spilled ale. Dice clattered against a battered wooden table, and a burly man in an oilskin cloak let out a foul curse as his opponent scooped up a pile of winnings.

Definitely not one of her brother's usual haunts. But he'd gotten banned from enough respectable taverns that it was only a matter of time before he tried a dodgy place like this. Emmett had an unfortunate habit of making cards and dice change to his favor more often than was plausible.

Emry spotted him immediately. He sat alone in a small booth, hunched over a table littered with empty mugs of ale, hair hanging in his face. At least he wasn't bleeding, which was a relief. And he still had his clothes on. He was wearing his new jacket, a fine blue velvet with silver buttons and fur trim. He should have known better. No, he did know better. But he never thought that rules applied to him, and he clearly hadn't started today.

"You're the worst," Emry grumbled, sliding into the booth. "I hope you know that."

Her brother merely gave her a tired smile, his chin propped in one hand. "I do love a good lecture," he slurred. "Go on, then."

Emry rolled her eyes. "What's the point? You've never listened to me before."

"That is entirely untrue," Emmett protested. "I listened when you said parting my hair down the middle made my eyebrows look uneven."

"Not what I meant." Emry shot her brother a glare.

Emmett shrugged. "Still counts." He lifted his mug and took such an enormous gulp of ale that Emry suspected he was trying to quench something deeper than his thirst.

"I'm probably going to regret asking, but why exactly are you—"

"Guinevere said we shouldn't see each other anymore," he blurted miserably.

So, that was the problem. She'd wondered when their foolish fling was going to end.

"Well, you shouldn't," Emry said. "She's engaged."

"To Arthur." Emmett waved off the crown prince as though he were merely an annoyance. "But I don't see that making a difference to you."

"Of course it does. Why do you think I'm keeping my distance?"

"You are?" Emmett frowned. "I thought you'd just gotten really good at sneaking."

Emry fought to keep her voice steady as she said, "I'm his wizard, and that's all." That was all she ever could be. Even though it was hard. Especially because it was hard. Anything more would only make her feel smashed into a million pieces when it ended. Which it inevitably would, because apprentice wizards didn't wind up with royals. Because—*oh*.

She bit her lip, staring across the table at Emmett, her twin in more ways than she could count. No wonder he'd parked himself here, at this disreputable tavern, sinking deeper into his cups as he delayed his return to the castle.

"I'm sorry about Guinevere," she said softly. "You'll find someone else. You always do."

"Not this time." Emmett stared down at his empty mug of ale, considering it with a sad smile before adding it to the collection. "Is it supposed to hurt like this?"

"Being incredibly annoying? I wouldn't know."

"Having your heart torn to shreds by the most flawless woman to ever live."

Emry snorted. "She's hardly flawless. Her lips move when she reads. And she's overly obsessed with her hair."

"Hey!" Emmett looked betrayed.

"It was never going to last."

"Still." He sighed, looking lost. "I'd hoped."

"And I'd hoped you'd learned to stay out of trouble by now."

"You didn't have to come," Emmett said.

"Of course I did." Emry sighed, hating that she had to spell it out. "If you get dismissed from the castle, do you think the king will let *me* stay?"

Emmett looked taken aback, as though this was the first time he'd considered that his foolish actions might have consequences for anyone besides himself.

Emry glanced around the tavern and noticed a table of dockworkers glaring at them. Four nasty-looking brutes, each of them big enough to grip a broadsword one-handed, and strong enough to make it look easy. The largest one cracked his knuckles without breaking eye contact, and another bared his teeth and drew his rough-spun cloak aside, flashing a sharpened blade.

Emry swallowed nervously. Tristan's alarm that she would march into the Tipsy Merchant by herself, not knowing what trouble her brother was in, seemed slightly less unwarranted now.

"Friends of yours?" she asked.

Emmett shifted guiltily. "They seemed all right before I won their purses at cards."

"You didn't." Emry groaned.

Emmett's face scrunched. "They're waiting to follow me out. I've been desperate to piss for an hour, but haven't dared. Those chamber pots on the floor are absolute torture."

Emry drummed her fingers against the table, trying to think. "How's your magic holding up?"

"It's not."

She'd figured as much. "Don't suppose you've got a knife?"

Emmett had the good sense to look embarrassed as he confessed, "It ruined the lines of my jacket."

Unarmed, drunk, and out of magic. Not to mention dressed like his pockets were lined with gold. What a mess. Emry sighed.

"This is the last time," she grumbled, glancing around for something that could cause a commotion. And then she spotted the casks of ale behind the bar. A dozen of them, stacked nearly to the ceiling. Perfect.

Transigo, she urged.

Six enormous casks of ale burst open, spraying fountains of amber liquid across the tavern. The place quickly descended into chaos. Men rushed forward, mugs held aloft, shoving each other out of the way, and swinging angry punches at anyone who shoved them back. The barkeep shouted in protest, scrambling for rags that he could use to plug the holes.

Emry admired the melee for a moment before turning to her brother with a grin.

"Exit stage left," she said grandly, grabbing her brother's arm and dragging him from the tavern.

The air still smelled of rain, but the downpour had stopped. Hopefully it would hold until they got back to the castle.

"Come on," she snapped, squelching down the alley.

But Emmett didn't follow. Instead, he ducked down a narrow footpath, stopping outside a bricked-up window and fumbling with his trousers.

"What are you d—" Emry started to ask, as her brother began pissing against the wall with a dramatic sigh of relief. "Ew, Emmett!"

"I told you I was desperate!" he protested. "Don't watch!"

"Wasn't going to!"

Emry stomped around the corner, grumbling. "Hurry up," she complained, only to be met by a long, ominous stretch of silence. "Emmett?" she called, with growing concern. But her brother didn't answer.

She marched back toward the tavern to check what was going on. And then a rough hand snaked out of a shadowed alcove, catching her around the throat.

"Goin' somewhere?" her captor growled, the tip of his dagger sharp against her side.

She swallowed down a scream, her heart hammering, as the man's fingers pressed bruises into her neck.

"Not anymore," she said in her best boyish tones.

It was the menacing dockworker who'd flashed his knife at her. And his companions had her brother. The bald one held Emmett's arms behind his back, and the thickset one had a blade at Emmett's throat. The third, a wiry, brown-skinned lad who couldn't have been older than sixteen, stood lookout.

Sard. So her distraction *hadn't* worked.

"We don't appreciate bein' cheated," growled the bald one.

"How exactly did I cheat?" Emmett retorted. "Magic?"

"Shut yer smart mouth." The man landed a blow to Emmett's jaw that had him spitting blood.

Emry winced. At least it had been a fist and not a knife.

Her captor seemed to be the leader, since the rest kept looking to him for approval. All of them were armed and angry and drunk enough to think a knife fight in an alley was a good idea. Her brother's magic was spent, and they didn't have a weapon between them except her magic.

Which meant she'd have to get creative. And she hated to get creative.

"Stealin's a terrible crime," said the leader. "At sea, a man would lose a finger. As would any who helped him."

He grabbed Emry's hand and pressed his dagger across her knuckles, drawing a thin line of blood. She hissed in pain.

"Well, well," he said, breaking into a rotting grin as he peered at her more closely. He stank of ale and fish and unwashed linen, and Emry's stomach twisted with disgust. "This lad's a lass."

"Keep your hands off my sister!" Emmett shouted, struggling against his captors.

"Sister? Even better." The man stroked his thumb across Emry's jaw, and she twisted away in revulsion.

"You're going to regret that," she warned.

"Is that so, girly?" He grabbed her chin and forced her gaze on his, an unabashed hunger in his eyes. "Forget the finger. I'll take a bit o' rough with the lass."

"Don't touch her!" Emmett cried, struggling against his captors.

The bald man landed a swift punch to his gut, and Emmett doubled over, coughing. Before he could straighten, the man's fist connected with his jaw, hard, and he went down on his hands and knees. A cruel smirk bloomed across the thickset man's face as he twisted his filthy boot into Emmett's back.

"My coat!" Emmett cried.

The man sneered, delivering a vicious kick that sent him sprawling facedown in the mud.

They were out of time. Emry didn't have a plan, but some hasty magic would have to do.

An illusion of fire should scare them off.

Before she could cast a spell, she felt a foul hand on her arse. Every nerve in her body went white-hot, and a strange, icy magic burst from the silver scars on her palms.

Emry gasped as purple flames sprang to life, twisting up her arms and hovering above her hands. Ropes of fire shot out, engulfing the four men in a very real blaze.

No. She hadn't meant to do this.

The magic pulsed through her veins, cold and wrong. It was the same power that had flowed through the stones the night she'd opened the door to Anwen, the world beyond hers. A power she didn't want, and had tried so hard to ignore.

But there was no ignoring it now. Emry watched in horror as the men stamped and shouted, desperate to snuff the searing flames.

"Extinguo!" she cried, but the flames didn't even flicker.

Come on, Emry thought. *Extinguo!*

The cold, bright magic pulsed again, and silver sparks danced at the edges of her vision. She stumbled as the flames shot out again, hitting the nearest building. Emry winced, but thankfully, the building was too wet to catch fire. Instead, the damp thatch gave off a thick, pungent smoke that filled the alley.

"Stop it! Please!" Emry cried, shaking her flame-coated hands and blinking back tears.

The flames faded, and she drew in a shallow breath, her whole body trembling. It was over. The heavy scent of charred wool filled the air, and dimly, through the smoke, she watched as the men staggered away, coughing and moaning but no longer on fire.

She felt light-headed and strangely hollow as she bent over her brother, giving him a gentle shake. "Emmett, it's over," she said.

His eyes fluttered open. He groaned and spat out a mouthful of blood, pushing to his knees.

"What happened?" he asked, wincing. "Was there fire?"

If he didn't know, she certainly wasn't going to tell him. "I cast an illusion," Emry lied. "Scared them off."

"Must've been some illusion." Emmett leaned on her as he

struggled to his feet. He was caked with grime. A nasty bruise was blooming along his jaw, and his lip was bleeding.

"Thanks, by the way," he said, "for whatever you did back there."

"Don't mention it," Emry said tightly.

What she'd done was the last thing she wanted to talk about. She'd set four men aflame with a dangerous spell she hadn't cast. And she didn't know how, or why, or when it would happen again. She'd thought she had a handle on the unfamiliar magic that surged through her, that she could keep shoving it down. But it had broken through her defenses.

"Let's just get back before we're missed," Emry said.

The king's threat came back to her, making her shiver under her cloak: *Give me a reason, and you're gone.*

Chapter 2

Arthur Pendragon stifled a yawn and raised his broadsword. It was just before dawn, and most of the castle was still asleep. Which meant it was the perfect hour to train without drawing any unwanted attention.

Or it would be if he weren't so exhausted. But the nightmares he'd suffered in the month since he'd nearly died beneath St. Paul's weren't going away. And between the sleepless nights and the long days, he was the kind of tired that had settled deep in his bones.

He adjusted his grip on the pommel just as Lancelot lunged forward in attack. His parry was weak, and Lance disarmed him in an instant. Arthur grimaced as his sword flew from his hands, clattering to the floor of the armory with an embarrassing clang.

"Wake up!" Lance scolded. "It's like sparring with a practice dummy."

"Sorry." Arthur yawned as he went to retrieve his sword. "Late night."

"Really?" Lance looked impressed, and a little proud. "Can I guess who you took to bed?"

"*Comparative Political Philosophy*, volume two." Arthur tried to ignore his friend's delighted torrent of laughter.

"For a moment I thought you meant you'd—"

"Definitely not." Guinevere was his betrothed in name only. After it became clear they weren't getting out of their forced engagement without risking the alliance between their kingdoms, they'd agreed to turn each other down at the altar.

And Emry . . . he'd thought fighting Morgana would bring them closer together, but in fact, it was the opposite. He didn't understand what had happened. It was like, overnight, a wall had gone up between them, one that he was unable to scale. And whenever he tried, he only succeeded in making things worse. It probably would do him good to take his mind off things with some willing courtier. But he doubted he could stand the gossip. So, books it was.

Books and an exhausting cycle of jolting awake in the middle of the night, soaked with sweat, reliving that horrible moment when he'd hesitated with his sword to Morgana's throat, and she'd stabbed him. He could still feel the sharp plunge of her dagger twisting into his gut. He'd nearly died. He would have died, if it weren't for Emry and the strange magic that had flowed through the stones to save him.

Belatedly, Arthur realized that his friend was watching him.

"You don't get a pass for terrible swordplay because you stayed up late reading," Lance said, closing his visor and raising his sword. "You asked me to spar, so let's spar."

Lance was right. Arthur had insisted on the practice session mostly because they saw each other so rarely these days. Lance's squire duties were no joke, and Arthur's father insisted he sit in on every council meeting, and review every new piece of legislation.

Perhaps, Arthur thought as he adjusted his stance, he should have suggested they go for an early-morning jog instead. At least no one expected him to be exceptional at jogging. But it was too late now to change it. So, he took a deep breath and tried to get his head in the game.

"En garde," he said, raising his sword.

Their blades clashed, and Arthur pushed, gritting his teeth as Lance bore down on him. His stance broke, and his back leg began to slide.

"Hold your footing," Lance instructed.

Arthur tried and failed, stumbling as Lance's sword slashed through his defenses. Lance spun, bringing his blade about, and landed a sharp hit to Arthur's shoulder.

"You died," said Lance.

"Well aware. Go again."

They went again. And again. Until Arthur's arms felt like rubber, but his lunges were surer and his blows rang solid. The sun rose while they sparred, and when Arthur set down his sword, he was surprised to find the first gray streaks of dawn brightening the sky. He glanced over at Lancelot, watching as his friend executed a complicated pass with his sword, hefting the blade with the ease of a born fighter.

"You've gotten even better," Arthur said admiringly.

Lance shrugged off the compliment. "I've had to. The squires have more training and better skill than the guards."

"I bet Percival could hold his own," Arthur said with a knowing smile.

"Well, sure, but Perce has always been head and shoulders above the rest of them." Lance grew wistful at the mention of the handsome guard who had once been his rival. And whom Arthur suspected Lance wanted to conquer in a completely different way.

"You should ask him out for a drink on your day off," Arthur suggested.

At this, Lance gave a bitter laugh.

"What's funny?" Arthur asked.

"I haven't had a day off since I became a squire."

Arthur frowned. That couldn't be right. He knew he barely saw Lance anymore, but surely Sir Kay wasn't working him that hard?

"Not even Sundays?"

Lance shook his head. "Squires attend to their knights at tournament, even on Sundays. And I swear Sir Kay is hiring himself out for parties with the amount of backwater jousts he agrees to. I haven't had time to visit the barber in weeks."

"Thank god," Arthur said with considerable relief. "I thought you were wearing your hair in a bun on purpose."

Lance shot him a dark look. "It's a topknot."

"It's exactly how Emry ties her hair back when she's brewing a potion." Before Lance could needle him for noticing, he added, "If you can't take Perce out, you could always invite him to supper in the Great Hall."

"Supper?" Lance choked.

"You're entitled to a guest, same as every eligible noble who resides in the castle."

He was right, and they both knew it. Lance would never call himself an eligible noble, not after he'd spent two years as a castle guard, stripped of his honor and his status over a malicious lie. But everything had been put right, and he was a squire now—for the King's Champion, no less.

"You're going to annoy me until I ask him, aren't you?" Lance asked.

"Daily. I'm having Lucan add it to my schedule."

"You know what else you could do daily? Practice broadsword. You're terrible."

Arthur sighed. "I had no idea I was so rusty. I've mostly been training with Excalibur."

These days, the legendary sword felt different in his hands. Bonded to him, somehow. Like the blade recognized a power inside him that hadn't been there before.

And it made him supremely uncomfortable. Because he hated the idea of what the sword meant—of the battles he was fated to fight, and the men whose lives he was destined to take on his path to becoming the one true king. A destiny that he wished he could delay indefinitely. Or at least until he was better with a weapon. Except his skill with a sword wasn't the problem. The last time he'd faced an enemy, it wasn't his footwork that had failed him. It was his nerve.

The silver scar on his stomach twinged, and he tried not to think about it, or the worrying way it glowed brighter when he held Excalibur, as though connecting him to the legendary blade.

"Everything all right?" Lance asked.

"Fine," Arthur lied. "Just tired."

"For the most boring reason." Lance closed the door to the weapons cabinet with slightly more force than was necessary.

There was an ominous clatter, and the loud clang of what sounded like a shield hitting the ground. Followed by a half dozen practice swords.

Arthur snorted.

"Whoops," Lance said, pressing back a grin.

The doors to the training room burst open, and Brannor rushed in. The guard brandished his sword, ready to fight off a deadly assailant. And was confused when he didn't see one.

"Morning, Brannor," Lance said cheerfully.

Brannor looked around, his sword raised. "I heard a noise, Your Highness."

Honestly. Ever since Arthur had snuck out of the castle and returned covered in blood and refusing to say where he'd been, the old guard had taken his job as the crown prince's protector even more seriously.

"As you can see, I'm not dead, injured, or in mortal peril," Arthur said.

"Yet," Lance returned, cracking his knuckles.

Brannor scowled, and Arthur bit back a laugh. "Don't worry," he said cheerfully, unbuckling his padding. "There's always next time."

Chapter 3

Emry slouched at the battered wooden table in the wizard's workshop, trying to concentrate on her notes. Master Ambrosius was testing them on magical transformations that morning, but she couldn't stop glancing toward the door, anxiously awaiting her brother's arrival.

Emmett had better show up soon, or else Master Ambrosius was going to lose it.

The ancient wizard brooded by the hearth, his eyes narrowed as he stared into the crackling fire. Overhead, bundles of drying herbs gave off pungent scents, and firelight flickered against the glass bottles and jars that lined the shelves. The cabinets were crammed with volumes of herb lore, magic spells, and anatomical renderings.

The wizard's workshop was Emry's favorite place in the castle. She never minded climbing the narrow, twisting stairs to the tower at sunrise. Yet Emmett always acted as though showing up was an inconvenience.

Emry still remembered the first day she'd come, disguised as her brother. Master Ambrosius had been surprised that she could work magic without speaking the spells aloud or using a wand to direct her magic. And he had known immediately that she wasn't who she was pretending to be. Her father, the great wizard Willyt Merlin, had only ever boasted of his daughter's abilities to do such magic, never his son's. But Master Ambrosius had kept her secret and taught her anyway, even knowing the truth.

King Uther will never accept a woman as his court wizard. But Arthur, perhaps, might feel differently, the old wizard had said.

Except Arthur's feelings wouldn't matter if anyone found out about her new powers from Anwen.

Her dangerous, uncontrollable powers.

She sank down in her seat, chewing her lip, and trying to put them out of mind by focusing on her notes, even though she'd memorized these spells long ago.

Finally, her errant brother stumbled into the workshop. The tavern fight hadn't done him any favors. His jaw had bruised purple and black, his lip had swollen to twice its normal size, and she could tell from his tight, pained expression that he was hungover besides. He gripped a mug of coffee as though it were the only thing keeping him upright. And he hadn't brought his books or his notes, which meant she'd have to share hers.

"You're late, boy." Master Ambrosius's lips pressed into a thin line.

"Don't suppose I could have any healing salve?" Emmett asked hopefully.

"That will depend on your exam results," the old wizard replied.

Emmett looked horrified. "Exam?"

Oh no. He'd forgotten.

"On transformations," Emry whispered.

"Did you study at all, boy?" Master Ambrosius demanded.

"I—well . . ." Emmett stalled.

"How would you proceed if I asked you to enlarge that bowl to twice its size?" Master Ambrosius questioned, pointing to a large wooden bread bowl that Chef was no doubt missing.

This one's easy, Emry thought. *Come on.*

But her brother pasted on a smirk and dropped into a chair as if he were a lord sitting down to his supper.

"My father was the greatest wizard to ever live. He wouldn't want me studying such demeaning spells."

Emry closed her eyes, wishing she could sink into the floor and disappear. Her brother had a tendency to act hotheaded, but she'd hoped he'd learned when to keep his mouth shut. And judging from Master Ambrosius's furious expression, Emmett really should have.

"If you find my teaching beneath you, no one is forcing you to remain my apprentice," Master Ambrosius said coldly. "Show up tardy and unprepared again, and I'll speak with King Uther about having you dismissed."

No, he couldn't! Emry fought to keep her composure, but her brother looked unfazed by the threat.

"You wouldn't," Emmett said, calling the old wizard's bluff.

"Try me." Master Ambrosius had never looked so fierce, and Emry didn't doubt for a moment that the old wizard would make good on his threat. "What are you so afraid will happen if you apply yourself?"

"Afraid?" Emmett echoed, incredulous. "I'm not afraid! I'm bored to death with these trivial household spells. Light a candle! Boil water! Mop up a spill! Am I a court wizard or a kitchen boy?"

"Kitchen boy is a wonderful idea," Master Ambrosius said. "You can spend the day working for Chef as your punishment."

Emmett barked a laugh. "You've got to be kidding!"

"Report to the kitchens," Master Ambrosius ordered. "Perhaps tomorrow you'll arrive on time, and able to cast a passable enlargement spell."

Emmett pushed to his feet and slunk from the tower.

Emry watched him go, burning with resentment. If Emmett got himself dismissed from the castle, it would be a disaster. There was no way the king would keep her around as the sole wizard's apprentice.

No, the king would find some other boy who had a bit of magic in his blood. And if by some miracle Emry was allowed to stay, she'd have to play apprentice to a talentless amateur. Or worse, face torment from a smug boy who thought he was her better. And that was if her own magic problems didn't get her dismissed first.

Telling Master Ambrosius about her uncontrollable Anwen powers was out of the question. What if the old wizard insisted on reporting it to King Uther? And even if he didn't, she worried he'd treat her like she was made of glass. Or worst of all, refuse to let her practice magic.

There was too much at stake, and she had worked too hard to get this far. She'd just have to make sure she didn't reveal there was anything wrong with her magic.

Belatedly, she realized Master Ambrosius was staring at her. And that he'd said something.

"Sorry?" she replied hastily.

"I asked you to cast the same spell," the old wizard repeated, an edge to his voice. "Don't think you're getting out of this exam just because it was meant for your brother."

"Yes, sir," Emry said, reaching for her wand, and hating the dread that sat heavily in her stomach as she did. She couldn't be afraid of a simple spell. Magic was the one thing that defined her, and without it, she didn't know who she was. Nothing was going to go wrong, she promised herself. "*Amplius*," she said, waving her wand in the direction of the bread bowl.

The bowl grew to twice its normal size, creaking as it expanded. When it stopped, Emry lowered her shoulders from where they'd scrunched up around her ears, and looked to the old wizard.

"Good. Now, smaller," he prompted.

This was the test? Emry almost snorted. It was laughably easy. *"Minutus."* She flicked her chin in the direction of the bowl, folding her arms across her chest as she watched the bowl shrink.

"Use your wand, apprentice," Master Ambrosius corrected.

"I don't need it," Emry insisted. "Besides, I need to be able to work magic without it." In the cave, Morgana hadn't used a wand. Relying on one was a liability.

"You need to do as you're instructed, apprentice," Master Ambrosius returned. "A wand isn't merely a guide, it's a warning to others that magic will be occurring."

"That's exactly the problem!" Emry protested. "In a fight, I can't—"

"When exactly will you be fighting with magic?" Master Ambrosius demanded.

The old wizard didn't know the full extent of what had happened in the battle with Morgana, and Emry certainly couldn't tell him about last night's tavern fight.

"I don't know. I just want to be prepared."

"And you will be, for the duties of a court wizard," Master Ambrosius assured her.

Emry sighed.

Master Ambrosius studied her for a moment, then proclaimed, "Since you've mastered the basics of transformation, I suppose we can try something a bit more complex."

Emry's heart fluttered with excitement. This. This was what she was here for. Not to learn the introductory magic she could find in her father's books, but for real instruction. She watched eagerly as Master Ambrosius got down a glass beaker and set it on the table next to the bowl.

"The bowl smaller, and the beaker larger. At the same time," he commanded.

"The same time?" she repeated.

"A problem?" The old wizard lifted a bushy eyebrow.

"I've never attempted two spells at once," Emry admitted. "I'm not sure I know how."

The old wizard gave her a small smile, as if he already knew that. "Visualize both spells and both objects, then choose one to begin with," he instructed. "Switch without a pause, and enunciate clearly."

Emry nodded, wondering if she could pull it off. Two spells at once. It would be a useful skill, if she could master it. She took a deep breath for focus and reached for her magic. "*Amplius*," she urged. And then, shifting her attention to the bowl, "*Minutus*."

She watched hopefully as the beaker enlarged and the bowl grew smaller. "Ha!" she said, grinning.

Master Ambrosius blinked at her in shock. "You got it on your first try," he said, as though he couldn't believe it.

"Wasn't I supposed to?" She frowned at the two objects, considering. "Can I try it again, without my wand?"

"Sarding hell, girl. Do you have any idea how difficult it is to work two permanent magical transformations on separate objects at the same time?"

"Not that difficult, clearly, since I managed on my first attempt," Emry said.

The old wizard shook his head. "In my best days, I accomplished it only a few times. Your father struggled for weeks to master it."

And there it was. Once again, Master Ambrosius had assigned her a spell he thought she wouldn't be able to cast, just like the poison antidote she'd used to save Arthur's life. And he hadn't done it because he wanted her to learn. He'd done it to put her in her place. Because he didn't want her racing ahead of his lesson plans.

Oh, she was furious. For a moment, she'd believed he was showing her new, exciting magic, but really, he was waiting for her to fail.

"So, my father could do it," Emry snapped, resentment flaring, "but you're surprised that I can, even after you explained the mechanics of the spell."

"That's beside the point," Master Ambrosius said.

"That's exactly the point!" Emry said hotly. "My brother may be a screwup, but I'm not! And when I prove myself, all I get is grief. You're the one who told me to cast the spell!"

"Not without your wand!" the old wizard returned. "What's next? Without saying the spell aloud?"

Emry bit her lip. That was precisely what she'd been planning. "If I'm capable of it, then why not?" she asked.

"Because it's not done!" Master Ambrosius argued. "At least, not by any wizards I've met. If you keep this up, what you seek to learn will soon be beyond me. Perhaps beyond any who use magic for worthy purposes."

Emry's stomach twisted. "I'm not going to turn out like Morgana."

The old wizard flinched at the name. "I didn't mean—" he protested, but Emry didn't want to hear it.

"Yes, you *did* mean it. Girls with magic go bad. It's in all of the legends. The evil witch of Anwen. The reason the Lady of the Lake is trapped on Avalon. Even my father's former apprentice. No one ever believes that a woman with ambition and power can use it for anything but evil." Emry's hands were clenched into fists, and she was breathing hard.

Master Ambrosius's lips tightened into a thin line. "Power corrupts those who have it, no matter their gender."

"If I were a boy, you wouldn't be saying any of this," Emry grumbled.

"If you were a boy, you'd be enjoying the spoils of a royal apprenticeship, like your brother," said Master Ambrosius. "But yes, it is true about Bellicent and Nimue and Morgana. They are cautionary tales. And I expect you to learn from them."

Emry nodded, trying to push away the voice in the back of her head that whispered, *What about last night? What about the magic you carry that frightens you? Magic you weren't able to keep in check.*

"I will," she promised.

Master Ambrosius gave her a long, hard look. "Now try the tandem spell again. *With* your wand. But from twice the distance."

Emmett stomped down the dark, rough-hewn servants' staircase to the kitchens, cursing under his breath. So he'd forgotten about the exam.

Master Ambrosius should have taken one look at the bruises and cuts on his face and understood that he ought to be excused. But no. Instead the old wizard had embarrassed him, refused to give him healing salve, and sent him to the kitchens like a servant.

It wasn't fair. Emmett banged open the ancient wooden door with more force than was necessary. Chef sighed, looking up from the enormous fish he was gutting.

"Oui, Monsieur Merlin? Have you come to return my mixing bowl?"

"No. Master Ambrosius sent me to work."

Chef muttered under his breath in French. "Ze old wizard is punishing *me*." He jerked a thumb toward a wooden table piled high with produce from the gardens. "Shell ze peas. And no magic."

Emmett pulled up a stool, staring helplessly at the pea pods. "How on earth do you do this?" he wondered aloud.

Two pretty scullery maids across the kitchen, their heads bent together in gossip, spared him a glance, and then giggled.

"You look lost," said the freckled blonde.

"I'm completely out of my element, I'm afraid," he said, turning on the charm. "I don't suppose you could show me, er, what I'm supposed to do?"

The two girls exchanged a glance again, giggling. The blonde got up and demonstrated, brushing ever so softly against his arm with the front of her pinafore.

Emmett swallowed. Sard, pretty girls would be the death of him one day.

"What's the black eye from, then?" the girl asked.

"Tavern fight." Emmett winked, and then winced in pain.

"You should put some meat on that," the girl suggested. "Takes away the swelling."

Emmett gave her a hopeful look. The girl told him to hold on, then went away and came back with a fine-looking chop.

"You 'ent got that from me," she said.

"Course not."

The girl beamed.

Emmett pressed the meat to his eye, which did seem to help, and clumsily went about shelling pea pods one-handed. Most of them shot across the room. Chef, thankfully, didn't notice.

Serving lads and serving girls came and went, fetching trays for different nobles, and Emmett heaved a sigh, wishing he hadn't skipped breakfast.

"The tea for Princess Guinevere?" a girl asked, and Emmett's head snapped up.

"I can help carry that," he said, surging to his feet. "It looks heavy."

"Fine," said Chef. "But I expect you right back here to peel ze carrots."

Emmett nodded, trying not to let his disappointment that Chef hadn't dismissed him show. At least now he'd get to see Guin. He picked up a platter of iced cakes and followed the maid, who looked at him with suspicion.

"Did you just eat a cake?" she demanded.

Emmett swallowed thickly, hoping there wasn't icing on his lips. "Nope."

When the girl knocked demurely at Guin's door, Emmett snatched up a second cake before following her inside.

"You may set everything on the table," Guin said grandly, turning a page in the book she was reading. She was curled on the sofa, a basket of embroidery at her feet. Two court ladies sat opposite her, daintily sewing flowers onto silk handkerchiefs.

"Yes, Your Highness." The girl curtseyed and lowered the tray, gesturing for Emmett to bring his. She shot him a glare before adding, "He ate some of your cakes on the way up."

Guin caught sight of him and glared. "Those were for my guests."

"I didn't know," Emmett said guiltily. "Besides, you don't like the lemon ones."

She shot him a warning look.

"I mean, girls never like the lemon ones," Emmett corrected.

The two court ladies were watching them in fascination.

"May I speak with you outside?" Guin asked prettily, smoothing her skirts as she stood.

It was a move, Emmett knew, that meant she was furious. With him. Again.

Guin followed him into the corridor, and the moment the door closed, her eyes flashed with anger.

"What are you *doing* showing up at my room?"

"Helping deliver tea! I didn't know you had company."

Guin shook her head. "Do you at least have the healing salve you promised?"

She lifted her hair off her neck, revealing the very telling mark from Emmett's enthusiastic kisses, an oversight that had made her angry enough to break up with him.

"No," Emmett said, hanging his head. "Master Ambrosius got angry because I didn't study for an exam."

"Emmett!"

"I was a little preoccupied getting beaten up outside a tavern!" he said, gesturing to his face.

Guin bit her lip, taking in the bruises. And then she sighed, disappointed. "No doubt because you were gambling. And drinking. And cheating honest men out of their hard-earned wages."

"They weren't honest! They were scoundrels and thieves," Emmett insisted. "Besides, no one talks politics freely at the castle. If I want to hear what's truly going on, I have to seek out places where men have loose lips and travelers pass through." He shrugged. "Is it so wrong to reward myself with a little compensation when I do?"

"I don't care what you do!" Guin actually stamped her foot. "I'll stay out of your way, and you stay out of mine."

"Gladly, Princess. If you're done with me, I'll go."

"I am," said Princess Guinevere, "*completely* done with you."

"Good."

"Good." Guin lifted her chin. "This was a stupid fling, and I regret it entirely."

"My thoughts exactly," snapped Emmett.

And with that, he stomped back to the kitchens.

Chapter 4

Emry stared up at her bedroom ceiling, her heart and her thoughts racing.

It had been four days since the incident at the tavern, and she still didn't know what was wrong with her magic. Thankfully, no similar incidents had happened again. Which was a relief. Master Ambrosius would never keep her as an apprentice if there was a risk her magic could get away from her. Especially if it could cause harm to those around her.

But keeping her problem a secret while figuring out how to fix it was proving trickier than she'd expected. She'd tried to borrow some likely looking books from the wizard's workshop, but the old wizard had come up behind her, asking what she was searching for, and she hadn't dared to take anything about Anwen. Instead, she'd pretended to be interested in a dreadful potions book, and had mumbled a flimsy excuse about wanting to lengthen her hair.

Perhaps there was a book in the castle library that might help explain her problem. The magic section was vast, and Master Ambrosius had just as often sent her there for books as he had pulled volumes from his own shelves.

It wouldn't hurt to check.

Emry dressed quickly, pulling on the boy's clothes that were still draped across the back of her chair. And then she crept down the darkened castle corridors and pushed open the grand double doors of the library.

A single candelabra was lit, and in its dim glow, a familiar figure sat at one of the long tables.

A handsome young man, pale and brown-haired, with an angular face made sharper in the candlelight. He was dressed in just a tunic and hose, a lock of hair dangling over one eye. He looked up in alarm, clearly not expecting anyone.

"Sorry," Emry apologized. "Didn't mean to sneak up on you."

"It's all right." Arthur's mouth lifted into a grin. "I probably wasn't going to do much with the year of my life I just lost to fright." He leaned back in his chair, stretching. "Didn't realize anyone else was up so late."

"Couldn't sleep."

"Same."

As Emry got closer, she could see the dark circles beneath his eyes, and the resigned weariness of his posture. This wasn't the first night he'd spent reading late in the library, she realized. Just the first night that he'd been caught.

He gestured toward a chair. "Join me?"

Emry bit her lip. She hadn't expected to see him here, like this. For the two of them to wind up alone in the place where she had given in, and kissed him back. She could still remember how the spines of the library books had dug into her back the night of the ball. And how naive she had been, going along with it, and thinking that princes ever wound up with girls like her as anything more than a secret dalliance.

I want you to be my court wizard, he'd said. *Isn't that enough?*

But that *wasn't* what he wanted—not really. And if she was being honest, it wasn't what she wanted, either. But it was the way things had to be.

"I'd appreciate the company," Arthur urged, sensing her hesitation.

"Is it so difficult for you to find company, Your Highness?" Emry replied, breaking into a grin.

Arthur glared. "Shut up and grab your books, wizard," he ordered.

"I will. What are you reading?" she asked, her voice echoing through the cavernous library.

Arthur lifted a finger to his lips, looking nervously to his right. For the first time, Emry noticed the second figure a few tables away: Arthur's loathsome guard, Dakin, who was fast asleep with his legs propped on a table, his mouth hanging open. The guard let out a nasal snore.

"I'm trying to find out what happened to Morgana," Arthur admitted. "Or, at the very least, determine whether she still poses a threat."

Emry's eyebrows shot up in surprise. "What have you learned so far?"

"Not much." Arthur sighed. "I can't understand half the magical terms without stopping to look them up, and my Old English is incredibly rusty."

"Mine isn't."

"Does that mean you're offering to help?" He looked so hopeful, as though he very much wanted her to say yes.

Dangerous, a voice warned. *You're supposed to stay away.* But Arthur had exactly the books she was looking for. If there was an answer to her magic problems, it was in those books. And helping him would be a convenient excuse for her to pore over them. But more than that, she couldn't leave him to this task alone.

"I suppose," she said.

"Well then." He gestured toward a chair, and Emry took a seat.

"You're dressed as a boy again," he pointed out.

"Oh. Yeah." Emry shrugged. Some days dresses didn't feel right, but she didn't want to explain that, so she simply said, "Less buttons."

A corner of Arthur's mouth lifted. "I like it. Reminds me of old times." He pushed a stack of books across the table. "Take a look at these. Let me know if anything jumps out."

They read in companionable silence for a while. Emry had forgotten how easy it was to be around Arthur, and how impossible. He had saved her life, risking his own, and the future of Camelot. And now the two of them were alone, and she wasn't prepared for it.

She wished he'd stop looking at her like that. Like he was still the boy she'd mistaken for a librarian all those months ago. Like he would ride off to her rescue, consequences be damned. Like the only future he wanted was one by her side.

His fingers brushed hers as they reached for the same book, and he didn't move them away.

"Arthur," she warned, her voice barely more than a whisper. Her traitorous hand stayed where it was, touching his.

"What?" He unleashed the full force of his grin. "It's only Dakin here, and he's asleep."

Dakin, who would certainly report to the king that he'd found the two of them together in the library together late at night.

Emry pulled her hand away. "I told you. We shouldn't."

"Even though you want to," Arthur accused softly.

He was right. She did want to. And she couldn't pretend otherwise. Which was why she couldn't wind up in compromising positions like this one. Alone in the library, in the dim candlelight, with the dreamy-eyed prince who made her heart beat faster and her insides go molten. It only made things harder.

There was nothing back for her in Brocelande. This job was her father's legacy. And she couldn't put it at risk because she had feelings for someone she could never be with. She wasn't throwing away her shot just because Arthur was a good kisser. Fine, an excellent kisser. One who knew exactly how to make her—

No. *Focus.*

"What I want," Emry snapped, "is none of your business."

"My apologies, wizard."

Arthur sighed and went to return a stack of books to the shelves. Emry glared at his back, flipping the page of her book with perhaps more force than was necessary. The vellum sliced into her finger, and a line of blood welled up.

"Ow!" she whined.

Dakin gave a startled snore, and Emry's heart lurched in a panic. He couldn't wake up and find her here. It would be a disaster. She needed—oh no—belatedly, she felt the icy prickle of Anwen's magic.

And then she looked down, horrified. A small flame burned over each palm. Her skin was unharmed, but the sleeves of her tunic were beginning to singe. *Stop that!* Emry begged of the unfamiliar magic. *Go away!* She closed her fists, but the flames curled through her fingers undeterred. She could feel the magic rushing through her veins.

Arthur poked his head out of the stacks. "Is something burning?"

"No," Emry replied, trying to shove the unwelcome magic back down. But it didn't work. The room was too hot. No, not the room. She was too warm.

The magic wouldn't stop until it got what it wanted. And it wanted to be used.

She needed to get out of there—now. She grabbed her cloak and rushed out of the castle, heading for the royal hunting grounds. She didn't know where she was going, but it didn't matter. All that mattered was getting as far away from the castle—and everyone in it—as she could manage.

The night air was a welcome relief against her burning skin. She darted through the trees, trying to ignore the hum and rattle of insects. *You're a wizard,* she reminded herself. *The forest should be afraid of you.* Besides, it wasn't a real forest. Not like the woods back home behind their cottage, wild and dangerous and unknown.

Finally, she came to a clearing that held the crumbling remains of an old church. Not a church of the current faith, she realized, noting the runes carved above the lintel, and the odd, circular roof. A thin stream trickled past, silver in the moonlight.

Emry pushed back her hood and took a deep, steadying breath. The purple flames pulsed impatiently in her palms, and then turned into swirls of black smoke.

This was new.

The magic shot out, thickening and swirling, until the entire clearing was coated with darkness. Emry couldn't see anything, not even her own hands. The strange darkness pressed against her, filled with whispers too faint to make out. Emry's chest clenched as she shuffled through the darkness, her hands out in front of her. Suddenly, she tripped over a tree root and stumbled beyond the edge of the magic. Her strange Anwen powers had created an enormous dark cloud, and she had no idea how she'd created it, or why.

"Go away," Emry tried. "Shoo, cloud."

Nothing.

She waited, counting the agonizing seconds until the darkness finally began to shrink. Soon, it was just a plume of smoke, and then nothing at all. The unfamiliar magic slithered obediently away, and Emry gasped as the familiar prickle of her own power returned.

She sagged against a tree trunk, breathing hard, her hands shaking. Perhaps all the magic had wanted was to be used, and now everything would be fine. But somehow, she doubted it.

Chapter 5

Guinevere stabbed her embroidery needle through the fabric, pretending to enjoy the mindless activity. Across her sitting room, Isolde and Branjen eagerly attacked their own embroidery, their expressions smug and Issie's dress revealing far too much bosom for afternoon tea.

"Is something the matter, Your Highness?" Issie asked, blinking her large blue eyes in concern.

"You've hardly made any progress on your handkerchief," noted Branjen, frowning at her own elaborate stitching.

"Not at all," Guin said, giving the courtiers a fake smile, and wishing she could get rid of them.

Two weeks ago, the horrid Lady Elaine had been married off to a minor country lord, and Guinevere had been thrilled to be rid of her tiring companion. Until the next morning, when Elaine's former minions had knocked at her door, latching on to Guinevere as their new leader. Guin hadn't had the heart to turn the crestfallen court ladies away. So, she had rung for tea and made conversation about the weather, considering it charity. Then the girls had turned up the next afternoon, with their baskets of embroidery, expecting tea, and Guin had realized she was stuck with them.

At least their presence stopped her from slipping through the passage that connected her rooms with the handsome wizard's. Her cheeks flushed thinking about their forbidden liaison. He was like a hero from one of her stories, a little bit dangerous, a little bit magic, and utterly gorgeous when he flashed his pirate's grin in close range, daring her to make the first move.

Which she had.

Again and again and again.

But no more.

She was done with such things. And she was done with Emmett Merlin. He didn't know how to be anything more than a good time. And even a good time got tiring after a while.

There was a knock at the door, and Branjen looked up eagerly. "I do hope that's our tea."

It wasn't their tea. It was Emry. The apprentice wizard wore a plain blue dress overlaid with a brown kirtle. Her short hair was braided behind each ear, with wisps coming loose around her face. Guin ached to give her a makeover, yet every time she broached the subject, Emry took offense. Honestly. Were all wizards so frustrating, or just Merlins?

"Emry!" Guin said, smiling.

"You'll never guess what—oh." The young wizard's face fell as she surveyed the crowded sitting room. "I didn't know you had company."

"You're welcome to join us." With Emry around, the afternoon wouldn't feel nearly as dull.

"At embroidery?" Emry sounded doubtful.

"It's an important skill for all marriageable young ladies to learn," Issie pronounced.

Guinevere bit her lip to keep from laughing.

"I'm not much of a marriageable young lady." Emry tossed the blonde girl a flirtatious wink, and a blush rose to Issie's fair cheeks.

"Did you not turn down such a proposal from Lord Gawain?" Branjen inquired, and then looked horrified at her boldness.

Emry looked taken aback. But she hid it quickly. "He wasn't being serious. He was mostly insulting my fashion sense. Only it came out sounding like a marriage proposal."

"A reasonable mistake," Guin said, pressing back a grin. "Branjen, pour the apprentice wizard some tea."

"No, no, I can't stay," Emry said. "I just came by to lend you this." She held up a small leather-bound volume.

"A book?" Issie wrinkled her nose.

Guin's eyes lit up. "Is that the next one with the pirates who—"

"Yup," Emry said. "In painstaking detail. Enjoy." She set the book on a table and stepped into the corridor just as a maid staggered past with their tray.

Guin's stomach rumbled as the table was set. She reached for a small sugary confection covered in pink icing. Usually she avoided sweets, but lately, she'd been craving them. And she might as well indulge her cravings. There wasn't much else to do at Castle Camelot. Honestly, she was starting to see why Arthur adored his books.

Over the past few months, Guin had developed a surprising enthusiasm for them as well. She hadn't realized there were ones with kissing in them, or that the kissing was described in salacious, shocking ways. Back home in Cameliard, where the royal family attended religious services each morning and night, such books weren't found in the castle library. Not that she'd looked particularly hard. She'd been far more concerned with flirting with the hapless young nobles who fumbled their words around her, and tormenting the royal tailor with requests for scandalous gowns.

Which she had the good sense not to wear to tea.

"Would you care for a slice?" Branjen asked, reaching for a large flaky pie decorated with intricate swirls of puff pastry.

"What kind is it?" Guinevere asked.

"Chef's specialty." Branjen cut a large slice. "Jellied eel."

Guinevere shook her head, not trusting herself to talk as a vinegary stench assaulted her nostrils. She'd never particularly disliked the dish, but she suddenly found it revolting. She swallowed thickly as Branjen raised a bite to her lips, a small slippery eel's head dangling from a gloopy reddish sauce.

"I do hope there will be harp music at supper this evening," Issie said.

"As do I," Guinevere replied tightly. "I—excuse me."

She abandoned her embroidery, bolting for the garderobe not a moment too soon. Her stomach twisted as she heaved her breakfast into the privy. She leaned back on her heels, wiping her mouth with a spare scrap of linen. She took a couple of deep breaths, feeling much better.

And then, much worse as she did some rapid calculations. Her courses were nearly two weeks late. Her maid had brought it up just yesterday, and she'd done her best to dismiss it as no cause for concern, smiling through her own anxiety. Perhaps it was stress, she had hoped. Or just an irregularity. But that had been before she'd bolted for the garde-robe at the stench of eel pie.

Oh no. *No no no.*

She couldn't be—she couldn't even think the word—pregnant.

Her stomach lurched again at the thought, as if in confirmation.

"Princess?" one of the girls called worriedly.

"A moment," Guinevere called.

The girls were clever, and she didn't trust them to keep their mouths shut. Often, she caught them with their heads together whispering, or trading meaningful looks when they thought Guin couldn't see. And the last thing she needed was two social-climbing courtiers discovering her situation before she'd really processed it herself.

Actually, the last thing she needed was to be knocked up by Emmett Merlin, but too late for that now.

"Princess Guinevere?" Issie called, her voice thick with concern. "Are you well?"

"Perfectly," Guin replied, climbing to her feet and smoothing her gown. She pinched some color into her cheeks, and emerged from the garderobe with what she hoped passed for an embarrassed smile. "Although I hope you didn't try the oysters at supper. My stomach kept me up half the night. I thought the worst was over."

Issie's brows knitted together in concern. "I did have a few," she said worriedly.

"Oh dear." Guin shook her head. "You should return to your rooms, in case yours is a delayed reaction."

Both girls hurriedly bobbed curtseys, and rushed out in obvious distress.

After the girls had left, Guinevere paced her room, her hands clenched into fists, her chin trembling.

A baby. She was going to have a baby.

Guin sat down on the edge of her bed, putting her head in her hands.

She'd been so stupid, dallying with that flirtatious wizard as though it were all a game. And maybe it was, for him. But not for her. Not when the risks and consequences rested entirely on her shoulders. She wished she'd had the good sense to acquire the herbs that prevented pregnancy in the first place, but she'd been too embarrassed to ask.

She hadn't wanted to raise any suspicions with the court physician, especially since Arthur made no secret of spending his nights in the library, and hardly glanced in her direction.

Foolishly, she'd assumed Emmett had taken care of things. That he'd cast some kind of protective charm. But she hadn't known how to bring it up, in case that wasn't actually a thing, and now . . .

Now it was too late.

She flopped back on her bed, staring up at the canopy, decorated with a peach fringe. She wished she were in her own bedroom back home, with her soft embroidered pillows she'd had since she was a girl, and her view of the rose garden, and her true friends, not these scheming courtiers who couldn't care less about her. She was just a guest here. Not even a guest—a gift, to the kingdom of Camelot. A thing her father had tried to trade for his precious treaty.

She was all alone. Or, not alone. And that was precisely the problem.

A hot tear trickled from one corner of her eye, sliding down her cheek, and she didn't wipe it away, even though it would ruin her powder.

Let it, she thought bitterly. She'd already ruined everything else.

Chapter 6

For the fifth night that week, Arthur strolled back to his room from the library, a stack of books tucked under his arm. Even though he was exhausted, he knew he wouldn't be able to sleep for a good while yet. Emry hadn't appeared again as he'd hoped, and he was no further in his research on Anwen than when he'd started.

The castle was peaceful at night, in the soft glow of low-burning torches and banked fires. The quiet was punctuated only by the slap of his boots against the stone floors. And, unfortunately, the boots of his guard. Dakin let out a loud yawn, and Arthur rolled his eyes. The young guard had slept for hours in the library, and Arthur had a strong suspicion the moment he closed himself inside his room, Dakin would go right back to sleep outside his door.

Not that Arthur feared a middle-of-the-night attack in his bed-chamber, but it was the principle of the thing. Dakin acted as though his duties got in the way of sleeping, chasing after kitchen maids, and bulking up his biceps on the training fields.

"I could send for some coffee, if you're tired," Arthur offered.

Dakin cracked his neck. "Nah, that stuff makes me shit."

Arthur groaned, wishing for the thousandth time that he could choose his own guards.

But no. His father insisted on picking them personally, so Arthur was stuck. If only he could rescue Tristan and Percival from gate duty and dungeon patrol . . . set them up with some stools and a little table in the antechamber where they could play cards and eat snacks, and where Arthur could sometimes join them.

They reached the royal wing, and Arthur frowned.

Something was wrong.

The guards stood at the ends of the hallway, not outside his father's door. A maid was having hysterics, and another girl was trying to calm her. Then the royal physician's assistant, still in his nightshirt, hurried into his father's apartments, carrying a medical bag.

"What's going on?" Arthur asked the serving maids.

They stared at him with wide eyes, bobbing twin curtseys.

"The king has collapsed," one of them whispered.

The king's bedchamber was stifling. A fire burned high in the hearth, with enough logs to heat an entire wing of the castle in winter. Arthur felt ill and light-headed from the heat as he pushed past his father's guards.

"Father?" he called.

The curtains were drawn, and the windows closed, as befitted a sickroom. Gold and silver adornments glinted in the firelight, and the air was thick with a cloying, smoky incense.

"What are you doing here, boy?" King Uther called irritably.

Arthur's heart slowed its frantic pace. Perhaps nothing was truly the matter. He made his way forward, taking in his father's scowl with considerable relief. "I saw the commotion and worried," Arthur said.

"I'm perfectly well," the king said. "I just tripped over that blasted stool and hit my head."

Arthur frowned. That wasn't what the hysterical maid had said.

Bruwin, the royal physician, bent over the king with a jar of leeches. King Uther was propped up on a mountain of silk pillows, looking sallow and unwell.

Arthur's frown deepened. "You're bloodletting for a head injury?"

"To rebalance the humors from the shock, Your Highness."

Arthur held back a sigh. His father's eyes were yellowed and glassy, and his stomach was thick with bloat. He doubted the cause was a bang on the head. Which meant the royal physician was lying. Or was shockingly wrong in his treatment.

Arthur wished the man would leave. Perhaps then he could open a window, bank the fire, and do away with the royal physician's superstitious nonsense. But his father preferred Bruwin's traditional methods of purging and bloodletting to the healing potions Master Ambrosius brewed in the wizard's workshop. Most of the castle did. A magical tonic to help with digestion or ensure a good night's sleep never bothered anyone, but they were mistrustful of what they didn't understand. And it wasn't as though the ancient, eccentric wizard, or his troublemaking teenage apprentices, inspired much confidence.

"What an interesting remedy," Arthur said carefully. "I'd love to learn more about it."

"As would I," said Lord Agravaine, striding into the room.

The king's closest advisor should have looked ridiculous in his nightclothes. But between the somber black of his dressing gown and his glittering dark eyes set against the deep brown of his skin, Lord Agravaine conjured an air of imperious disapproval.

"Of course, my lord," Bruwin said, motioning for his assistant, a pale, nervous lad with a shock of red hair, to continue administering the leeches. "We may speak in the hallway."

"We most certainly will not," Lord Agravaine chastised. With a disapproving scowl, he pushed open the door to the king's study, a room that Arthur knew well. The chamber was empty, with just a guttering candelabra left on the desk, and a banked fire burning low in the grate.

Once they were all inside, Lord Agravaine clicked the panel shut behind them. The physician was fidgeting, his face ashen.

"Well?" Lord Agravaine asked, an edge to his voice. "Has it gotten worse?"

"Has what gotten worse?" Arthur asked.

Bruwin grimaced. He looked nervous as he whispered, "His Majesty suffers from liver insufficiency."

A shadow passed across Arthur's face. He'd always known his father drank more than he should. Yet the news that it was more than a vice—that it had become a condition—struck him like a blow.

"And yes," Bruwin said to Lord Agravaine, "it has gotten worse."

"So, he didn't trip over a footstool," Arthur pressed.

"No." The single word was delivered with such force that Arthur winced. The physician went on, "I had to think of something after the chambermaid found him unconscious on the floor."

"We will have to make sure the footstool remains in his chamber, so he may trip over it again," Lord Agravaine said carefully.

The royal physician nodded.

"Surely liver insufficiency is treatable," Arthur pressed, not understanding.

Bruwin and Lord Agravaine exchanged a look. "In the early stages, yes," said the royal physician. "But the king has ignored my advice to abstain from drinking, and his condition is now advanced."

"How advanced?" Arthur asked, dreading the answer.

The physician looked away. Swallowed thickly. And when his gaze returned, his expression was grave. Even before the man spoke, Arthur knew.

"He has a year. Perhaps less."

No.

In that moment, Arthur's heart was made of glass. And he felt it shatter.

His father was going to die.

His chest clenched, and everything warped, and suddenly, he couldn't breathe. The walls of the study felt like they were pressing in. He was going to lose his father. Not someday, but soon. He was going to become king. And there was nothing he could do to stop it.

He could feel the pressure of the two men's stares, and how they weren't looking at him so much as looking to him. And he hated that he was expected to be something more than a heartbroken son who was reeling from the news of his father's terminal illness. That, in this moment, he needed to be their future king.

He forced himself to take a breath, and then another. To be here, in this moment, instead of bolting from the room and finding somewhere private to let out the tangled sob that was lodged in his throat.

"I see," Arthur said shakily. "Could you be mistaken?" He hardly dared to hope.

Bruwin shook his head. "I know this affliction well, Your Highness. He will get worse, not better." Belatedly, the physician added, "I'm sorry."

Arthur nodded, though the words meant nothing. Everyone had been sorry when his mother had died, but it didn't bring her back, and it didn't dull the pain, and it didn't change what he was going through. What he'd go through again, barely two years later.

His father had always drunk himself to excess. Arthur had thought nothing of it, yet now the memories assaulted him. All the times attendants rushed forward to fill his father's cup. The constant bottle of wine on his desk. The way Lord Agravaine handled more and more of his responsibilities.

Why hadn't he suspected? The truth had been right there in front of him: The way his father had summoned an apprentice court wizard, and been so insistent on arranging a politically advantageous marriage. The way he'd thrown himself a lavish birthday party, inviting the heads of all the surrounding kingdoms so that he might be seen in good health. None of it was an accident.

His father had been preparing to hand over the keys to the kingdom. Not because he wanted to, but because he had no other option.

"Why wasn't I informed of this earlier?" Arthur demanded of Lord Agravaine.

"His Majesty does not wish you to know."

The words struck him like a blow.

"But I'm his son," Arthur said, incredulous. Surely his father didn't hold him in such low regard. "Perhaps he's just waiting for the right time?"

"His instructions were clear," Lord Agravaine said apologetically. "You were not to be told until the very end. He wishes to keep his dignity."

"I would not take it from him," Arthur whispered.

He'd hoped—foolishly, it now seemed—that one day, his relationship with his father would improve. That they would bridge the chasm that divided them. Instead, Uther wished that distance to be even greater. Was it so difficult to be both a king and a father?

Or perhaps, Arthur thought glumly, the problem rested with him. He knew he wasn't the son his father had hoped for, despite everything he had done to try and prove himself. He'd pulled the sword from the stone, a blade that could only be freed by the rightful king of all England. He'd recovered Excalibur, the sword of the one true king. And his father's thunderous disapproval still rained over him.

"His Majesty can't learn that you've found out," Lord Agravaine warned. "You must pretend you believe he tripped."

"You're joking," Arthur said, but it was clear that Lord Agravaine was serious.

"It will be better this way. For all of us."

Arthur shook his head. "I can't just . . ."

Lord Agravaine put a hand on Arthur's shoulder, his expression grave. "Yes, you can. I worry he will steer Camelot toward disaster in his anger if all is not as he wishes."

He hated that Lord Agravaine had a point. The last time his father had flown into a temper, he'd called for Emry to be publicly executed. And before that, he'd strong-armed Arthur into a betrothal, threatening to make him a prisoner in the castle if he refused.

"Keep your silence, for Camelot," Lord Agravaine advised.

The royal physician nodded in encouragement.

"For Camelot, then," Arthur agreed.

Lord Agravaine's eyes met his, and for the first time, Arthur saw a deep sense of worry there.

"You will inform me of my father's condition," Arthur stated. "Whether he desires it or not. I will keep the knowledge to myself, but if I'm to take charge of this kingdom, I wish to be prepared."

Somehow, Arthur managed to hold it together long enough to return to his rooms. There, he collapsed on his bed and willed himself not to go to pieces.

Chapter 7

Arthur tried not to be too obvious as he stared at his father across the table during the royal council meeting.

Other than being even more irritable than usual, the king seemed to have recovered well enough from his collapse the evening before. Arthur, meanwhile, was still reeling. He didn't understand how Lord Agravaine was carrying on as though it were business as usual. Though the king's most valued advisor had always kept his cards, and his emotions, close. And now Arthur would have to do the same. He tried to drag his attention back to what the royal advisors were saying.

"The Duke of Cornwall is becoming a problem," Lord Agravaine insisted. "My spies report a large swath of Lansdowne Forest has been razed."

"Perhaps he is building a new addition to his castle," said the king, with a dismissive wave of his hand.

"Perhaps he's fortifying his castle," Lord Agravaine suggested.

"To what end?" questioned the king. "Gorlais wouldn't dare to attack me."

Arthur grimaced. His father didn't know the half of it. At the sword-fighting contest during the king's birthday, the duke had slipped poison into Arthur's wine. It had only been Emry's quick spell work that produced an antidote in time. Arthur had nearly died. He just hadn't been able to prove the duke was behind it, so he told no one. And he worried that such a failure had only infuriated and emboldened a man like the duke.

"He might be fortifying against King Yurien," Arthur suggested. "It's possible he fears an attack."

Uther drummed his fingers against the table, considering this. "Is there any reason to suspect Yurien will launch one?" he demanded.

"His army grows by the day, but no one knows which direction he will turn it," reported Lord Agravaine.

"Is there any news from France?" Arthur asked hopefully.

"Nothing definite," said Lord Agravaine.

Arthur knew Lord Agravaine feared King Yurien's boy, Mordred, would be betrothed to Princess Anne, cementing a worrying alliance. It was why he had dispatched his eldest son, Gawain, to French court, to dissuade King Louis from making such an agreement.

"Although the Lothian queen is not accounted for," Lord Agravaine continued, "and could have the French queen's ear."

Only Arthur's closest friends knew the truth of what had happened to her, that she had gone through the portal to Anwen. It was possible she would never return. It was also entirely possible that she would return with a vast magical army at her disposal. And he hated not knowing.

"Morgana is of no concern to us, surely," Arthur lied, watching his father for any reaction. But the king didn't so much as blink at the name. He had forgotten her, and what he had done. When Arthur had learned why the Lothian queen was so set on taking down King Uther and his heirs, he had almost confronted his father about it, but in the end, he'd kept the knowledge to himself.

The same way his father had kept the knowledge of his own illness to himself.

As the meeting progressed, Arthur couldn't help but think how these problems would soon be his. How he would be the one to sit at the head of the large rectangular table, which seemed ridiculously unnecessary, not to mention unbalanced, in the space.

Camelot was prosperous, but it shared borders with both a kingdom and a duchy that couldn't say the same. And while Cameliard was friendly, Cornwall was a small but definite threat.

"The duke isn't trustworthy," warned Lord Agravaine. "Not so long as there's a possibility his son will inherit the throne and he could rule as regent."

It was an unfortunate twist of fate that thirteen-year-old Maddoc was next in line after Arthur. And if the duke snagged hold of the throne, it would spell disaster for Camelot.

Arthur realized that everyone was staring at him. "Er, right. That," he said weakly.

His father had been clear about his expectations that Arthur would take Guinevere as his wife and immediately produce an heir, whose rightful claim to the throne would shuffle Maddoc further down the line of succession.

What a mess.

There were so many expectations pressing in on him from every side. He didn't want this. He hadn't asked for it. And yet, he knew he had no choice.

After the council meeting, Arthur helped himself to a gelding from the knights' stables while no one was watching. And, for a rare moment, he was free.

He rode hard and fast through the royal hunting grounds, the trees and sky blurring past. Daylight filtered through the treetops, and he felt the solid reassurance of a leather saddle beneath him. He needed this. To get away from the castle and clear his head. He took a deep breath, and then another.

His father hadn't said so much as two words to him after the council meeting. He had swept from the room complaining loudly of a headache, and demanding that no one bother him with anything else for the afternoon. Arthur didn't know why he'd held out hope that his father would change his mind. That he would look to Arthur, request a word in his chambers, and set right what felt so disastrously wrong. But his father hadn't. And perhaps, in the time they had left, he never would.

Arthur's horse jumped over a fallen log, and he leaned forward, encouraging the beast to go faster, even though it was hopeless. He couldn't outrun his future. He'd thought he would be ready to lead the kingdom, when the time came. But then, he'd thought there would be more time.

When he reached the circular clearing that held the old stone chapel, he knew it was no accident he had ridden to this place.

His mother's tomb.

Before she died, she had loved coming to this clearing. She'd brought picnics for them, and asked Arthur to point out the different types of trees and plants as they walked, and smiled as he recited the names. But that had been a long time ago. Back when the other noble sons had called him Prince Bastard the Spare when they thought he couldn't overhear. Lance had gotten himself a month of kitchen duty for punching the lad who'd started it.

Arthur had come here even after his mother grew too frail and ill to join him. In this private place, he had hidden himself away from all the gossip and the noise, and imagined so many things. But most of all: a life outside the castle walls.

And now it was never going to happen.

Arthur slid from his horse and pushed open the door of the ancient stone building. There was a crumbling altar set beneath a stained glass window, covered in wax drippings from ancient candles. And at the far end of the space, his mother's stone sarcophagus. It was carved of

white limestone, with the reclining effigy atop, an artist's approxima-
tion, cold and distant and nothing at all like Queen Igraine had been.

He slid down against the wall, the stone rough against his jacket,
and put his head in his hands. "I can't do this," he said. "Any of it."

He had never felt so alone. How could his friends possibly understand what he was going through?

His friends. He didn't know how to tell them. And when he did,
everything would change in an instant, even worse than it already had.
Lance was barely a month into his squire's training, and Emry was no
more ready to be a court wizard than he was to be a king.

But maybe he didn't have to tell them right away. Maybe he could
pretend, for a little while longer, that he wasn't about to lose his father
and inherit a kingdom.

Arthur sighed. He'd never noticed before, but the old church was
covered with runes, not unlike the stone slab beneath St. Paul's. No
wonder he'd always been drawn to this place. It belonged to a time of
monsters and myths, when heroes rode noble steeds and performed
deeds of derring-do.

Emry would love it.

He pictured bringing her here. The bright spark in her eyes as she
realized what he had planned. There would be a picnic, all laid out. And
the two of them, alone in this quiet clearing, with cakes and wine and
perhaps a stack of books to read. Emry with her head in his lap. With
her soft mouth—

No.

He was going to be king. And kings didn't plan secret, romantic
picnics with their court wizards. They planned treaties, and legislation,
and wars.

I'm going to miss everything, he realized. Everything that's supposed
to happen when you're nineteen. He'd already missed so much that

he hadn't quite realized there was even more that could be taken from him. All his dreams, gone: University. Raucous nights out at the tavern. Stirring trouble with his friends. Dating.

Instead, there would be council meetings and petitioners and a constant, suffocating sense of responsibility. For an entire kingdom. No—thanks to the prophesy and Excalibur, for more than that.

For all of England.

Chapter 8

Morgana stumbled through the forest, shivering as another gust of icy wind howled through the trees.

That first night, she had gone back to the stones, flinging every spell she could think of in their direction, but nothing had worked.

The passage was gone.

And so was her magic.

Without it, she felt curiously hollow, like a vital piece of her had been scraped away. And the parts that were left no longer fit together in the way they were supposed to.

For years she had dreamed of this world, and the treasures it contained. She knew its stories by heart: Tales of a castle in the clouds with an invisible drawbridge. Of sisters who heated a magical cauldron with their breath and stole away to the vanishing tomb of a lost saint. Of enchanted beasts, unbeatable swords, and magic with a mind of its own.

Yet if those things were here, she hadn't found them. All she'd found was the pain of an empty stomach, parched lips, and a torn dress that she had worn for days.

She was stranded in this endless forest, weaponless, without even a whisper of magic, in a world brimming with so much power that she could taste it on the air. She was starved for magic, and all the while, it taunted her.

Her skirt snagged on a fallen log, and she swallowed down a scream of frustration as she ripped it free.

She hated it here. Hated feeling powerless and small and trapped.

And then, she heard the soft burble of running water. She plunged forward, licking her cracked lips, branches scraping against her arms, until she found the stream. She fell to her knees at the water's edge, cupping the cool liquid in her hands and drinking greedily. The stream was narrow enough to jump across, but perhaps it grew wider. Perhaps it led somewhere. She meant to find out.

Behind her, shadows shifted in the forest. An unnerving sensation of something moving—something enormous—shuddered up her spine. She whirled around to face a monster. The creature was enormous, with thick leathery wings, and the legs and claws of a lion, but twice as large. It growled, revealing rows of dagger-sharp teeth.

"μαχαιριά!" she cried, hoping desperately the spell would work.

It didn't.

Panic tore through her, along with another, less familiar emotion: fear.

She was utterly defenseless. The creature pawed the ground, one sinewy wing torn and hanging. Morgana felt hollow as she realized that there was something *worse* than this beast, something that had injured it.

The creature let out a bone-shuddering screech, and Morgana ran.

Tree branches scratched at her like feral animals as she batted them aside, her breath coming in gasps. The creature crashed through the forest after her, until the distance between the trees became too narrow for it to follow. It roared in frustration.

She was safe, for now.

And then, through the thinning trees, she spotted a long stone wall. A village. She stumbled toward it, worrying what she would say to the guards at the gate. But there was no one. The gates stood open, the road into town unnervingly silent.

The wrongness prickled at her, and she ignored it. It was a town, with food and warmth and beds. Nothing else mattered. Yet the sense of wrongness grew stronger. The silence was thick and consuming. Her footsteps were the only sound she heard.

She came upon a sleeping man slouched at the bench of an apple cart, a crop of fruit in the back. Her stomach gnawed with hunger. She crept forward and reached in to snatch an apple, but the fruit was stuck, as if by magic. And then she realized that the man was not asleep, but bound by the same strange magic.

Something was wrong with this town.

She pressed on, but everyone and everything in it was the same. Every hearth was covered with frost, every piece of food stuck fast, every person cursed into a state that was neither life nor death, but a nightmarish in-between.

Suddenly, a small creature that was a cross between a rabbit and a fox bounded past. Another streaked across the road after it. Everything was under an enchantment, Morgana realized, except, apparently, the magical creatures.

She knew better than to stay in this place and become ensnared by the same curse. There was a road beyond the gate, and roads had to lead *somewhere*.

She sighed, despairing at the thought of more famished, freezing nights in the forest as she walked toward the gates. And then she stopped short as the enormous beast from the forest sprang through them with a ravenous screech.

It had followed her.

Chapter 9

Emry crouched in the clearing, blood trickling from her nose as three enormous boulders swirled over her head.

She was trying to provoke Anwen's magic by expending her own, but it wasn't working. She sighed, and one of the boulders dipped perilously low. "Don't you dare!" she snarled, flicking her wrist.

The boulder floated up to join the rest. Her arms were shaking from the effort, and she felt dizzy, which meant it was only a matter of time until her own magic began to misfire.

"*Pessum,*" she said, bringing her hands together and letting the boulders drop.

Anwen's magic had stayed strangely silent since the night in the library, but she could feel it coiled within her.

"You want out, then get out." She extended her wrists and turned her palms toward the sky, expecting the magic to rise up, but nothing happened.

"Come on," she muttered. "I dare you."

She drew more of her own magic than she ever had before, flinging spells silently, and without her wand. She threw out her hand, and a tree branch cracked and fell. Flicked her wrist and sent the fallen branch flying across the forest. Bent down and ran a line of fire along the parched earth, then snapped her fingers and extinguished it without a word.

She stopped, hands on her knees, gasping for breath. She felt depleted, and faint, but Anwen's magic still lurked just beyond her grasp.

And she was no closer to understanding why, or figuring out how to use it.

"Ugh!" she complained, biting at one of her fingernails in frustration. A corner of it ripped off, and a small line of blood welled at her fingertip. Suddenly, the cold, thrilling magic was there, and she gasped with understanding.

She'd been bleeding on the way home from St. Paul's, when she had first felt the magic trapped inside her. And that scoundrel outside the tavern had sliced her knuckles with his knife. There had been the paper cut in the library. And now, she'd accidentally torn her nail, and there it was, the magic that she could feel in her veins, literally at her fingertip.

Blood magic.

Of course. It had been blood that had opened the doorway in the first place.

Flames flickered to life above her palms—above her scars—twisting up her arms.

"No, not fire," Emry begged, looking around in horror at all the dried brush. She let out a breath as the fire changed to ice. She shivered as the ice twisted up her arms, and then shot out, engulfing a tree. The tree crackled as it froze, icicles dripping from its boughs. One of them fell, smashing onto the ground at Emry's feet.

"Stop," she cried. *"Prohibere! παῦε! Stoppian!"*

The words of command did nothing. She stood there, shivering, waiting for the ice to melt back into the scars on her palms. The veins on her hand stood out, a bright silver against her skin. She'd figured out what summoned Anwen's magic, but she still had no idea how to stop it.

◑ ◑ ◑

"That will suffice, squire!"

It was about sarding time, Lancelot thought, lowering his shield. He was soaked with sweat, and beyond exhausted. All the other knights had finished an hour ago, but Sir Kay was always the first one on and the last one off the training field.

He wasn't the king's champion for nothing.

Lance offered Sir Kay the customary bow before gathering the swords and equipment that lay strewn across the field. He tried to hurry, since he'd taken Arthur's advice and invited Percival to join him for supper in the Great Hall. And he still didn't know what he was going to wear, or how he was going to endure the knowing smirks from the insufferable first-year squires at his table. Not all of them were awful, but there were rotten apples in every bunch, and this year's crop of squires seemed to be more rotten than most.

Don't panic, Lance scolded himself. *It'll be great.*

He sheathed the final sword, and Sir Kay grinned, running a hand through his honeyed blond curls that were an exact match for Lance's own. The knight was his father's younger brother, and their resemblance was pronounced. Over the years, many had made the assumption that Lance was Sir Kay's son, to Lance's embarrassment and Sir Kay's horror.

"A moment, squire," Sir Kay said, and Lance suppressed a sigh.

When Arthur had finally spoken up for him, insisting King Uther reinstate him as a squire, he still hadn't believed it would happen. And when he'd been assigned to Sir Kay, he had nearly laughed aloud. His uncle had never wanted him, and still didn't.

He was a cold and exacting master, but he was inarguably the best knight in Camelot. So, Lance gritted his teeth and did what was asked of him. Even if he suspected he had triple the tasks assigned to the other squires. Even if Sir Kay never gave him a turn on the training field, like he saw the other knights doing. Even if he was so exhausted from his duties that half the time he fell asleep with his boots still on.

"Did you need something else, Sir Kay?" Lance asked blandly, checking that the sheath was secure.

"See to it that my armor is polished by morning. And my longsword sharpened. At the whetstone this time, not with paper."

Lance nodded. Polishing the armor alone would take hours, and the knight knew it.

"Also, there's a rent in my chainmail," said Sir Kay. "I assume you're handy with such things?"

"Well, no—"

"Then you'll need to take it to the smithy. And watch while it's repaired, to learn how it's done."

Lance gave another bow, not trusting himself to speak. Sir Kay's armor, his sword, and his chainmail. There was less than an hour until supper. And he couldn't turn up at the Great Hall in his sweat-stained squire's tunic. But the smithy would close if he didn't hurry. And Sir Kay would make his life hell—or dismiss him on the spot—if he failed to complete his duties.

Lance walked across the tilting fields toward the forge, passing the familiar path to the guards' barracks along the way. As the barracks came into view, Lance had the strange feeling he had never been gone, and that his cot would be waiting for him.

But of course it wasn't. These days, he had a finely decorated suite, where a maid came each morning and evening to light the fire in the grate and provide a pitcher of fresh water, and a stack of soft linens. A suite he was desperate to get back to, so he might wash up, and run a comb through his overlong hair, and choose a jacket that showed off his broad shoulders to their best advantage.

Except the visit to the blacksmith took longer than Lance had hoped. The gruff, gray-haired smith insisted not only on showing Lance how to mend the armor, but how to forge the links as well. *Come on*, Lance thought, staring impatiently at the old craftsman as he slowly pressed the last link closed with a set of needle-nose pliers. When it was finally over, Lance looked to the clock tower in despair.

He was late. And there was no helping what he was wearing. Lance raced toward the Great Hall, brushing soot and grime from his tunic.

Percival was waiting outside, looking extraordinarily handsome in blue hose tucked into knee-high boots, and a soft fawn-colored jacket that set off the deep brown of his skin. He stood stiffly in the corridor, chatting with the guards who stood on duty at the door. Morian and one of his dim-witted, closed-minded cronies, Lance saw. Truly the worst of the castle guards.

Percival spotted him and waved with obvious relief. "There you are," Perce called. "I was beginning to worry."

Sard. He hoped Perce didn't think he'd meant to stand him up.

"I'm really sorry." Lance gestured at his sweaty, soot-covered tunic. "I got here as soon as I could."

"I can see that. Well, I'm glad you didn't go to any effort on my behalf," Perce joked.

"It actually took significant effort to look this terrible," Lance said.

"You don't look terrible," Percival murmured, leaning so close that Lance got an enticing whiff of clove-and-cedar cologne. "You look like a knight."

Lance swallowed nervously. "I think you mean a blacksmith," he corrected.

He knew he should offer Percival an arm, so they might enter the Great Hall together, but both of his were currently in a state of deep repugnance.

"Coming?" Percival asked, gallantly offering his.

"I'll get soot all over you," Lance warned.

"That better be a promise, squire." Perce winked, and Lance felt his cheeks go pink.

They stepped inside, and Lance pretended not to notice as Perce took a sharp intake of breath at the finery. The royal family sat at the front of the hall, their table raised above the others. Long communal tables of courtiers and nobles flanked the walls, the silver candelabra and serving platters glinting in the light. A harpist played in the corner, and young pages, who hoped to one day become squires, stood in their fresh-pressed livery, serving at table.

"This way," Lance said, nodding toward the wall where the pages waited with basins and fresh linens so they might wash their hands before dining. Lance's linen came away stained with grease and grime. The page gave him a withering glare when he handed back what was now an unfit rag.

"Right, shall we hope Arthur saved our seats?" Percival asked, nodding his chin toward the royal table.

It took Lance a moment to realize he was kidding.

"I'm seated with the first-year squires," he said. "It's assigned by rank."

Ordinarily, he was so thrilled to dine in the Great Hall that he didn't particularly mind being squashed at a table of snobbish boys two and three years younger. But tonight, he wished he sat anywhere else.

As he'd predicted, the other squires smirked and exchanged meaningful glances at his arrival. "A guest, Lance?" asked Fergus, a freckle-faced earl's son with a nasty sneer and deadly precision with a blade.

"Everyone, this is Percival," said Lance.

Percival nodded hello.

"We've already met." Fergus tilted his chin imperiously. "Surely you remember?"

"It's difficult to forget someone vomiting on your boots," Percival replied, his smile tight.

"Oh, is that where we know you from?" drawled tall, brown-skinned

Degor with a disarming grin. "So clumsy of Ferg to do that. A gentleman always aims for the gutter."

"I thought I was," Fergus replied coolly.

Lance's hands balled into fists. And then he felt the warning pressure of Percival's hand on his back.

"Don't," Perce warned.

Thankfully, the food arrived as a distraction. A hearty capon broth with roasted vegetables, fresh white rolls still steaming from the oven, and a platter of herb-encrusted guinea fowl.

"I'm sorry about them," Lance whispered. "They've—well—"

"Not yet taken the oath of chivalry? Nor heard of it, it seems," Perce finished, biting into a roll. He let out a soft moan. "I could house an entire basket of these."

"Be my guest. Although I should warn you, it's only the first course."

Perce shook his head in wonder. "You must've hated the guards' mess," he said, no doubt thinking of their nightly pottage, a hearty but bland stew, which was served with coarse loaves of barley bread.

"I was only a page before," Lance explained. "We served at table and ate our supper cold in the kitchens once we were through, before the platters went on to the staff."

Percival grinned.

"What?" Lance asked.

"Nothin'. Just picturing this lot serving at table and eating cold supper in the kitchens."

"I'm sorry I missed it," Lance said.

He tried not to let it get to him, the way the others held themselves apart. The boys from Lance's days as a page had already attained their knighthood. Most had left the castle on quests, and some had returned to their family estates upon the deaths of their elder siblings, since they now stood to inherit titles and lands.

Knighthood was a profession of younger sons, and, in Lance's case, illegitimate sons grudgingly recognized by their fathers. Which meant that even within their ranks, there was a hierarchy. Fergus and his friends should have served Lance at table. Instead, they had watched with glee as the prince's favored companion had accepted guard's duties, banished to the barracks in shame. And now he had returned, pardoned and squiring for the king's champion. He should have been their leader. Yet the others treated him as though he were of lower rank for having been a guard.

Lance glanced over at Percival, who was eating another roll smeared with fresh butter, and tentatively making conversation with droll, easygoing Dryan about the differences in their training regimens.

Percival gave him a small smile and pressed his leg against Lance's, keeping it there.

Lance went pink.

Screw what the arrogant squires thought. None of them had a handsome guard by their side, who could shoot arrows with alarming accuracy and run faster than anyone in the castle and who resembled a Greek statue beneath his tunic.

"Look at that guy," Percival whispered, flicking his chin toward an old, pot-bellied earl who was clapping his hands in time with the unmemorable harp music as though he'd never heard anything so rhapsodic.

Lance smothered a grin. "Look at his wife, who's clearly plotting to murder him."

Percival snorted at the glowering, pinch-faced woman by the man's side. "The poison she tipped into his soup should kick in any moment."

Lance laughed. "To deflect blame, of course, she's had to poison the entire table."

"Including herself," Percival added. "But she's spent the past five years slowly building up an immunity to the poison."

"Or so she thinks."

They'd entertained themselves just like this during endless hours of gate duty, making up ridiculous stories about the people who passed by. Yet somehow, it felt more charged tonight. More flirtatious. Lance glanced at Percival, tipping him a smile, and could see the guard felt it, too. And in an instant, the rest of the table melted away, and it was just the two of them, in their own private world.

After supper ended, Percival caught Lance's arm.

"I traded with Safir, so I've got the rest of the evening free," he began shyly. "Maybe we could go to a tavern . . . or you could show me your fancy new room," Perce ventured, looking adorably horrified at how forward he'd been.

Lance was about to suggest they start at the tavern, but then he remembered the unfinished tasks still ahead of him. "I still have to polish Sir Kay's armor," he said glumly.

"Oh." Perce seemed to deflate.

"But this was nice," Lance said. "I don't often, um . . ."

"Invite handsome boys to dinner?" Perce grinned. "I'd hope not."

"When's your next day off?" Lance asked.

"Not for a while, since I traded."

"Whenever it is, we'll go to a tavern," Lance promised. "My treat."

"I'll hold you to it, squire." Percival tossed him a wink and disappeared down the corridor. Lance watched him go, wishing he could follow.

Chapter 10

Arthur glanced around his father's study, trying to smooth his nerves. He had no idea why he'd been summoned without warning, and was being made to wait in the empty chamber.

Perhaps, he thought hopefully, his father had changed his mind about keeping his illness a secret, and was going to confide in him. Or, his treacherous brain whispered, perhaps his father had discovered that he had found out, and was furious. It wasn't as though he had ever been summoned for anything good.

The door opened, and Arthur's eyes widened in surprise as Guinevere rushed in, looking absolutely panicked. She glanced around the room, seeming relieved that the king had not yet arrived.

"Good afternoon, Your Highness," she said, bobbing a pretty curtsey in Arthur's direction.

He suppressed a sigh as he bowed in return. He'd thought they were past such formality, but apparently not.

"Do you have any idea—" she began.

"—why we're here?" Arthur finished. "No. I was hoping you did."

Guinevere shook her head and swallowed nervously, smoothing the bodice of her gown. She was trembling. And she looked pale.

"Deep breaths," Arthur told her. "It'll help."

"I see Your Highness has failed to notice that current court fashions involve tightly laced corsets," Guinevere replied.

"Oh, er, right," Arthur said, feeling foolish. He truly hadn't noticed. "So, how have you been?"

"Very well," Guin murmured politely. "And yourself?"

Arthur rolled his eyes. "How have you been, really?"

Guin's lips twitched with the barest hint of a smile. "Bored," she confessed. "I got desperate enough to read those pirate books Emry's become so obsessed with."

Arthur's expression turned to one of horror as he realized which books Guin meant. "The ones from the library?"

"You know of them?"

"Well, yeah, I bought them."

"They're *yours*?" Guin let out a delighted cackle, just as King Uther burst into the chamber.

She quickly dropped into a deep curtsey. Arthur bowed, his heart pounding as he straightened and took note of his father's expression. Not angry. A small mercy.

"You sent for us, Your Majesty?" Guin murmured.

"I did," said King Uther, dropping into his chair. He took up the waiting wineglass, drinking deeply. "There's no sense in delaying your wedding any longer. The ceremony will take place in two months."

Arthur stared at his father in disbelief. He'd known this was coming, eventually. But he'd assumed they would wait until the spring. He hadn't realized their engagement was to be so short. Although, knowing what he did, he should have anticipated his father would do something like this.

He looked to Guinevere, expecting to find a twin expression of horror on her face. Instead, the princess was grinning ear to ear.

"How wonderful, sire," she enthused.

"Doesn't two months feel a little soon?" Arthur asked, trying to tamp down his panic.

"If anything, it feels too long a wait!" Guinevere interjected.

Arthur stared at her, betrayed. He'd expected her to back him up. Instead, here she was, cheerfully throwing him under the horse for no reason that he could determine.

"I agree. This treaty, and this marriage, has been delayed too long," said Uther.

"Perhaps we could wed even sooner," Guinevere suggested. "Is next month possible?"

Arthur choked.

"The joining of Camelot and Cameliard is an auspicious event," said the king. "And my advisors inform me it will take some time to handle the preparations."

Arthur's stomach sank. The preparations. Right. Of course. Because their sham of a wedding needed to be announced throughout the kingdom, and celebrated in every village as Camelot welcomed their future queen. Little did they know that the toasts they'd make would be to a marriage that would never happen.

They hadn't quite worked out the part where they shook hands and went their separate ways in front of a horrified priest, but it seemed they had better do that soon.

"Those invited will need to make preparations as well," the king went on. "We'll want all the royal families of England present."

"Are you sure that's a good idea?" Arthur asked, thinking of the last time his father had assembled such a crowd.

"Of course, there will be a few exceptions," his father allowed, with a dismissive wave of his hand. "But it has been a long time since Camelot has had a royal wedding. There will be celebrations. Feasts."

"Perhaps even commemorative mugs sold in the markets," Arthur said dryly. "Painted with our likenesses."

"Is that the custom in Camelot?" Guin asked.

"It is now," Arthur insisted.

"We will announce it to the court this very week," said Uther.

After the king dismissed them, Arthur cornered Guin in the corridor. "What was that?" he demanded.

"What was what?" she asked, frowning prettily.

He'd thought they shared a plan. But Guin had gone rogue, and he couldn't fathom why. "You practically begged to walk down the aisle tomorrow!" he accused.

"So what if I did?" Guin retorted. "The sooner our kingdoms sign this treaty, the better. King Yurien could attack Cameliard any day."

"He won't," Arthur said confidently.

The Lothian king wanted magic on his side, that much was clear. Far more than just the enchantment that made him unkillable in battle. And as long as Morgana was in Anwen, he doubted Yurien would make his move.

If Morgana was in Anwen. He wished he knew.

"Have you forgotten that, until our wedding takes place, I'm stuck here?" Guin went on, growing emotional. "I miss my friends. I miss my brother. I miss my *life*." She was practically in tears. Arthur hadn't realized she was so miserable. But then, he hadn't thought to ask. "And you stood there cracking jokes about commemorative mugs!" she accused. "You agreed you'd pretend!"

Arthur lowered his voice to a whisper. "I'm pretending I'll go through with the wedding. Isn't that enough?"

"Hardly. You act indifferent about me!" Guinevere accused.

"How else am I supposed to act? It's a forced marriage!"

"I don't know!" Guinevere retorted. "But spending every night in the library isn't it."

"What do you care where I spend my nights?" Arthur asked, flabbergasted.

"The courtiers gossip!"

"They would do so even if you came to my room in your nightshirt, carrying a riding crop," said Arthur.

Guin gasped. "That is shockingly graphic! Apologize at once!"

"All right. I'm sorry," Arthur said.

"No, you're not! You're just apologizing because I demanded it," Guin said, furious.

Arthur frowned. "Is there a difference?"

"Oh my god!" Guinevere let out a small scream of frustration and stomped away, quite unprincesslike.

Chapter 11

"Wizard!" Arthur called, hurrying down the corridor after supper. "A moment!"

Emry stopped, wondering what he wanted, and all too aware of the curious glances that were being thrown in her direction as the prince called after her.

He was dressed handsomely, in a black jacket with silver buttons, and his best circlet. Whenever he dressed to impress, it meant he was nervous. And she hated that she knew that.

"You require something?" she asked, folding her arms across her chest.

"I've been trying to catch your attention since dessert," Arthur said.

"Strange, I hadn't noticed." In truth, she had noticed. She'd just forced herself to ignore him.

A corner of Arthur's mouth hitched into a grin. "I was wondering what you're up to."

"Oh, the usual," Emry said airily. "Being magic and doing crimes."

"Perhaps you could postpone those thrilling plans and join Lance and me instead?"

She should refuse, she knew. But the sarding jacket and crown. And the tension at the corners of his eyes. And the urgent way he was looking at her, as though he very much hoped she'd say yes.

Besides, she reasoned, nothing had happened after they'd run into each other in the library. And Lance was coming along. She so rarely got to see him. "What exactly will we be doing?" she asked.

"Hanging out," Arthur said. "It's been far too long since it's just been the three of us."

"You're sure he's free?" Emry frowned. It seemed Sir Kay was working him to the marrow as a squire.

"He probably has to polish a pile of armor," Arthur admitted. "But I thought you might know a spell to take care of that."

"I might," Emry admitted, as Lance rounded the corner along with a few younger squires, who were animatedly discussing an incident on the training field.

The boys fell immediately silent when they saw Arthur. They bowed obsequiously, while Lance rolled his eyes. A few of the boys threw curious glances at Emry. She tried to look fierce, just in case they weren't suitably intimidated.

"Can you r-really . . . y-you know?" one of them stuttered.

"Turn your nipples into garden slugs?" Emry finished. "Do you truly want to find out?" She drew her wand from her sleeve, and the squire looked as though he might faint.

"Um, I meant make magic swords," the boy ventured.

Emry threw a disgusted look at Lance. "You told them?" she asked, betrayed. The last thing she needed was a line of entitled squires outside her bedchamber, begging her to magic their training weapons.

"She absolutely can," Arthur said, adopting his most princely tone. "Whenever I command it. And only when I command it." He shot the boys a meaningful look, and they deflated.

"But the nipples thing is still on the table, if you'd like," Arthur went on as Lance choked.

"Practice makes perfect," Emry said sweetly, tapping her wand against her palm.

Lance's choking grew more strangled as the squires mumbled excuses and fled.

After they were gone, Emry rolled her eyes. "You enjoyed that," she accused, whirling on Arthur.

Arthur shrugged. "Squires are such easy targets."

"Speaking of squires," Lance said, heaving a long-suffering sigh, "if you need me, I'll be polishing Sir Kay's armor."

"Not tonight," Emry said. "I'm taking care of that. We're forcing you to hang out with us."

"Really?" Lance asked, brightening.

"And if Sir Kay gets upset that you outsourced, he may blame me," Arthur promised.

"That I'd love to watch," Lance said.

"I just—er—have to dispose of this first," Arthur said, gesturing sheepishly toward his circlet.

Lance raised an eyebrow. "Staying in the castle, are we?"

Arthur grinned. "Not if I can help it."

"What about this one?" Arthur suggested, as they passed a loud, shabby tavern where upbeat fiddle music spilled out of the open window.

Lance snorted. "Do you want to drink water but pay for ale?"

Emry craned her neck to read the sign. "I want the name, so I can send my brother here."

Arthur laughed at that. He couldn't remember the last time he'd been in such high spirits. It was exciting wandering the city in the company of his friends, every tavern sign promising a good time. He hadn't really thought Emry would agree to come and was pleased she had.

Her cheeks were pink from the cold, and her eyes were bright as she drank in the city sights. Arthur did the same, not bothering to put up his hood. He had needed this. Badly. And now that it was truly happening, he couldn't believe his good fortune.

"There's always Madame Becou's," Emry joked, naming Gawain's favorite brothel.

"Don't worry, I know a place," Lance promised.

He steered them down the Strand, toward a two-story brick building with a small wood sign shaped like a shield that proclaimed the tavern the Gilded Lion.

Lance wrenched open the door to a cozy, low-ceilinged room with heraldic symbols painted across the walls. A troupe of musicians played a popular tune on a dulcimer and tabor. Nearly all the tables were full, the atmosphere lively with conversation and laughter.

"Best beer in the city," Lance promised, as a short, dark-skinned man with a pointed beard and an elaborately ruffled jacket rushed forward to greet them.

"Welcome, welcome!" the man enthused. He ran a critical eye over Lance's purposefully shabby cloak. "We're awfully full tonight—would you mind sitting at the bar?"

"That's fine," Lance said with a shrug.

"Sure," Arthur agreed.

The publican caught sight of him and nearly choked. "Your Royal Highness!" the man fawned. "What an honor! An absolute honor!"

The room went silent. Even the musicians faltered. Arthur wished the floorboards would open up and swallow him whole.

"Please," the man went on, "allow me to show you to our very best table."

The publican flapped his hands at a seductively dressed blonde, who rushed to boot a party of young noblemen from a prime booth with an unobstructed view of the entertainment.

"That isn't necessary," Arthur said hurriedly. "Any table will do."

It was too late. He recognized Lord Dagonet's tiresome sons and a haughty young viscount as the patrons who had lost their seats. The lads protested their dismissal as the girl coaxed them toward a small corner booth. The girl must have said something, because all heads swiveled in Arthur's direction, and then the group went silent.

Arthur winced, hating how it looked. He managed a thin smile as the publican ushered them to the booth.

"I shall fetch a bottle of our establishment's best wine for His Highness," the publican said, snapping his fingers impatiently at the wide-eyed lad behind the bar.

"Actually, we'll take a pitcher of beer for the table," Arthur said.

Surprise flickered across the publican's face. "Of course," said the man with a deep bow.

After he'd gone, Arthur slouched down in the booth with a groan.

"Sorry," Lance said, making a face.

"It's fine," Arthur said tightly, even though it wasn't. It seemed the entire establishment, from the musicians to the barmaid to the patrons couldn't stop whispering about and gawking at their table.

The publican arrived with the beer, and Arthur took a sip, his eyes widening in appreciation at the fragrant and fresh drink, with a hint of citrus mixed in.

"Good, right?" Lance said knowingly.

"You're still in trouble," Arthur grumbled, trying to ignore the press of everyone's stares.

"When am I not?" Lance shrugged. "You've clearly gathered us for a reason. Out with it."

Arthur scrubbed a hand through his hair. "My father set a date," he said glumly.

"A date?" Lance asked with a frown.

Emry was quicker on the uptake. "For your wedding to Guinevere."

"I believe it's just being referred to as 'the royal wedding' to make things as impersonal as possible," Arthur replied sourly.

"When?" Lance shot him a sympathetic look.

"In two months."

"That soon?" Emry sounded surprised.

"Why can't the wedding wait until the spring?" Lance asked.

Because there isn't time, Arthur thought despairingly. "My father has always done what he wants," he said instead. "Why should this be any different?"

The table fell silent. It was like the opposite of a toast, Arthur thought. But he appreciated that they were acknowledging his misery and giving it space.

"At least you're not actually going through with it," said Lance.

"Still." Arthur sighed. "The money could be put to such better use. But my father wants to flex in front of a bunch of nobles and foreign royals—again."

"Since it went so great last time," Emry said sarcastically.

At that moment, the young viscount who had lost his table took the opportunity to approach. "Your Highness," he said, straightening from a deep bow. "A couple of lads and I have a game of dice going—terribly high stakes—and I would be remiss if I didn't invite you to join our fun."

"Another time, perhaps," Arthur said. After the viscount was gone, he pressed back a sigh. "Anyone mind if we get out of here?"

Emry reached for her cloak, and Lance finished his drink in one gulp.

Arthur raised his hood and slapped a gold coin on the table.

"It was a pitcher of beer," Emry said, incredulous.

"Doesn't matter." Arthur practically bolted for the back door.

The cool night air was a welcome reprieve from the overly warm tavern. He hunched his shoulders against the wind. His jacket was silk, and his cloak too thin, and it seemed Emry's was as well. Lance, who had stood guard outside the castle gates many a cold night, seemed unfazed.

Arthur was suddenly and unaccountably furious. It had taken so much to get one night out, and it had gone terribly. "'Don't worry, I know a place,'" he muttered, with an accusatory glance at Lance.

"That wasn't my fault!" Lance protested.

"Of course it was! All I wanted was some anonymity. I didn't want to be fawned over and treated like a royal!"

"Too bad, because you are one!" Lance bellowed.

"How could I forget?" Arthur shot back, stepping forward, his hands clenched into fists. Excalibur pulsed at his side, as though asking whether its services would soon be needed. He reached for the sword, breathing hard and fast.

"Enough!" Emry bellowed, shooting silver sparks into the air from her fingertips.

Both boys turned to look at her. She cleared her throat theatrically. "Stop squabbling, or else I won't share my spoils," she said, pulling her cloak aside to reveal a bottle of the publican's finest wine.

Lance let out a delighted laugh.

"You didn't," Arthur said, smothering a grin.

"Grabbed it on my way out." Emry shrugged. "Now, can you two stop fighting and help me find a good place to drink this?"

Arthur felt his anger dissipate. He looked over at Lance, who was cracking the tension from his neck. Emry was smirking at them, as though she knew precisely what she'd done.

"Remember when we were fifteen, and that nun . . ." Arthur began.

Lance shuddered at the memory. "I still have nightmares about frogs. Yeah, that should be around here."

"Boys," Emry muttered, as Lance led them along a narrow pathway between a grand estate and what looked like a convent.

"I haven't been here in ages," Arthur said, when the empty wharf came into view. "Do you think the old nun is still around?"

"I sincerely hope not," said Lance.

They sat down on the edge of the wooden planks, feet dangling above the dark water of the Thames, watching the thin lantern light of the wherry boats cut through the fog. It really was a wonderful view. The kind where you felt as though you were in the middle of everything, but still invisible to the world.

Emry uncorked the wine bottle with a snap of her fingers and took a swig before passing it to Arthur. He drank deeply, and when he was done, he saw that Lance was watching him with a crease between his brows.

"What's going on?" Lance demanded. "You're acting . . . off."

"No, I'm not," Arthur protested.

"Yeah, you are. You almost pulled Excalibur on Lance!" Emry accused.

Arthur felt his resolve crack. He'd thought he could keep the king's illness from his friends, so nothing would change, but now he felt if he didn't tell them, he'd go mad. "My father's dying," he confessed.

Lance choked. "Wait, what?"

Emry had a hand over her mouth, her expression somewhere between horror and panic.

"Liver insufficiency," said Arthur. "The royal physician says he has a year, maybe less. And I'm not supposed to know. He didn't want me to know. I found out by accident, and now I'm supposed to pretend that I didn't." He took a deep, shuddering breath.

Somehow, without his realizing, Emry had placed her hand on top of his. "Oh, Arthur," she said. "I'm so sorry. No wonder you're upset."

Lance passed him the wine. "You need this more than me," he said.

Arthur took a swig and stared out at the Thames, hurting, and for once not trying to pretend otherwise.

"We're here for you, if you need anything," Emry said, and Lance nodded.

"Just let us know," said Lance. "It can't be easy, losing your mother, then father . . . and gaining a kingdom."

"Thanks." Arthur nodded gratefully. His friends were acting normal about it. And he wondered why he'd ever thought they wouldn't. "What if I'm a terrible king?" he wondered aloud.

"You won't be," said Emry. "You'll probably be annoyingly good at it."

"Of course he will," said Lance. "With us advising him, it'll be the golden age of Camelot." Lance motioned for Arthur to pass him the bottle. "A toast. To King Arthur."

"Nope," said Arthur.

"Why not? A toast is a great idea," Emry insisted.

"Sadly, we've finished the wine." Arthur turned the bottle upside down and shook it to demonstrate.

"Stop that," Emry scolded. "You'll get your clothes stained and want me to fix them."

"Which you will. 'Cause you're my laundry wizard," he said solemnly.

"Better a laundry wizard than a master of the privy," said Lance.

Arthur shot him an appalled look.

"A what?" Emry asked.

"Someone to wipe his—"

"Oh my god!" Arthur put his head in his hands. "Stop!"

"Hold on," Emry said. "I'm still processing this. It's an actual job for someone to wipe the king's arse?"

"A customary title, and one that shall remain vacant, I assure you," Arthur said with clenched teeth.

"What happens when he's unavailable?" Emry asked.

"Excuse me?"

"Like, let's say it's his day off, or it's three in the morning—"

"I hate both of you!" Arthur ground out, as Lance cackled.

"Don't worry, the feeling is mutual," Emry grumbled. "Laundry wizard indeed."

Her hair had come loose from its braid, and her cheeks were pink from the cold and the wine, and Arthur couldn't help but imagine what her lips would taste like if he leaned in and kissed her.

Sard, he really had drunk too much.

The stars were starting to spin. But at least he didn't feel that horrible pressure in his chest anymore. For the moment, all his problems were far away. And his friends were right here, lying with him at the edge of the docks, drunk on stolen wine.

And he wouldn't have it any other way. He needed them by his side, and more than that, he wanted them by his side.

"I'm going to miss this," he said.

"Torturing me?" Emry suggested.

"Being able to escape," Arthur corrected.

A heavy door scraped open, and an ancient, furious-looking nun poked her head out, holding a broom like it was a poleax. "You there!" she yelled. "Get off that dock before I tan your hides in the name of the Lord!"

"Sard!" Arthur said, his eyes wide. "It's the nun!"

The nun rushed forward, beating her broom against the edge of a small pond.

Ribbit! Ribbit!

A hundred frantic frogs poured out of the water and surged toward the dock.

"Frogs," Emry said in horror.

There was only one thing to do.

"Run?" Arthur suggested.

"Run," Lance agreed.

Chapter 12

"I'm here about your wedding gown, Your Highness," said the royal tailor, bustling into Guinevere's parlor. His arms were full of fabric samples and designs, and behind him, an assistant trailed with even more.

Guin blanched. Ordinarily, she would have loved the chance to design a showstopping gown. Something scandalous and modern, perhaps with only one sleeve, or a neckline that plunged to her navel. Yet ever since King Uther had set the date for their wedding, all she wanted to do was curl into a ball, eat cake, and cry.

The last thing she wanted to do was choose a wedding dress, much less be measured for one.

"Do any of these catch your eye?" asked the tailor, spreading out a sheaf of sketches. "Or did you have a particular style in mind?"

Something that will still fit in November, Guinevere thought despairingly. Already, the bodice of her favorite dress was noticeably tighter than usual. She had expected her stomach to expand, not her bosom.

"Something ethereal and flowing," Guin said, "so I might resemble a Greek goddess."

Her maid, who was tidying Guin's vanity, stopped and frowned. The royal tailor looked suitably taken aback. His assistant actually gasped.

"But that's not the current fashion!" the man protested. "This season's bodice is tight, with boning at the sides, and a low neck, like so." He gestured to his sketches.

She would never get away with a dress like that. Guinevere scrambled, trying to think of a credible excuse.

"But surely, to wear something tight and suggestive in a house of God . . ." she said, making her voice small. "I couldn't."

The royal tailor's lips pressed into a thin line. "Very well," he said. "A modest gown for the ceremony."

"Wonderful." Guin breathed a sigh of relief.

The tailor reached for his ell, a wooden stick marked with divisions, and took out a few strips of parchment. "Please disrobe, so I may take measurements for the pattern," he instructed.

"Why can't you use the measurements you have?"

"The gown you are wearing is too tight. See how the bodice is straining at the seams?"

She'd hoped he wouldn't notice.

Dorota, her maid, came to unlace her bodice and remove her skirts, the girl's expression bland as always, but still, Guinevere's panic rose. She stood in only her shift, pasting on a smile as the tailor held up his stick and scribbled out measurements.

"I could let out your gown," the maid suggested shyly, from the corner. "It wouldn't be any trouble."

That was the last thing she needed. What if her maid whispered of the task? Or Issie and Branjen came to visit while she was letting out the seams?

"That isn't necessary," Guin said coldly.

She would start ordering large quantities of sweets from the kitchen to explain her weight gain, or else her maid would suspect soon enough. The girl was too demure to say, but there had been panic in her eyes as she'd laced Guin into the too-tight gown that morning. Guin had pricked her finger on an embroidery needle the other week, letting the blood drip onto her bedsheets, but she suspected Dorota hadn't been fooled. Perhaps she could send for her maid from home, after she married Arthur.

The thought shocked her.

They weren't actually going through with the wedding.

But perhaps they should.

She couldn't very well return home four months pregnant, having been rejected at the altar. To turn each other down for lack of love was one thing, but a baby would complicate such matters immensely.

Cameliard was a far more religious kingdom than Camelot, and women were expected to remain pure until marriage. In Camelot, Guin knew an unmarried pregnancy would be a scandal—Arthur himself was proof of that—but back home, it would be a true disaster. She would have no hope of finding a good match after being publicly rejected and ruined by the crown prince of Camelot. No matter if she'd rejected him as well.

And everyone would believe her child was Arthur's. It would turn their kingdoms against each other and do the exact opposite of what they hoped to accomplish.

She didn't want to marry Arthur. He felt more like a childhood playmate than a handsome suitor, but it was the easiest solution.

As for the baby . . . Arthur himself had been a scandal, born just a few months after his own parents' wedding.

Perhaps, if she convinced him the child was his, she might also convince him to go through with their arranged marriage. She remembered his off-color joke, about her coming to his bedchamber in her nightshirt.

Actually, that wasn't a terrible idea. He was a nineteen-year-old boy. She doubted he'd turn her away. Or question her when, a few weeks later, she revealed that their night together had created a complication.

After the men left, Guinevere took a deep breath, wondering if she could really go through with it. Seduce Arthur, lie to him, and then marry him.

She'd have to. Because she didn't see another choice.

◑ ◑ ◑

Emry sighed and flipped another page in the library book just as a hard knock sounded at her door.

"Arthur, I swear to god, I'm still having nightmares about frogs," she complained.

"Emry?" a girl's voice replied.

Emry opened the door, her cheeks burning as she came face-to-face with an enormous armload of fancy dresses.

"May I come in?" the stack of clothing asked.

"Er, be my guest," said Emry.

To Emry's surprise, Princess Guinevere staggered into her bedroom and dumped an avalanche of clothing onto her bed.

Emry sighed, expecting her cleaning services were needed.

"I hope I'm not interrupting," Guin said, trying to catch her breath.

"Not at all." Emry looked around, wishing she had a second place to sit that wasn't her bed. "I was just reading the most dreadful book."

"Oh no! Do the pirate captains not find the treasure and sail off together on their own ship?" Guin said with dismay.

"Spoilers," Emry warned. "Actually, it was a potions book by a former court wizard. Seemed he had a bit of trouble, uh, *performing*, and attempted to remedy it with a magical solution."

Guin giggled. "Ugh, why on earth are you reading that?"

Emry shrugged. "I'm trying to find the answer to a magical problem," she said. And then she realized she'd said too much. "Something Master Ambrosius assigned me. I'm sure he'd love to know he accidentally sent me down a rabbit hole on male performance anxiety."

"I'd love to see his face when you tell him," said Guin.

"Magical applications are nothing to be laughed at, girl," Emry said, in an impression of the old wizard.

"Oh! That's him exactly!" Guin beamed. "Do another."

Emry frowned, thinking. And then she raised her chin and declared with a devilish grin, "Why should I learn such humiliating spells? My father was the greatest wizard who ever lived."

Guin looked taken aback. "Emmett," she said softly. A mix of emotions flittered across her face.

"I'm sorry," Emry apologized. "I know you two aren't in the greatest place right now."

"It's whatever," Guin said. "It's—he's—oh, I can't stand men!"

"Whenever I feel that way, I go and find a pretty girl to obsess over," Emry advised. "Makes me forget that boys exist entirely."

Guin shook her head. "It's just boys for me."

"No fun." Emry remembered the pile of dresses. And Arthur's joking accusation that she was his laundry wizard. "So, I'm guessing you need some stains removed?"

Guin went pink. "It's a bit more embarrassing than that. I'm, um, having trouble fitting into some of my dresses."

Emry brimmed with sympathy. She'd put on a few pounds herself from all the rich foods at the castle. And with her limited wardrobe, the situation was entirely inconvenient.

"The same thing happened to me," she assured Guin. "It's no wonder, with all the butter Chef puts in everything."

Guin nearly laughed, looking far less embarrassed.

"He uses pounds of it," Emry insisted. "In the vegetables, even! I keep getting pimples!"

"So do I," said Guin miserably.

"And Emmett said it was all of the potion-making seeping into my face." Emry scowled.

Guin laughed. "Sorry," she said. "Was it mean to laugh?"

"Not at all." Emry gave her a small smile. "It's nice to have someone to talk with."

"It really is," Guin agreed, sitting down on the bed and running a hand over one of the dresses.

"So, you want me to let these out for you?" Emry asked.

Guin looked relieved. "If it isn't too much trouble."

"Just a simple enlargement spell," Emry said, reaching for her wand. She pushed up her sleeves and reached for one of the gowns. "About an inch in the bodice?"

"Two, please, so I might actually be able to breathe," said Guin, leaning in to watch as the dress grew larger. "My goodness, that's fascinating. The original seams are intact. You can't even tell anything was done."

"Magic," Emry said with a smile.

"I'm going to be nosy, if you don't mind," said Guin, walking over to Emry's wardrobe and opening it. Her brow creased as she surveyed its meager contents. "Is this everything?"

"I'm no courtier," Emry defended. "Magic is messy, and it's impractical wasting coin on fine dresses I can only wear for supper."

"But you wouldn't only be wearing them for supper," Guin said. "You'd be wearing them for yourself." She picked up a lovely goldenrod gown with a velvet bodice from her alterations pile. "I don't wear this one very much. You should have it."

"Me?"

"And this one doesn't suit my coloring at all," Guin went on, plucking out a dark gray linen with pale edging and trailing silk sleeves.

"Are you sure?" Emry said, running a hand over the gray dress. It was so soft. And it had little seed pearls around the neckline. "These are beautiful."

"I have more that I never wear," Guin said. "I'll have my maid send them over."

"Thank you," Emry said, surprised by the girl's generosity.

"I do have one condition." Guin smiled mischievously. "You have to wear this one to supper tonight. And let me arrange your hair and do your makeup."

"That sounds suspiciously like a makeover," Emry grumbled.

"Does it?" Guin batted her lashes. "I can't imagine why."

Emry sighed. "All right, have at me."

Guinevere squealed.

Chapter 13

Emry slipped into the seat next to Emmett, who was deep in conversation with some of the jovial young nobles who sat at the far end of their dining table. Emry sighed, hoping her brother wouldn't spend all night conversing about some dreadful game of dice with his friends.

"Hi," she finally said.

Emmett glanced over at her and choked. "Good lord, what happened to you?"

"Guinevere gave me a makeover. There's soap in my eyebrows, and it looks amazing, and I'm incredibly upset over it."

"You are not," Emmett returned. "Lads, let's have your opinions."

The young nobles all swiveled around, and Emry fidgeted at the attention.

"Princess Guinevere attacked my sister," said Emmett. "Should Emry challenge her to a duel?"

"Absolutely not," said bearded Elian, with a booming laugh.

"She is to be commended. You are a vision, Miss Merlin." The elder of the red-haired brothers, whom Emry thought might be named Lionel, tossed her a wink.

"Our table is beautified by your presence," agreed his brother.

"Would the cosmetics have the same effect, do you think, applied to Emmett?" teased the athletic, dark-skinned lad, flashing a grin.

"We should find out!"

"They are twins, after all."

"Oh my god, stop," Emry begged, trying to sound angry, despite her helpless laughter.

The king stood and gestured for quiet, and Emry frowned. What was going on?

"A toast," said King Uther, "to my son, and his future bride."

Arthur's smile looked pasted on, and Guinevere's hand that held her goblet was trembling.

"The royal wedding will take place the first weekend in November," continued the king, "and all are invited to celebrate this joyous occasion. To the bride and groom!"

Arthur and Guinevere looked shocked by the announcement. They sat frozen as everyone in the Great Hall raised their goblets.

"To the bride and groom," Emry murmured, elbowing Emmett, who had remained silent.

"So, it's really happening," Emmett said mournfully. "Guin's leavi— I mean, getting married. Ow! Did you have to kick me that hard?"

"No," Emry said with a sweet smile. "Be nice, or I'll use magic next time."

"I'll use it back," Emmett threatened.

"You'll lose," Emry told him.

"Did I mention that you look very pretty this evening, sister?" Emmett said.

"I wholeheartedly agree," said Lionel.

As supper went on, Emry was determined to finally learn the boys' names, so she didn't embarrass herself. Lionel and Cal were the ginger-haired brothers, and the brown-skinned boy was Gary, a distant cousin of Gawain's.

Actually, they weren't such bad company, for entitled young lords. Sure, Elian's loud laugh turned heads, but it was Gary's quiet observations that set him off.

It was strange, but Emry's new dress and hairstyle and courtier's cosmetics really did make a difference. The boys kept eyeing her with interest, and as they dug into their dessert, Gary asked if she was enjoying the harp player, or if she preferred her music on-key, which had her choking on her wine. Four months, and not a word. But throw on a nice dress, pin up her hair, and apply a smoky eye, and suddenly she was on the receiving end of wry conversation. Noted.

After supper, Lionel hesitated. "My lady, I don't believe we've been introduced," he said, clearing his throat nervously. He was tall and pale, with a fiery mop of curls and a rather prominent chin. He was perhaps twenty, though his clothes were so fine that they made him seem older.

"You're Lionel, Lord Griflet's eldest son," she said. "We do dine together."

His smile faltered. "Right, but we haven't been *introduced*," he said, putting emphasis on the last word.

"Emmett!" Emry called. "Do you want to introduce me to Lionel Griflet?"

"You realize you're literally talking to him," Emmett yelled back, already halfway down the hall.

Emry tilted her head. "Does that count?" she asked.

Lionel sighed. "If it must. Perhaps I might be permitted to take you for a stroll through the castle gardens?"

Emry almost laughed at the absurdity of having to take his arm and make polite conversation. "Permitted by whom?" she asked, her smile growing sharp.

"I'll permit it," a cool, mannered voice said.

Emry whirled around, and sure enough, Arthur was leaning against the wall, hands thrust in his pockets, watching them with an unmistakable gleam in his eye.

She shot him a glare, but he forged on, enjoying the spectacle.

"I hear the stargazing is lovely in the hedge maze," he added with a wicked grin.

"Surely my new silk slippers would get ruined walking outside in the dirt!" Emry protested.

"Oh." Lionel's face fell.

Arthur looked as though he was choking back a laugh, and Emry felt certain he'd observed she was wearing her usual battered boots beneath her voluminous skirts.

"Another time, perhaps?" Emry suggested, not wanting to be unkind.

Lionel brightened. "I shall hold you to it," he promised. "I bid you a good night, my lady." He bent forward in a formal court bow, reaching for her hand and drawing it to his lips.

The situation was just as unpleasant as she'd expected. She could actually feel the press of his teeth, and when he pulled away, his mouth had left a bit of a wet spot.

After the boy left, Emry turned on Arthur. "You're a scoundrel," she accused, jabbing a finger into his silk doublet.

"Am I?" he replied. "I'm confused. Are you not interested in the lovesick ministrations of the eldest Griflet?"

"You know I'm not." Emry folded her arms and glared.

"My mistake." Arthur smirked, enjoying himself.

And then Lancelot appeared in the corridor. "Did I miss it?" he asked, grinning widely. "Is that dull lordling still making a pass at Emry?"

"No, he's gone," Emry said, pleased.

Lance pinched a bit of her skirt fabric between his fingers. "This is lovely. I've never seen you dressed so fashionably."

"That's it? You're not going to say anything mean?" Emry asked, surprised.

"Why would I?" Lance protested. "Now that you've got your bosom out, I can finally tell you and Emmett apart."

Arthur shook with laughter.

"And there it is," Emry muttered. "You know what? I give up. This is the last time I let Guinevere put soap in my eyebrows."

"Soap?" Arthur asked with interest. "You mean you didn't use magic to—" He waved a hand vaguely in her direction.

Emry bristled. "Guin attacked me with her cosmetics bag. Do you honestly think I would *magic my face?*"

"Er," said Arthur, fidgeting.

"Stepped in it, haven't you?" Lance added smugly.

"Excuse me." It was one of the king's personal guards. The one with the mustache as thick as a sausage.

"Can I help you?" Emry asked with a frown.

"His Majesty wishes to speak with you." The enormous, sausagey mustache wagged as he said it, which ordinarily would have been a delight. But not now.

The king wished to speak with her.

Sard.

Emry nodded and followed after the guard, trying not to panic. She had done nothing wrong. Other than accompany Arthur to a well-heeled tavern in the city, where she had stolen a bottle of wine. Other than keep her misbehaving magic a secret. Other than meet with the prince in the library late at night and read books that even Master Ambrosius would find incriminating.

The king stood with his back to the door when she entered, and motioned for the guard to leave them alone.

The guard hesitated a moment to shoot her a mustachioed glare before crisply pulling the doors closed behind him.

Emry bobbed a curtsey. "You sent for me, Your Majesty?"

The king regarded her with a deep frown. His eyes traveled from the twisted plaits in her hair to the bodice of her dress to the full silk of her skirts with blatant displeasure.

"I told you to stay away from my son," growled the king.

"I have, Your Majesty."

"You have not. You were seen in his company at a tavern!"

Emry winced. This was bad, but not damning. "I was protecting him. Or would you rather he went into London alone?"

Uther bristled. "He doesn't need your protection."

And he doesn't need you controlling our lives, Emry thought. Now that she knew the truth, she'd expected the king would look different. Sickly, somehow. Weaker. But he was still just as terrifying.

"And tonight," the king went on, "you are dressed entirely above your station as a castle apprentice."

Emry bit her lip. Emmett wore silk doublets and fur cuffs and pearl buttons, which the sumptuary laws designated only for nobles, yet she doubted he would ever get called into the king's chambers for a wardrobe violation.

"Princess Guinevere insisted I wear it," said Emry.

The king grimaced and paced the length of the room, stopping and staring into the hearth as though the flames held answers.

"Is it wealth and status you're after?" he asked. "A rich merchant to marry, and a grand household of your own?"

Emry spluttered, at a loss for words.

"I assume you wish to breed," the king went on. "Perhaps you will produce sons, of Merlin's bloodline. Would that not be a triumph? To watch them train to be court wizards?"

Emry stared at the king, indignant. "I have no desire for a husband. I came here to study magic!"

"Then do so," growled the king. "And stay out of the way otherwise. Remember, girl, you'll get no second chance."

Chapter 14

Emry pressed the point of the dagger against her wrist. She was in the king's hunting grounds again, and it was nearly supper, and she would have to stop soon.

She didn't want to stop.

Blood welled and dripped onto the dirt, and she winced at the pain. Anwen's magic surged to the surface, the way it had been doing for the past hour. The scars on her palms glowed bright, and tentative flames appeared, hovering just above her fingertips.

"Not fire," she grumbled. *"Smoca?"*

Latin didn't work, and neither did Greek. She'd racked her brain for the Old English, yet that was also proving useless. Nothing in any of the library books helped, or even hinted at what she needed to do. She had no idea how to control this magic. And until she did, it was nothing but a liability.

"Come on," she groaned, flapping her hands uselessly. "*Forst?* Ice? You've done it before." The flames responded by growing long and thin, until they stretched above her head. "Stop it," she cried. "Someone will see!"

At that, the tall purple flames crackled, then turned into beams of violet light. They shot upward, into the treetops. Emry winced, waiting for branches to fall, but thankfully, it appeared to be nothing more than harmless purple light.

"Fine, then," she muttered, folding her arms across her chest and tucking her hands into her armpits.

Nothing was working. Not commands or questions, not Latin,

Greek, French, or Old English. She could summon the magic, but she still couldn't make it obey. She bit her lip, blinking back tears. Her wrists were slashed with half a dozen shallow cuts, she was exhausted, and she wanted desperately to scream and to break something.

And then she heard footsteps in the forest, and a boy's voice calling, "Hello?"

Her heart pounded in distress. "Who's there?" she demanded.

"Emry?" Arthur stepped out of the woods.

"What are you doing here?" Emry grumbled.

"Visiting my mother's grave. What are you doing here?"

Emry stared at him in horror. "Your mother's grave?"

"Why are your armpits glowing?" he asked.

Emry looked down. Her hands were still folded across her chest, and her armpits were pulsing with a bright violet light. How inconvenient. "Magic," she snapped.

Arthur burst out laughing. "I can see that," he said. "Dare I ask why you're visiting my mother's grave and magicking your armpits purple?"

"None of it is on purpose," she said, dropping her hands to her sides. The light shot out from her palms, and Arthur's eyes went wide at the sight. She balled her hands into fists, willing the magic to go away.

It didn't.

"You're bleeding," Arthur said suddenly, noticing the cuts on Emry's wrists.

"Don't worry about it. I was just experimenting with a magic thing."

Arthur sighed. "Are you going to tell me why you're alone in the woods with glowing hands and self-inflicted knife wounds?"

Finally, the pulsing light faded, along with Anwen's magic.

"Nope," Emry snapped. "Now go away."

"Absolutely not," Arthur protested. "First you were avoiding me. Then you bolted from the library without warning. And last night, you were practically marched off to my father's chambers. Now this? What's going on?"

"Nothing! I—" Emry started, searching for a lie. But she didn't have one. And she was tired of lying. "There's been something wrong with my magic ever since that night in the cave," she confessed, explaining about the men she'd set on fire, and how she'd figured out her blood was what summoned the magic, but she still couldn't control it.

He listened thoughtfully, and when she was done, he frowned, considering. "Why didn't you *tell* me?"

"I didn't want to worry you."

"I would have welcomed the distraction! Finally, a way I can be of use, instead of made to stand in the wings, waiting for my cue."

"Was that—did you just make a theater reference?" Emry asked.

"Don't get used to it, wizard," Arthur warned. He leaned back against a tree and scrubbed a hand through his hair. "So, this magic problem of yours. Who else knows about it?"

"Just you," Emry confessed. "I'm afraid Emmett will forget and say something. And Master Ambrosius . . ." She trailed off, swallowing hard. "I can't screw up. Or else your father will send me back to Brocelande like he threatened."

"Threatened?" Arthur's brows knit together, his expression turning grim. "What exactly did he say to you?"

"That if I mess up even once, I'm done," Emry admitted. "And he warned me to stay away from you. Which I got a lecture about not doing the other night. I believe the lads whose table we stole at the tavern complained."

Arthur thought about this a moment. "When did my father give you this threat?"

Emry bit her lip. "Pretty much the moment we returned from fighting Morgana."

To Emry's surprise, Arthur laughed. It was the kind of laughter that came out when something wasn't funny at all, and it rang hollow. "So that's why you've been avoiding me," he said. "Why didn't you tell me?"

"Because if you talked to him on my behalf, he'd only dig in harder," Emry said. "Uther doesn't want me as an apprentice, and he's made that clear."

"But I do," Arthur said fiercely. "I want the Camelot we're going to build together. And I'll fight anyone who stands in the way of that."

"So, everyone, basically," Emry said with considerable sarcasm.

"I'm serious," Arthur insisted. He knelt in the clearing, reaching for his sword. He drew Excalibur, which pulsed with a familiar bright light, and laid it across his palms.

"You have my loyalty, my trust, and my sword, always," he said. "No matter how small the battle."

Emry gazed down at him, this beautiful boy on bended knee, offering so much of himself. Offering so many things she'd dreamed about and thought she could never have. "That was entirely unnecessary," she said, "but thank you."

"Anytime." Arthur smiled shyly. "Now, wizard, how can I help with your magic problem?"

"You can't," Emry protested. "I'm trying to protect you from this. I could hurt you—"

"I don't care," Arthur said, reaching for one of her hands. "Emry, don't you get that?"

"Don't you get that my magic is *broken*?" Emry retorted, blinking back tears. "In the moments when I'll need my magic the most, when everyone is counting on me—when *you're* counting on me—I'm going to let you down."

"Then we'll fix it. Together."

"You don't have to help me," Emry said. "I mean, I'm sure you have so many other things to worry about, now that—"

"Not more important than this," Arthur promised. "I need you by my side, remember?"

He stared at her, and Emry wanted nothing more than to press her lips against his. But they couldn't—they shouldn't. He had promised her his sword, not his heart.

"The Lady of the Lake speaks in riddles," she reminded him, remembering their unsettling journey to the Isle of Avalon.

Suddenly, Arthur's eyes went wide. "The Lady of the Lake," he said. "That's who you should talk to. She knows more about Anwen and its magic than anyone else."

Emry blinked at him in surprise. "That's not a bad idea."

"It's a brilliant idea," he corrected.

Emry grumbled, hating that he was gloating about it.

"And there's a chance she'll know what's happened to Morgana," Arthur mused. "To think I've been wasting my time in the library when we have an even better resource."

"Wasting your time in the library?" Emry raised an eyebrow at the unlikely phrase.

"You know what I meant," Arthur said tiredly. And Emry realized just how much weight Arthur had been carrying these past few months, between Morgana, and his father, and his engagement to Guinevere.

He was right, though, about the Lady of the Lake, and Emry couldn't believe it hadn't occurred to her sooner. The Lady guarded the island that divided the two worlds, a place that belonged to neither, and contained magic from both.

The last time Emry had visited Avalon, she'd seen for herself that magic worked differently there. The Lady of the Lake might truly be able to help her.

"Would your father let us go?" Emry asked doubtfully.

"No," Arthur said, a muscle feathering in his jaw. "So, we won't tell him."

"Won't you be missed if you just . . . disappear?" Emry asked.

"Unfortunately. But I'll come up with a credible excuse to explain your absence."

"You're not coming?" Emry asked, surprised.

"I would love nothing more than to ride off on a quest with you and Lance." He bit his lip, thinking. "You'll bring Emmett along, since you really are the only one who can keep him out of trouble. And a guard who knows the terrain."

That didn't sound too bad. "When I tell Emmett we're going to Avalon, he'll want to know why."

Arthur thought about that a moment. "I suppose someone ought to tell the Lady of the Lake what happened to the scabbard," he mused. "How's that?"

Emry hated to admit it, but it sounded as though it would work.

Chapter 15

In another world, in a cursed town, Morgana was running for her life. The monster was gaining on her, all fangs and claws and rage, a dark shadow at her heels.

A shadow that was going to tear her apart.

Morgana's breath clouded the icy air as she skidded around a corner, scrambling down the packed-dirt road. She had no weapon to defend against the monster, and a shiver raced up her spine as the creature roared in anger.

She needed somewhere to hide. Somewhere with supplies, where the creature couldn't follow. And then she saw the tavern, with its high, peaked roof, a dragon painted on its wooden sign. She threw herself inside and slammed the door shut, pressing her back against it.

Her breath came in ragged gasps, and she was shaking so hard she could barely think.

The tavern was small, with three long tables that took up most of it, bodies slumped over each one. Some still clutched mugs of ale, others were facedown in their plates. Even the cobwebs had turned to ice.

Everything and everyone was cold and still. Trapped. Frozen between one moment and the next.

There was no one to help her here. She didn't realize she'd been hoping there would be until the disappointment knifed through her.

At least she'd found warmer clothes. She reached for a thick woolen cloak clasped around a woman's shoulders, but it didn't move. And then she spotted a dagger at a man's waist. She grabbed for that, but it too stuck fast.

Something large and angry hit the door with a tremendous bang, and the entire building shook. Morgana tensed.

The creature had found her.

She looked around for something—anything—she could use to defend herself. Two swords were mounted above the hearth. She didn't know if they would come down, but she had to try.

She stretched on her toes, her fingers brushing the tip of one pommel. Just a little more, and there—the weapon fell to the ground. She scrambled for it, her knuckles scraping against the rough stone floor as she clasped the hilt with shaking hands.

The door slammed open, and the monster burst inside, forcing its way through the narrow opening. It caught sight of her and loosed a growl, lowered its scaly head, and then it charged.

Please, she thought. *Please don't let me die here, like this. I'll do anything.*

The sword rippled in her hands, and she wondered briefly if the blade was magic, and if it had heard her thoughts. She clenched her teeth and held the blade tight as the creature rushed toward her. *Not yet, not yet*, she told herself, though her every instinct screamed for her to run.

She lunged, thrusting the blade forward. She sliced only air as the creature reared back on its hind legs in fury. The monster let out a roar—that it never finished. Its limbs froze first, and then its jaws, trapped wide open.

Morgana stared at it in disbelief, still holding the sword in both hands.

Then one of the bodies at the closest table twitched. It sat up, twisting toward her in a way that didn't seem human. A girl, perhaps eleven or twelve, in rough-spun wool, blinked, a homemade doll clutched in her hand.

The girl's eyes were clouded with a dark, swirling fog, and Morgana had the strangest sensation that someone else was looking out of them. Someone powerful.

"Who are you?" demanded the child, climbing stiffly to her feet. Her voice was a child's voice—high and sweet—but there was an echo behind it that made Morgana shiver from more than the cold. An echo of another voice, which belonged to a grown woman.

"I am Morgana le Fay," she said. "A sorceress from another world."

"Your magic does not work here." The child's lips pulled into an unnaturally taut smile. "But mine does."

Chapter 16

Emry dropped her pack at her feet, her heart racing with excitement at the prospect of their journey. In the cold, gray fog of early morning, the castle courtyard felt as if it should have been still and silent. Instead, it was far too busy.

The castle guard ran their daily drills, the thunder of their feet punctuated by the clang of the blacksmith's forge. A cluster of kitchen maids carried pails of fresh milk and baskets of eggs across the lawn. And on the far-off tilting fields, Emry could see the squires hurrying to set out their knights' equipment. She squinted, standing on her toes and trying to catch sight of Lance.

"He's in the stables, saddling Sir Kay's destrier," Arthur said, coming to join her.

Emry wrinkled her nose. "Is that why you smell like horse?"

"I was inspecting your mounts," he said, pressing back a yawn with his fist. "Someone had to warn the poor beasts they'd be carrying wizards."

Emry rolled her eyes. "I'm not going to magic the horses," she promised. And then she bit her lip. "I wish you were coming with us."

"So do I." He looked as if he meant to say something else. "Good luck, wizard."

Before Emry could reply, Arthur was gone.

"Too early," Emmett complained, tossing his pack next to hers. He was eating a slice of toast, his hair a mess, his eyes puffy from lack of sleep. And under his traveling cloak, he had traded his courtier's finery for a brown wool jacket and breeches he'd worn back home.

"Oh god, we match," Emry said, realizing. Her hair was secured back in a braid, and her cloak was of green wool instead of dark blue, but she was wearing a similarly colored boy's jacket and trews tucked into knee-high boots.

Emmett groaned. "Go change," he insisted.

"Into what? A ball gown?"

"Someone less annoying?"

"I will if you will." Emry smiled sweetly.

"There you are!" a cheerful boy's voice called.

Tristan waved in their direction, leading three slim gray palfreys loaded with provisions. He was dressed plainly, in a traveling cloak and dark breeches and mud-splattered boots that had definitely seen better days.

"You're coming with us?" Emry asked, delighted. She hadn't expected the excitable young guard, who had often followed Percival and Lance around the training field like a hopeful puppy. In fact, she'd been bracing for dreadful company.

"Yep!" Tristan said, beaming. "I volunteered. Sounds far more interesting than tower duty. And anyway, one of my sisters married a Cornishman, and they live less than a day's ride from Avalon. My mum insisted I try to visit."

"I'm sure you'll be able to while we're on the isle," Emry said.

"Oh, good," Tristan said, relieved. "Because she gave me all sorts of baby things she knitted." He gestured to his bulging pack. "I tried to tell her, 'Mum, I can't undertake a royal quest with a satchel full of baby booties,' but she insisted."

Emry stifled a laugh. "We can and we will undertake a royal quest with a satchel full of baby booties," she pronounced.

Tristan grinned. And then he glanced between Emry and Emmett with a frown. "Is there a reason you're dressed to match?"

◑ ◑ ◑

That night at the inn, Emmett waited until Tristan had fallen asleep. Quietly, so he wouldn't disturb the young guard, he picked up his boots and his jacket and tiptoed to the door.

And then he noticed Tristan's bed was empty as well, his pack creatively tucked under the covers in imitation of a sleeping body.

Clever. And a trick he knew well.

Three guesses where to find him, Emmett thought wryly. He'd seen Tristan eyeing the tavern just as he had, and marking its place in the village, just three doors down from the inn.

He could hear the tavern before he could see it. He pushed open the door to the cozy, crowded place with fresh rushes on the floor and candles dripping wax onto the bar, and felt as though he were back in Brocelande, at the Prancing Stag.

And then he spotted Tristan hunched over a game of dice, sweating profusely. The young guard had a problem with gambling, Emmett knew. He had once famously returned to Castle Camelot wrapped in a friend's cloak and nothing else, having lost the clothes off his back in a bad wager.

"Mind if I join you lads?" Emmett asked, sauntering up to the table and hoping the young guard would have enough sense to keep his mouth shut.

The players mumbled their assent, and Emmett pulled up a chair, shooting Tristan a wink. He made sure to lose a few hands and display some nervous tells, convincing the others that he was no threat. When he started winning, he'd play it off as though he were shocked, laughing incredulously. He was just about to change a roll to his favor when he realized Tristan was down to his last few coins, and looked faintly green with panic.

Sard it all, Emmett thought. If Tristan had lost their money for lodgings and horses, they'd really be in trouble.

He let his own hand fall as fate dealt it—an unimpressive five—and then sent Tristan a winning roll. And another. And another.

The guard's eyes grew wide at his sudden luck, and his shoulders relaxed as his lost coins began to flow back to his pile of winnings.

"What brings ye out this way?" asked a large bearded man who, from the grease on him, seemed to be a blacksmith.

"Headin' toward Cornwall, to visit my sister and her new baby," Tristan lied smoothly. "Don't suppose you know of an honest day's work I could pick up along the way?" He gave a self-deprecating laugh. "Could use some coin, the way this night is going."

"Ye might check with the sheriff of Lansdowne," one of the men said. "The duke's fortifying his castle. Lookin' for men to cut the trees, men to build the battlements, and men to join his army."

"His army?" Emmett asked, and then, trying to sound disinterested, "Who is he planning on fighting?"

"That's the question, 'ent it?"

Emmett glanced uneasily over his shoulder before leaning forward and asking, "You don't think he's going to turn on King Uther?"

The man shrugged and drained his tankard of ale. "The duke's had his eye on that crown a long while."

A few of the others grunted in agreement. "He's prob'ly worried about King Yurien," grumbled the blacksmith.

"Then why 'ent he gone to Uther for aid?" one of the men retorted. "My brother in Cornwall says his taxes have tripled. His sons had to join the duke's army to keep food on the table. They're taking lads young as thirteen."

"Clever man, the duke," grunted the blacksmith. "He might become king yet."

Emmett nearly dropped the dice. "What makes you think that?" he asked.

"What good's a magic sword against an entire army?" The man shrugged.

" 'S what I've been saying all along," one of the men insisted, pounding his tankard of ale against the table for emphasis. "One sword can't defend a kingdom."

Emmett made his excuses and left the men to their game. But he didn't dare to go back to the inn. Instead, he hung around outside, practicing levitating a coin in his palm. A couple of minutes later, Tristan emerged.

"Thank you," the young guard said. "I nearly lost a month's wages."

"Don't mention it," said Emmett.

"Half's yours," Tristan said, holding out a handful of coins. "It's only fair."

Emmett reached for the money, but thought better of it at the last moment. "Keep it."

"Thanks," said Tristan. The young guard bit his lip for a moment before he blurted, "D'you think it's true what the men were saying about the duke?"

"I hope not. But I'm not fool enough to dismiss it."

"Me neither," Tristan said, worry darkening his gaze.

Emry glared at her brother the next morning, hoping he'd offer an explanation of where he'd snuck off to. But by midafternoon, it became clear that he wasn't planning on it.

How annoying.

Well, if he wasn't offering, she wasn't asking.

So Emry concentrated on the road, remembering many of the landmarks from the last time she had undertaken a quest to Avalon. And finally, as the sun started slanting toward the horizon, the lake came into view.

Across the water sat the magical isle, barely visible through the mist. An isle apart, her gran had called it, telling stories from her childhood growing up there. Until she'd visited the island herself, Emry had always thought she was exaggerating. But now she knew Gran's stories were only the half of it.

"There's a decent inn up the road," she told Tristan, remembering how she and Arthur and Lance had tested Excalibur in the woods behind the stables. "We'll meet you there in four days."

"Four days?" Tristan said with a hopeful grin.

"I hope your sister enjoys the baby booties," Emry said.

Emmett shot Tristan a meaningful look that Emry couldn't quite decipher.

Tristan nodded and gathered their horses. "Good luck," he said, and then he was gone.

Emry raised an eyebrow at her brother. There was no priestess to greet them this time. But Emry knew her way. And hopefully, Emmett would learn his. "Well, come on," she said, climbing into the rowboat.

"Do we have to row?" he asked, making a face.

"It would serve you right if we did," Emry said, as the boat shot out from the shore, zipping across the lake in the fading light. "But no. It's a self-rowing boat."

Emmett held tight for a moment, and then relaxed, peering over the side in obvious interest. "Weird. Is it an enchantment?"

"Obviously," Emry said. And then, before she could stop herself, "I know you and Tristan went out last night. I warded the door of your room."

"Then you should know that we didn't go out together." Emmett bristled. "He went out—I'm sure you can guess why. And I followed, since he has care of our journey's finances."

"Oh," Emry said. She probably would have done the same.

"Besides," Emmett went on, "everyone knows the best place to overhear news is at the tavern."

"You could have told me that's what happened before I spent the whole day annoyed with you."

"And you could have trusted me," Emmett retorted. "I got up to absolutely no trouble, and I rescued Tristan from a very poor game of dice. Even gave him some luck to win back his lost wages."

"You did?"

"He's a good lad," Emmett said. "Just needs to rein in his vices."

"You're one to talk," Emry told her brother.

"My vices are flourishing by design," Emmett said offhandedly. "And it seems the Duke of Cornwall's are as well."

Emmett related what he'd found out about the duke, and Emry's alarm grew. "You have to tell Arthur," she said.

Emmett blanched. "Me?"

"You're the one who overheard it."

"He likes you better," Emmett wheedled.

"Course he does. I didn't sard his fiancée in the hedge maze," Emry retorted.

Emmett went red. "He doesn't know about that?"

"Thankfully not," said Emry. "But the way you keep making eyes at her isn't at all discreet."

"I can't help it. You try looking at a gorgeous woman in a low-cut gown and not reacting."

"I do it all the time! You're just a rake."

Emmett stretched back, pillowing his head in his hands. "Arthur looks at you the same way," he said. "Even when you're in a plain old dress that comes up to your chin."

"He does not!" Emry bristled.

"I would duel him over it, if he wasn't the crown prince," Emmett said seriously.

"He has Excalibur," Emry pointed out.

"And my father was the most powerful wizard who ever lived." Emmett smirked. "Now, before we reach Avalon, tell me about these virgin priestesses. Fair game, or no?"

Chapter 17

The wizards had been gone for days, and Arthur was trying to occupy himself with other things besides worrying. Annoyingly, Lance had no time to spare. Even worse, a steady rain caught hold, flooding the gardens and placing horse riding and archery off the table.

It actually made Arthur miss Gawain. Not that his cousin was such a dear friend, but at least his presence at the castle had always been entertaining.

On Friday night, Arthur was carrying a tall stack of books that he'd tucked beneath his chin for balance back to his room. Dakin, who was slouched outside the door, stifled a snort.

"Something wrong?" Arthur asked.

"Nothing at all." Dakin smirked. "Have fun."

Arthur frowned, wondering what Dakin was on about.

The guard flung open the door, and the first thing Arthur noticed was all the candles. The second was the scent of orange blossom perfume.

"Hello?" he called.

"In here."

Princess Guinevere was waiting for him in his bedchamber. Her hair was down, and she wore just her nightdress, and Arthur had no idea what to make of it. Evidently, neither had his guard.

"Hi?" he said, confused.

Guinevere handed him a goblet of wine. "I thought you might like some company."

"Sure. Uh, let me just put these down," Arthur said, maneuvering his books onto the desk. The stack wobbled, but thankfully didn't tip. Arthur accepted the wine and drank appreciatively.

Guinevere watched him, a small smile on her lips.

"It's very good," Arthur said.

"I'm glad." Guinevere tilted her head, one sleeve of her nightdress slipping off her shoulder. "Sit, relax. Take off your boots and jacket."

"All right," Arthur said, taking another sip of wine and sitting down in his favorite chair by the fire. "What's going on?"

"Nothing's going on." Guin pouted. "We've spent so little time together, and I got tired of waiting for you to come to me, so I thought I would surprise you."

"I'm definitely surprised," Arthur said warily.

Guin had never acted like this before. It was almost as if she was trying to . . . seduce him. He watched her recline back on his bed, letting her thin nightdress slip from the other shoulder.

Sard. She was definitely trying to seduce him.

"And why is that?" Guinevere asked, looking up at him through her eyelashes. "Haven't you ever considered asking me to your bed?"

Arthur choked. "I—um—" he spluttered, wondering how on earth he'd wound up here.

"That's what I thought," Guin said. "You see? No one believes for a moment that we wish to be married. I hoped we might fix that."

"By doing what, exactly? Going to each other's rooms at night and pretending?"

"Who said anything about pretending?" Guinevere rose from the bed and closed the distance between them. She pressed her lips against Arthur's. They were soft, and she smelled sweet, and he was so startled that he gave in.

It was nice, kissing her. Because kissing was nice. Guinevere leaned into him, making it clear that she didn't mean to pull away, and it had been so long since anyone had done that. He groaned, pressing back.

"Come to bed with me," she whispered, tugging on the laces of his tunic as though they were a bridle and he her prize stallion.

He followed her, thinking that he clearly didn't understand girls at all. If he'd known Guinevere desired to sleep with him casually, to dispel court gossip, perhaps he wouldn't have ignored her so thoroughly.

"You kiss well, Your Highness," Guinevere purred, sliding a hand down the front of his trousers. "I wonder what else you do well."

Arthur sucked in a breath. This was madness. But after the wine at supper and what Guinevere had given him, madness seemed like a very good idea.

"A moment," he said, opening a desk drawer and quickly sifting through its contents. Finally, his fingers closed around the small potion vial filled with a bright pink liquid. "Here. Drink this. It prevents pregnancy."

Guinevere stared at the proffered vial, eyes wide. "Oh, I don't need that."

"Take it anyway, just to be safe," Arthur insisted. "Imagine what would happen if you went home to Cameliard and discovered you were with child."

Guinevere took the vial with a trembling hand, but she didn't uncork it. Instead, she sat down on the edge of the bed, her arms wrapped around her bodice, looking ill with regret.

"If you've changed your mind, you can tell me," Arthur said gently.

And then, to his acute horror, she burst into tears. "I'm so sorry," she wailed. "I never should have done this."

"That's all right," said Arthur, sitting down next to her on the bed.

Guin sniffled. "I should have known it wouldn't work."

"In case you missed it, I said yes." Arthur frowned, unclear on what was the matter. Then a thought occurred to him. "Guinevere . . . are you . . . without experience?"

Guin laughed, wiping away her tears. "No," she said wryly. "I've had plenty. Which probably isn't something to say to one's betrothed."

"It isn't like we're actually getting married."

"Right," Guinevere said, her voice small. She stared down at the vial in her fist, her chin trembling. And then she began to cry again.

"Um," Arthur said, standing up and tugging back on his tunic. "Would you like me to send for some tea and cakes? I've got a deck of cards around here somewhere. A chess set, too."

"No," Guinevere insisted. "I didn't mean to ruin it. I—take off your tunic and kiss me some more."

This wasn't like Guinevere. Arthur was certain of it. The prim and proper girl who had stepped from the carriage a few months ago, who always had her hair arranged just so, and whose speech rarely veered from formal court language into casual conversation, never would have come to his room to ply him with wine and kisses. To discuss the treaty between their kingdoms, sure. But not this.

"I think you had better tell me what's really going on," he said.

He stared at her, waiting.

Guinevere sniffled. "Oh, Arthur, I'm so sorry. It was a wretched plan, and I should never . . ." She trailed off, shaking her head.

"It's all right. Whatever it is."

"No, it isn't!" Guin blinked back tears. "I didn't know what to do, so I thought—I thought—" She went very quiet for a moment, and Arthur thought she might not say anything else, until, in a small voice, she said, "I thought if we slept together, you'd think the baby was yours."

Arthur gaped at her, hoping he'd misheard. "Guin," he said, his voice barely more than a whisper. "Are you pregnant?"

Miserably, she nodded.

And Arthur's entire world fell apart.

The way Guin had been desperate to have their wedding date moved up. How strange she had been acting lately. If she was pregnant now, he was fairly certain she hadn't been when she'd arrived. "How did this happen?" he demanded.

"It was an accident," Guin whispered. "We didn't use anything, and I—I didn't know about the potion."

"Everyone in this castle knows about the potion," Arthur said flatly. "Some for more honorable reasons than others. So, who was it?"

He nearly thought Guin wouldn't answer. But then she mumbled, "Emmett Merlin."

That sarding wizard.

Arthur had known the lad would be nothing but trouble from the moment he laid eyes on him. He and Guinevere had always seemed friendly, and Arthur hadn't thought anything of it. But now it seemed painfully obvious that the two of them were far past friendly.

Their bedrooms, Arthur realized. Emry had kept her father's quarters, which meant Emmett was right next door to Guinevere. And there was the old passage that led between, the one Arthur had played in as a young boy.

Oh, he'd been a fool not to see it sooner. "How long has that been going on?" he asked.

"It's long over," Guin said. "And it was just an amusement."

"An amusement," Arthur repeated, incredulous. This got worse and worse.

"He doesn't know," Guinevere pressed anxiously. "It's—you're the only one who knows."

Arthur frowned. It wasn't as though they'd made any promises to each other. They'd never even courted. Their engagement was nothing more than a political promise, one that they planned to see ended with a bit of thoughtful diplomacy, rather than a marriage.

"You could have told me outright."

Guin bit her lip. Looked away. "I couldn't," she said, her voice small.

Arthur had a terrible thought. "Guin," he said, his voice low with warning, "why did you want me to think the baby was mine?"

"I know we promised to turn each other down at the altar . . ." Guinevere went very quiet. "But I can't do that anymore."

Arthur had never felt so betrayed.

He wiped sweat from his brow as he lashed his sword at the practice dummy. It was late, and he was in the armory, trying to distract himself from this terrible problem with Guinevere.

It wasn't enough that he'd almost died—twice—or that he was going to become king far sooner than expected. It wasn't enough that his father tried to arrange every aspect of his life.

Guin had put him in the worst possible position.

And he knew what everyone would think. That he had followed in his father's footsteps, repeating the very same scandal of producing an heir who wasn't conceived in marriage. And if Arthur swore the child wasn't his, there would be an even bigger problem.

He lunged at the target again, landing a satisfying hit to the dummy's groin.

To mutually call off a betrothal was one thing. To refuse marriage to one's pregnant fiancée was quite another. Especially when the friendship between their kingdoms hung in the balance.

He couldn't turn her down now that she was with child. That much was clear. Perhaps, if they were lucky, the child would be a girl. But if it wasn't, many would consider the boy the rightful heir to the throne, which would absolutely destroy the goodwill between Camelot and Cameliard.

Oh, he wanted to strangle that smug, insufferable wizard.

Before he could think better of it, he let his longsword clatter to the ground and reached for Excalibur.

The legendary blade glowed fiercely as he removed it from its sheath. There was a faint ringing sound, and a ripple that traveled up his sword arm, rushing through him. He no longer felt like he was holding a sword at all. The blade was simply part of him, and he was part of the sword. He lifted his arm, his movements lightning fast, his footing impossibly light as he struck at the practice dummy again.

The arms came off first, followed by the head. Arthur spun and struck, cutting the torso neatly in half, until all that was left was an iron cross and a cloud of feathers.

Arthur stared down at the glowing blade, a shudder running up his spine. He wasn't even out of breath. He tried a complicated pass, executing it easily.

If this was his future, it could go hang. He didn't want it. Any of it.

As an experiment, he took up the longsword once again. Compared to when he'd wielded Excalibur, he felt clumsy and slow.

There was a sharp knock at the door.

"What?" Arthur ground out.

Dakin stuck his head in. "Still at it?" the young guard asked.

"No, I jumped out the window five minutes ago," Arthur replied dryly.

"After I bed a girl," Dakin boasted, "I tend to fall asleep, not work out."

"Are you sure you're not asleep to begin with?" Arthur asked.

The joke sailed over the young guard's head. "What happened to the practice dummy?" Dakin asked.

"The same thing that will happen to you, if you don't return to your post," Arthur threatened.

After the guard closed the door, Arthur put away the longsword and stared at the mess he'd made of the armory.

No matter how he figured it, he didn't see a way out of this.

He had to marry Princess Guinevere.

Chapter 18

Lance barely dared to breathe as Sir Kay examined his work with the whetstone, going over every inch of his newly sharpened blade.

"Good," the knight finally pronounced.

Lance let out a sigh of relief. He had plans with Percival this Sunday, and had worked hard to make sure Sir Kay could find no fault in his work before his day off.

"Thank you, Sir Kay. Is there anything else?"

"There is, in fact. I've decided to throw into the Kent tournament this weekend after all. You'll need to make the preparations. We leave for Cameliard at dawn."

"Another tournament?" Lance fought to keep his expression neutral as he thought despairingly of all the armor that would have to be polished, and all the equipment checked, sharpened, and packed.

"You tire of them," Sir Kay accused.

"No. I just . . ." He trailed off, unable to explain how much this Sunday had meant to him. How much he had been looking forward to spending time with Percival.

"You just what?"

"Had plans on my day off," Lance admitted. "A date."

"Reschedule it." Sir Kay sniffed. "I'm sure the girl will understand."

"Boy," said Lance.

"You're still messing about with lads?" Sir Kay's expression made it clear he didn't approve.

"We're not messing about."

"And you'd wear his favor at tournament?" The knight smirked, as though the thought was absurd.

"If he gave one to me." Lance lifted his chin. Why wouldn't he tuck Percival's handkerchief inside his breastplate for good luck? It was just a custom, one that had nothing to do with the gender of either partner.

Sir Kay's expression turned hard. "Then teach him what it is to court a squire. Your duties come first, always."

"Yes, Sir Kay," Lance said, picking up the knight's breastplate and polishing cloth. "I'll have everything ready by tomorrow."

After Sir Kay had gone, Lance leaned back against the wall, tipping his head up until all he saw were the ancient beams in the ceiling. He desperately wanted to become a knight. But he didn't know how much more of this he could take. He couldn't help but notice that the other knights trained their squires, instructing them in tilting and jousting. Sir Kay used him more like a servant, giving him chores instead of lessons.

Yet he knew that he had to take it. No matter how tough Sir Kay was, or how close the knight pushed him to his breaking point, it would be worth it in the end, to become a knight.

Still, with every weekend bringing a new tournament, he wanted to ask, *Why do you ride like you're running out of time?* But of course he knew the answer. Sir Kay was a decade older than every eager young knight he bested. And when he was forced to retire from the tournament circuit, there'd be no more late nights boasting of his victory in crowded taverns.

Just a long, empty future of training others to do what he still wished he could. There was nothing left for Sir Kay to become but a washed-up former champion who went home to an empty bed.

And Lance could feel that future pressing in on him. The way Sir Kay prepared for hours before tournaments with freezing baths and endless rounds of stretches. The potions to relax his muscles that

Master Ambrosius made for him, and which Lance was forced to rub into his back after each joust.

There was nothing Lance could do but take the extra duties and endless errands and hope that it would all be worth it.

"Where were you?" Percival demanded when Lance rushed into the guards' barracks late Sunday night. "I waited for hours."

"I'm sorry," Lance said. "I thought I'd make it back in time."

Percival's jaw went hard, and he motioned for Lance to join him outside. "From where?" Percival asked, his eyes flashing with anger, as though he already knew.

"Kent," Lance admitted.

Perce shook his head. "You should have told me you had to squire this weekend," he accused, "so I could have done something with my day off other than waste it."

Percival had a point, but Lance didn't want to admit it. "This is what being a squire is," he tried to explain. "My duties come first."

He'd said exactly the wrong thing, he realized, judging from Perce's incredulous expression. But too late to take it back.

"Being a squire is having no days off? Not even a moment to change for supper? Working through the night at menial tasks? None of the others have such responsibilities."

"None of the others have to prove themselves twice over," Lance snapped, realizing he was only digging an even bigger hole, but unable to turn back now.

"You shouldn't have to prove yourself at all."

"Becoming a knight is everything I've worked for. It's who I'm meant to be."

"And then what?" Percival demanded. "After you're a knight, what will you have gained, except a moving target you can never hit?"

Lance frowned. He hadn't thought past the part where he became a knight. But it was clear that Percival had.

"I don't know," Lance said finally.

Perce sighed. "I'm no stranger to ambition," he said. "My father's a plowman. It's a good and honest living, and it was mine if I chose it, but I wanted more. So, I came to London and worked hard to join the guard. And to one day become captain."

"You will," said Lance.

"I *might*," said Percival. "But I wouldn't hurt someone I cared about to see it happen."

Lance winced. "What other choice did I have? I'm out of chances, Perce. Everything I've worked for balances on the tip of a blade."

"Everything?" Perce repeated. "What about happiness? After you become a knight, and you have a squire polishing your armor, and crowds cheering your name at tournaments. After the day is done, what then?"

"I . . ." Lance trailed off miserably.

"Think about it, and let me know."

Lance watched in despair as Percival stalked back into the barracks.

Chapter 19

The Lady of the Lake stood waiting on the shore of Avalon. She was as ethereal and otherworldly as Emry remembered, with her long cascade of dark hair, deep copper skin, and eyes that seemed to swirl with mist, as though they saw not just the present, but also the future, in this world and the other.

"My Lady," Emry said, dropping into a curtsey and elbowing her brother to bow. He did, a moment too late.

"Children of Merlin," she said. "I have been expecting you."

I thought you might come to me sooner, the Lady said, her voice clear as a bell in Emry's head.

Sooner? Emry thought.

After your encounter with Morgana.

Oh, Emry replied. *Um, I hope it's okay that I have come now?*

It is your life. And your journey, replied the Lady.

She motioned for a young brown-haired and dark-skinned priestess to step forward. The girl did with a small curtsey.

"You will show this young wizard around the cloister," the Lady said, gesturing toward Emmett.

"Yes, my Lady," murmured the girl.

"Whatever you do, don't use the soap," Emry warned her brother in a low voice.

"The soap?" Emmett frowned.

Before Emry could say more, the girl led him away.

"Walk with me," said the Lady, gesturing toward the forest.

Emry dutifully fell into step beside the ancient priestess. Mist curled at their feet as they walked silently between the ancient oaks.

"You have come to ask me about the nature of magic," said the Lady.

Emry frowned. That wasn't what she had come to ask at all. But she was curious what Nimue would say.

"I guess?"

"You saved young Arthur's life, and the stones rewarded you with all the power they could spare," said the Lady of the Lake.

"I don't want it," Emry protested. "I was doing just fine with my own magic. Unless, do you know how I might control this new magic?"

"I do not," said the Lady.

Emry's heart twisted with despair. She hadn't realized how much she'd been counting on finding answers here until this moment, and now she felt as if the Lady had dashed her dreams into the lake.

"Magic is not always a gift. Sometimes it is a curse," warned the Lady. "I told you not to dwell on Morgana. Not to pursue that path."

"It's not like I went looking for her," Emry protested. "She came to me. She—she made me believe I could have my father back. You said she took his life, but she claimed she didn't kill him. That he's merely trapped in the Otherworld."

"There are ways to take a life beyond ending it." The Lady walked more briskly, and Emry hurried to keep pace. "The hour grows late. You should join the priestesses in preparation of the evening meal."

A young priestess stepped forward, dressed in the simple white gown and plaited hairstyle that all the girls seemed to wear. She bowed and took Emry with her to the kitchens, where Emry was put to work peeling carrots.

"I don't suppose you'd want to peel yourselves?" Emry asked the carrots.

One of them shot across the kitchen in protest.

"Guess not," she muttered.

As she worked, she went over her disappointing conversation with the Lady of the Lake. She'd come all this way for nothing. Nimue couldn't help her.

But her problem had come from opening a door to Anwen. And her magic had come from the stones. Perhaps, if she opened another door, she might fix everything.

It was worth a shot. If her father was beyond the doorway—and Nimue couldn't help her with her magic problems—then she was going through the stones.

She was going to Anwen.

It was past midnight when Emry unlocked the door to her chambers and magicked a light at the tip of her wand. She'd hastily scribbled a note to her brother, explaining. He'd be furious, of course, but he'd understand. She slid the note under her brother's door and crept from the cloister.

She was going after their father, and she couldn't take him with her. Not to Anwen. It was too dangerous, and anyway, she needed to leave Arthur a court wizard. One whose magic did what it was told.

The moon was new that night, just a mere sliver in the sky, like the needle that stitched the seam between worlds.

"Show me the way to the henge," Emry commanded of the forest.

She shifted her bag of provisions, pleased to find a glowing symbol shaped like two sides of a triangle on a tree trunk. *Kenaz*, the rune for a guiding light.

That worked.

Emry made her way through the forest, guided by the glowing symbols. Nerves and doubt clawed at her with every step. Something about this didn't feel right. The unfamiliar magic inside her pulsed urgently as she came to the stone henge. In the dark, the pale white stones seemed to glow from within.

Find your father, fix your magic, Emry reminded herself, taking a deep breath.

No, a voice inside her head whispered. *Don't.*

She tried to push it away.

Emry took a deep breath, and then sliced her palm with a knife, breaking the silvery scar that already marked where she had opened a doorway between worlds before.

Anwen's magic surged to her fingertips in a swirl of purple smoke. The smoke twisted higher and higher, until it drifted beyond the tree-tops.

Emry coughed. It was like inhaling pungent spices. She pressed her blood to the altar stone, gasping as a deep, teeth-chattering vibration rippled through her. This time, when the stones called to her, they spoke different words than they had before:

I know what you want.

I know what you desire.

I know what you seek.

Emry's magic rose to the surface with a jolt. Everything started to spin, and her heart was hammering against her rib cage, and—

"Stop!" cried the Lady of the Lake, stepping from the shadows. *"Anoishe ta porta!"*

The air between the stones rippled and went still.

Emry backed away, the smoke gone, her hands throbbing in pain. The magic had never hurt before. She grimaced, hoping it would stop.

"I thought you might come here," said the Lady. "But I hoped you wouldn't."

"I'm sorry," Emry said. "I just—I have to find my father."

"You must not," said the Lady. "You must promise me this. You cannot interfere with Anwen's doorways again. Knock three times, and it's as good as a summons."

"A summons?" Emry frowned. "I don't understand any of this! And I'm not making a promise to stop looking for my father based on vague riddles."

The Lady of the Lake nodded. "Come with me," she said, holding up her lantern and picking a path through the forest. "And I will show you."

They walked in silence until they reached a silver pool.

"What do you see?" the Lady asked.

Emry stepped forward, peering into the strangely still surface. Faintly, she could see a sleeping woman, laid out on a stone slab in a pale cave. The woman was perhaps in her fifties, with long silvery hair, and bronze skin.

"Who is she?" Emry asked.

"My sister," said Nimue. "Bellicent."

Emry had heard the name before, and she frowned, trying to place it. "The Sorceress of Anwen," she said, remembering the children's stories about an evil witch and her cauldron that forged magic blades. Stories her gran had told her, and which she should have guessed held more truth than fantasy.

Nimue nodded. "She rests in an enchanted sleep. As does your father." She leaned forward and grabbed Emry's hand, guiding it until her fingertips brushed the surface of the pool. The liquid rippled, then stilled, showing Emry's father. He lay slouched on the ground of a cave, covered in a cloud of shimmering mist, his eyes closed in a fitful slumber.

"To awaken one is to free the other," said Nimue. "And Bellicent is a grave danger not just to the Otherworld, but to ours. So long as they both slumber, your world is protected."

"But Morgana—" Emry began, realizing.

"Morgana travels her own path," the Lady snapped. "She will make her own choices and will face the consequences. You never should have let her through the stones."

"I'm sorry," Emry said. "I didn't know."

"Now that you do, you must promise me that you will not open a portal there again. It could ruin everything. You must not turn the tide of history while we still wade in its most crucial depths. Promise me."

"I promise," Emry said, never taking her eyes off her father's sleeping form. He was alive, yet not. Right there, but impossible to reach. And she *hated* it.

"Good." Nimue nodded, pleased. "As for your magic, child, there is yet hope. If you wish it, I can take that which you don't want from you."

"You can?"

"You will be as you were. Or, there is another choice you might make," said the Lady. "You could learn to use what you were given."

"How?" Emry asked.

"By going to France," said the Lady. "I do not know how you might control this magic, but there is one who can help you."

"You should have told me that in the first place!" Emry retorted.

"You did not ask," replied the Lady, as calmly as if they were discussing the weather.

Emry seethed with frustration. "Who will help me?" she asked.

"A wizard called Flamel will help with your magic. You will find this wizard if you go to Paris."

"Paris?" Emry said, trying not to think of Gawain, with his handsome smile. Gawain, who had once asked her to join him.

Wear a nice dress, and I'll introduce you at court as my fiancée.

Emry blinked away the memory.

"Should you choose this path, bring Arthur with you. There are things he must learn about how to be a good king. He will find answers there, and if he is fortunate, allies."

"You want me to go to France," Emry said, making sure she had it right, "with Arthur?"

"I want you to choose your own future," said the Lady. "Your journey will not be easy. And much will be required of you, whatever you choose. What will it be, child of Merlin? Do you wish to master this magic that ails you, or be rid of it forever?"

Emry sighed. The thought of getting rid of it was certainly tempting. Everything could go back to the way it had been. And she wouldn't have anything to hide from Master Ambrosius, or from King Uther.

But she couldn't just throw away an opportunity to master a type of magic that might prove useful. She had never turned away from hard work, and she certainly wasn't about to do it now. Especially if this magic could give her an advantage over those who stood against Arthur . . .

"I would like to see Paris," she ventured.

The Lady of the Lake nodded.

She passed a hand over the silver pool, and the images faded. She gestured for Emry to follow her back to the cloister. In the lantern light, she looked relieved as she turned to Emry and said, "You have chosen a most fascinating future, child of Merlin."

When Emry met her brother at the dock the next morning, he was pacing the shore, a piece of paper clutched in his fist, his jaw tight with anger.

When he spotted her, his eyes went dark. "I thought you'd left!" he accused.

"You got my note," Emry said.

Belatedly, she realized that, perhaps, running off in the middle of the night with just a few hastily scrawled sentences in explanation had been a bad idea. Emmett looked awful. His hair was a mess, his jacket unbuttoned, his pack hastily stuffed and coming untied.

"Of course I got your sarding note!" He dropped his pack and stalked toward her. "Going after Father, to Anwen! Are you serious?"

"The Lady of the Lake caught me and forbade it," Emry said.

Emmett shook his head like he couldn't believe what he was hearing. "I thought you'd left without even saying goodbye! You're all I have at the castle. You can't abandon me like that."

There was a real fear in her brother's eyes, and she could see that he meant it.

"I'm sorry," she said. "I wasn't thinking."

"No, you weren't," Emmett said harshly.

Smart as spades, but foolish as hearts.

That's what her father had always said about the way Emry tended to run straight into danger with half a plan and even less of a prayer.

Emmett's shoulders slouched in a way that made him look younger, and more vulnerable. He swallowed thickly before admitting, "I lost our father, I don't even remember our mother, and Guinevere wants nothing to do with me. I can't lose you, too."

Emry hadn't realized Emmett felt like that. But she should have. And she felt awful. "It was horrible of me," she said. "I won't do anything like that again."

"Please don't. I don't want to be the next court wizard. That's your thing. I'm just . . . being supportive."

"And taking advantage of the spoils," Emry added, with a hint of a smile.

"I said I was being supportive, not selfless," Emmett pointed out. He folded his arms, some of his usual swagger returning. "So, anyway, what's this about the Lady of the Lake catching you trying to run away to Anwen?"

"Oh." Emry shrugged. "Yeah, she was mad."

She couldn't tell him about what she'd seen, about their father in that cave. Emmett had already grieved that loss and moved on. She couldn't rekindle his pain, only to tell him there was no hope.

"Why did we really come here?" Emmett pressed. "I know it wasn't to tell the Lady of the Lake what happened to Arthur's scabbard."

Emry stared at her brother, who had raised his chin and was trying to recover from his moment of emotional vulnerability. This, at least, she could tell him. "You're right," she said. And then she explained about her magic problem, and how Arthur had found out and suggested she ask the Lady of the Lake.

While she explained, Emmett stared at her in disbelief. "I knew something was up!" he cried.

"You did?"

"Ever since that tavern fight. There was no way you scared those guys off with some illusion. Plus, it smelled like something had been burning."

"Oh." Emry bit her lip.

"I've been waiting for you to say something," Emmett said. "But you've been off in your own world, like always."

"I have not!" Emry protested.

"I came by your room to ask for help with a spell, and you weren't there," he said. "Apparently you were out at a tavern with Arthur. So much for keeping your distance."

"I am," Emry said, and then amended, "I was."

"So, you told him what was going on, but not me?" Emmett accused.

"He found out by accident!" Emry defended. "I wasn't going to tell anyone. It's—well, private. If you were having magic problems, what would you do?"

"Probably try and fix them before anyone found out," he admitted. "So, did the Lady of the Lake fix everything?"

"No." Emry sighed. "But she told me what I need to do. So, I suppose we got what we came for."

"That's good." Emmett glanced at her sideways, and she could tell he was trying not to be angry at her. "Now come on, let's get back to Tristan before he gambles away his clothing."

"A moment, children of Merlin," said Nimue, stepping from the forest. Emry winced, hoping the Lady hadn't been listening to their conversation.

"Yes, my Lady?" Emry said.

"You understand what I have told you."

"As well as I can," Emry said.

"And you, son of Merlin."

Emmett blanched. "Yes?"

"You should heed the passage of time, in all its variations. It might be of some help to you. As might I. Should you find yourself in need."

"Right," Emmett said doubtfully. "Thanks."

Emry elbowed him.

Emmett sank into a bow. "I mean, thank you, my Lady, for your, er, crystal-clear wisdom."

Chapter 20

Emry was dismounting her horse when Arthur reached the stables. His heart lurched at the sight of her. Dusty and travel worn, wearing a boy's jacket and trousers. Her cloak flowed from her shoulders, and her hair had come loose from its braid. She wore the dagger he'd given her at her waist, and he didn't think he had ever seen her look more appealing.

"Miss me?" she asked with a smirk.

"Hardly," he protested. "The castle was peaceful with you gone. I'm merely inspecting the state of my horses."

"Not green. No wings. Still terrible," Emry reported, untying her pack.

"May I?" A groom stepped forward.

"Yes, please," Emry said, happily divesting herself of the horse.

"Your Highness," Tristan said. "I was just coming to find you." He squared his shoulders, looking every inch the castle guard, despite the travel grime and his lack of uniform. "It's urgent."

"I'm listening." Arthur folded his arms across his chest and waited.

Tristan's eyes darted uneasily toward the grooms.

"Walk with me," Arthur commanded.

The young guard fidgeted. "Emmett ought to be the one to tell you," he said, motioning for the wizard to join them.

Arthur's mood darkened as Emmett sauntered over, greeting him with a nod instead of a bow.

What had possessed Guinevere to sleep with this smug, arrogant wizard?

Once they were inside the king's hunting forest, and Tristan made no move to begin, Emmett cleared his throat.

"We overheard some troubling news at a tavern," he confessed.

"About the Duke of Cornwall," Tristan blurted. "He's not just fortifying his castle. He's building an army, and has tripled taxes to force men to join."

Arthur frowned. "You're certain of this?" he asked, looking between the two of them. The young, eager guard wasn't the most credible source. And Emmett he wanted to turn out of the castle the first chance he got.

Yet both of them nodded without hesitation. And neither would lie about something like this.

"I asked around in the village where my sister lives," Tristan went on. "Said I was looking for work. Got told to speak to the Sheriff of Lansdowne about joinin' up with the duke's army by nearly everyone."

Arthur ran a hand over his face. Truly, this news couldn't have come at a worse moment. There was only one reason the duke would build an army without coming to Camelot for aid. He wasn't building a defense against King Yurien. No, the Duke of Cornwall meant to make a play for Camelot.

"I'll make sure your information is put to good use," promised Arthur.

If the duke was truly planning an attack, then Camelot's alliance with Cameliard would become even more necessary.

Lord Agravaine looked up in surprise when Arthur entered his study unannounced. The king's advisor sat behind his desk, a quill in hand, the royal seal at his elbow.

"Your father remains stable," he said, removing a piece of parchment from a precariously high stack.

"I'm glad to hear it, although that's not why I'm here." Arthur gestured toward a chair. "May I?"

"Of course."

Lord Agravaine set down his quill, his expression shrewd. "Have the young wizards returned from Avalon?"

"They have," Arthur confirmed.

"And as to the true reason for their venture," Lord Agravaine prompted.

"My visit is related to that, yes," Arthur confirmed, which of course wasn't what the man was asking.

Lord Agravaine bit back a smile at how Arthur had twisted his words. "You do your tutors credit."

"I believe the weapons master would disagree." Arthur smoothed the front of his jacket. "As you know, the journey to Avalon runs close to the border with Cornwall."

Lord Agravaine raised an eyebrow.

"Fascinating what a young castle guard can overhear in a tavern on the edge of both territories," Arthur went on.

"And?"

"The Duke of Cornwall is amassing an army, as you suspected," Arthur confirmed. "Tristan saw it for himself. And it's no small defense force. Gorlais is taxing his people beyond their means, and those who can't pay must fight."

Lord Agravaine nodded slowly.

"You knew of this," Arthur accused.

"I suspected. You confirm what my spies report."

"Then why are we doing nothing?" Arthur demanded.

Lord Agravaine raised an eyebrow and waited.

"My father." Arthur shook his head. "How can he justify such denial?"

"He believes building an army will make him look weak. He does not wish to appear afraid of a mere duke."

"Damn his pride," Arthur fumed. "What harm is it to look weak, if in that weakness, you strengthen your kingdom's defenses?"

Lord Agravaine inclined his head. "Well said, Your Highness."

"We can't do nothing."

"I agree. But we must not appear to go against him. And if Cameliard chooses to amass their own army, that will be to our advantage, with your upcoming wedding to their princess."

Arthur winced. "Right, that."

Lord Agravaine frowned. "Have you not come around, Your Highness? I understood that the two of you are recently . . . of an intimate acquaintance."

Oh god. He would rather sink through his chair and disappear than discuss his fictional sex life with his father's closest advisor. But the man wasn't wrong—somehow, the entire castle knew Guinevere had come to his rooms. Arthur suspected Guin's maid of spreading the gossip. And he suspected Guin had made sure of it. It had been clever of her.

"I believe I've taken up enough of your time," Arthur said, rising from his seat. "Thank you for your counsel."

"Are you there, wizard?" Arthur called, knocking at Emry's door.

"Yes, but—" she called, and Arthur didn't wait for more. He pushed open the door, and his face turned pink.

"I'm not dressed," Emry finished, glaring at him.

She wore only a linen tunic that fell mid-thigh, and her hair was wet from the bath. Arthur stared at her bare legs, swallowed, and tried to stare anywhere else.

"Um," he said.

"Oh my god, you're *impossible*. Go wait outside if you're going to be weird about it."

"I'm not being weird about it," Arthur protested as Emry reached for a pair of boy's breeches and stepped behind the wardrobe door.

"You had me attend to you naked in the bath that one time," she called.

Arthur winced, hating that she'd reminded him. "Only because I thought you were a lad."

Emry emerged with her tunic tucked into the trousers. "You still kissed me, even thinking I was a lad."

Arthur felt his blush deepen. He had kissed her, and the resulting misunderstanding had been mortifying.

"You made a very appealing boy. Are you going to wear that around the castle?" he asked, alarmed at the thought. Her legs were entirely on display, which was somehow much worse than the low-cut gowns the court ladies favored.

"Of course not. Your father would never allow it. So, how were things while I was gone?"

Arthur stiffened, filled with guilt. He didn't know what to say. He knew she'd find out eventually, but he desperately hated the idea of telling her about Guinevere, and the change in their wedding plans. Emry was finally talking to him again, and he didn't want to ruin it.

So, he shrugged as if his entire life hadn't been upended in her absence. "Boring," he said. "What of Avalon? Did the Lady of the Lake fix you?"

"No." A shadow passed across Emry's face. "It's not that simple."

"Oh." Arthur bit his lip. He'd thought she would have good news, and he didn't know how much more disaster he could take.

"She showed me my father," Emry said, sitting down on the edge of the bed.

"She what?"

Arthur listened as Emry explained about the pool, and what she'd seen there. "The Lady of the Lake is the Sorceress of Anwen's sister?" he asked.

Emry shrugged. "Makes sense why she's confined to the isle. And why magic and time flow differently there."

"So, Morgana is alive, and in Anwen," Arthur summarized. "And so is your father. But you can't go after him."

"Correct," Emry said, sounding heartbroken. "And seeing him like that—so helpless and stuck—just made me want to save him even more."

Arthur didn't remember sitting down next to her, but suddenly he had his arm around her, and her head was on his shoulder. "I'm so sorry," he said. "About everything."

Emry gave him a sad smile and pulled away. Her damp hair was falling into her face, and Arthur couldn't help but smooth a piece behind her ear.

Oh, he had missed her. He wanted to draw her into his arms and tell her it would be all right, but he didn't know if she would let him.

"It's not all bad news," she said. "The Lady of the Lake knows someone who can help me learn how to control this new magic."

"That's wonderful," Arthur said. "Why didn't you lead with that?"

"Because I'll have to go to France," she added. "There's a wizard at French court. Goes by the name Flamel."

Arthur tried to remember where he'd heard that name before. "King Louis's court wizard. He's something of an experimenter in magical objects. I read his pamphlet on alchemy."

"The Lady of the Lake said you should come with me," Emry finished.

"To the French court?"

"She said you would find answers there, and if you are fortunate, allies."

Allies. Arthur's head snapped up at the word. Allying with the French would solve a large sum of his problems. And, by extension, Camelot's.

The only snag was King Louis. From everything Arthur knew of the man, he was impassioned and impulsive, quick to welcome those he prized into his inner circle, and just as fast to dismiss them.

But the Lady of the Lake hadn't steered them wrong yet. And his heart leapt at the thought of going off on an adventure with Emry. Of sailing away from Camelot, and spending these final few weeks before his wedding with the woman whose company he truly wished for.

"What are we waiting for?" asked Arthur. "Let's go to France."

"You want to go *where?*" bellowed King Uther.

The room still smelled faintly of incense, and the windows in the king's apartments were all firmly closed, which Arthur itched to say something about.

"The Lady of the Lake insisted that I accompany Apprentice Wizard Merlin to French court. To find allies." He made sure to stress this last part.

"She did?" The king frowned.

"She did," Arthur said firmly. "And I don't think I should discard such advice lightly. Wouldn't it be a triumph for the French to take our side in any future conflicts?"

He gave a meaningful pause, but before his father could reply, he went on, "I can write to King Louis immediately. He *is* a distant cousin, and we're not so far apart in age." They weren't so close in age, either. The French king was approaching thirty, and they were third cousins, which was hardly any relation.

"You would be home within two weeks," King Uther said, and Arthur could hardly believe his good fortune.

"Three," he bargained. "It's a long journey."

"Very well," said King Uther. "So long as you are back well in advance of your wedding. Your guards will go with you."

Arthur made a face at the thought of bringing tiresome Dakin to France. "About that," he began.

"Take your valet as well," finished the king. "Lance stays with Sir Kay."

Arthur sighed. It had been worth a shot.

"See to it that you and Merlin's boy make good use of this trip."

"Perhaps I wasn't clear," said Arthur, even though he'd misled his father deliberately. "I will be going with Emry, not Emmett."

"Absolutely not!" The king's face went red as he realized he had already agreed to the journey. "I forbid it."

"On what grounds?"

"I am the king. I don't need a reason."

"Do you truly wish to leave behind such a legacy? Uther Pendragon ruled Camelot solely by whim, never taking into account the good of his people, or the betterment of his kingdom?"

The king bristled. "How does a trip in the company of that—that girl—better my kingdom?" Uther demanded.

Arthur shrugged. "The last time we traveled together, I recovered Excalibur."

The king spluttered.

"I'll let you know when the arrangements are set," said Arthur.

Guinevere was nearly asleep when she heard her maid tiptoe across the adjoining chamber. There was some frantic whispering, and then

Dorota stuck her head into Guin's bedchamber, looking panicked. "It's the prince!"

"Arthur?" Guinevere frowned, wondering what he was doing here. "I suppose you can let him in."

"But—but—you're not dressed," the girl spluttered.

Guin glanced down. She was in her nightdress, her hair loose. She shrugged on a silk dressing gown and fluffed her curls. "Send him in," she ordered, lifting her chin.

She wondered what Arthur wanted. Her plan to seduce him had gone horribly, and they'd tiptoed around each other in such awful silence for the past few days. Perhaps he meant to tell her that he couldn't go through with it. That he would expose her secret.

Guin's heart hammered nervously at the thought.

Arthur entered through the double doors, a small parcel under his arm. He didn't look furious, merely resigned. He closed the doors to her bedchamber behind him.

"To what do I owe the visit?" Guin asked tentatively.

"Keeping up appearances." Arthur replied, holding out a wooden box. "I brought you something."

"It's not a riding crop, is it?" Guin asked nervously.

Arthur choked back a laugh.

Guinevere opened the box, revealing a pouch of fragrant dried herbs. She looked to him with a frown.

"Ginger tea," he said curtly. "For nausea."

"Thank you." If he was bringing her a gift, perhaps there was no need to worry.

"Listen—" Arthur began.

"No, me first," Guinevere insisted. "I'm so sorry. Truly, I am. I thought—I thought Emmett was taking care of things."

"He should have," Arthur said flatly. "But so should you."

"I know," Guin said. "It was a foolish fling, and I never should have been so careless. I believed I was leaving in a few months, and there was no harm in . . ."

She trailed off with a sigh, nibbling her lip. That wasn't what she'd meant to say.

"I hate how we left things," she tried again. "The other night, in your bedroom . . ."

"That's why I'm here," Arthur said. "I'm bound for France as soon as I can make the arrangements. And I won't be back for three weeks."

"For that long?" Their wedding was scarcely more than a month away.

"I have business at court," Arthur said. "As does Emry. And—"

"Emry is going with you? To France?"

"Technically, I'm going with her," Arthur said. "But yes. Along with my valet and my guards. I aim to persuade the French crown toward an alliance."

Guin frowned, twisting her hair over one shoulder. "Why would Camelot need an alliance with the French?" she asked, taking a seat on her bed and settling her dressing gown around her legs.

Arthur leaned back against the mantel, crossing his arms. "Because I don't trust the Duke of Cornwall. He's building an army, and my father is too proud to do the same in response."

"You don't think he'll invade?" Guin asked. Most kingdoms didn't keep standing armies, her own included. To gather one was tantamount to declaring war.

"I don't know," said Arthur truthfully. "But the people of Camelot shouldn't have to risk their lives in its defense if there's another way."

He sounded so much like a king that it made her heart ache. Here he was, caring for his subjects. Protecting them. She'd never seen this side of Arthur before. The confident politician, putting himself at risk to maintain peace. Far more often, he was dressed as plainly as any gardener, books tucked under his arm, and herb clippings in his pockets, ducking off to hang out with Lance or Emry. It was easy to think him weak, but he wasn't, he was merely quiet and insightful.

And here she was, standing between him and any future happiness.

"Well, what do you think?" he asked.

Guin had never been so flattered that her opinion counted, because it never had before, at least, not to anyone important. "It's a clever plan," she said approvingly.

"Thank you." Arthur hesitated a moment. "Before I go, I wanted to make sure you'll be all right. Considering."

Guin lifted her chin. "I'll be fine."

"If you need anything, go to Master Ambrosius, not the court physician," Arthur went on. He drew a sharp breath. "And when I return, we'll be married."

"We will?" Guin asked nervously.

"We will."

He reached for her hand, raising it to his lips with a dull, rehearsed sense of duty. His expression was bleak as he said, "Here's to a continued alliance between our kingdoms, bound by the terms made by our fathers."

They were trapped, and both of them knew it.

Chapter 21

Morgana kept hold of the sword as she endured the cold press of the child's unnatural stare.

"Who are you?" Morgana asked.

"A sorceress."

"Then we have that in common. In my world, I am the same."

"But we are not in your world, we are in mine." The girl frowned, as though offended by the comparison. "You came here through the stones?"

Morgana thought quickly. She didn't want to admit that someone else's magic had opened the doorway. Not before she knew what she was dealing with. She nodded in confirmation.

"I'll tell you how if you teach me to use Anwen's magic."

The girl's expression twisted into one of displeasure. "You dare to bargain with me? I saved your life, yet you desire more favors!"

So it had been the sorceress's magic that had frozen the creature. Which meant the woman could do the same to Morgana. "I thought it was the curse."

"I commanded the magic to take the creature, just as I commanded it to give me control of a body, so I might see who had come into this world."

Commanded the magic to give her control of a body. Morgana's blood ran cold at the thought. That was strong magic, yet the sorceress spoke of it as though it were nothing.

"Is all of Anwen like this? Not just this village?" Morgana asked.

The sorceress scowled. "The whole world," she confirmed. "As to the debt you owe me, you shall repay it by freeing me."

"How?"

"We will travel to my real body, and you will break the enchantment that holds us in this frozen thrall."

Morgana prickled with dread over being tethered to this volatile sorceress. Especially since the woman believed she could open doors between worlds. But she didn't see another way out of this. And she didn't wish to freeze or starve to death in this cursed world that was nothing like she'd imagined. "All right," she said.

The girl's smile turned sharp. "Then it is agreed. Swear it on that sword. Swear you will free me to repay your debt."

Morgana dutifully repeated the words, her hands around the hilt of the sword.

"Good," purred the child. She pulled heavy fur cloaks from around the shoulders of two sleeping villagers, and daggers from their belts.

One cloak and weapon she held out to Morgana, and one set she kept for herself.

"I swear on my blade to protect you," said the girl. She lifted a bowl of stew from the table, its contents suddenly steaming. Morgana's stomach gurgled at the rich smell of broth and meat. The sorceress handed her the meal.

The broth burned her tongue, but Morgana didn't care. She ate greedily, and when she was done, she frowned. "What do I call you?"

"My name," said the child who wasn't a child at all, "is Bellicent."

Chapter 22

Emry stood on the deck of the great ship, London disappearing behind her. The high tide of the Thames lapped against the hull, and a hearty wind filled the sails.

She was headed for France to meet the wizard who would help her gain control of her new, unpredictable magic. A shiver of adventure ran up her spine, and she had the strangest sensation that the girl who returned to Camelot wouldn't be the same as she was now.

The three-mast ship was a merchant vessel, and though it flew Camelot's crimson flag, they were only borrowing passage to Calais. The journey was short, and the wind was in their favor.

Emry watched with amusement as Arthur's prim and proper valet fussed with the luggage. Instead of sturdy sailing clothes, Lucan had stubbornly worn his royal livery, including his silk cravat. His dark hair was immaculate, his boots without so much as a scuff. She smothered a grin as a wave slapped against their boat, and the valet turned green, rushing to the side to heave the contents of his stomach overboard.

Dakin let out a nasty laugh at the valet's expense. He'd roped some of the sailors into a card game and was gleefully amassing a large pile of coins that he no doubt planned to spend on company and drink at his earliest convenience.

Brannor stood at the prow with his own compass, a sailor's oilskin coat over his royal livery, seeming truly at home at sea.

Emry looked over at Arthur. He stood on the deck, his hands on the railing, the wind ruffling his hair. He was dressed plainly, in a sturdy traveling jacket and cloak, but somehow, he still looked very like a prince.

It was the sword, Emry decided. Even in a plain sheath, Excalibur still managed to give off an undeniable vibe.

"So," Emry said, coming over to lean against the rail beside him. "How's your French?"

"Better than yours, I'd wager."

"We'll find out soon enough," she said. "Ever been to the Continent before?"

"I've never even left Camelot, other than our quest to Avalon." Arthur leaned over the rail, staring pensively at the churn of the dark waters below. "So, I suppose it will be an adventure."

"Hopefully the kind with coffee," Emry said. "And indoor plumbing."

"You're hopeless," Arthur accused.

"No, I grew up in a cottage. You grew up in a castle. I'm just being pragmatic."

"You're being something, all right," Arthur joked.

He was standing closer than he had been a moment ago, Emry realized. His arm bumped against her sleeve. She had never been so aware of the scratchy fabric of her jacket before.

"A bit forward, don't you think, Your Highness?" she teased.

Arthur's warm brown eyes met hers, and she swallowed nervously. "If I was being forward, you'd know," he promised. "I merely slipped."

His arm was still against hers. The slight pressure of it left her breathless. On the rail, his fingers twitched, and Emry wondered if he would move his hand to cover hers, but he didn't.

This was madness. She tried to draw her attention anywhere else. But there was no ignoring the fact that they were sailing off together, at each other's side.

Overhead, the sales billowed in the wind, and sailors scurried about on the rigging, casting lines and calling to one another.

This connection between her and Arthur wasn't going away. If anything, avoiding his company had only made her feelings more intense.

Every time she saw him after her return from Avalon, her heart fluttered, and she felt his presence whenever he entered a room. Emry glanced over at him, at his dark hair ruffled in the breeze. At the faint stubble on his cheeks, and the sharp angle of his jawline.

She could almost forget that they weren't truly alone. That Dakin and Brannor kept watch just as vigilantly as they had back at the castle. That just because she had an excuse to spend time with him didn't mean she could let her guard down and act as she wished. No matter how much she wished she could.

"One last adventure," he said sadly, staring out to sea.

"It only feels that way," she promised. "You'll see. This trip will fix everything."

He merely gave her a melancholy smile, as if he was guarding something that he wasn't quite ready to share.

As their ship pulled into port, Emry leaned across the rail, gazing out at the bustling city in fascination.

A long, solid wharf ran around the edge of the harbor, with smaller docks where galleys and barks sat alongside other two- and three-mast vessels. The quay was lined with warehouses, and beyond that, travelers' inns and pubs of varying repute, their lanterns glowing invitingly in the twilight.

Please, she thought, *let this journey be worth the trouble.*

She was still worrying when they left Calais and set off along the post road early the next morning. The weather was gray and cloudy, and only got grayer and gloomier as the day progressed.

Emry shivered beneath her cloak, wishing she owned a warmer one.

Dakin kept insisting that he felt raindrops, even though no one else did. Brannor, at the front, kept nearly nodding off in his saddle after having kept watch the night before. Arthur rode next, shooting Emry knowing looks whenever her horse went astray. And Lucan made up the rear of their party, entirely out of his element. The beleaguered valet kept swatting away flies and asking when they would stop for lunch, as though he expected to dine at table.

When they finally did stop, at the edge of a thick, primordial forest, it was for a brief picnic of bread and cheese they'd bought from the innkeeper's wife that morning.

"We shouldn't linger," said Brannor, gazing uneasily into the woods. "The innkeeper said there'd been reports of bandits."

"Of course he did." Arthur brushed crumbs from his lap. "Right before he offered to rent us a carriage with damage insurance for an exorbitant amount."

"I wish we'd taken him up on it," Emry said. Her legs felt wobbly, and her thighs ached, and she couldn't imagine enduring days of this.

"Come now, wizard, where's your sense of adventure?" Arthur teased. "Horses, nature, the crisp autumn air. What could be more thrilling?"

"A cushioned seat in a warm carriage?" Emry suggested.

Arthur sighed.

"We should get back on the road shortly," Brannor advised.

"I might need a moment," Lucan said apologetically.

Emry and Arthur exchanged a grin as the valet hurried off, looking vastly uncomfortable at the prospect of emptying his bowels in the woods.

"Is there any bread and cheese left?" Dakin asked.

"*Fleoges*," Emry muttered, waving her hand at their picnic. A heel of bread lifted off the ground and smacked Dakin in the chest, followed by a rind of cheese, which landed a little lower, and a little harder.

Arthur snorted.

"Catch," Emry said belatedly.

"You did that on purpose," Dakin accused.

Suddenly, an arrow landed in the middle of their picnic. For a moment, Emry stared at it, her eyes wide with disbelief.

Then another arrow slammed into the tree trunk inches above Arthur's head.

"*Bandits!*" Brannor cried, scrambling to his feet and drawing his sword. Dakin did the same, with considerably less urgency.

Three men in oiled cloaks stepped out of the forest. Two were brandishing swords, and another held a crossbow pointed straight at Brannor's heart.

Oh god, Emry thought.

The man with the crossbow grinned, showing off his blackened teeth. "This is where you part ways with your belongings and possibly your lives, English swine."

"Our luggage is merely laundry and stale bread," Brannor scoffed. "You would have better luck waylaying a washerwoman."

"We shall see," said one of the bandits, slashing a heavy pouch that hung from one of the horses. Gold coins spilled to the ground.

The bandits exclaimed in French. Arthur winced.

The man with the crossbow rapidly loosed an arrow. Brannor cried out in pain as the arrow pierced his shoulder. He crumpled to the ground, clutching at his wound, his face pale.

"I hate liars," the man snarled, calmly reloading his crossbow. He pointed it at Dakin next. "Drop your weapons. All of you."

To Emry's horror, the young guard let his sword clatter to the ground without hesitation. "Don't hurt me," Dakin pleaded. "It's them you want as hostages!"

The man turned his crossbow on Emry and Arthur. "Your weapons," he snarled, his finger on the trigger.

Emry glanced at Arthur, whose expression was calculating as he surveyed the bandits. His eyes met hers, and he inclined his head, one hand on the hilt of his sword. Emry nodded. Together.

"*Arcesso!*" she cried, raising her fist. The crossbow flew into her hands, and she smirked, aiming the weapon back at its owner.

At her side, Arthur drew Excalibur from its sheath. The glowing sword pulsed with a white-hot light that lit up the forest.

"Run while you can, or prepare for deadly consequences," warned Arthur, with a slice of his glowing sword.

The men stood frozen in place, transfixed by the glowing weapon. And then, they began to laugh.

Four more bandits stepped from the forest brandishing swords.

"You were saying?" asked their leader with a mocking grin.

Emry swallowed thickly. They were hideously outnumbered.

An arrow shot from high in a tree, and Arthur brought his sword up in a swift arc, knocking it to the ground.

Seven men and an overhead archer, Emry realized, her stomach sinking. The odds were impossible.

"Get ready," Arthur murmured, sinking into a fighter's crouch.

Emry threw aside the crossbow and drew her wand as the bandits rushed toward them. Everything was a blur, and it was all Emry could do to shoot blasts of fire from her wand, pressing the men back as Arthur fought them off with his glowing blade. Her heart pounded, and her breath came in gasps, but she couldn't stop.

The men stubbornly kept coming. There were too many of them. She sent a boulder flying into one, and the effort left her panting. She lowered her wand a moment, trying to catch her breath as an arrow clipped her arm, and she hissed in pain.

Oh no.

She felt Anwen's magic rush to the surface, purple flames crackling above each palm. No, not flames, Emry realized with horror. *Lightning!*

The bolts shot out, hitting the trees. There was a sharp snap of a branch, and a shout as the archer tumbled from his perch, landing with a sickening thud. The horses reared, neighing in fright as Emry's lightning kept coming. Another tree branch snapped, and then another. The forest was falling on them, and she couldn't stop it. Branches snapped loudly, crashing down on the bandits.

Not just the bandits—their entire company.

"No!" Emry cried. "No, please! *Contego!*"

But the protection charm didn't work.

She looked up as a heavy branch plummeted toward her and Arthur. There was no time to move. They were going to be flattened.

Suddenly, she felt Arthur's arm around her. He held his sword above them, its blade glowing brighter than it ever had before. The branch exploded into harmless wood pulp. Sawdust rained down around them, like they were caught in an impossible snowstorm.

Finally, the lightning bolts stopped. There was a terrible, silent pause, and Emry braced herself, waiting.

"I think it's over?" Arthur said, his sword still above his head.

She looked around, surveying the damage in dismay. Fallen tree branches had crashed down on top of already-injured bandits. Half a dozen bodies lay on the ground. Wounded, unconscious, stabbed, or worse.

She felt sick.

This morning, she had never killed a man. And now she couldn't say the same.

"I lost count," Arthur said softly, his voice cracking. His glowing blade was tinted a ghoulish red.

"So did I," Emry replied, her voice small. And then she remembered. "Your guards!"

"Brannor!" Arthur called. "Dakin!"

"Over here, Your Highness," Brannor called, his voice thin.

"Help me see to them," he said. With the sword in his hand, it came out as a ringing command. Usually, Emry would have rolled her eyes, but this time, she only nodded and followed as Arthur wove through the sickening path of fallen tree branches and men.

"This is all my fault," Arthur said as they walked.

"What else could we have done?" Emry retorted. "Sailed a royal great ship into the harbor and traveled with crimson banners?"

Arthur's lips pressed into a thin line.

Brannor was propped against a tree, the arrow still imbedded in his shoulder, a dark stain spreading over the cloth of his jacket. Dakin lay on the ground nearby, one leg trapped beneath a fallen branch. "Get this thing off of me!" he complained.

Emry waved a hand, and the branch flew sideways. Dakin groaned, examining his leg.

"It looks broken," Arthur said grimly. "Don't move."

Emry bit her lip, blinking back a torrent of hot, frustrated tears. She had done this. Not the bandits. She had broken Dakin's leg because she couldn't control her magic.

"I can heal it," she promised, even though she'd never mended a broken bone before. "The arrow wound as well."

"You can?" Arthur asked, as though he'd hardly dared to hope.

He shifted, and Emry saw a bloodstain on the side of the prince's tunic that she hadn't noticed before.

"You're hurt," she said.

"I'll manage," he said tightly. "See to the guards first."

"I wondered why you weren't putting away your sword."

Fine. If Arthur wanted to play the hero, she would let him. Not that he was playing. He had been magnificent back there. Nothing at all like the quiet boy from the library. He had been brave, and bold, and wonderful.

And she had been a disaster.

Lightning bolts, in a forest. Falling branches that had nearly injured them all. It had only been Excalibur that saved them. No, not Excalibur. Arthur.

Emry rolled up her sleeves. "Brannor, do you trust me?"

"What are you going to do?" the old soldier asked warily.

"Fix your shoulder."

"With magic?" Brannor looked uneasy.

"She's healed me plenty of times," Arthur said.

"You were injured, Your Highness?" Brannor gasped, looking horrified.

"Worse than this," Arthur said cheerfully. "So, you have nothing to worry about. Wizard, on your mark."

Emry took a deep breath, gathering her magic. "*Angsumnes*," she whispered.

The spell released, leaving her gasping. The arrow snapped in two and slid from Brannor's shoulder, and his wound stitched itself closed. Color returned to the guard's face.

"Easy," she bragged, and then she wobbled.

Arthur had her in his arms in a moment. She looked up at him with a small embarrassed smile.

"All right there?" he asked.

"I'm fine," she promised, even though she was impossibly dizzy.

She didn't want him to let go of her. If he could have held her forever, right there, in the middle of the post road, she honestly might have let him. She took some deep breaths, waiting a moment until the road stopped spinning and she could think clearly again.

"How's the shoulder?" she asked, frowning at Brannor.

"Good as new," the old guard said gravely. "Thank you."

Emry let out a sigh of relief. "You're up," she said, turning to Dakin.

"You 'ent using magic on me," he protested.

"Oh yes she is," Arthur said fiercely. "You're no use to us with a broken leg."

The guard considered this. "Fine," he grumbled.

"Excellent," said Arthur. "And once you've been healed, we're going to have a talk about how you dropped your sword and left us to fight."

The guard paled.

Even though she'd rather let him suffer, Emry mended the bone in his leg. It took more out of her than she'd thought it would. She felt awful. Exhausted, drained, and judging from the way Arthur refused to put away his sword, he wasn't faring much better.

"I'm fine," he muttered, digging out a jar of healing salve.

There was a rustling noise in the woods, and the snap of a twig.

Arthur tensed, raising his sword. Emry groaned and raised her wand.

Lucan emerged from the forest, adjusting his trousers. "What did I miss?" he asked. He caught sight of the clearing and fell to the ground in a faint.

"Whose idea was it to bring a personal valet?" Emry muttered.

"My father's," Arthur said with a sigh. "I was trying for Lance."

Emry rolled her eyes. "Should've tried harder."

Chapter 23

Emry stared at the room, hoping it was a mistake.

The space was clean and spare, with fresh rushes strewn across the floor, a small wooden table and chairs, and a stone fireplace that looked older than the half-timbered building. Tranquil blue shutters flanked the window, and the beams that ran overhead had been painted with fleur-de-lis to match.

There was just one problem.

"One bed," she announced, as though it were possible that such a situation had escaped Arthur's notice.

Perhaps it had. The prince didn't look well. He'd needed to sheath his sword to enter the inn, and he'd been pale and unsteady as the innkeeper had shown them to their rooms—the smaller for le personnel, and the larger adjoining chamber for monsieur et madame, which was where they were now.

"So, magic another one," he suggested weakly, sinking into a chair and withdrawing Excalibur. He sighed with relief, a small amount of color returning to his cheeks. "Much better," he murmured, tipping his head back and closing his eyes.

Emry folded her arms. "Let me see it."

"I'll use more healing salve. You're in no shape to fix me up."

"How do you know what kind of shape I'm in?" Emry arched an eyebrow, even though he was right—she *was* exhausted.

Arthur reached for his pack and winced. "Because I fought alongside you today."

Emry bit her lip, hating the reminder. She'd been reliving the horror of it for hours.

"How can you even stand to be around me after what happened?" she blurted.

"What are you talking about?"

"I broke Dakin's leg!" Emry said. "And I nearly killed us both with that falling branch!"

"Dakin deserved it," Arthur returned. "Throwing down his sword as he did. Besides, he's fine now, and so am I."

"You're not fine, you're injured!"

"By a blade, not by your magic."

"A *blade*?" Emry didn't think she'd heard him right. "How are you standing?"

Arthur chuckled weakly, gesturing at his chair. "I'm not, if you hadn't noticed. I used quite a bit of healing salve earlier."

Emry had once applied the same to a stab wound and knew just how little it did to dull the pain. Especially after a long day in the saddle. "You should have *said* something."

Arthur shrugged pragmatically. "There wasn't much point. Lucan would have fussed, and you would have collapsed from overextending yourself."

"But you got *stabbed* by *bandits*!"

"Don't," he said, his voice breaking with exhaustion. "I would have had far worse if you hadn't ended that skirmish with your magic."

"It wasn't my magic, it was Anwen's magic!" Emry said, nettled. "And I couldn't control it." She shook her head, blinking back tears at the memory. "You needed me at your side, and when I was, the tiniest cut had me shooting lightning bolts from my hands. I could have killed the horses. Or any of us!"

Emry sat down on the edge of the bed, her shoulders trembling in misery.

Arthur got up with a grimace and sat next to her, Excalibur still in hand. "You can't blame yourself for what happened. We were attacked by bandits, and we did our best to come out of it alive."

"Except for Dakin," Emry said with a devastated laugh.

A muscle feathered in Arthur's jaw. "I spoke with him privately. He won't dare try anything like that again. And he won't be saying a word to my father about anything that happens on this trip, either, if he expects me to hold my tongue about his cowardice."

Emry couldn't believe it. "Truly?"

Because that meant—that meant Dakin wouldn't be watching her every move, ready to report back to the king. It meant Uther might never learn of her misbehaving magic. Or any other misbehaviors.

"Truly," Arthur promised, reaching for her hand. "My father should never have made you feel that your place at the castle could be taken from you at his whim. Threatening Dakin is the least I can do, for my wizard."

His wizard. Emry closed her eyes, blinking back hot tears. "I'm your wizard, and that's all," she said sadly, remembering.

Arthur shook his head. "You're my wizard, and that's *everything.*"

Before she knew it, she was closing the distance between them, her lips seeking his. And then his mouth was on hers, soft and hungry. His hand curled against the back of her neck, and her breath went shallow as the rest of her went taut with desire. His fingers tangled into her hair, bringing the kiss deeper. It was the sort of kiss you could drown in, and for a few glorious moments, she did.

Arthur leaned eagerly forward and then winced, clutching his side in pain.

"Tunic off," she insisted. "That's an order."

A corner of Arthur's mouth hitched up. "Is it, now?" He laid down his sword and pulled his tunic over his head.

Emry swallowed thickly, taking in his smooth chest, his broad shoulders, and the starburst-shaped silver scar on his side. An inch above the scar was a tender red wound, which gave off the unmistakably spicy scent of healing salve.

They were so close. Her heart was pounding, and her skin felt too warm, and her lips were swollen from their kiss. All she wanted to do was throw her arms around this brave, impossible boy who could somehow manage to both make her laugh and go weak in the knees.

"If I swoon, you better catch me," she warned.

"My shirtless presence does tend to have that effect on women," Arthur teased, a wonderful smile curling over his lips.

But there was pain tightening the corners of his eyes, and when she laid her hand over his wound, she had the briefest sense of sadness.

She gasped as the magic flowed out of her, the scar on her palm filling with light.

Excalibur suddenly lit up as well, flashing so bright that Emry closed her eyes, momentarily dazzled.

When she opened them, she was staring up at the prince, her palm flat against his ribs. She didn't feel dizzy or weak in the slightest. And he certainly wasn't grimacing in pain. Instead, he was staring down at her through his eyelashes, looking pleased.

She removed her hand, and the red, tender wound was gone.

"Healing salve?" she said, arching an eyebrow. "Really?"

"I guess not." He ran a hand over the space where he'd been stabbed, testing. "It's hard to believe the things you can do."

"Likewise," she whispered.

His eyes lifted to meet hers, and neither of them looked away. She swallowed and wet her lips, all too aware that he was staring at her with an intensity he usually reserved for books. A shiver ran up her spine as he pulled her toward him, his warm hands stroking up and down her sides.

As their lips came together, she knew, somehow, that they both had the same glorious idea at once. Neither of them held back, or pulled away; instead, they pressed deeper, further.

She wanted this, had wanted it for a long time—to be alone at an inn with Arthur, shirtless, glorious Arthur, and for there to be absolutely nothing she could think of to keep them apart.

Flamel would help her to control her magic. When they returned to Camelot, Arthur and Guin would turn each other down at the altar.

Arthur's lips moved from her mouth to her neck, his clever fingers hiking up her skirts and skimming against her thighs, and Emry gasped. "I suppose just the one bed will do," she decided.

"Will it?" Arthur looked startled but pleased. When Emry blushed, he lifted an eyebrow. "Hardly seems fair I'm the only one without a shirt on."

"Then even the playing field, Your Highness."

Arthur reached for her lacings as their mouths crushed together in a searing kiss. She was lighting up from the inside, her entire body was made of heat and fire and pleasure, and, oh, she adored it. Her dress fell to the floor, and the cool air felt magnificent against her warm skin.

When the kiss softened, Arthur lifted her chin with his fingertip, staring at her in the candlelight, his eyes blazing with desire.

"Your move, wizard," he whispered, a corner of his mouth rising in the most infuriating grin. "Better make it a good one."

She spun them around, their bodies melting together as they fell onto the bed.

Arthur propped himself up on the pillows as Emry hovered over him, bracing her hands on either side. She took in his lean muscles and hard jaw, the bare expanse of his chest, the taut line of his waistband, the way he was straining against the front of his trousers.

She pressed her mouth and her body flush against his, feeling her against him. He gasped, and she smiled, moving her mouth to his jaw, then his neck, his heart hammering against her own.

"Good move?" she asked, her lips skating against his neck.

"Very," he whispered, grabbing her hips.

They rolled until she was no longer on top of him, and they were both lying with their heads on the pillows, their noses inches apart, staring into each other's eyes.

Arthur's dark eyes were serious. "There's something I should tell you," he said.

And then the door flew open, and Lucan bustled in with a pitcher and basin.

"I thought you might want to wash up before bed," said the valet.

Emry grabbed for the covers, horrified.

"Thank you, Luc," said Arthur, with absolutely no trace of embarrassment.

"I'm afraid the water's cold," the valet went on.

"Not a problem," Arthur went on serenely, resting one hand behind his head, entirely nonchalant.

"Very well. Goodnight, then," said the valet, his expression perfectly neutral as he bowed and exited the room.

"Oh my god," Emry said after he was gone.

"What?" Arthur asked, the picture of innocence.

"You know what!"

"He's my valet de chambre, Emry. Better let him do something, or else he'll sulk."

Emry scowled. "Maybe the interruption was for the best," she said, detangling herself from the quilt and pulling on her linen shift.

This thing between them—it wasn't supposed to be there. Even though the king wasn't watching, if they took it too far, the moment they returned to Camelot, it would be obvious that they burned for one another in ways that were entirely improper.

Emry didn't want the whole of Castle Camelot whispering *she* was the reason Arthur was turning down Guinevere at the altar.

"What do you mean?" Arthur asked.

"After all, what are we even doing?" Emry said. "It's—you and me, it never goes well."

She bit her lip and stared at him, wishing he'd correct her. Wishing he'd insist she was wrong, and promise that it would.

Instead, he rose from the bed and went over to Lucan's washbasin.

"Heat this up for me?" He said it as if issuing orders was the most natural thing in the world.

How easily she had forgotten that he was soon to be a king, and she was merely an apprentice wizard who intrigued him.

"That's much better," Arthur said, wringing out a damp linen cloth.

"You wanted to tell me something?" she said.

Panic flashed briefly across Arthur's face. "I—nothing. It's nothing."

Chapter 24

E mmett gritted his teeth and tried the attack spell again.

It went wide, missing the archery target entirely, and hitting the castle wall with a bang. Thankfully, the battlement held, with just a few pebbles shaking loose. He winced, hoping no one had noticed his errant spell. He lowered his wand, barely daring to breathe for fear of being discovered.

The dark silhouette of a guard with a helmet and halberd emerged from the nearest tower, and Emmett's stomach sank. "Who goes there?" called the guard.

Emmett swallowed nervously, hating how it looked. "Sorry!" He hadn't realized anyone was in the tower. "It's—er, I'm a castle apprentice, not an attacker."

"Emmett? That you?" The guard pulled off his helmet, revealing a splash of freckles and a thatch of ginger hair.

"Hey, Tristan," Emmett said with considerable relief. "Sorry about that. Bad aim."

Tristan leaned down over the edge of the wall. "You're practicing magic?" he asked eagerly. "Can I watch?"

"Er, sure," Emmett said.

"Best thing to happen all night," Tristan said. "Morian's abandoned me. There's no way he needs the jakes for an hour. I know he's back in the barracks playing cards with his friends and having a laugh at my expense."

Emmett made a face. "Knew I never liked him."

"What kind of spells are you casting?" Tristan asked, resting his elbows on a crenellation.

"Combat," said Emmett. "Found the instructions in a book. It's a bit like flinging an invisible rock."

"An invisible rock? Are you serious? I'm coming down," Tristan said. Emmett heard echoing footsteps, and then Tristan joined him on the lawn, out of breath, and tucking his helmet under his arm. "Is this about—you know? What we overheard on the quest to Avalon?"

Emmett nodded grimly. "I want to be prepared for what's coming. I hate how no one is doing anything."

"I feel the same way," said Tristan. "Perce and I were talking about it at supper. Did you know there's no plan to defend the castle from an attack?"

Emmett hadn't known that. "There's not?"

The guard shook his head. "I brought it up with Captain Lam after we got back, since I thought I'd forgotten what we were supposed to do. He, uh, well . . ." Tristan gestured toward the guard tower with a sigh. "I've either got tower duty or dungeon patrol for the rest of the month. Apparently, my question was 'purposefully stirring unrest.'"

A muscle feathered in Emmett's jaw. "You need a new captain."

"We'd all vote for Perce in a heartbeat. Well, most of us. But it's the king's choice, and Lam's been in his post for twenty years." Tristan frowned, and then brightened. "Show me that spell again?"

"Sure." Emmett raised his wand, sending a blast of magic at the archery target. It knocked over, and Emmett whooped.

He had that hollow, empty feeling that warned him his magic was almost spent, which was a shame. "So, you're out here most nights?"

"Unfortunately. Why?"

"If there isn't a plan to defend the castle, then we should make one," said Emmett.

"The two of us?" Tristan looked skeptical.

"No one else is going to, so why not us?" Emmett pressed. "We'll get Percival to help. And—and Lance. And anyone else you think is trustworthy. That way, if there's an attack, you won't have to wait for captain's orders. You'll already know what to do."

Tristan grinned. "We'll be like a secret order of guards."

"Exactly!" said Emmett.

"When Arthur gets back from France, he'll be so pleased," said Tristan.

Emmett pressed back a sigh. He knew the young guard worshipped the crown prince, but he didn't need the reminder that his sister had run off to the Continent with the guy. Even if it was on the Lady of the Lake's advice. Even if it was to help sort out Emry's magic. Even if they did have two guards and a valet traveling with them.

"When's the next time you're posted in the dungeons?" Emmett asked.

"Thursday," said Tristan.

"Are there any prisoners, or would we be able to use the space?"

"There's no one," Tristan said. "Uther would rather sentence someone to hang than keep them languishing in the dungeons, so it turns over pretty quickly."

Emmett made a face.

"Sorry," Tristan said hastily. "But it's the truth."

"Well, then," said Emmett. "We'll meet in the dungeons. And figure out how to defend Camelot if no one else will."

Chapter 25

In the soft twilight, the streets of Paris teemed with life. Arthur stared up at the grand, gothic stone buildings that towered above the rest of the city. A cathedral, shaped like none he had seen before, with two soaring towers dwarfed everything in its shadow. Beyond that was the university district, he knew from studying a map, a warren of closely packed stone-and-timber buildings.

There were more people crammed into the walled city than Arthur had thought possible, the streets choked with carts and carriages and horses. Parisians slopped chamber pots out the window, aiming half-heartedly for the gutter, and more often than not missing it entirely. Lucan looked horrified the first time it happened. Brannor looked resigned. Emry pressed back a grin, especially after some of the offending slop splattered across Dakin's cloak.

They had spent three days on the road since leaving Calais, and the nearer they got to Paris, the scarcer the lodgings. For the past two nights, everyone had crammed into the same room, and Arthur had lain awake until the others were asleep, nearly dying of frustration.

Emry was right there, and all he wanted to do was find a dark corner and kiss her until it was impossible to stop. And sometimes, when their eyes met, he thought she felt the same way. But sometimes, he worried she didn't.

Her words at the inn haunted him: *What are we even doing? You and me, it never goes well.*

She was so wrong—she was the only thing in the world that ever went well for him. It was everything else that went to hell. He knew he should tell her about Guinevere, and his promise to go forward with the wedding. But telling her would make it real. And he wanted to pretend, just for a little longer, that it wasn't truly happening.

They had their whole lives to be torn apart by circumstance. But they only had these few weeks before the future pressed in on them.

And maybe, just maybe, they might find themselves alone in a room with one bed again. It didn't even have to be a room, he thought, glancing at her. A dark alcove would do.

"I believe it's this way," Brannor said doubtfully, gesturing toward a narrow lane lined with bakeries and tailoring shops whose signs were in both French and Hebrew.

"Then lead on," Arthur said. They might as well get this reunion over with.

At Lord Agravaine's insistence, they were staying with his son Gawain. Not that Arthur minded his perfect cousin so much these days, but they had spent most of their lives forced into an unasked-for rivalry as spares to the throne, with Gawain always smugly coming out on top. Until finally, they had established a tentative truce.

It turned out Gawain wasn't quite the unprincipled rake he always pretended to be and was doing his part as a spy for Camelot at French court. Though he hadn't passed much intelligence to his father lately. Arthur wasn't sure whether that was a good or a bad sign.

He tried to put it out of mind as they wound through the narrow lanes of the fashionable Marais, in search of the d'Orkney townhouse. They found it without too much trouble. The house stood nearly edge-to-edge with its neighbors, hidden from the street by a wide entrance screen, which was helpfully propped open. Beyond that sat a large forecourt and a three-story house, lit up with music and laughter spilling from open windows.

"What is this?" he wondered aloud.

"I believe, Your Highness, this is what's known colloquially as a house party," said Lucan, trying to be helpful.

Dakin snickered, and Brannor let out a long-suffering sigh.

"Are you sure he's expecting us?" Emry frowned.

"He's supposed to be." Arthur swung off his horse. "Come on." He knocked, bracing himself. A tall, snobbish-looking manservant opened the door.

The man took in their travel-worn clothes, horses, and luggage, and sniffed, as though he would strongly prefer to close the door in their faces and suggest they find a lodging house.

"Bonsoir—" Arthur began.

"Ah, yes," said the man in a heavy French accent. "Lord Gawain's English guests. This way."

Emry exchanged a confused glance with Arthur as the manservant led them through an elegantly appointed townhouse that was deep in the throes of a wild soiree, as though pretending nothing was amiss.

Scandalously dressed revelers darted through the rooms, sloshing wine out of their goblets as they laughed and flirted. A troupe of musicians with brightly painted faces, who wore very little in the way of clothing, performed in a marble foyer.

"Seigneur d'Orkney is upstairs," said the man, leading them past a group of well-dressed lords, who spun a shirtless gentleman wearing a bearskin rug across his shoulders in dizzying circles before pushing him toward a crowd of giggling young women.

The shirtless gentleman let out a growl. The manservant pretended he hadn't.

Emry laughed aloud. Arthur knocked against her shoulder and grinned. A maid carrying a tray of drinks passed them on the staircase, and Emry floated two goblets off her tray.

"Mon dieu!" exclaimed a lad in a profusion of pink ruffles, his mouth hanging open at the sight of the flying drinks.

"Grab one, quick," Emry murmured.

Arthur did, raising the goblet with a wink in the lad's direction that had him blushing the same color as his outfit.

"This is amazing," Emry said, not knowing what to look at first. She couldn't remember the last time she'd been to a real party, and certainly she'd never been to one as grand as this.

At the top of the stairs, the manservant knocked smartly on a set of exquisitely carved double doors.

"Entrez," came a bored voice.

They did and found themselves in a large sitting room draped with sumptuous silks. Naked men and women posed seductively about the space with leaves pinned in their hair and other places. Three men in their shirtsleeves frowned behind easels as they sketched and painted the scene.

Among them was Gawain, in bare feet and a beautifully embroidered dressing gown. He was even more handsome than Emry remembered, with his flashing dark eyes, high cheekbones, and smooth brown skin. He had the same wide, clever grin as Arthur, but on Gawain, it seemed haughtier and more self-possessed. Tonight his cheeks were dusted with stubble, and he held a goblet in one hand, and a dripping paintbrush in the other.

Come to France. Wear a nice dress, and I'll introduce you at court as my fiancée. Emry remembered all too well when Gawain had made her that offer. But she hadn't come. Hadn't so much as said goodbye. Anyway, he hadn't been serious. He rarely was, about anything.

"There you two are," he said, slurring slightly. "Now the party can really get started."

"I believe it's well underway," said Arthur.

Gawain's infuriating grin stretched wider. "Good. I do have a reputation to maintain." He pitched his voice low as he stepped forward to add, "And of course, it is quite convenient to blackmail young nobles for their indiscretions when they commit their sins under my roof."

Emry choked on a sip of wine.

"Follow me," he said, throwing open the doors to a smaller chamber, a study, which was mercifully unoccupied, and pulling out a half-empty bottle of wine from one of the desk drawers. "Is the young vicomte mauling anyone while pretending to be a bear yet?"

"They've turned it into a party game," Emry said.

"A pity." Gawain sighed, uncorking the bottle of wine with his teeth and taking a swig.

"You live here by yourself?" Emry asked.

"As a temporary caretaker," Gawain said. "The house belongs to my father's family. As do the staff. By the way, they think you're both my cousins. I can explain away a prince, but not an unmarried, unchaperoned woman."

Emry rolled her eyes. "This house is literally full of unmarried, unchaperoned women," she pointed out. "Half of whom are drunk and undressed."

Gawain shrugged. "Yes, but they'll be gone in an hour or two. Otherwise the comte next door will have my head." He sat down on top of his desk. "He thinks I throw too many parties. And he may be right. But if I end them early enough, then tant pis, vous savez?" Gawain seemed unaware he'd lapsed into French.

Emry shot Arthur a look. Gawain was behaving like his worst self. And she didn't understand why.

"What are you doing?" Arthur asked.

"Whatever do you mean?" Gawain replied serenely.

"You're entertaining a house full of guests in your dressing gown!"

Emry swallowed back a laugh.

"I'm misbehaving, my dear cousin," Gawain said, as though it was perfectly obvious. "As to the reason, well, you'll never guess who's run away from his boarding school."

"Again?" Arthur winced, wondering when Gawain's younger brother, Jereth, would stop making a menace of himself.

Gawain nodded. "Father's furious. Blames me for not checking up on the lad. I am sick of all this responsibility. Perhaps, if I act irresponsibly, he will give me less of it."

Arthur looked annoyed. "Well, you better sober up and take this seriously. You're to be my introduction at court."

"Impossible. I cannot show my face at court for a month at least. Not after the Comte de Montaigne found me in bed with his horrible wife. Ghastly woman. Rather resembles a goose." Gawain shuddered. "My father needed some documents from the comte's study, and I had to gain admittance to his house while he was away." Gawain laughed bitterly. "Now he's set on challenging me to a duel. So, you see, I can't go. But you'll be fine on your own. Just stay on the king's good side."

"I'm relieved to hear he has one," Arthur replied.

"Go and enjoy the party," Gawain said, shooing them from his study. "I have a painting to finish."

The curtains were drawn when Arthur arrived at breakfast the next morning.

Gawain, who was seated at the head of the long wooden table, looked awful, despite his immaculate brocade coat and matching vest. Tension pulled at the corners of his eyes, and he was gripping some sort of tonic and staring miserably at a plate of toast and eggs.

"Morning, cousin," Arthur said brightly, making Gawain wince. "Didn't expect to find you up so early."

Gawain groaned and gripped his head as a maid tiptoed past, setting a platter of fruit on the sideboard. "Through no desire of my own. I have business with the Vicomte de Lorraine."

"Where's Emry?" Arthur asked.

"Plotting my demise, I'm sure," said Gawain. "I sent a maid to attend to her toilette."

Arthur choked. "She hates that sort of thing."

Gawain grinned. "I know."

Arthur piled his plate high, enjoying the novelty of a buffet service. "Is there any coffee?" he asked hopefully.

"None. Haven't been able to find any in Paris. I'm starting to think you invented it."

Emry arrived with a yawn, and Arthur dropped a piece of fruit back to the platter in surprise.

She was dressed like a proper lady. Her lips were painted red, and her hair seemed to have doubled in volume, and was piled elaborately on top of her head. The dress she was wearing wouldn't have looked out of place at court.

She looked wonderful, but she didn't look like his wizard.

"Don't laugh," she threatened. "Or I'll turn your tea into bathwater."

"Why would we laugh?" asked Gawain. "You are the picture of elegance."

Emry glared, furious over the compliment. Arthur, at least, knew to keep his mouth shut. "Is there coffee?" she asked.

"No," Arthur and Gawain said simultaneously.

Emry sighed and piled her plate with eggs and toast before joining them at the table.

"Did you enjoy yourself at the party last night?" Gawain asked.

Emry grinned. "Very much."

Gawain leaned forward, propping his chin in his hands. "Do tell."

"Yes," Arthur said, raising an eyebrow. "Do tell."

"I learned a game where you toss a ball into your opponent's beer. If it goes in, they have to drink it, and you win." She laughed.

"You didn't," Arthur said, pressing back a smile.

"Serves them right," said Emry. "If you're so horrified to be bested by a girl, it's your own fault if you keep calling for her to play again."

"Making enemies wherever you go, I see," said Gawain.

"Hardly. I got them too drunk to remember any of it," Emry promised.

Gawain motioned to the staff for some privacy, and they were shut inside the dining room.

"Here," Arthur said, withdrawing Excalibur from his scabbard and handing it to Gawain. "Hangover cure."

Color returned to Gawain's cheeks the moment he gripped the sword. "That's much better," he said. "I hope you don't mind the subterfuge with the staff. I didn't want them gossiping over who was staying here."

"Wait, am I supposed to be his sister?" Emry demanded. Arthur choked on a mouthful of toast. Like Emry, he had just made that connection.

"Yes," Gawain said mildly. "My apologies if you believed you'd be sharing a room."

"Of course we didn't," Emry said, her cheeks red.

Arthur sank down in his seat. So much for stolen kisses in darkened corridors, unless they wished to cause a scandal.

"When are we expected at court?" Emry asked, pouring herself some tea.

"Tomorrow," Arthur said.

"My tailor will be here this morning," promised Gawain. "I've already given him instructions."

"And this is the current fashion in Saint-Germaine?" Emry asked, gesturing toward Gawain's fitted ice-blue damask.

"You mean the fashion in Paris," Gawain corrected. "The king is currently in residence at his Palais de la Cité, just a short walk from here." Gawain sipped his tea, winced, and stirred in a spoonful of sugar. "He rotates between his many royal residences as the whim strikes."

"Seems wasteful," Arthur put in.

"Oh, he means it to be," said Gawain. "His real aim is forcing nobles to acquire expensive residences all over the kingdom. The more debt they take on to impress him, the more desperately they need to stay in his favor. And, of course, the less likely they are to have the means to amass an army and rise up against him."

It was clever, but terrible. And it made Arthur even more apprehensive of meeting the French king. He sighed. "I wish my father had thought of that. Might have saved us all a lot of trouble with the Duke of Cornwall."

Gawain frowned. "What's going on with the duke?"

Arthur explained about the army and the fortifications.

"So that's why you're here," he said. "What's Merlin's excuse?"

Emry scowled into her breakfast. "The Lady of the Lake said the French court wizard could help me with my magic."

"Maître Flamel is supposed to help you?" Gawain laughed. "Good luck."

"What do you mean?" Emry asked.

Gawain merely shrugged. "You'll see."

Chapter 26

Arthur had always thought Camelot to be a prosperous kingdom, and its royal castle to contain great riches. But as he approached the Palais de la Cité, he wondered if he had miscalculated.

The moment he stepped inside the château, with its gilded corridors and stained glass windows, he felt as though he hadn't been raised in a castle at all, but merely an oversize guildhall. From the sumptuous clothing he saw on the passing courtiers, Arthur was glad he'd had the sense to let Gawain dictate his own wardrobe.

The other courtiers in the throne room eyed him curiously, and a few let their gazes linger, their stares a bit lower than he would have liked. Arthur tried not to fidget in his silk brocade. The trousers were rather tighter than he was used to, and without a codpiece for privacy.

It's the fashion, he told himself, even if none of the others he saw wore their trousers quite as close-fitting. And having Dakin and Brannor along in their Camelot royal guards' uniforms was certainly drawing looks.

Finally, the doors at the end of the hall were flung open, and a hush fell over the crowd as King Louis entered.

He was a tall, commanding man of about thirty, with dark hair, a prominent nose, and a deep brow that made him seem permanently unpleased. He carried himself as if he thought he was very handsome, and the coat he wore—one of burgundy velvet embroidered with golden flowers—dripped with jewels.

There was no mistaking him for anything but what he was—a king. A powerful one.

Arthur swallowed nervously as the king made his procession down the receiving hall, stopping in front of his courtiers who stepped forward and bowed before handing him a petition, or those who merely wanted a quick word. In Camelot, the courtiers bowed and stayed there as King Uther made his way to the throne, able only to speak with the king in front of a large audience. Perhaps, Arthur thought, when he was king, he would try something more like this.

"What if he stops?" Dakin muttered, as the king got nearer.

"He's not going to stop," Brannor whispered back.

Arthur was one of the very last who stood in the king's audience on his way to the throne. Yet, instead of sweeping past, King Louis stopped with a frown.

"Et tu es?" the king demanded. *And you are?*

Arthur gave a short bow, which sent a stir through the crowd. It was not how a subject bowed to their king.

"Arthur Pendragon, le prince héritier de Camelot."

King Louis gave Arthur and his guards a critical once-over.

"Mon roi," Arthur went on, "je vous presente les cadeaux, pour votre gentillesse." He gestured for Brannor to present the gifts.

The French king inspected the jeweled puzzle box and the golden pocket sundial as though he were surveying a meager breakfast spread of toast and jam. He raised a hand, and an attendant stepped forward, sweeping them into the sack along with the petitions asking for more land, or a divorce from an unfaithful spouse.

The king regarded Arthur with a small smile, and Arthur tried not to fidget.

"Your French is tolerable, but I must insist upon English. I have an important guest arriving next week with whom I must speak it, and I wish to practice."

"Of course, Your Majesty," said Arthur, visibly relieved.

"I admit, I'm surprised," said the king. "After receiving your letter,

I could not determine if you were truly serious about making the journey."

"I am a man of my word," said Arthur.

"How rare." The king raised an eyebrow. "Since you have come all this way, perhaps you will join me for my luncheon?"

"I would be honored," said Arthur.

"Il n'est pas nécessaire d'amener votre gardes," replied the king. *It is not necessary to bring your guards.*

The king continued his procession to the dais and throne, and Arthur wished he could drop through the floor and disappear.

The castle was much larger than Emry had imagined, and the hallways were full of lavishly dressed courtiers. They clustered in a dozen different drawing rooms, playing cards, dice, and checkers, listening to music, weaving tapestries, and gossiping. The fashions were luxurious and far more daring than what she was used to back at Camelot, and suddenly Gawain's foppish outerwear and jeweled shoe buckles made far more sense.

Emry looked down at her own gown, a gray silk that had once belonged to Princess Guinevere. The bodice was laced with gold ribbon and edged with golden leaves. She had edited the sleeves to a looser fit, so she might have somewhere to stash her wand, added pockets, and brought up the neckline so she didn't feel half-naked bent over her alembic.

Gawain had pronounced it passable, which from him was a high compliment. But still, she worried. She wanted everything to be perfect, because without Flamel's help, she didn't know what she would do. And maybe, smoothing the wrinkles from her dress would also smooth the wrinkles from her nerves.

The wizard's study was in the oldest part of the castle, a short wing that jutted off the side, overlooking the castle's fruit and vegetable gardens. She almost missed the corridor entirely, but then she saw the runes and alchemical symbols painted over the archway in what looked to be real gold.

At the end of the corridor was a short, squat wooden door pressed against a crumbling wall of stone and flanked on either side by carvings of gargoyles wearing fierce frowns.

"Bonjour?" Emry called, knocking on the door of the wizard's study. "Hello? Maître Flamel?"

The door was flung open, and Emry came face-to-face with a scowling man who looked to be in his late thirties. He had pale skin and dark, slicked-back hair that curled around his ears. He was dressed entirely in black, from his billowing tunic to his skintight trousers, to his knee-high leather boots.

Charcoal was smudged around his eyes, and a collection of strange amulets hung around his neck, from pieces of bone to feathers wrapped with colorful cords and marked with runes.

He looked, Emry thought, like a conceited pirate who had fallen ill, and had grudgingly taken to penning poetry until his health recovered.

"What is it, girl?" the man snapped. "I'm awaiting the arrival of Camelot's apprentice court wizard."

"That's why I knocked," Emry tried to explain.

"Where is he?" the man asked, twisting around to peer down the corridor behind Emry.

Emry smiled. Waited.

"Absolutely not," the wizard growled. "There is no such thing as a female wizard!"

It hadn't occurred to her that Flamel might refuse. And now that he had, she couldn't believe she had been so foolish as to believe he might help her.

No one wanted a female wizard. Not her father, not King Uther.

Yet she had naively come all this way because the Lady of the Lake had suggested it.

Flamel wouldn't help her. However, he might help her brother. The idea was reckless and risky, but it might just work.

The wizard started to close the door in her face. She wedged it open with her boot.

"There's been a misunderstanding. Please, let me explain."

The wizard glowered at her. "Well?"

"Obviously I'm not the wizard you're meant to help," she said. "I apologize for the confusion, Maître Flamel. You will be working with my brother."

The door opened a bit wider. "Your brother?" the wizard said with a frown. "Then why are you here?"

Emry thought fast. "He's . . . indisposed. Too much wine. So, he sent me in his place to send his apologies and gather a list of materials he should bring when he arrives tomorrow."

"His apology is accepted," the wizard said gruffly.

Emry felt her shoulders relax in relief. "He'll be pleased to hear it," Emry said.

"See that he brings parchment, quill and ink, and his wand," huffed the wizard. "Good day, girl." He shooed her out to the corridor and slammed the door in her face.

It was fine. Everything was fine, she told herself as she retreated down the corridor. She would just have to play the role of her brother again, at French court. She had fixed it. Yet a small voice in the back of her head whispered that she hadn't, not really.

Who was Maître Flamel to declare that women weren't wizards, and to refuse to help her, though the king had ordered him to do so?

Emry didn't want to pretend to be her brother again. Not to learn magic. And what's more, she shouldn't have to. Before she could think better of it, she turned back around and threw open the door of Flamel's workshop with a wave of her hand.

The wizard gaped at her, startled by the intrusion, and the fact that the door had opened itself.

"I lied," she said. "I was going to come back tomorrow dressed as my brother. It's how I won my place as apprentice court wizard in Camelot. But I'm sick of everyone telling me I can't be something that I am. I'm a wizard, and I'm a woman, and I came all this way, so you're going to help me with my magic, because it's the honorable thing to do."

Flamel regarded her carefully. Emry was breathing hard, and she wished she'd raised the bodice of Guin's dress even higher. She lifted her chin, trying to look fierce, despite her panic and fancy dress.

"Bien," Flamel said, with a very French shrug.

Emry couldn't believe it. "Bien?" she repeated. "So, you're going to help me?"

"You are Camelot's apprentice court wizard, as you say." Flamel shrugged again. "I agreed to help this person. There was no condition of male, female, or anything else."

"Thank you," Emry said, feeling an enormous weight lift from her shoulders.

"Hmph," he growled, gesturing for her to step inside. "I suppose even an English girl can benefit from my vast array of knowledge and expertise. My wife is English. She is also insufferable, as you no doubt are."

Emry took a look around Flamel's study. It was like a parody of a wizard's lair. Animal skulls hung above fantastical tapestries. Poisonous herbs grew beneath a row of glass cloches, and a large wooden cabinet of various drawers, jars, and shelves took up one wall.

Emry realized she was staring, and quickly pulled her attention back to the wizard himself.

"Does the συνδέω charm still work if you wear it on an amulet? I thought it only affected objects," she said, nodding at his necklace.

He sniffed, tucking the amulet into the front of his tunic. "It depends on what you consider an object," said Flamel.

Emry took in more of the space with a frown. Perched in a brass cage on top of an ancient marble column was a stone gargoyle. The poor thing had a miserable expression, and was leg-shackled to the pedestal with real irons.

"Is that a statue?" Emry asked.

"It is a marvel," the French wizard said proudly. "I have given it eternal life!"

"Tuez-moi, s'il vous plaît!" moaned the creature.

"Er, I believe it just asked you to please kill it?" Emry said.

"It has a regrettable sense of humor." Flamel scowled darkly in the gargoyle's direction, and then, after a moment's thought, tossed his cloak over the thing.

"How did you make it?" Emry asked.

That was clearly the wrong question. Flamel glowered.

"He slopped a bad batch of potion out the window," the gargoyle called helpfully. "The next thing I knew, I was like this, and they were chiseling me off the castle walls."

"Because you made such a racket," Flamel snapped.

"Wouldn't have, if I'd known it would get me chained up." The gargoyle complained, and Emry stifled a grin.

She picked up a bottle labeled *Moste Potente Poison* and gave it a sniff. "Fish oil?" she guessed. "With some sort of purgative."

"Cascara," Flamel confirmed.

"What's in the *aphrodisiaca*?" Emry asked. "St. John's wort?"

"Goat piss and sea holly."

Emry snorted in amusement. Arthur would have the time of his life in here.

"You are an apprentice, no?" asked Flamel. Emry nodded. "Then, so long as you are here, you are my apprentice. Have you any skills besides running your mouth?"

"Some," Emry said modestly.

"Don't just stand there," Flamel said imperiously. "Show me."

Emry glanced doubtfully around the wizard's lair. There was so much furniture that there was hardly any room to move. And then she had an idea.

"*ψηλά*," she said.

Everything in the room lifted six inches off the floor. The chairs, the small reading table, the lectern topped with a heavy illuminated manuscript, the crates and trunks, the large wooden cabinet, even the marble column.

It was a lot. Emry groaned from the effort, her hands shaking. "*κάτω*," she gasped, and everything returned to its place.

Flamel swore under his breath.

Emry turned to the flabbergasted wizard and bowed.

"Acceptable," sniffed the French wizard, pretending he wasn't impressed. "I notice you don't use a wand."

"I do sometimes, if it's Corperus magic," she admitted.

"You can work magic upon another person without . . . I don't know it in English . . . une contre-attaque?"

"Blowback?" Emry supplied.

Flamel nodded and ran a hand through his hair, ruffling it just so.

"Master Ambrosius taught me how."

"Ah, the old potions master. I thought he'd retired decades ago."

"He, um, came back," said Emry. Master Ambrosius had been forced to return from his retirement after her father had gone missing.

"Perhaps he is whom I should consult about the elixir of life." The wizard crossed to his cabinet and pulled down a stoppered bottle of amber liquid that smelled of honey.

He bit off the cork with his teeth, and drank deeply from the bottle. "Mead," he said by way of explanation. "Now tell me, Mademoiselle Apprentice, what am I supposed to do for you?"

"The Lady of the Lake said you could show me how to control magic."

Flamel barked a laugh. "Controlling your magic is something you should have learned as a child."

"I did," Emry said, annoyed. "I'm not here about *my* magic. I opened a doorway to Anwen, and the stones left me with a . . . parting gift. My blood summons the power, but nothing controls it."

"Mon dieu." Flamel blinked at her. "You opened a doorway to Anwen? A corporeal doorway?"

"Twice," Emry said impatiently.

Flamel paled. "Non," he said. "You will leave immediately. You could be under the control of la Dame de l'Autre Monde."

He stumbled back, regarding her warily. Emry had never heard the term before, but she knew whom he meant. The sorceress she'd seen trapped in a magical slumber in Nimue's looking pool.

"She's not," called the gargoyle. "There's no witch's bargain or compulsion magic on her."

"How could you possibly know that?" Emry asked curiously.

"I can sense magic," boasted the creature. "Yours is fascinating, by the way. Very shiny."

"Thank you, I think," Emry said, looking to the French wizard.

Flamel had composed himself, though he still regarded her warily.

"You see?" Emry said. "I never even stepped through the doorway. So of course I've never met . . . whatever you call her. The High Sorceress of Anwen."

"This is most intriguing," Flamel said, staring at her with unabashed curiosity. "You carry power from a world you have not visited. And you can summon it? I would make a study of you."

"You may study me *after* you help me learn to manage this power," Emry bargained.

Flamel shrugged. "But of course. And while I think on how to help you, you will help me with my experiments."

"Experiments?" Emry asked, curious in spite of herself.

"I am distilling la prima materia." He paused grandly, perhaps expecting Emry to be impressed. She shrugged, having no idea what he was talking about. "The first step in the alchemical journey to create the elixir of eternal life," he finished, annoyed.

"Huzzah," drawled the gargoyle, from beneath Flamel's cloak. "Now, please kill me."

Flamel looked as though he wanted to kick it.

Chapter 27

Arthur had expected King Louis to dine publicly, in a grand hall full of courtiers, but the king only did so at supper, and took his afternoon meal in his private apartments.

Well-dressed servants admitted Arthur to the antechamber, indicating a basin where he might wash his hands, and a drop zone for his weapons. Arthur hesitated before unfastening Excalibur from around his waist.

"Et les autres," said one of the king's attendants, gesturing toward Arthur's jacket.

"C'est tout!" Arthur protested, since he carried no other weapons.

The attendant bowed, and then made a humiliating pat-down, divesting Arthur of a book, a jar of healing salve, a few pouches of herbs, and a pair of herb-cutting scissors no longer than his little finger. The objects were all placed unceremoniously into a painted wooden bucket by the door. Only the lack of lid distinguished it from a chamber pot.

Finally, he was admitted to a large gilded room. In the far corner, a musician plucked at a harp. A long banquet table was covered with a white cloth, and directly at its center sat King Louis, entirely by himself. By his side was an empty chair of much plainer build and lower suspension.

"Come, sit," demanded the king, raising a jewel-encrusted wine goblet.

Arthur took the chair, realizing belatedly that it was the same trick his father used—a less favorable seat, both more uncomfortable and lower than the king's own.

"Thank you," said Arthur, as an attendant poured him a measure of wine.

"What shall we toast to?" the king inquired.

"Friendship?" Arthur suggested.

"To our friends, then." The king raised his goblet as though he had not just twisted Arthur's words into a very different meaning, and Arthur smiled and did the same. This French king was too cunning by half.

Arthur set down his glass, staring at his plate, upon which sat a sprig of parsley. An ancient custom, one meant to demonstrate that a guest's food had not been poisoned. Not that Arthur was worried the king had such plans, but it was interesting that others might be.

"You must tell me what inspired you to come to France so suddenly," said the king, as an attendant stepped forward to place a platter of meat upon the table.

"My apprentice court wizard was determined to make the journey," said Arthur, waiting until the king had chosen his cuts of meat before spearing some for his own plate.

"How quaint, to accompany one's apprentice court wizard," said the king.

"I owe Merlin my life."

"And my chancellor tells me your wizard is consulting mine regarding a matter of magic?"

"That's right," said Arthur, hoping Emry was getting on all right. "The Lady of the Lake suggested it."

"The Lady of the Lake? But she is only a legend."

"You would not say that if you had met her," said Arthur.

The king laughed. "So, you are on a quest given to you by a fairy, and you travel with a wizard. I must have fallen into a storybook. Tell me, have you slain any dragons? Or come across a treasure map to le Sangreal?"

"You mock me," Arthur said.

"It is hard not to. You are, what, seventeen?"

"Nineteen," Arthur replied evenly.

"A grown man. Practically a king. Practically . . . que dit'on en anglais? Ah yes. The High King of all England."

Arthur desperately wanted to squirm under the king's ridicule. Instead, he forced himself to take a nonchalant sip of wine.

"I see my reputation precedes me," Arthur replied coolly.

"Reputation?" Louis scoffed. "It is just gossip. Clever little whispers, designed to fashion an unremarkable boy into an undeserving king."

"You do not like me, Your Majesty," Arthur said boldly. "May I know why?"

"I should think it obvious," said Louis. "You rejected my daughter's proposed hand in marriage."

Arthur's stomach twisted. He had put out of mind the ridiculous match between himself and seven-year-old Princess Anne. But it was clear that Louis had not.

Arthur winced in the deep silence that followed. "I meant no offense by the rejection," said Arthur. "I simply did not wish to be betrothed to anyone, much less a child."

"That is most perplexing to hear," the king went on, his smile turning sharp, "since I understand that, not a month later, you accepted a betrothal to the granddaughter of the King of Andalusia, my enemy."

Arthur's heart sank. He had never thought of Guinevere as such.

"Which is why I'm confused to find you in my court," King Louis continued, relentless. "And toasting to our friendship."

This couldn't have gone worse if Arthur had sent Emmett in his place. *Think*, he urged despairingly. There must be some way to fix this.

He couldn't very well deny the truth of the king's accusation, but perhaps he could make the man see that it was out of his control.

"My father insists on the match, since our kingdom shares a border with Cameliard," said Arthur. "He does not care that I am opposed. If you were able to escape a forced marriage while you were still le dauphin, I would appreciate knowing how you managed it."

The king's lips pressed into a line. They both knew that wasn't the case. The powerful Duke of Aquitaine had insisted on his daughter's betrothal to Louis from the moment of her birth.

"I was not," allowed the king. "Though I certainly tried. When is this joyous occasion?"

"Next month," Arthur said glumly.

"So, you have run away with your court wizard," replied the king.

Arthur's cheeks heated at the implication. "I intend to return. I know my responsibilities. I just . . . desired a moment of freedom, before."

"A wife is not as great a burden as you would fear. I keep mine elsewhere, with her own separate court. And here, I keep my mistress. And whomever else pleases me. Women are such charming playthings, no?"

"Er," said Arthur.

"Where are you staying?" the king asked.

"With my cousin Gawain."

"That would explain the outfit," said the king with a mocking grin. "He has made himself scarce lately. Is there to be a duel between him and the Comte de Montaigne? The rumors are inconclusive."

"I think you're out of luck," said Arthur.

"A pity." The king drained his wineglass and snapped his fingers for it to be refilled. "I was hoping to watch. I so enjoy when men triumph over those who have slighted them."

Arthur forced himself to let the dig pass unacknowledged. If he didn't get out of there soon, he thought he might perish of humiliation.

He made his farewell, his cheeks burning as he exited the dining room. The attendant passed him the bucket, and Arthur miserably fastened Excalibur around the waist of what were, as he'd suspected, an obscenely tight pair of trousers.

◖ ◖ ◖

Arthur spent the rest of the day in Gawain's library, brooding over his humiliation.

Emry still hadn't returned, and Gawain was nowhere to be found, and the solitude suited his mood perfectly. He'd been so certain that this would work that he couldn't wrap his mind around the fact that it hadn't. He slouched down in the chair by the fire, hating everything. He stayed there until the supper bell rang, and an insistent maid coaxed him downstairs.

Gawain sat alone at the table, calmly buttering a piece of bread. "The library," he said, rolling his eyes. "You are far too predictable, cousin."

"I try not to be. Where's Emry?"

"I'd assumed she was also in the library," said Gawain. "You two seem close these days. Is Princess Guinevere not to your taste?"

Arthur glared. "You know she isn't."

"A pity that you can't choose for yourself," Gawain said lightly. "The way you could if you were king."

Arthur frowned. "What do you know?"

Gawain's expression was innocent. "Is there something to know?"

"Of course not," Arthur said, wondering just how much his cousin was holding back.

The door to the dining room burst open, and Emry hurried in, out of breath. "Sorry," she said. "I lost track of time in Flamel's laboratory."

"I take it things went well?" Gawain asked as she hastily joined them at the table.

Emry laughed. "Actually, they did. Flamel's a disaster, but he's agreed to help me. He has a talking gargoyle, and all of these potions that sound impressive but are made-up remedies that do nothing at all. Arthur, you'd *love* it."

She turned to him, breathless and happier than he'd seen her in a long time. "How did it go with King Louis?"

He wished desperately that he could give her good news, instead of the truth. "Horrible."

"Why? What happened?"

"I rejected a betrothal to Princess Anne," Arthur said angrily. "And I looked a fool. Gawain dressed me as a fop."

Gawain shrugged. "Slim-cut brocade is the height of fashion. How was I to know you couldn't serve such a cutting-edge look?"

Arthur's lips pressed into a thin line.

"I'm sure it wasn't that bad," Emry said.

"I was treated as a court jester," Arthur complained. "The king will never respect me after this."

"You're not giving up?" Emry asked.

Arthur stared at his plate in silence.

"You have to try again," Emry insisted. "If you've already embarrassed yourself, what else could go wrong?"

"She has a point, cousin," said Gawain.

Arthur realized he'd shredded his slice of bread into crumbs. "I don't think I can face the king's throne room, especially without an invitation."

"There must be some other way to gain an audience," Emry said, looking to Gawain.

Gawain gave it some thought. "The king goes hunting every Friday in the Bois de Boulogne," he said. "You could meet by chance, if you went riding in the forest at dawn."

"Why not?" Arthur said with a sigh. "It can't go any worse than it did today."

Chapter 28

Morgana had always been fond of children's stories. She appreciated their violence and the unapologetic way the adults were so terrible to children. It made her feel as if she could be part of a story one day, after all she'd endured. And in fairy tales, monsters could be killed, treasures could be gained, and clever little girls could become queens.

Morgana knew the stories of Anwen, and so she knew of Bellicent. But she didn't let on that the sorceress's name meant anything to her. Instead, she hid that knowledge as carefully as she could, and followed the witch from her childhood cautionary tales through her frozen world.

But the longer they traveled, the more she couldn't shake the suspicion that something wasn't right. The thought pricked at her, and every time she dismissed it, it returned. Every town they passed through was the same as the last. Cursed, frozen, trapped by this strange enchantment.

"There was a wizard from my world, who came here," Morgana said lightly, on their third day traveling. "Went by the name of Merlin. Do you know what became of him?"

"The same that became of everyone in this world," snapped the sorceress, her child's eyes growing dark. "We are all cursed. Only the magical creatures are immune."

Morgana tucked that information carefully away, along with the knowledge that it didn't make sense. After all, *she* wasn't cursed.

"But who cursed you?" she pressed. "And how long ago?"

"It does not matter!" the sorceress shouted, losing her composure. "Do not speak of this again!"

Bellicent's eyes stormed, and her hair whipped back, as though caught in an invisible wind. Morgana gasped as the sorceress's will ripped through her, as though searching for something. Bellicent's power scraped against her bones, and Morgana gritted her teeth, desperate for it to end.

When it did, she felt curiously light-headed. A sense of calm settled around her shoulders, one she couldn't shake. Her pounding heart slowed to an even, steady pace.

It was almost as if she wasn't in control of herself.

As if Bellicent had snuck inside her mind and rearranged things, and Morgana kept tripping over them.

But that was impossible. Wasn't it?

Chapter 29

In the pale gray of early dawn, Arthur spurred his horse down the dirt path toward the Bois de Boulogne. He was dressed plainly, in his worn boots and favorite suede jacket, with Excalibur belted at his waist.

Please, he thought, *let this work.*

He had spent the past day reliving his humiliation as he locked himself in his room, reading every book he could find on hunting. And he worried that it wouldn't be enough to make up for so many years avoiding the activity. It was agony admitting to himself that his father's advisors had been right. He still remembered the sting of how they'd evaluated him when he was unexpectedly named heir.

A lad of eighteen should have long since mastered the arts of hunting, hawking, and combat.

Arthur cringed, remembering what he'd said in return—that his French was passable, his Latin excellent, and his knowledge of medicinal herbs first-rate.

Pathetic.

He had believed those things to be enough. Now he knew better. Ideas were only dreams, unless he could persuade others to share his vision.

King Louis saw him as a joke, and now he had one more chance to impress the man, with a skill he didn't have. Going forward, he would not be so quick to dismiss activities that others prized. He had already paid for the mistake when his father had entered him in the sword-fighting tournament, and now he was paying for it again.

He caught sight of the hunting party easily. They had traded court shoes for tall leather boots, but beyond that, it seemed everyone wore gold-threaded tunics and heavily embroidered velvet.

Apparently, hunting called for the same finery as a royal ball. A pavilion had been erected, the golden tent fluttering with decorative flags.

King Louis picked up his bow, notching an arrow. To Arthur's horror, an attendant held up an archery target.

"Cours!" yelled the king, as the attendant carrying the target ran back and forth.

Surely the king wasn't going to—

Arthur flinched as the arrow scraped the very edge of the target, inches from the attendant's hands. The members of the hunting party applauded politely.

"Baisse!" called the king, notching another arrow.

The attendant shakily lowered the target, exposing his face. Sard, Arthur thought, the man looked terrified. He trembled as he held the target, yet the hunting party gave no notice.

Thankfully, the king's next arrow hit the bull's-eye. The applause was much louder.

"Formidable!" called the king's chancellor. The man caught sight of Arthur, and his eyes narrowed. "What are you doing here?"

"Er, riding?" Arthur said.

"Then it is fortunate you have ridden into my hunting party, as I have a question for you." The king motioned for Arthur to come forward. "My staff informed me that they relieved you of a very unusual sword. Is that correct?"

Arthur frowned. "Yes, Your Majesty," he said, wondering where this was going.

"In order to accept my luncheon invitation, you left the sword in the stone in a chamber pot in my anteroom?"

So it had been a chamber pot! Arthur had thought so. "Worse, Your Majesty," said Arthur. "It was Excalibur."

The king drew in a sharp breath. The chancellor looked incredulous. A few nearby courtiers began to whisper.

"Excalibur? Impossible."

"A gift from the Lady of the Lake," Arthur replied smoothly.

"I should like to see this Excalibur. Where is it now?"

"Er, if you would permit me to draw my blade in your presence?" Arthur asked.

The king waved a hand in assent. Arthur drew Excalibur from its sheath. The blade glowed bright as midday against the pale gray mist that preceded the dawn, and the hunting party gasped. He felt the sword tug at something within him, and realized the blade wanted to show off.

All right, he agreed grudgingly, letting the sword yank him through an intricate series of passes with the glowing blade.

"Mon dieu," breathed the king. "It is just how the legends say. You should come hunting with us. Do you have a bow and arrow?"

"I don't," Arthur said. "I was merely out for a ride."

"How fortuitous," said King Louis. "It is a good thing, then, that I always bring a spare."

The hunting party had been riding through the royal forest for what felt like hours, and Arthur was starting to suspect that they'd return empty-handed.

He didn't know how he was supposed to prove himself while riding at the back of the group, but at least he was included in the hunt. That was what mattered.

Suddenly, an excited whisper rippled through the party. A deer stood still and proud not thirty feet from their group. They dismounted their horses, creeping through the forest.

The king stepped forward, softly, slowly, and notched an arrow. He drew it back and fired—at the same moment that another member of their party stepped on a twig, loudly snapping it in half. The deer spooked, bounding away.

It was half an hour before they found the animal again. This time, the energy was different. Charged. And far more determined. Arthur held back, his arrows still in his quiver, hesitating to take part in slaying such a beautiful creature.

But the king's chancellor had no such qualms. He stalked forward, raising his bow with a practiced movement. He loosed an arrow into the deer's neck. The animal wobbled, and more archers shot. The chancellor crept forward again, notching another arrow.

And then the hairs on the back of Arthur's neck stood up, and Excalibur pulsed in its sheath. He drew the sword, wondering what it wanted. And then he saw the wild boar charging through the forest, headed straight for King Louis. The animal was enormous, with glowing red eyes. It was practically the size of a horse.

"Watch out!" he called. "Gardez!"

But everyone was too focused on the deer.

The boar let out a scream, and the king whirled around, his expression one of pure horror as he spotted the beast charging toward him.

An archer fired an arrow, but it bounced harmlessly off the creature's thick flesh. The creature kept coming. Arthur didn't think as he threw Excalibur straight at the charging boar.

The glowing sword arced through the forest and caught the creature in the throat. The boar dropped to the ground less than an arm's length from King Louis.

The king stared down at the beast, and the unmistakable sword that had felled it.

Arthur's heart hammered as he went to retrieve his blade. He knew everyone was staring, and he caught snatches of whispers as he pulled Excalibur from the creature's throat as easily as if he were drawing the weapon from its sheath.

"I believe you just saved my life," said King Louis.

Arthur bowed. "Consider it a gesture of friendship, Your Majesty."

The king nodded, regarding him thoughtfully. "You are dressed like a peasant," he pronounced.

Arthur winced. "I thought my clothing adequate for horse riding in the forest."

"See that you change into something more suitable before returning to court," demanded the king.

"Thank you, Your Majesty, I will."

It had worked. Somehow, miraculously, he had impressed the king during the hunt. Not just impressed the man—saved his life. He couldn't believe it.

"We are of distant relation, are we not?" inquired the king.

"We are," Arthur confirmed.

"Then it's a shame that we are not better acquainted. You must stay at the castle, so I can further enjoy your company."

There was a threat behind the invitation, but Arthur didn't dare to refuse.

Chapter 30

Emry got down the alembic and set it on the worktable, frowning at the specks of leftover potion on the glass. "I thought I cleaned this before I left yesterday."

"I stayed late, experimenting," Flamel said.

"*Extergio*," Emry muttered, and then regarded the pristine glassware with a satisfied smirk. "Are we attempting the prima materia again?"

"Exactement."

"When are we getting to my magic problem?" she pressed.

It had been days, and still, the wizard showed no interest in anything other than his alchemy experiment.

"In time," Flamel said evasively. "Come now, the ingredients, girl."

Emry got out everything they had used the day before, placing the ingredients neatly on the table. And then there was a knock at the door.

"Entrez!" Flamel commanded.

The door opened, and there was Arthur. Behind him stood an impeccably dressed and glowering bald man.

"Monsieur Chancellor," Flamel said, with an obsequious bow.

"The young prince of Camelot wished to check on his apprentice wizard," said the chancellor. "Where is the lad?"

Flamel gestured toward Emry, and the chancellor looked suitably taken aback as she sank into a curtsey.

"I do hope Merlin isn't giving you too much trouble," said Arthur, with a grin.

"Not at all, Your Highness," simpered Flamel.

"L'existence est misérable," moaned the gargoyle.

Flamel winced.

"Er, did someone say something?" Arthur asked.

"Just the suicidal gargoyle," Emry replied innocently.

"I thought that creature was to be destroyed," said the chancellor, with a glare.

"Working on it," Flamel promised.

Arthur's gaze landed on the Moste Potente Poison. He went over to investigate.

"It's fish oil and purgatives," Emry whispered. Arthur put down the jar, looking disappointed.

"How'd it go this morning?" she asked.

"Surprisingly well." Arthur broke into a grin. "The king has invited me to stay at the castle."

"That's great," Emry said, even though a tiny part of her hated that he wouldn't be with her at the townhouse.

Perhaps more than a tiny part.

"It is," Arthur agreed. "And I'm to watch a tournament of a new sport called tennis, which apparently involves whacking people's balls."

"Are you sure you have that right?" she asked.

"Er, no, not exactly," Arthur admitted. "The gentleman who explained it did so in very rapid French."

The chancellor cleared his throat, and they sprang apart. Emry realized just how familiar they looked, their heads together, whispering over a shelf of potions, and she felt her cheeks go pink.

Arthur stepped back, straightening his posture. "Well, apprentice, what are you working on?" he asked blandly, clearly realizing the same.

"Distilling the first ingredient necessary for the elixir of eternal life," she said.

Arthur's eyes lit up. "The prima materia! Really?" He bent over to inspect her collection of herbs and potions. "I would not have thought frankincense."

"I see Your Highness has a keen interest in alchemy," said Flamel, puffing out his chest.

"A passing interest," Arthur allowed. "I read your pamphlet."

Flamel couldn't have looked more delighted. Emry rolled her eyes.

The chancellor cleared his throat once again. "His Majesty is expecting us in his game room," he said pointedly.

"Oh, right." Arthur looked torn. "I'll, um, endeavor to check in on your progress, Apprentice Wizard Merlin. And Monsieur Flamel?"

"Oui, Monseigneur?"

"I trust you're dedicating sufficient time to helping my apprentice?"

Flamel went pink. "But of course," he said, with a bow.

By that afternoon, Arthur was settled into a guest suite at the castle. Lucan bustled around noisily, humming under his breath as he unpacked Arthur's meager luggage, looking positively thrilled to be back in his element once again.

Brannor and Dakin had been given lodgings along with the rest of the castle staff, and permitted at Arthur's door during the night alongside a member of the king's own guard.

Arthur couldn't believe he'd managed to turn his failure into a resounding success. King Louis wished for him to stay at the castle, where he was sure to have the opportunity to win the man over to his cause. And Maître Flamel seemed willing to assist Emry.

All was going perfectly, yet Arthur still had a bad feeling as Lucan dressed him in stiff brocade to dine with the king's favored circle of courtiers.

He pasted on a smile and did his best to mind his verb conjugations and follow the rapid-fire conversation. After all, this was what he had come for. To endear himself to the French court and propose an alliance.

Yet the thought of Emry returning to the townhouse without him soured what should, by all accounts, have been a great victory.

Later that night, Arthur was reading at his desk when there was a commotion at the door.

Brannor appeared, looking alarmed. "The king sends his compliments," the guard reported.

"He does?" Arthur asked with a frown, as three scantily clad women dusted with gold paint filed inside and dropped into curtseys designed to leave little to the imagination.

"Bonsoir, Monseigneur," they cooed, rising in unison.

Arthur swallowed nervously as one of the girls stepped forward and trailed a line of gold paint from his temple down the front of his tunic.

"Non, merci," he said firmly, shooing the girls out the door.

They pouted theatrically, and one planted a bold kiss on his cheek before leaving.

Arthur warily returned to his desk, rubbing off the gold paint as best he could, and hoping that was the end of it.

A short while later, there was another commotion in the hallway, and his guard stuck his head in again, looking terrified.

"Not again," Arthur said with a groan.

A trio of well-muscled lads, wearing only skintight breeches, their chests bare except for swirls of silver paint, filed inside and bowed.

"À votre service, Monseigneur," they purred.

The shortest, a lad with dark brown skin and sharp cheekbones, stepped forward, a playful smirk on his handsome face. He opened his hand, placing it in front of his lips and blowing an avalanche of finely powdered glitter all over Arthur.

"Ça suffit!" Arthur complained, trying to brush the glitter from his tunic. "Please go."

The lads bowed and exited the room.

Some minutes after they had gone, there was a third knock at the door.

"What is it this time?" Arthur practically shouted. "Sheep?"

The door opened, and an elderly woman stepped through. Her gray hair was secured in a bun, her face lined with deep wrinkles. She dipped into a pained curtsey.

"Non, merci," Arthur said, suppressing his alarm.

But the woman pushed past him, dropping to her knees on the rug and adding another log to the grate.

Arthur watched with considerable relief as the elderly woman tended to the fire. She arched a knowing brow at him as she swept back into the hallway with a murmured goodnight.

After she was gone, Arthur put his head in his hands and laughed.

"Did you enjoy my gifts last night?" King Louis asked Arthur during his procession to the throne the next morning.

"They were very, er, unexpected," Arthur said diplomatically.

"I wasn't sure which you preferred." King Louis regarded him with an amused expression, and Arthur was painfully aware of the traces of gold paint, which he'd tried to scrub off, to no avail. And of the silver glitter that still clung to his skin. "Both, it seems."

Arthur went pink and scrubbed at his face with his sleeve.

The chancellor stepped forward, whispering to the king, "Monsieur le comte needs a word."

"I shall leave you to enjoy the hospitality and company of my half brother, Henri," said King Louis, gesturing toward a dark-haired, brown-skinned lad a few years older than Arthur, who stood off to the side with a group of lavishly dressed gentlemen of the same age. "I remember what it was to be young."

That statement didn't bode well, Arthur thought. But he pasted on a smile and approached the young royal and his crowd.

"I hear you saved the king's life," said Henri, in thickly accented English. "I can't decide if this is a disaster or a cause for celebration."

"Does one need a cause for celebration?" his tall, blond friend asked. Arthur recognized him from the hunt, and remembered his name to be Albon, or perhaps that was his title.

"I've never thought so," Arthur said, realizing both boys looked to him.

"Parfait," said Henri. "Come with us, if you want some real hospitality."

As Arthur followed the lads, he tried to recall what he knew of Henri—a younger son of the previous king and his royal mistress. And by all accounts, a scoundrel, a gambler, and a man of shockingly poor character.

As the day wore on, Arthur's suspicions were quickly proven true. The boys occupied a grand game room that glittered with gold and silver accents. Even their playing cards were edged with gold. Arthur's own cards, which he'd begged off a castle guard as a child, were worn and familiar and plain. He had no qualms about pulling them out at taverns, but he balked to reveal the shabby set in front of this discerning crowd.

After a few hours in their company, he was drunker than he'd ever been before lunch, and couldn't remember what he'd done with his shoes.

"Hold the game a moment," said a young, hawk-nosed vicomte, who staggered over to the fireplace and fumbled at the front of his trousers.

"You better not put it out," Henri called, unperturbed, as his friend pissed into the flames.

"Shall we take bets if he will?" asked one of the lads.

Steam, and the acrid scent of warm pee, drifted toward their card table. Arthur made a face, but everyone merely laughed.

"Have a care, Tourcy!" cried Henri. "You're traumatizing our new friend."

"I'm fine, really," said Arthur.

"You should try it," the boy called. "Far more satisfying than a chamber pot."

One of the lads called for yet another bottle of wine, and Arthur stifled a groan. "I have no head for drink, I'm afraid," he apologized, waving off what might have been a third or fourth refill from a pretty serving girl in a gown that was so low-cut as to draw everyone's attention.

"Merci, mon petit," whispered Tourcy, when the serving maid topped up his glass. He reached out and pinched the girl's bottom. "Allons-y."

The two of them disappeared into the hall, and Arthur heard the girl protesting. At the table, the others merely grinned, unbothered.

Arthur frowned. "Shouldn't someone check on them?"

"Why? Do you wish to watch?" asked Henri. His friends laughed.

"It doesn't sound as if the girl consents," Arthur insisted.

"Who needs to say yes? It is an honor to be desired by a noble," drawled one of the lads, draining his goblet of wine. The others gave emphatic nods.

"Don't worry," said Henri. "Should the girl find herself with child, she'll be taken care of. Or shipped off to a convent. Either way, she won't have to scrub chamber pots anymore."

Arthur choked.

Make a good impression, he reminded himself. *The king wished for you to spend time with these lads.*

And then he heard the girl give a loud protest from the hallway.

Before he knew what he was doing, he'd pushed to his feet. The lads stared at him, and Arthur tried to conjure a credible excuse.

"Where's your hospitality?" he asked, summoning his father's stern glare. "Don't guests get first choice of any desirable maids?"

Henri looked stunned at Arthur's change in opinion. "But of course. Have her, then, if you wish it."

"I will," Arthur said, lifting his chin and marching toward the door in his stockinged feet.

He half worried he would slip on the polished stone floor, but thankfully he made it into the corridor. Tourcy had the girl up against the wall, and was pawing at her bodice.

Her eyes were squeezed shut, as though she was trying to disassociate herself from the moment entirely.

"You may go, Tourcy," Arthur said coldly. The young noble regarded him with a strong measure of disbelief. "Prince Henri has graciously promised the girl to me."

"Fine, then. She's a cold one, anyway." Tourcy scowled, letting the girl alone and pushing past Arthur into the game room.

The girl trembled, her expression wary as she fumbled to pull up the neckline of her dress.

"I'm not going to touch you," Arthur promised. "I only came to help. You sounded upset."

The girl frowned, studying him as if to make sure it wasn't a trick. Finally, she bobbed a grateful curtsey.

"If you'd like to compose yourself, you may do so in my chambers," he offered. "You need not worry that I'll join you."

"Non, I can return to my work," she insisted, sniffling. "Thank you for the kindness." The girl curtseyed again, deeper this time, before hastening away.

Arthur leaned back against the wall, tipping his head back and closing his eyes. Sard, it was taking everything he had to make it through a day in this place. Now he just needed to make things believable. He cleared his throat and slammed his hand against the wall.

"If you're going to be like that, then go scrub some chamber pots, you useless, cringing girl," he said to the empty hallway.

He went back into the game room. The lads looked up in surprise.

"It didn't go well?" Albon asked, frowning.

Arthur raised an eyebrow, as if that much was obvious. "She failed to please me, so I sent her back to her work," he said. And then he looked around for his shoes. "I'll be off. I should probably check on my wizard."

"How amusing. Let's all go," said Henri, lurching to his own stockinged feet.

"Er," Arthur said, horrified at the thought of the lads bursting into the laboratory behind him, demanding magic tricks. "I'm sure they're very busy."

The last thing he needed was this crowd declaring Emry their new amusement.

"My father was the King of France," said Henri, raising his chin. "And I demand a magic show."

Arthur's stomach sank.

"Notice how he leaves out the part where he is the former king's bastard," said Tourcy, with an insouciant laugh.

Henri's expression went dark as he slapped Tourcy, hard. "If you wish to keep your family's lands, you'll kiss my shoe."

Tourcy cast around, panic in his eyes. "Er," he said, spotting the pile of everyone's court shoes and boots by the door. "Which ones are they?"

Henri grinned. "I can't remember. Better kiss them all."

Tourcy slunk over to the pile, looking as if he would rather do anything else.

"Go on," said Henri coldly. "Make amends."

Tourcy raised a shoe to his lips.

"Not like that!" cried Albon. "Use your tongue, man! You're kissing royalty, not your great aunt."

Henri's laugh was cruel.

Arthur winced. "Is this necessary?" he asked.

"I am insulted," insisted Henri. "And too drunk for a duel."

"What would you have him do instead?" demanded Albon.

All the boys looked to Arthur.

"That's right, you also have a dubious parentage," said Henri, with a mocking smirk. "What do you do when someone calls you a bastard?"

Henri was goading him, he knew. But Arthur had long gotten over the sting of such an unoriginal insult. He swallowed nervously, trying to figure a way out of this before the terms of Tourcy's punishment landed squarely on his shoulders

"I don't let it bother me," said Arthur, "but if my friends feel differently, they are welcome to their recourse."

Henri looked taken aback. "Truly?"

"I am the future King of Camelot. I don't waste my time with such pettiness."

"You misunderstand me," said Henri. "I meant, truly, you have friends?"

For the second day in a row, Arthur stood in a crowded balcony, watching the King of France play tennis. Across the court, in the women's balcony, ladies leaned suggestively upon the railing, promenading their bosoms as they feigned interest in the match below.

The sport wasn't at all what he'd thought. The balls in question were small leather ones, and the whacking was done with what looked like stiff fishing nets on sticks.

Certainly this would never catch on as entertainment in Camelot. Jousts and sword fighting were far more exciting to watch, and one wasn't expected to stand politely in a balcony, but rather to stomp, shout, cheer, and eat turkey legs with one's hands like delightful heathens.

Arthur had quickly deduced that anyone invited to play tennis against the king had better lose the match, and some did so far more believably than others. The young athletic lord who currently ran about the court looked as though he could swing a broadsword as easily as a tennis racquet.

"I know what you did, the other day," said Albon, sidling up alongside Arthur.

"I'm not sure what you mean," Arthur said.

"With the maid. You had no intention of keeping her for yourself."

Arthur sighed. "Was it so obvious?"

"Not to Tourcy and Henri. It was . . . good of you to stop it."

"Any one of you might have done the same," Arthur said pointedly.

Albon nodded. "Regardez," he said, gesturing toward the match. "It's about to get interesting."

The king was breathing heavily, beginning to tire. This young noble had better throw the match soon. And from the snatches of conversation Arthur overheard in the balcony, it seemed the others were in agreement.

"Va!" cried the king. "I will beat you yet!"

The lord swung a fierce backhanded hit, putting a spin on it. Arthur watched in horror as the ball ricocheted off the wall, heading straight for the bulge in King Louis's trousers.

A tremendous gasp went through the crowd as the ball connected with a matching set.

King Louis groaned and staggered back, and the horrified young lord dropped his racquet on the spot, sinking to his knees and making the sign of the cross.

"Il est mort," Albon observed.

"Surely not," protested Arthur. "It was an accident."

"Perhaps he will get lucky, and the king will merely strip him of his lands and title, and allow him to be a castle servant."

Arthur frowned, certain he had misunderstood. "Are there many servants here who used to be nobles?" he asked.

"Dozens," the young noble answered. "Thanks to the king's generous mercy."

Arthur suddenly felt sick.

"Look, it's his wife," said Tourcy, joining them.

In the women's gallery, a young woman was having hysterics. They waited nervously while the king regained his composure.

"S'il vous plaît, j'ai une famille," the young lord begged, still on his knees. The court was silent. Watching.

The guards stepped forward, waiting for instructions.

"Tue-le," said the king. *Kill him.*

A wail went up from the women's gallery as the young lord was dragged away.

A shiver ran down Arthur's spine. He'd just watched a man lose his life over a rogue tennis ball.

So this was why everyone in the galleries seemed to watch the dull matches in fascination. It wasn't the game that interested them. It was the consequences.

Chapter 31

As Guinevere watched that evening's musical performance, she couldn't help but notice Emmett noticing her. He shot her an arrogant wink, and she scowled. Honestly. The way he'd been trying to catch her attention ever since Arthur had left for France was entirely obnoxious. And she wanted none of it.

No, that wasn't entirely true. She burned with how much she wanted to drag him into her bedchamber and have her way with him. She was desperate for it. It was a most inconvenient feeling, and one that she did not wish to be having as she sat in the audience of a dull vielle concert.

"I think I'll go to bed early," she whispered to Issie and Branjen, slipping into the hall. A few moments later, Emmett appeared.

"I hate vielle music," he said with a grimace. "Why not the lute? Or better yet, nothing?"

Guin let out a yawn. "I wholeheartedly agree. Well, goodnight."

"Wait!" Emmett said. "Perhaps, since the music was not to your taste, I might walk you to the library to select a book that is?"

Guin bit her lip. It was a kind offer, and one that surprised her. "I wasn't aware you knew the location of the castle library," she returned.

Emmett grinned. "I was hoping you did."

Guin laughed, and then clapped a hand over her mouth.

"See? I'm far more entertaining than the vielle," he boasted.

"Merlin!" a boy's voice called.

Emmett turned around. A clutch of well-dressed young lords

waved at him. "Come out to the tavern!" one of them called. "Help us win at dice!"

Emmett groaned.

"Drinks are on us, come on," another wheedled.

Emmett turned toward Guin, a sheepish expression on his face.

"Oh, by all means, go," she said brightly. After all, he didn't owe her anything. He was eighteen years old, of course he would rather go out with his friends.

"I promise not to start any brawls," he said.

"I don't care what you do," Guin snapped.

"My mistake." Emmett smirked. "Great dress, by the way."

He wasn't even pretending not to stare down the front of it.

Guin scowled. She knew she was spilling out of the bodice, but she was quickly running out of gowns that fit. This one was definitely leaving the rotation.

Emmett bounded off to join his friends with a hearty laugh and some sort of boast that got swallowed up by their footsteps retreating down the corridor.

Guin yawned. She really was tired. Perhaps heading to bed early wasn't a terrible idea.

Then she saw the edge of Issie's pale green gown disappearing around a corner. She wouldn't have thought anything of it, if not for Branjen's whisper of, "Are you sure no one saw us?"

"Of course not," Issie replied.

A knob turned, and a door creaked open and shut.

What on earth was going on? Guin tiptoed to the door, listening, but all was quiet. Were the girls just standing in silence? That didn't seem right.

Guin pushed open the door, and found Issie and Branjen locked in a passionate embrace in the darkened music room.

Guin gasped.

Issie and Branjen pulled apart, their eyes wide with panic.

"Princess!" Issie said, her cheeks flushed. "I—we—"

"Were kissing," Guin finished, since Issie seemed at a loss for words.

"You can't tell anyone," Branjen said fiercely.

"If you keep our secret, we'll keep yours," Issie bargained.

Guin's heart sped up. "I have no secret," she said indignantly, drawing the door closed behind her.

"Oh yes you do," said Issie. "And you'll need our help if you mean to keep hiding the fact that you're with child."

Guinevere went red. "What a ridiculous accusation," she said indignantly.

"She's right," Branjen continued. "That dress practically gives it away. You need something that goes straight down from under the bust, like the one you wore yesterday."

"An overskirt could work as well, if you fastened it high enough," said Issie. "We'd copy you, so it looked like the latest court fashion. In a week, everyone will be wearing it."

Guinevere blinked at the two of them. "You'd help me?"

"Of course," said Issie. "It's rotten of the prince to put you in such a position. Summoning you to his bed before the wedding. How could you have refused?"

Guinevere fought to keep from laughing. The girls believed the child to be Arthur's. And what's more, they wanted to help her.

"Why are you being so kind to me?" Guin asked.

"You're our future queen," said Issie. "And we are your future ladies-in-waiting."

She lifted her chin, daring Guin to say otherwise. It was a bold move, and Guin admired her for it. So few women at court admitted to their ambitions aloud. Perhaps she had misjudged these girls. She'd certainly misjudged why they were always exchanging meaningful looks and whispering.

"Please say yes," Branjen begged. "Our fathers will marry us off otherwise. We were sent to court to find wealthy husbands. Instead, we found each other. Staying here as royal ladies-in-waiting is the only way for us to remain together."

"My father has already found me a match," Issie said, her voice raw with emotion. "A widowed viscount of five and fifty. He's to inspect me at your wedding, as though I'm a prize horse."

The wedding. Guinevere blanched at the thought.

"If I lose her," Branjen said, taking Issie's hand, "I'll lose the will to go on. My heart beats only for her, and has since the moment we met."

"Mine does, too," Issie said.

"Oh, of course I'll help you," Guin promised.

"Truly?" Issie squealed.

"I won't see my friends forced into loveless marriages when they already have everything that will give them happiness," she said.

Branjen was beaming. "I told you," she whispered, squeezing Issie's hand.

"So, we are to be your ladies-in-waiting," said Issie shyly. And then she added, "Are you sure you don't mind that we're . . . together?"

Issie looked to Branjen with a soft smile.

"Not at all!" said Guin. "And shame on anyone who does."

Issie and Branjen beamed.

"You heard our future queen," said Branjen.

Future queen. Guin's stomach twisted at the thought.

"We're running low on healing salve, squire," said Sir Kay. "See that Master Ambrosius gives us an extra pot this time."

"I'll try," said Lance doubtfully, "but he says—"

"Never mind what he says," Sir Kay snapped. "I'm the king's champion. Remind him of that."

Lance promised he would. Yet as he climbed the spiral staircase to the wizard's workshop, he doubted it would make much difference to the old wizard. Still, he couldn't imagine disappointing Sir Kay, especially since they were to leave for yet another joust that weekend. Lance was exhausted just thinking about it. He pressed back a sigh and knocked.

Emmett sat at the battered wooden table, mixing some spicy-smelling concoction of herbs with intense concentration. The old wizard peered over his shoulder, nodding.

"Good, boy. Not too much tansy, now . . ."

Lance cleared his throat, and Master Ambrosius looked up. "Yes, squire?"

"Er, Sir Kay sent me—" Lance began.

"Absolutely not," said Master Ambrosius. "I gave you a jar of salve last week."

"I know," Lance said miserably, "but—"

"You can remind Sir Kay that if he uses it too often, he'll build up a resistance," cautioned the old wizard.

"He won't want to hear that," said Lance.

The old wizard shook his head. "If it's sore muscles, he can use a chamomile infusion." He disappeared into the storeroom.

Lance scrubbed a hand through his overlong hair. Sir Kay wasn't going to be pleased.

Emmett pushed aside his pile of notes. "He's been in a mood ever since Emry left to consult a court wizard he considers 'an overly dramatic faker.' Don't tell him I gave this to you," he said, reaching into his pocket and holding out a small jar of salve.

"Thank you," Lance said gratefully.

"It's half-empty."

"I'll mix it with lip salve, and he won't know the difference," said Lance.

Emmett snickered. "Listen, I've been meaning to ask," he said, dropping his voice to a whisper. "A group of us are meeting in the dungeons tonight, to figure out how to guard the castle in case of an attack. You should come."

Lance blinked at the young wizard in surprise. "All right," he said.

"If there are any squires who might be interested, let them know," Emmett continued.

"I will," Lance promised, as the door to the supply room swung open. He pocketed the jar of healing salve just in time.

"Is this everyone?" Lance asked skeptically, glancing around at the small group that had gathered in the dungeons.

Emmett and Tristan, of course. Soft-spoken Ywayne, the new lad Safir, and Percival. Only six of them. It wasn't much, but it was something.

"Guess so," said Tristan cheerfully.

And then a cacophony of footsteps sounded on the stairs, and a cluster of well-dressed young lords descended with merry grins. There were Lionel and Cal Griflet, then Gary, and loudmouthed Elian, with whom Lance was of distant relation.

"We come bearing refreshments!" Elian announced, holding up a cask of ale. "Are there to be officers in this club? And if yes, who will be our master of revels?"

Emmett had the good sense to look embarrassed at his friends' theatrics.

The Griflet brothers spotted Lancelot. "Figures you'd be here," said Cal. "Been keeping yourself well, Lance?"

"Yep," said Lance.

"Shame you have to sit with the other squires at supper," said Lionel. "We'd have the best table in the Great Hall, between you and the Merlin twins."

"Shame," Lance echoed. The young nobles were being friendly. And he couldn't remember why he'd ever thought they wouldn't be.

And then there were footsteps on the stairs, and everyone stopped.

Dryan, who had changed back into his squire's tunic, grinned. "This must be the right spot."

Cal waved. "You made it!"

"Told you I would." Dryan nodded at Lance. "Knew I'd see you here. And Percival, too. Is this your idea, then?"

"Afraid not," Lance said. He had left supper early to polish Sir Kay's armor, just so he could make it. And he hated that he knew Dryan hadn't done the same.

But it wasn't the lad's fault that his knight treated him fairly, while Lance's didn't.

"This is definitely everyone," said Emmett. "We've gathered you all here because we want to make sure Castle Camelot has a proper line of defense, should it need one," said Emmett.

"Captain Lam doesn't believe there's any threat," Tristan added. "But he's wrong. And you're here because you think so, too."

"Actually, I'm here because Percival said I—ow!" Safir whined, as Percival elbowed him.

"I was merely curious to see the dungeons," said Lionel. Everyone stared at him in horror. "It was a joke! We all saw what the Duke of Cornwall was up to at the king's birthday celebrations."

The other nobles nodded.

"And King Yurien was horrible, gifting that painting of all the dead peasants," put in Cal.

"Hear! Hear!" said Gary. "It's our family's lands at risk as well, should Camelot fall."

"You're right," said Lance. "Camelot isn't just a castle. It's our kingdom, and we have a responsibility to defend it."

"Tell me those aren't words for a toast," cried Lionel.

"One toast," Emmett allowed.

"All right," Lance said, when everyone had drunk their ale. "Who can tell me the castle's weakest points?"

"The gates," Ywayne said shyly.

Lance nodded.

"The servants' entrance?" ventured Tristan.

Lance hadn't even thought of that. They spent the next half hour hashing out various plans of defense.

"All of this is well and good, so long as we can fight off an attack," said Elian. "I don't know about you lads, but all I'm good for is hitting archery targets and fencing."

"It's the same in the guard," said Tristan. "We're not expected to have skill, only strength."

"I remember," said Lance with a grimace.

"So, beyond defense strategies, we should actually learn to fight," Emmett summarized.

"I nominate Lance and Percival," said Tristan.

"Dryan's a squire," called Cal.

"I'm barely a season into my training," Dryan protested. "I agree, it should be Lancelot and Percival."

Lance exchanged an uneasy glance with Perce. They hadn't spoken since their fight. Not because Lance hadn't wanted to, but because he hadn't known what to say.

"I'd be honored," said Perce. "What do you say, squire? You up to the task?"

Perce flashed him a competitive grin, and Lance couldn't help but match it.

"Always," said Lance.

◐ ◐ ◐

As they parted after training, Lance was glad he'd let Emmett talk him into coming.

"Wait," someone called, as Lance headed up the stairs.

It was Percival. Of course. Looking more handsome than he had any right to.

"Hey," Lance said, stopping so Perce could catch up.

"You were great, back there," Perce said tentatively.

"So were you." Lance stuffed his hands in his pockets. "I didn't expect Emmett to rope in a bunch of silly nobles."

"They're not silly," Percival protested. "Just spoiled."

"We grew up the same."

"You were never the same. Not even the first day you turned up at the barracks, begging for a place in the guard, even though the sword at your waist was worth triple our yearly wage."

Lance winced. "You remember that?"

"It was a great sword." Percival grinned.

Lance grinned back. "It was my father's. I would have rather starved than sold it."

"Stubborn," Perce accused lightly.

"Very," said Lance. They were standing so close together. Lance leaned in. And Percival leaned away.

"You still owe me an apology, squire," said the guard.

Lance bit his lip. "I know," he said. "I'm sorry. Truly, I am. I wish I could explain how important it is that I become a knight. You'll have to take my word for it that I only need to endure it a little longer. But I don't expect you to wait."

"There's something you're not telling me," Percival said with a frown. "And I believe it has to do with why the prince and Emry have run off to France."

"It might," Lance admitted.

"Just how sick is King Uther?" Percival pressed.

"How could you possibly know about that?" Lance spluttered, before realizing he was meant to deny it.

"The guards gossip." Percival shrugged. "Especially when the court physician pays the king a visit nearly every night."

Lance shrugged miserably. "Arthur's my best friend. And he's going to need me when—so yeah, I put up with whatever Sir Kay asks of me. It's nothing compared to the burden Arthur will have to shoulder. The least I can do is make sure I'm worthy of being by his side."

"He's the reason you stayed at the castle," Perce said softly, realizing. "I'd always wondered why you became a guard. It's because you're in love with him."

Perce's expression was heartbreaking.

And Lance couldn't believe the handsome guard had it so wrong.

"Arthur's like a brother to me," he protested. "I'm in love with *you*!"

"Me?" Percival shook his head, as though that was impossible. "But you just said you wanted to be worthy of being by his side."

"In battle," Lance ground out.

"Oh," Perce said. "In which case, you'd have to be a—right. What a mess."

"I'm sure we could get it ironed out over a drink," Lance offered.

A corner of Perce's mouth hitched up adorably. "I'd like that."

Chapter 32

"We're out of mercury," said Maître Flamel, handing Emry a list the moment she walked in the door. "I need you to go to the apothecary and fetch these supplies."

Emry stared down at the scribbled list of ingredients, half of which were in shorthand, and the other half in French.

"Er, I don't know where it is," she said.

"I have written the address on the list." Flamel sniffed. "You should have no trouble finding it."

"And when I return, you'll help me with my magic?" Emry asked.

Her patience was growing thin. She'd spent the past four days distilling and discarding bad batches of la prima materia, and Flamel seemed set on a fifth day of the same.

"Yes, yes, we'll get to that," promised the wizard with a wave of his hand. "But first, my supplies, Mademoiselle Apprentice."

"Oui, Maître Flamel," Emry said, bobbing a curtsey.

"You're going to love the apothecary," the gargoyle called.

"How would you know?" snapped Flamel. "You've never been."

"Anywhere's better than here," replied the creature.

Thankfully, the apothecary wasn't far. Just a few blocks south of the castle, on a slim winding street lined with gothic stone buildings. Battlements and gargoyles protruded overhead, and the shop fronts looked ancient. Some bore iron signage shaped into scissors or animals, advertising their wares with pictures rather than words, as they had back in the Dark Ages.

The front was painted black, with golden alchemical symbols around the doorway. It reminded her very much of the entrance to Flamel's lair. The window display showcased an appealing array of dried herbs arranged in metal bowls.

Emry pushed open the door and was met with the heady scent of drying herbs, and an apothecary that reminded her of a library. Shelves filled with stoppered glass bottles stretched two stories high, and a ladder ran the length of the shop. Candles flickered from inside glass jars, ensuring that the wax did not drip onto the carefully swept wooden floor, which was painted with a map of astrological constellations. The shop smelled pleasantly of herbs, and of something else, something familiar . . .

"Coffee!" Emry blurted.

It was the first time she had found any outside Castle Camelot, and she was starting to believe Arthur was the only person who drank it.

"You have a good nose. I bought it from some Ottoman traders just last month," said a woman's voice, in native English. "The university students seem to crave it."

The curtain was swept aside by a beautiful lady in her late twenties. She had soft brown eyes, deep brown skin, and long black hair twisted back into an intricately spiraled braid. She wore a leather apron over a sturdy but fashionable wool dress, and a small pair of brass goggles perched on top of her head.

Emry stared in admiration, both at the woman's beauty and her eccentric ensemble. "A friend of mine has been desperate to find some," said Emry. "And so have I."

"You must be the horrible English apprentice who has been torturing my husband this week," the woman said brightly. "Please, accept my heartfelt thanks for your efforts. It is so tiring tormenting him on one's own."

"You're Flamel's wife?"

"Pernelle Flamel, à votre service," said the woman, removing her goggles and apron, and offering her hand.

"Emry Merlin. I'm the apprentice court wizard in Camelot."

"So I've heard. I visited London as a child," Pernelle said. "I'm from Lothia originally, but my family moved here when I was very young. And the new Lothian king . . ." She shook her head. "The less we say about him, the better. Now, what brings you to my shop?"

"This is your shop?" Emry asked, surprised.

"My family owns most of the apothecaries in the city," Pernelle said. "That's how I met Nicolas. He was very handsome, but very thin, and I knew money was dear to him. He kept coming in for the strangest, most expensive herbs, and finally I asked whom he was trying to poison, and if he'd allow me to suggest a more cost-effective alternative."

Emry grinned. "Did he accept?"

"Not at first." Pernelle gave a private smile. "And of course I had to convince him the substitutions were his idea."

Emry rolled her eyes. "Boys."

"I know. But the handsome ones are worth the effort," said Pernelle. "I assume he sent you for more supplies. Is it still the prima materia, or has he moved on to the red stone?"

"Still the prima materia," Emry confirmed, handing her the list.

"There must be something wrong with his formula. Or his preparation." Pernelle sighed and stepped onto her ladder, which began to move on its own.

Emry gaped. "That's—that's magic!"

"Clever, isn't it?" she said, reaching for a jar of a sooty-looking powder. "I've enchanted it to move whenever it senses a person's weight."

Emry's mind was spinning over the possibilities. Perhaps she could animate the ladders in the royal library to move on their own. Or, even better, a carriage that didn't need horses.

"How did you do it?"

"The enchantment's infused into the varnish," she said. "It was an experiment I designed some years back. I can dig up the formula, I'm sure."

"Flamel never mentioned that his wife is a wizard," Emry said.

"I'm not." Pernelle gave her a strained smile. "I'm a scholar of magic, but I have no ability as a practitioner."

"I've never met a . . . scholar of magic before."

"And I have never met a female wizard, so it seems fate has determined that we'll be friends."

Pernelle reached for a jar just as a high-pitched scream sounded from behind the curtain. She fumbled it, and the jar began to fall.

Emry quickly cast a silent spell, rescuing it. She floated the jar back harmlessly into its place with a flick of her hand.

The screaming continued.

"Thank you," Pernelle said, climbing down. "I thought the little gargoyle was asleep."

"Another gargoyle?" Emry muttered as Pernelle disappeared back behind the curtain, cooing in French.

She returned a moment later with a sobbing boy no older than two on her hip. He had light brown skin, and a fluff of dark brown curls, and his face did resemble a gargoyle, crumpled up like that.

"Maaaaaamaaaaaa," he wailed.

Pernelle sighed. "Mon petit Nicolas. His nurse has a case of the morbid sore throat this week, so here we are." She smoothed a hand over his hair, soothing him. "Would you mind holding him?"

"Um," Emry said, as the child was thrust into her arms. "Hi there? Bonjour?"

He was very warm and solid, and heavier than she'd expected. He stared up at her and then nuzzled his head against her chest, sucking his thumb.

Not so bad.

Emry had never been particularly good with children, nor did she dream of having one of her own. Not in the way Emmett did. She stood, holding the now-content child as Pernelle set a collection of jars and pouches on the counter.

"That's everything," said Pernelle, taking back Nicolas. "Did you want some coffee as well?"

"Yes, please," Emry said.

"I shall sell you half a bag, to ensure you come back and visit soon," said Pernelle.

Emry was making her way back to Flamel's lair, the parcel of apothecary supplies tucked under one arm, when she caught sight of Arthur. He was in a crowd of nobles who leaned over the edge of a double-tiered balcony, watching the king and his challenger play a game of tennis in the court below.

"Arthur!" she called, waving. She couldn't wait to tell him she had found his precious coffee.

But he didn't notice her.

King Louis gave a fierce swing of his racquet that sent the ball ricocheting around the courtyard. His opponent swung and missed, and a victory cheer went up from the crowd.

"Arthur!" Emry called again, pushing toward him.

She had just about reached him when a guard stepped into her path, blocking it.

"Laissez-moi passer!" she cried. *Let me through.*

A man put a hand on Arthur's shoulder and asked a question with a frown. Arthur turned and spotted her. His eyes went wide, and he shook his head, flapping his hand for her to leave.

Screw that. The guard was shouting at her in very loud French, which she could only half understand, something about the wrong balcony. And then she looked across the courtyard and realization dawned. Men and women were given different areas from which to watch the match.

Sard. She mumbled an apology, and was just about to leave, when a shout went up from the courtyard. King Louis had hit a rogue ball, which ricocheted high on the wall, and then flew toward the women's balcony with alarming force.

Emry didn't think, she just threw out her hands, stopping the ball in midair. It floated there, rotating slowly, as a gasp went through the crowd. Emry let the ball drop harmlessly onto the court below.

She realized that Arthur was watching her. As was the tall man at his side. "It was you," the man said loudly, pointing a finger in Emry's direction.

"I—"

"You could have killed the king!" he accused.

Panic bloomed in Emry's chest as she scrambled to find the words in French.

The whole men's gallery was staring at her.

And then the king's chancellor stepped forward.

"This is, I believe, your wizard, Monseigneur?" he asked Arthur.

Arthur gave a grim nod. "I'll handle it," he said, pushing his way toward Emry and dragging her around the corner.

He was dressed in another fine outfit of matching silk brocade, and he was wearing his hair parted down the middle, in imitation of the king, the way the other courtiers did. He looked nothing like himself, except for the furious expression on his face.

"What are you doing?" he snapped.

"Saying hello. I haven't seen you for days!"

"I haven't been able to get away," said Arthur. "How's Flamel?"

"Irritating." Emry sighed. "Every time I remind him that he's supposed to help me, he makes an excuse. How're things going with you?"

"I wish I knew." Arthur rubbed a hand against his neck, and Emry noticed that he was wearing a large ruby ring on his pinky that she'd never seen before.

"What's with the ring?"

"I won it at dice," Arthur said curtly. He glanced back toward the balcony. "Emry, you can't behave like this here."

"Like what?"

Arthur blinked at her incredulously. "Pushing your way through a crowd of courtiers. Using magic. And you called me Arthur in front of people."

Emry snorted, but he didn't seem to be joking. "Are you actually serious?"

"We represent Camelot. *I* represent Camelot."

"I know that."

"*Do* you?" Arthur pressed. "Our kingdom's fate hangs in the balance. I can't be myself here. And we can't act familiar with each other in public if I'm to be taken seriously."

"So, you want me to curtsey and call you Your Highness?" Emry asked in disbelief.

"I don't want you to," Arthur said, "I *need* you to."

Emry couldn't believe what she was hearing. This didn't sound like the boy she knew at all.

"What's going on with you?" she demanded.

Arthur drew himself up to his full height, and when he spoke, it was with a haunting echo of his father's stern command. "I'm the future King of England, and I need them to believe it. If you hope to be my court wizard, then prove yourself worthy of the position."

"Prove myself worthy? I already have," Emry retorted. "You're the one who pushed for me to be *more* than just your court wizard. Or is that only where no one can see?"

Arthur clenched his hands into fists and looked away, his jaw tight.

"I cannot risk losing Louis's favor. Why don't you understand?"

"Oh, I understand perfectly," Emry fumed. "If that's all, I'll be on my way back to Flamel's laboratory, Your Highness, as soon as you see fit to dismiss me from your royal presence." She bobbed a curtsey and stood there glaring.

"Very well, you're dismissed," he snapped.

Chapter 33

Emry felt as though she'd been reading in the townhouse library for hours. She was determined to get through Flamel's pamphlet on alchemy, so she might understand what they were actually trying to accomplish, but the French was slow-going. She didn't know how Arthur had managed it. Not that she would ask him. She wasn't planning on talking to him in the foreseeable future. Not until he apologized.

She couldn't believe how he'd spoken to her. Like their friendship was something he could call off according to his whims. He had taken back everything between them without so much as a warning, and had acted as though he was the one who had been wronged.

Oh, it was infuriating. *He* was infuriating.

If he wanted to keep the company of awful boys and wear his hair in that unflattering style and make everyone bow and call him Your Highness, then fine.

Just fine.

She didn't need a friend like that. She just needed Flamel to help her gain control of Anwen's magic, and then they could go home and go back to their lives, where she would be more than happy to follow King Uther's demands and stay away from Arthur.

Emry sighed, glancing out the window. At this hour, Paris was quiet, except for the occasional burst of merriment or rumble of a passing carriage. She turned another page. The door to the library opened, and Gawain poked his head in.

His forearms were streaked with paint, his sleeves rolled nearly to his elbows. And he reeked of wine.

"Fun night?" Emry asked.

"Marvelous." Gawain grinned. "Come out with me next time. You can borrow an easel. Or not. Anything goes at Madame Girard's."

A brothel. She should have known.

"Maybe I will," Emry decided. "Did you drink the entire contents of their wine cellar, or merely bathe in it?"

"I do have a bachelor's reputation to maintain," Gawain said, sloppily leaning against the doorframe. "Come on, wizard, let's see what sustenance we can rustle up in the kitchens."

"It's nearly midnight," Emry said. "Aren't the staff asleep?"

"Yes, but I'm terribly drunk, and bread is an excellent hangover preventative." He looked at her with a hopeful expression.

"Oh my god, I'm not making you a sandwich," Emry said sternly, leading the way through the great room and down the narrow stairs to the kitchen. The townhouse was dark, and she muttered a spell that lit the tip of her wand so they didn't trip.

"What would I have to give," Gawain bargained, "for you to reconsider?"

"What are you offering?" Emry returned.

"A kiss?"

"Pass."

"Your loss. I'm a very good kisser."

"Anyone who says that usually isn't," Emry pointed out.

Gawain scowled.

And then there was a scuffle at the door. A boy's voice, shushing. A rattle of the knob.

"Someone's trying to break in," Gawain said incredulously.

"Maybe it's Arthur?" Emry said, gripping her wand tightly.

"He would have knocked," Gawain said, withdrawing a dagger from his boot.

"Do you always carry knives around?" she asked.

"Every good scoundrel does." Gawain put a finger to his lips and flung open the door.

A familiar figure knelt on the steps, scrabbling with a makeshift lockpick. Jereth's head had been shaved since Emry had seen him last, though it was quickly growing back. He looked disheveled, as though he had been some days on the road. But he still bore those same haughty cheekbones and Gawain's rich brown skin. Behind him, a blond, rosy-cheeked lad in what was once a very fine silk coat, but now resembled rags, hovered nervously.

"Hello, little brother," Gawain said disdainfully. "Is there a reason you're breaking into my kitchen?"

"It's not your kitchen," Jereth protested, lifting his chin. "The house is Father's."

"He placed it in my care. Aren't you supposed to be at school?"

"I left," Jereth said.

"I know that," Gawain said. "Everyone's been worried. What did you do this time?"

"It wasn't me! I didn't do anything!" Jereth protested. "The priests believed I needed to be reformed!"

"You do," Gawain said harshly.

"For liking boys," Jereth finished miserably.

Gawain's grip on the knife tightened. "Those bastards."

The blond boy let out a terrible coughing fit.

"This is Prince Hugo," Jereth said casually. "We were roommates back at the monastery school in Cameliard."

"So this is your fellow arsonist," Gawain said with a sigh.

"Delighted . . . to . . . meet you," Hugo said between coughs.

"He needs to get warm," Jereth said. "Perhaps a hot drink? He hasn't been well."

"I can see that," said Emry.

"Who's this?" Jereth asked imperiously.

"Oh, we've met," Emry said.

"Good lord, it's the apprentice wizard! You didn't—you're not actually betrothed to her?"

"Of course not," Gawain snapped.

"A wizard?" Hugo said, looking at her curiously.

"That's right," Emry replied.

"If the constabulary calls, tell them we're not here," Jereth said, sweeping inside. "Now, wizard, fetch us some hot brandy."

Emry rolled her eyes and stayed put.

"It really would be wonderfully good of you," Hugo said, catching his breath and offering her an embarrassed smile.

"Fine," Emry grumbled, waving a hand at the hearth and conjuring a roaring fire.

Jereth and Hugo startled, and Hugo coughed again, scrambling to press a linen cloth to his lips. When he lowered it, it came away splattered red with blood.

Emry reached for the brandy, then thought better of it and boiled a few mugs of peppermint tea.

"For your cough," she said, passing one to the golden-haired prince, who smiled his thanks. He was dressed quite expensively, Emry noticed, the cuffs of his jacket decorated with seed pearls. Or, they had been, but most had been torn off. The buttons were missing as well.

Jereth was dressed as a simple scholar, and was carrying both their packs. His stomach let out a loud gurgle, and Emry rustled up a plate of bread and cheese, which the boys fell upon as though they hadn't eaten in days.

Emry and Gawain exchanged a look.

"I think you had better tell me what you're doing here," said Gawain.

Jereth pouted. "I wrote to Father about what was going on, but the monks didn't send my letters." He shuddered. "They beat me and made me fast every day until sundown, to 'break me of my unnatural tendencies,' they called it. I was desperate. So, I wrote to Hugo using our old code, and it worked. He rescued me from that wretched school."

"I ran away," Hugo said proudly. "My health has never been great, but lately, my parents treat me as an invalid. The court physician insisted I must be confined to bed. That I have brought ill health on myself, through impure thoughts of other boys. I could not bear to know Jereth suffered similarly."

"You see!" said Jereth. "We had no other choice! We meant to make new lives for ourselves, but our money ran out, and Hugo has been sick, and we skipped out on our last lodgings without paying. I wouldn't have bothered you otherwise!"

Anger flashed in Gawain's eyes. "You should have bothered me to begin with! I would have come immediately and unleashed hell on that holy order for daring to mistreat you as they did."

Jereth frowned. "You would?"

"Of course!" said Gawain. "You were foolish to run off! And without sending word to myself or Father to reassure us you were alive and well!"

Jereth hung his head. "I thought—"

"Hang what you thought!" Gawain snapped. "You cannot keep tormenting our family like this."

"I'm sorry," Jereth mumbled. "I expect you'll inform our parents that I'm all right."

"And if I refuse?" Gawain challenged.

"I did tell him to write," Hugo put in. "He swore he had. Just as he swore we'd be welcome here. If that isn't the case, we'll go."

"I'm not putting you out," Gawain said wearily. "But you better write to our parents immediately. And while you're here, I won't allow you to be idle. You'll either enroll at the university, or work to pay back the landlord you owe."

Jereth looked horrified. "Work?" he repeated.

"That sounds fair," allowed Hugo. "Right, Jer?"

Jereth glared. "I suppose."

Gawain sighed. "And the next time you run away—together or apart—for god's sake, have a plan."

Chapter 34

"This doesn't look right," Emry said, staring at the violently bubbling flask of sludgy black liquid. "I think we're using too much heat."

"Keep going," Flamel said.

"Er, if you're sure." Emry gave the potion a doubtful glance.

Once again, she was in Flamel's workshop, helping him to brew a batch of prima materia that would inevitably wind up slopped out the window. The poor plants beneath looked ill, and Emry was convinced a few had sprouted tentacles instead of vines.

Whenever she brought up Flamel helping with her magic, he merely shrugged and promised that he would get to it. But he never did. And she didn't know how much more of his experiments she could take.

Without warning, the flask exploded.

Emry twisted out of the way, but she wasn't quick enough. The black sludge splattered across her dress, and the glass shards nipped against her arm.

"I told you!" she said.

"We shall try again, after you get cleaned up," said Flamel.

Emry picked a shard of glass out of her forearm with a grimace. A bead of blood welled, and she sucked in a breath.

"Maître Flamel," she said, trying not to panic. "I was cut. I—" The twin flames appeared in her palms. "It's—look—"

"Mon dieu," said Flamel, his eyes wide as he stared at the flames dancing above Emry's palms. "Get rid of that!"

"I can't," Emry said, her voice tight. "I can't control it, remember?"

"I didn't expect it to be purple," put in the gargoyle. "Is it always purple?"

"Always," Emry confirmed, hurrying to the hearth, so she might aim whatever the magic conjured into the fireplace.

Flamel stood frozen, gaping at the bright fire floating above Emry's palms. "Anwen's magic," he breathed.

"Don't just stand there," Emry snapped. "Help me!"

The flames blazed a bright purple, then turned pale and crystalline. A thick layer of ice coated her hands, twisting up her arms. Then the ice shot out, spraying into the hearth. The fire went out, and icicles formed.

"*Prohibere*," Emry said. *"Aqua! Wæter!"*

The entire hearth was starting to ice over. Without the fire, the temperature in the room dropped dramatically, and Emry's teeth were chattering.

"You see?" she said angrily. "Nothing works. Not with Latin or Greek or Old English or new."

She stood there, trembling, waiting for the spell to wear itself out. Once it finally did, she wrapped her arms around her chest, shivering. A muttered spell and a wave of her hand had the fire crackling in the grate once again.

"Fascinating." Maître Flamel's brows knitted together as he considered the problem. "You have tried spells and what else?"

Emry frowned. "I don't understand what you mean."

"Charms, potions, hypnotism?"

"Who on earth tries hypnotism?" Emry returned. "And no."

"I shall solve this," Flamel proclaimed. "The prima materia can wait."

"Finally," Emry said under her breath.

Flamel clasped his hands behind his back as he paced the length of the bookshelf, muttering to himself in French.

Emry caught snatches of words, but it all sounded like nonsense. The wizard pulled down a book, flipping through what looked like diagrams of old buildings, and then slammed it shut with a curse.

"Have you tried leeches?" Flamel asked.

"Not yet," Emry said doubtfully.

"We shall consider it," Flamel said, reaching for another book.

"Are you allergic to snake venom, by any chance?" he asked after a few minutes.

"Isn't everyone?" Emry replied, disliking the direction this was going.

She muttered a clothes-cleaning spell and began to clean up their exploded potion, thinking that between leeches and snake venom, hypnotism was starting to sound less terrible.

Flamel was lost in his stack of books, so Emry pulled out his alchemy pamphlet, slogging through the dense descriptions. She could almost understand what it was they were looking to accomplish in the alembic.

"I have a question about the tree of life," Emry said.

"Don't interrupt," Flamel snapped.

"Sorry." Emry went back to the pamphlet, deciding that she loathed alchemy. It was like guesswork and chemicals made mathematical. And there were so many unnecessarily creepy diagrams of snakes.

Some time later, Flamel looked up, his eyes bright.

"Blood always calls it?" he asked.

Emry nodded. The wizard unfastened the knife from his belt and held out the handle. "Then cut yourself again. I have a theory."

"It's not always the same thing," Emry warned. "It could be fire, ice, smoke, lightning . . ."

"The risk is the cost of the knowledge," said Flamel.

Emry took the dagger and pressed the tip against her palm. It took a moment before the purple flames appeared again.

"Bien," said Flamel.

He began to unlace his tunic, and Emry winced. But he merely pulled out the tangle of amulets and rapidly sorted through them. "Try this one," he said, removing a charm and placing it around Emry's neck.

Immediately, the flames went out.

"Huzzah!" proclaimed the gargoyle.

Emry stared down at her hands in shock. "What did you just do?" she demanded.

"I have proven a most unusual theory."

"It's very clever of him, too," put in the gargoyle.

Emry examined the necklace. A polished piece of black stone hung from an ordinary leather cord. One side of the stone was chiseled with the rune *Elhaz*. To protect.

"Runes," she said, realizing. *"Of course!"*

Morgana had used runes on the stone to trap Emry and let the altar drink her magic. Excalibur's scabbard had carried runes along its shaft; there were runes carved into the old churches. Emry had even seen them in the woods in Avalon when she had tried to look for a path.

There was just one problem.

"But runes don't work on people," said Emry. "They only work on objects."

"Is magic not an object?" Flamel asked.

"I—" Emry thought about it. "I suppose it could be. But that's very theoretical."

"That is why it was only a theory, until now," said Flamel. "Never mind the elixir of life. I wish to test the effects of runes on Anwen's magic."

Emry grinned. "So do I."

❶ ❶ ❶

"Do you have any idea what time it is?" Pernelle scolded, banging open the door to Flamel's laboratory.

Emry looked up in surprise as the frowning apothecary folded her arms across her chest.

"Go again, girl," Flamel said, gesturing toward Emry. "The same pattern as before."

Emry nodded, Flamel's blade hovering above her palm. She took a deep breath, centering herself.

"Don't you dare!" said Pernelle. "I forbid any more nonsense about the elixir of life!"

"But it's—" Emry tried to explain.

Pernelle held up a hand. "Tu as une famille, Nicolas," she said, folding her arms across her chest.

"I know," Flamel snapped. "But today, I have done something no other wizard has done before me!"

"And what is that?" Pernelle asked sourly.

"I have proven that magic is an object!" Flamel boasted.

"We're not working on the elixir," Emry put in. "Well, we were, but Maître Flamel figured out how I might control Anwen's magic."

Pernelle looked shocked. "He has?"

"Show her," Flamel said greedily. "Mon chou, you will not believe this!"

Emry pricked the pad of her finger with the dagger. She could feel the power gathering inside her, demanding to be let out. She held it back for a moment, just to prove that she could, before letting Anwen's magic flow to her fingertips. The purple flames danced above her palms, and she focused on her breathing, on lowering her shoulders and relaxing her jaw.

"*Isaz!*" she insisted, tracing her hands in the shape of the rune. The fire turned to ice.

"*Laguz!*" she demanded, using just her left hand this time. In her hand, the ice melted into water. Her right hand still bore the shard of ice.

"*Kaunan,*" she said, bringing both of her hands through the shape for fire. Flames leapt from her palms. She shot a ball of purple fire into the hearth.

"*Elhaz,*" she murmured, snuffing the flames, and the magic vanished.

She grinned, steadying herself on the edge of an overstuffed armchair as Flamel applauded. She felt breathless, and her heart was pounding as if she'd just run across the city, but she had done it. *She had controlled Anwen's magic.*

Emry gave a bow, which might have been a mistake, based on how much the room was spinning.

"There," Flamel said smugly to his wife. "You may apologize for scolding me now."

"I may, but I won't," Pernelle retorted. "I never would have thought to use runes. How curious that it works." She bit her lip, thinking. "Have you tried making the different elements interact?"

"You mean like creating a fire in one hand, and putting it out with water from the other?" Emry said excitedly. "No, not yet."

"Let's try it," said Flamel.

Pernelle gave him a horrified look. "I forbid either of you from lighting this laboratory on fire!"

"It would only be a small fire," Flamel grumbled.

"You know the rules," Pernelle snapped. "If it's dangerous, it happens in the dungeons."

"Fine." Flamel sulked. "Come along, Mademoiselle Apprentice."

"Not tonight!" Pernelle scolded. "Unless you mean to miss supper?"

At the mention of supper, Emry's stomach grumbled. She was exhausted from all the spellcasting, and had worked up quite an appetite.

Flamel shot his wife a dark look.

"Have you dined at the castle yet?" asked Pernelle.

"No," Emry replied, "but I'm not dressed for it." She gestured to her wool kirtle, which was good enough for mixing potions, but certainly not a courtier's gown.

Pernelle laughed. "You're dressed just fine," she promised. "Now, come with me. Nicolas unfortunately will eat his supper cold, after he's done tidying the mess he's made of his lab."

Flamel's mouth fell open.

"Bon appétit!" called the gargoyle as Pernelle swept Emry into the hall.

Emry followed her through the castle and frowned when they passed the Great Hall.

"I thought we were going to supper?" Emry said.

"We are," said Pernelle, opening a door to a servants' stairwell. "It's this way."

They arrived at a cozy, low-ceilinged room in the castle undercroft, where benches flanked long wooden tables set with platters of food. Most seats were taken, but a cheerful-looking woman with a long red braid waved them over.

Emry suddenly felt foolish she'd worried about her dress. She tried to mind her French and keep everyone's names straight as she met a music tutor, a secretary, and Marie, the castle midwife who had waved them over.

"You were expecting something different," Pernelle observed, as Emry buttered a slice of seeded bread. "Do you not dine similarly at Castle Camelot?"

Emry's cheeks went red. "I, well, it's usually in the Great Hall," she tried to explain.

Across the table, Marie choked on a mouthful of stew.

Pernelle's eyebrows rose. "The royal family dines with commoners?"

Emry knew the castle staff ate separately, and the guard had their own "mess" as Lance had called it. Come to think of it, she hadn't seen any of the other apprentices in the Great Hall. And certainly Emmett's friends at her table were all of noble birth. "Um . . . I guess not."

She'd never noticed it before, but she and Emmett were given favor at court above the other apprentices. And it wasn't just Arthur's doing. Even before they'd met, she had been shown to her father's old chambers and invited to dine in the Great Hall.

"Where are you staying in Paris?" asked Claudine, the curly-haired music tutor.

"With a friend from back home. Um, Gawain d'Orkney?"

Pernelle frowned. "Seigneur d'Orkney? But he's a bachelor. It's just the two of you?"

The other women looked curious.

"His staff believes we're cousins," said Emry.

Marie tittered, and Claudine bit her lip to press back a smile.

"Ah," said Pernelle. "I was certain a talented maid had arranged your hair. But I'm confused. I thought you were an apprentice, not a lady."

"I am definitely not a lady," Emry protested. "I'm a wizard!"

"Is it not possible to be both?" ventured Claudine.

Emry frowned, considering. "I suppose," she said. "But I certainly didn't grow up as one."

"None of us did," said Marie. "We are all . . . I'm not sure how you say it in English—we made ourselves?"

"Self-made," Pernelle told her. "And exactly. My family immigrated here, and now I run my own business."

The others all had similar stories, of following their passions, and working hard, and leaving behind small towns or poorer kingdoms. Emry listened with admiration.

"But of course you've heard these same tales, from your friends at Castle Camelot," said Marie, blushing.

"Not really," Emry admitted. If anything, these other girls reminded her of Marion, her best friend back home, who was the theater troupe's seamstress. She hadn't realized quite how much she had missed the company of other girls. Not that it wasn't a good time, hanging around with Arthur and Lance, but it was different. Perhaps there were other girls at Castle Camelot, who weren't just silly courtiers prowling for rich husbands, whom she had never met.

"Because all of your friends are handsome, noble bachelors?" Pernelle teased.

Emry blushed. "Some of them are guards," she mumbled.

"The next thing you'll say is that you are good friends with your prince," joked Marie.

Emry sank down in her seat. "He's a pompous arse, and I hope he chokes on his sword," she muttered.

"There's a rumor that he saved King Louis's life the other day, in the forest," Claudine said.

"He did what?" Emry frowned.

"With his magic sword. This is why he's favored at court, and spends his time with Prince Henri and his friends."

"A word of advice," said Pernelle. "If you see Prince Henri coming, run the other way."

"Why?" Emry said.

"Half the nuns in Paris were once palace maids," Marie said.

Emry couldn't imagine Arthur hanging around with someone like that. But then, perhaps she didn't know him as well as she thought.

"Your prince is the same way, non?" Marie asked.

"Arthur?" Emry snorted. "Hardly."

"For a pompous arse, he is quite handsome," Claudine added.

Emry went pink. "I hadn't noticed," she mumbled.

"It's hard to miss," Pernelle insisted. "Perhaps, with some coaxing, he'll be willing to unsheathe that magic sword of his."

Marie giggled. "I believe the king has tried."

"What?" Emry choked on a mouthful of stew.

"He sent men and women to tempt him," Pernelle explained.

"To Arthur's bedchamber?" Emry laughed.

"He turned them all away," Marie said sadly.

Emry couldn't help but smile at the thought of Arthur shooing unwelcome visitors from his chambers, who had come to seduce him. They must have interrupted his reading.

"How curious, that you call him Arthur," Pernelle observed. As she sipped her drink she asked, "Did he enjoy the coffee?"

"I haven't given it to him yet," Emry answered automatically, and then blushed, realizing her mistake.

Chapter 35

Guinevere was surprised to find that she actually missed Arthur's company. He had left for France two weeks ago, and every night since, she'd sat stiffly at supper, wishing he was by her side.

Still, she supposed she could count herself lucky. The wedding was only a few weeks away, and so far, no one suspected her secret beyond Issie and Branjen, who had been true to their word, and had started quite an enthusiasm for flowing dresses with wide, trailing sleeves. They had even convinced some of the young lords to adopt the baggy style, with ballooned trousers and bloused tunics, much to the horror of the royal tailor.

But the deception had worked. And Issie and Branjen had bullied Guin's maid into letting them dress her, under the guise that they might all wear complementary colors. Clever girls.

Issie had even started embroidering a pair of baby booties with the sweetest swirls of silver vines, and every time Guin saw them, her heart fluttered with excitement instead of dread.

There was another concert after supper, and between the overly warm hearth and the soft tones of the harp, Guinevere nearly nodded off. She took the intermission as an opportunity to excuse herself, and was nearly back to her room when she felt someone following her.

"Who's there?" Guinevere asked sharply.

"It's just me," Emmett said. "I guess we both had the same idea to sneak out at intermission."

"I won't tell if you won't," Guin said.

"Do you think anyone was enjoying that terrible music?"

"Perhaps it is more pleasing if you suffer from insomnia," Guinevere offered.

Emmett laughed. "I nearly started snoring aloud," he agreed. "It's a pity King Uther never hires players."

"I asked Arthur about it, and he said the players were so terrified to perform at the court that they flubbed their lines and made a misery of the material."

"Most players do that anyway," said Emmett, and Guinevere bit back a laugh. "At least, the troupe back home was dreadful about it."

"You were a player?"

"On occasion. Mostly, it was my sister. But the lads and I were friends. Got up to a lot of trouble at the Prancing Stag after the performances." He shot her a wink. "And thanks to the kindness of the other patrons, we never had to pay for a single pitcher of ale."

"It sounds like a lot of fun," Guinevere observed

"I miss it sometimes," Emmett said wistfully. He gave her a sad smile. "May I walk you back to your room, since we're going the same direction?"

"All right," Guinevere agreed.

Emmett grinned, looking pleased. He offered his arm, and Guin took it, wondering if his biceps had always been so firm. The jacket was lovely, a bright blue velvet with yellow trim, and buttons done over in brown leather.

"I haven't seen you wear this before," she said, and hoped he wouldn't take it to mean she'd been watching him. Which she hadn't. Much.

"It's new," he said. "Hold on, let me show you the best part." He reached across and drew his wand from a clever bit of trim along a front seam.

"A secret compartment!" Guin enthused.

"There are others as well," said Emmett. "I got into a bad tavern brawl a while back. Didn't have my wand on me. It really is a nightmare trying to figure out where to stash it. So, I designed this. There's a holder on the sleeve, too. The appliqué comes up."

"It's wonderful," Guin said admiringly.

"Not as wonderful as having you talk to me again," Emmett said earnestly. "Guin, I've missed you. It breaks my heart that you're going back to Cameliard in a few weeks, and I'll never see you again."

"Cameliard. Right," Guin said. Emmett still thought she wasn't going through with the wedding. That she was going home.

"Well, this is you," he said, stopping outside the door to her chambers.

Guin felt a stab of regret. The corridor was empty of guards, with everyone back at the performance. It was just the two of them. "Would you like to come in?" she blurted.

Emmett's grin was a beautiful thing to witness. "Really?" he said. "I mean, yes, Princess, I'd like that very much."

Guin fumbled behind her with the doorknob. The chambers were dark; the maid hadn't yet come to light a fire in the grate.

"I've got it." Emmett strode toward the fireplace, leveling his wand at the grate and speaking a word in Greek. A flame crackled to life, throwing a warm, cozy glow across the space.

Guinevere swallowed. He was so handsome in the firelight. She looked up at exactly the wrong moment, and saw Emmett staring back at her with an impish grin.

"I don't mean to presume," he said, "but you look like you very much want to kiss me."

Oh god, she really did.

Before she could think better of it, she strode forward and pressed her lips to his.

Heat pooled low in her belly, and for a moment Guin was ravenous at the thought of being with him again, of slaking this fire that raged within her whenever he was near.

His lips brushed her neck, and she shivered.

"This is unexpected," he whispered against her throat.

"Don't stop," Guin begged him.

"As you wish, Princess."

They fell back onto the bed, Emmett insistently tugging at the laces of her new gown.

It had been so long, and his lips were so soft, and he smelled like leather and soap and boy, an intoxicating combination. She let her dress fall to the floor as she reached eagerly for his trousers.

Emmett frowned, taking her in. The fire burned low, but not low enough. His eyes went wide.

"Guin, are you pregnant?" he asked, his voice the barest whisper.

Guin didn't deny it. She merely bit her lip, waiting for him to back away in horror. To abandon her like the eighteen-year-old rake he was.

Instead, he looked exactly as he had when she had broken up with him. Utterly heartbroken.

"It's Arthur's, isn't it?" he went on, defeated. His shoulders were slumped, and he sounded absolutely miserable. "No wonder he was so—I didn't know that the two of you were . . . I'm sorry, Guin, I am such a fool." He put his head in his hands, looking for all the world like a man who had professed his love and been informed it was entirely one-sided.

And Guin knew she should tell him that the baby was Arthur's, but for some reason, she couldn't. "You're not a fool," Guin said. "Arthur's just a friend. You're the only one I've—well . . ."

"It's mine?" Emmett said, as though he'd hardly dared to hope. He stared at her in wonder, reaching for her hands. "Truly? We're going to have a baby?"

This wasn't how it had gone in her head. Why wasn't he screaming? Why wasn't he bolting for the door, protesting that it couldn't be true, and making terrible accusations as to her honor.

"I didn't know how to tell you," she said.

"This is perfect." Emmett took her hand, a tender look in his eyes. "Don't worry, I promise to be there for you. For both of you."

Guin stared at him, shocked. "What are you talking about?" she asked.

"I don't have much, but I can provide," he assured her. "If you don't wish to stay at the castle, there's always my family estate. It's only a cottage, but the land is mine, with tenants who farm it. I'm sorry, I wish there was more to my name than that. I know you're used to so much more."

"Emmett, stop," she said firmly. "You don't have to pretend you want any part of this."

"Who's pretending? I thought I was going to lose you forever."

He wrapped her in a hug, holding her close. *This doesn't make any sense*, Guin thought.

"Are you feeling all right?" Emmett asked. "Nothing strange?"

"Strange?" Guin asked.

"Well, magic runs in my bloodline."

"Magic," Guin said, horrified. She hadn't even thought. But of course. Their baby would be a wizard. And that would complicate things immensely.

Before she could help herself, Guin put her head in her hands, her shoulders trembling as she burst into tears.

It wasn't fair. In two weeks, she would marry Arthur and take her place as the future queen of Camelot. They would recite a loveless and painful promise to help their kingdoms. They'd spend the next five months desperately hoping the baby was a girl, and the rest of their lives trapped. If it was love they wanted, they'd have to look elsewhere, with the entire court watching and whispering if they did.

She let out a loud, blubbering sob.

"Guin, what's wrong?" Emmett asked, rubbing a hand in small circles on her back. He muttered something, and a small linen handkerchief floated from the wardrobe and landed in her lap.

"I don't want to marry Arthur," she sobbed. She reached for the handkerchief, drying her tears.

"I didn't realize you were going to," Emmett retorted. And then he went very still. His hand dropped from her back. "Guin, no."

"I have to say yes," she whispered. "This treaty is too important. Could you watch your kingdom fall to King Yurien, knowing it was your fault that no one came to their aid?" Her chin trembled at the thought.

"My sister was right," Emmett muttered. "There is nothing I don't ruin."

"That isn't true," said Guin.

"Yes, it is." Emmett shook his head, disgusted with himself. "You'll say the child is his, right?"

Guin bit her lip.

"So, if you marry Arthur, I've ruined all of our lives, and screwed up the royal family," Emmett summarized. "And if you don't?"

"I return to Cameliard, where it soon becomes obvious that I'm pregnant. And there will be no match I could make to save my kingdom, or my reputation."

"There has to be another way," said Emmett.

"There isn't."

"Of course there is." A corner of Emmett's mouth lifted, and he reached for her hand. "We'll elope. You can't marry Arthur if you're already married to me."

Guin laughed. "Marry you? But you don't even love me."

Emmett looked taken aback. "How do you know that?"

"You've never said anything!"

"How could I, when you made it so clear we were just amusing our-selves until you returned home?"

"*I* made it clear?" Guin spluttered.

"You made me sneak!" Emmett insisted. "I couldn't be seen with you, I couldn't take you out, I couldn't even visit your rooms. And when you ended things, you called it a stupid fling and said you regret-ted it entirely!"

"Oh," Guin said, biting her lip. She had been so foolish, denying what was between them to everyone, including herself. "Do you love me?"

"Of course I do," Emmett said fiercely. "I've loved you ever since you tripped over me in the gardens. My heart and soul ache for you, and I am a wreck at the thought of losing you. I've never felt like this before, and I don't think I will ever feel this way about anyone else. All I want, and all I have wanted since we met, is to spend the rest of my life with you."

Guin put her head in her hands. "I feel the same way," she con-fessed.

"Well, then," Emmett said. "I guess we're in love."

"I guess we are," Guin said wonderingly.

If she married Emmett, she would never again have to deal with the stress of being a perfect princess, or bearing heirs to a throne, or having a husband whose political obligations always superseded their family. She could be mistress of her own household, instead of queen of a kingdom. It sounded wonderful.

The more she thought about their life together, the more she wanted it. Not just for herself, but for their child. No, children. They would have a big, loud house full of them. Little wizards with her curly hair and Emmett's grin.

Perhaps she would try penning some salacious romance novels

herself. Guinevere Merlin. She rather liked the sound of it. It was certainly less of a mouthful than Guinevere Pendragon.

It was a perfect solution. If she was already married, there was no way she could marry Arthur. They could turn each other down as planned, and the peace treaty would move forward, and perhaps, they could each get a happily ever after, instead of being trapped in the misery of a forced marriage.

Guinevere realized she'd been silent a long while.

"So, um, what do you think?" Emmett said shyly. "Do you want to marry me?"

Guin threw her arms around him. "More than anything in the world."

Chapter 36

In the cool dungeons beneath the château, Emry was trying to master Anwen's magic.

She could control it with talismans, and by tracing the shapes of runes with her hands, but that wasn't good enough. She wanted it to work no matter the circumstance.

And she knew she could do it. She just needed practice. Which was why she had come down here in the first place. It had been hours, and she was exhausted, but she wasn't going to stop. Not if she didn't have to.

So she raised her dagger, seeking the magic that swirled within. She focused on her breathing, on lowering her shoulders and relaxing her jaw. And then she pricked her finger once again.

She felt for the magic, and when a whisper of it shivered through her, she stared into the shadows, imagining Morgana with her dagger plunging into Arthur's stomach. Remembering the way the sorceress had grinned when she had trapped Emry and tried to drain her magic.

Flames crackled to life above her palms, and she threw them against the far wall with as much strength as she could manage. The torchlight flickered as the fire flew past. She did it again and again, until her breathing came in ragged gasps. Until she was certain she would not miss a target.

"*Isaz!*" she demanded, the command echoing through the space. The flames changed to shards of ice, and she hurled those as well, then tried to change it back to fire with just a thought. The ice melted, and her vision tunneled as she stumbled, losing control.

"Sard," she muttered.

She should rest, she knew. But after not knowing how to control this for so long, she was determined to get it right. To master it, so it was no longer a weakness, but a strength.

She raised her trembling hands once more and tried again.

Arthur stewed quietly as he stood in the balcony of the horrible tennis tournament. He had hardly exchanged more than a sentence with King Louis all week, much less found any opportunity for a conversation with him. Instead, he was forced to watch this grim sport, and expected to keep company with Prince Henri and his loathsome friends.

He was beginning to regret how he had squandered the opportunity to have the king's ear on his first day at court. And he couldn't stop wondering how Emry was getting on, and if Flamel had helped her make any progress with her magic. Arthur didn't trust that self-centered court wizard one bit. He doubted Emry would appreciate seeing him right now, but if he stayed in the tennis balcony any longer, he thought he might scream.

He excused himself and hurried through the castle corridors, trying to remember the way to the wizard's laboratory. Finally, he reached the strange, rune-surrounded hallway.

"Entrez," called Flamel.

The wizard was bent over a glass apparatus, distilling a black, sludgy solution into a flask. In the corner, the gargoyle was still chained to a marble column. But Emry was missing.

"Oui, Monseigneur?" said Flamel.

"I'm looking for my apprentice court wizard."

"She is in the dungeons," Flamel said sourly.

"The dungeons?" Arthur choked. "Why wasn't I informed of this?"

"My wife was convinced your wizard would burn down the castle," Flamel muttered, tipping a packet of black powder into his flask.

"I have to go," Arthur said, his heart pounding.

Emry was in the dungeons. Not of Castle Camelot, but at the Palais de la Cité.

And it was all his fault. He had brought her here, and abandoned her in favor of his own pursuits. An alliance with the French didn't matter. Nothing mattered except rescuing her.

Arthur tamped down his panic as he hurried through the castle, trying to find the way to the dungeons. Finally, he came upon a doorway blocked by two royal guards. "I'm here to see a prisoner," he said.

"On whose authority?" a guard demanded.

"I—she's my wizard! I'm here on my own authority, as the crown prince of Camelot, and I demand that you release her at once!"

The guards exchanged a look and burst out laughing.

"We cannot," the shorter one said, his tone mocking.

"Immédiatement!" Arthur shouted, drawing his blade. Excalibur pulsed with light, and the guards squinted.

They had to release her. He didn't know what else to do. He didn't even know how long she had been there, just that there wasn't anything he wouldn't do to see her set free.

"Arthur?" a girl's voice called. "Why are you shouting?"

He turned, and there she was. She stood in the corridor in a green velvet dress, scowling at him.

She wasn't imprisoned. Not even a little bit. Arthur didn't think, he just rushed forward and wrapped her in a hug. "Oh thank god," he murmured.

"What's going on?" Emry asked.

"Flamel said you were in the dungeons!"

"Practicing magic!" Emry retorted.

"I thought you were imprisoned," Arthur said.

A smile tugged at the corner of Emry's mouth. "I know. I heard you shouting."

"I was afraid I was going to lose you," Arthur said. "And I couldn't bear the thought. I—forgive me, my behavior at the tennis match was appalling. I acted like an arse, and I deeply regret every word I said. I was awful and selfish and not at all the man I want to be."

Emry folded her arms, arching an eyebrow and making it clear she meant for him to go on.

"You've proven yourself a thousand times over, and have saved my life more times than I've deserved, and I'm honored to have you by my side, in any situation." He stared at her with a pleading expression, willing her to accept his apology.

To his horror, Emry sank into a curtsey and said prettily, "I must thank you, Your Highness, for your attempted rescue. It was most ardently appreciated."

Arthur snorted. "You've made your point, wizard."

"Have I, Your Highness?" Emry simpered. "I am glad to hear it. How do you find the weather this afternoon?"

"Stop it, please," Arthur begged.

"So you don't want me to curtsey and call you Highness?" Emry asked with a smirk.

"God no. I want you to be horrible and call me Arthur, the way you always have."

Emry grinned. "Good," she said. "Then yes, I accept your extremely late apology, but only because I'm in an excellent mood."

"You are?" Arthur replied, and then frowned. "Why?"

"Gawain took me to the most amazing brothel last night," she said. "Have you ever had a rose oil massage?"

Emry sighed happily, and Arthur spluttered.

"I never should have left the two of you together," he mumbled.

"But you did," Emry said, grinning. "Did I mention Flamel figured out the problem with my magic?"

"He did?"

"Yep. And he's sent me down here to practice, where I can't get into any trouble."

Arthur's expression was bland as he said, "Wizard, there's nowhere you can't get into trouble."

"Well, you and I know that, but we can't go around telling people."

"So your magic is truly fixed?" Arthur asked.

Emry's grin stretched wider. "Come on, I'll show you."

She went through the same pattern she had shown Pernelle. The only difference was that now she could change the magic silently, sketching the runes in her head. When she was done, and had extinguished the magic, she gave a small bow.

Arthur applauded. "Very impressive. Does this mean there aren't going to be any more rogue lightning bolts?"

"Not unless you're mean to me," she threatened, and then she shook her head. "I can't believe it worked, coming here."

"Perhaps for you." Arthur sighed. "I'm so far out of my depth that I feel as if I'm drowning."

"Gawain told me about the courtier King Louis had killed," Emry said.

"Everyone just stood there, watching." Arthur shuddered. "And that's not the only time I've had to bite my tongue. I don't want to go back and pretend I find it all a charming amusement."

"Then don't," Emry said. "The king isn't going to ally with Camelot just because you stood in the audience of some game, or played dice with his brother."

Arthur looked at her with surprise. "You're absolutely right, wizard," he said, and then a smile flickered across his lips. "In that case, do you want to get out of here?"

"Can we?"

Arthur shrugged. "I don't see why not."

Emry couldn't remember the last time she'd felt so free. She smiled, glancing over at Arthur, whose nose was pink from the cold. The sun was starting to sink behind the rooftops of Paris, and the city felt alive and magical.

It had been surprisingly easy to slip away from the castle. Though Arthur's clothing was too fine, his cloak was plain enough to avoid attention. They were completely alone, without even a guard trailing them.

"Hold on," she said, reaching over and mussing his hair.

"What was that for?" Arthur asked.

"You were wearing it with that horrible center part," Emry explained. "Now I can stand to look at you again."

"And?" Arthur asked with a grin.

"Oh my god, I'm not saying you look handsome." Emry rolled her eyes.

"But you're thinking it," Arthur said, pleased. "I can tell."

She was thinking it, and she wished she wasn't. She watched as Arthur took in the city in fascination, his eyes bright and happy. They stopped to buy candied nuts from a street vendor, and hot spiced wine from a market, which they drank out of tin cups chained to the stand.

As they did, Arthur caught Emry up on everything that had happened at court, though she noticed he left out the parade of men and women that Marie and Pernelle seemed certain had been sent to his bedchambers.

"So," he said when he was through. "What's life been like at Gawain's?"

"Unexpected," Emry replied, taking a sip of her spiced wine and thinking that a warm mug in one's cold hands was the most wonderful feeling in the world. "Did I tell you Jereth turned up with his boyfriend?"

"You're joking," said Arthur.

"We caught them trying to break in."

Arthur laughed. "Why on earth would they do that?"

Emry explained, and Arthur heaved a sigh. "As much as I dislike him, at least he's found someone worth running away with."

"Hugo is delightful," Emry said. "It's such a nuisance."

She shivered, and Arthur quirked an eyebrow. "Cold, wizard?"

"Underdressed is more like it," she complained. "I need a warmer cloak."

"Then come on," Arthur urged, motioning toward all the vendors in the market. "Let's buy one."

This was what Emry had been afraid of. Walking arm in arm through the market with Arthur, licking sugar off their fingers and laughing and browsing the merchants' shops.

"How about this?" Arthur teased, holding up a pink cloak edged in white, which had some sort of fussy pearl clasp.

"C'est parfait pour mademoiselle," the shopkeeper insisted.

"Just so you know, I can magic it a different color," Emry threatened.

"But I'd know it was secretly pink, underneath," Arthur replied, grinning.

Emry spotted a thick black cloak with leather edging and silver buckles. The hood was dramatic and oversize and lined with plush black velvet.

She ran a hand over the fabric, thinking she'd never seen anything so fierce looking. When she tried it on, Arthur grinned. He negotiated with the vendor, pulling some coins from his pocket.

"Happy now, wizard?" Arthur asked.

"Very," Emry said, admiring her new cloak. "Thank you." She hadn't realized how thin her old one was. "Oh no, don't look."

Arthur's expression was stricken. "Have my guards found us?"

"Try and contain yourself, but I seem to have spotted a vendor of used books."

Arthur laughed and pulled her along. She watched him sort through the books, reluctantly buying only three. With the parcel under his arm, he turned toward her, his face lit with happiness.

"Where's that apothecary of yours?" he asked.

"I think that's enough for one day," Emry said. "Eventually, Flamel's going to realize I'm not still in the dungeons."

"One last stop," he bargained. "I can't face going back just yet."

She didn't have the heart to turn him down.

When she saw what Arthur had in mind, she frowned. Notre Dame, the twin-towered cathedral, was under construction, but the edifice soared over the rooftops of Paris, eclipsing even the Sainte-Chappelle inside the Palais, which only the king was allowed to visit.

"A church?"

"Notre Dame isn't a church," Arthur protested. "Come on, I've always wanted to do this."

Arthur took her hand in his, a simple action that felt like so much more. They climbed endless staircases, snuck through the wooden structure of the bell tower, and then up more narrow stairs, until they finally reached the roof.

Paris stretched out below them, a walled city surrounded by woods and farmland, glittering with lanterns and humming with life.

"Wow," Emry said.

Arthur grinned. "Good, isn't it?"

A cold wind whipped past them, fluttering Arthur's hair. His cheeks were pink, and his eyes were bright, and as he stood there with the parcel of books under his arm, it felt as though he belonged with her, and she with him.

"Cold?" he asked.

Emry shrugged, taking a knife from her pocket and pressing the tip against her thumb. Blood welled, and she smiled.

"*Kaunan*," she whispered, summoning a purple flame that hovered over each palm. She closed one fist. "*Elhaz*," she murmured, until she was left with just the one flame. Concentrating, she nudged it upward with her palm, until it floated freely around shoulder height.

"Stay there," she warned the flame, "or I'll put you out." The flame obligingly stayed where Emry had nudged it.

Arthur pressed back a smile. "I can't believe you're scolding fire."

"Why not? It works."

They sat on the edge of the rooftop, their feet dangling, the purple flame burning at Emry's side, keeping them warm.

"I wish it could always be like this," Arthur said sadly.

There was something weighing on him. Emry could see it now, and she suspected it had been there for a long time.

"You can tell me," she said softly. "Whatever it is. Whatever you're afraid to say. It can't be that bad."

Arthur turned toward her, the heartbreak clear in his eyes. "It is," he whispered. She could see him steeling himself before he added, "I have to marry Guin."

Emry frowned. "What happened to giving everyone a heart attack by calling it off at the altar, and then very cleverly proposing your diplomatic solution?"

Arthur flinched. Looked everywhere except at Emry. And she suddenly had a very bad feeling about what was weighing on Arthur's mind, and why he had so quickly agreed to run off to France.

"No longer an option."

"Why not?" Emry pressed.

"The marriage has to go forward," Arthur said, "because . . . Guin's pregnant."

Whatever Emry had been expecting Arthur to say, that wasn't it. She stared at him, stricken. For a moment, she hoped he would break into a grin and confess he was joking, but he didn't. His shoulders slouched, and his expression was downright tragic.

Guin was pregnant. And he had to marry her.

Emry felt tears prickle at the corners of her eyes at what that meant for them—for all of them.

"Arthur Pendragon," she accused. "How could you be so careless?"

"I wasn't!" he insisted. "We never—she tried to seduce me, so I'd believe that I was the one at fault, but she panicked and confessed."

"She what?" Emry said, horrified.

"If I reject her now, she'll be ruined, and I'll be thought heartless. The best thing to do is pretend the child is mine."

"Whose is it really?"

"Emmett's," Arthur said tightly.

Emry had never been so furious at her brother. "So stupid," she muttered. "I warned them."

"You knew?" Arthur shook his head in disbelief. "And you didn't tell me?"

"That my brother was hooking up with a girl who eagerly came to his bed?" Emry retorted. "Of course I didn't. You would have had Emmett dismissed. And Uther would have sent me along with him."

Arthur winced. "You still should have told me."

"Are we really playing that game?" Emry asked.

Arthur sighed and ran a hand through his hair. "No, we're not." He stared out at the city below them for a moment, thinking. Just when Emry thought he might not say anything else, he said, "If I don't marry

Guinevere, it will be some other princess. My father will make sure of it. Some princess from some resource-rich kingdom who thinks me a monster for jilting Guinevere, but is willing to overlook it to become a queen."

Emry hated that he was right. He'd thought this through—of course he had—and there wasn't a better path forward. There were only parallel paths of misery.

"That's why you wanted to come to France," she said, realizing.

Arthur nodded. "I didn't know how to tell you about any of this. It isn't my doing, but it's my responsibility to see this marriage through. There's no way out that doesn't lead to worse circumstances for both of us." He let out a heartbreaking sigh. "This is what it is, to be a prince. I suppose I'd always known that, but after I met you, I hoped— I wished—that is, I desired for things to be different."

Emry stared out over the rooftops, feeling as though she had lost something she'd been convinced she could never have, but had let herself dream about, just for a moment. "I desired that, too," she whispered.

"If you wish to turn some sensitive part of my body into a rotting fruit or a small woodland creature, I wouldn't blame you," said Arthur.

"Those are the options?" Emry asked incredulously. "A moldy tomato or a bunny?"

Arthur laughed hollowly. "They are. Take your pick, wizard."

Emry shook her head. "What I want is honesty. I wish you'd told me what you were going through, so you didn't have to suffer alone."

Arthur's dark eyes were serious. "Just as I wish you'd told me of your magic problems, and my father's threats, so you didn't have to suffer alone."

"No more keeping secrets?" Emry suggested.

"Never again," Arthur promised.

Chapter 37

"Wonderful, my English-speaking visitors have finally arrived," said King Louis, as his inner court walked back to the castle from the tennis match the next afternoon.

Arthur turned, and couldn't believe what he was seeing.

Not what, whom.

His uncle Gorlais, the Duke of Cornwall, stood resplendent in a coat of gold brocade. Behind him was his son, Maddoc, a gangly, sour-faced lad of thirteen who looked as though he could use a poultice for his angry spray of acne. He wore a suit of burgundy velvet, which wasn't helping matters.

Thankfully, the duke didn't notice Arthur amid the crowd of courtiers. Instead, he dropped into an obsequious bow before the French king. "Je suis at votre service, mon roi," he began, the French garbled on his tongue.

"Your Grace," the king said, "don't strain yourself. I cannot bear to hear you mangle my language any further."

The duke looked relieved. He bowed again, in assent. "Your English is excellent, Your Majesty," he said.

"I have spent the past fortnight practicing." Louis motioned toward Arthur, who pasted on his best smile as he stepped forward. "I believe you're already acquainted with Prince Arthur of Camelot?"

The duke choked.

"Uncle," Arthur said coldly. "And Maddoc, how well you look in burgundy."

"I—I didn't realize you'd be here," began the duke.

"Yes, I believe we are equally full of joy at this unexpected meeting," Arthur went on. "How are the renovations to your castle coming along?"

The duke blanched. "Renovations?"

Arthur frowned. "Do I have it wrong? I'd heard you were making improvements to the fortifications."

"We are only adding more garderobes," said the duke with an oily grin. "Many of the staff fell ill last winter having to use the outdoor privies in the cold."

"How thoughtful of you to remodel on their behalf," said Arthur.

"The duke is a very thoughtful man," said Louis. "He wrote to me about his son, for whom he is trying to arrange a betrothal. I understand Maddoc is second in line for Camelot's throne."

Arthur suddenly had a very bad feeling. "At the moment," Arthur said tightly.

"I invited His Grace to visit and bring his son where I may inspect him, in hopes he's a match for my daughter."

Arthur swallowed hard. It was as he'd feared—the Duke of Cornwall was at French court to secure a betrothal between his son and Princess Anne.

This was an unmitigated disaster.

"Hello?" Arthur called, racing up the stairs of the townhouse. "Where is everyone?"

He pushed open the door of the bedroom he'd been staying in and stumbled back in surprise.

The room was occupied. Very occupied.

"Aghhh!" a boy shouted. "Get out!"

"Sorry!" Arthur ducked into the hallway, his cheeks burning.

A moment later, a familiar figure joined him, tucking a tunic into his breeches.

"It is customary to knock, isn't it?" Jereth asked, scowling. "Or are you so important that you've forgotten?"

"I thought it was still my room," said Arthur.

A skinny, rather unwell-looking blond boy stepped into the hall, wearing his tunic back to front, and nothing else. "Is everything all right?" he asked nervously. "It's not the constabulary?"

"No, just my cousin," said Jereth.

The blond boy tilted his head, studying him. "You wouldn't happen to be the crown prince of Camelot?" he asked.

"I would," Arthur replied gravely.

"Thought so." The boy gave him an embarrassed smile. "Please excuse me a moment."

The blond lad disappeared back into the bedroom, and reemerged in a rather shabby pair of trousers and a worn jacket.

"Prince Hugo," he said with a bow. "Of Flanders. At your service. I thought it best to delay introductions until I could find my trousers."

So this was Jereth's former roommate from boarding school. The one with whom he'd managed to burn down the scriptorium naked and get summarily expelled. He wasn't what Arthur had been expecting. But then, people so often weren't.

"Er, a pleasure to meet you," said Arthur. "I can—er, if you want to finish?—I'll be in the library."

"It's a very good library," Hugo said earnestly.

"Very flammable," said Jereth.

Arthur went pale.

"That was a joke," Jereth told him. "Oh my god, go away."

That evening, in the library, Emry and Gawain got Arthur up to speed on the whole Jereth and Prince Hugo situation.

After they had, Arthur pressed his fingers to his temples and sighed.

"I don't understand how anyone can be so closed-minded," he said. "It shouldn't be up to society to say we're safe. Safe should be expected."

"Ooh, are you going to give one of those 'when I'm king' proclamations?" Emry asked.

Arthur scowled. "No, but I like that you thought I would."

"They can't stay here forever," said Gawain. "Jereth certainly, but we've got a runaway Flemish royal who's supposed to be convalescing, not gallivanting around Paris."

"If I anger yet another foreign king, I don't think I'll be able to bear it," said Arthur, slouching back in his chair.

"Did something happen with King Louis?" Gawain asked.

"Nothing I shouldn't have foreseen." Arthur grimaced. "It's all right if I stay here through the weekend, isn't it? I just—panicked. So, I made up an imaginary dinner party to escape the castle, where I intend to become ill with imaginary food poisoning."

"I could give you real food poisoning, if you like," said Emry.

"You're offering to make him a sandwich?" Gawain complained. Emry glared.

"May I ask why you intend to become conveniently food poisoned at my dinner party?" asked Gawain.

"So I don't get actually poisoned by my uncle, the duke," said Arthur. "Because he just turned up at court as an honored guest of the king."

Emry and Gawain wore twin expressions of disbelief.

"You're kidding," said Emry. "The Duke of Cornwall is *here*?"

"And his son," Arthur reported. "Who is apparently to be a match for Princess Anne."

Gawain groaned at the news. "We have to prevent this. If the duke believes himself to be backed by the French, there's no telling what he'll do."

"From the way he's been fortifying his castle and building an army,

I fear the threat to Camelot lies far closer to home than we had thought," said Arthur.

"Perhaps we can stop it ourselves," Gawain agreed.

"Stop what ourselves?" asked Jereth, who had materialized in the door to the library.

Hugo stood behind him, carrying a tray of sandwiches. "We weren't sure how long you would be in here, so we made sandwiches."

"Look, maybe you will get food poisoning after all," Emry said brightly, and Arthur shot her a glare.

"That's very thoughtful," said Gawain.

"Also we were eavesdropping in the hall," said Hugo. "We didn't mean to. We just didn't want to interrupt—"

"—right as you were about to finish," Jereth said pointedly.

Arthur coughed.

"So, what's up with the Duke of Cornwall?" Jereth asked, sitting down and motioning for Hugo to do the same.

No one touched the sandwiches.

"Since when do you care?" asked Gawain.

"Since I learned that he tried to poison Arthur!" said Jereth. "It was a total dick move."

"It was," Emry agreed, pressing her lips together to keep from laughing.

"And what if he doesn't stop there?" Jereth went on. "What about the rest of us? Gawain's next in line for the throne after Maddoc, and then me, and I—I don't want anyone to be poisoned, okay?"

Arthur blinked at his cousin, having been previously unaware that the lad had any feelings on the matter.

"I also don't want anyone to be poisoned," Hugo said sincerely.

"Then you can understand why we're hesitant to try your sandwiches," said Emry.

Arthur couldn't help it. He burst out laughing. He knew it wasn't funny, yet somehow it was. And before he knew it, everyone was in hysterics, except for a rather wounded-looking Prince Hugo.

"So we just have to make sure Maddoc seems like a bad match?" Jereth asked.

"That seems the easiest solution," said Gawain. "And it would ensure that such an alliance never takes place."

Emry arched an eyebrow. "And how do you suggest we make Maddoc appear unsuitable for marriage? Magic?"

"I once found it very effective to pretend that attentions I'd asked for were made without my consent," said Jereth.

"We remember," Arthur said coldly.

"I'm not seducing a thirteen-year-old," Emry said.

"It was just a suggestion," Jereth muttered.

"The only problem is, what if we ruin this only for King Louis to choose someone worse?" said Gawain, looking worried.

"You mean King Yurien's son," Arthur supplied. He frowned and then suggested, "Perhaps Prince Hugo could try his suit."

Everyone turned to him, surprised.

"Me?" said Hugo.

"You're a neutral third party," Arthur went on. "It's not every day you have an eligible young prince at your disposal. That is, if you'd be amenable."

Hugo made a face, considering. "This Princess Anne is how old?"

"Seven," said Arthur.

Hugo's frown deepened in thought. "I'd be down for it," he said.

"Truly?" Arthur asked.

"She cannot marry younger than fifteen?" Hugo asked. Arthur nodded. "So I'll have eight years to get out of this. Perhaps eight years is more than I'm granted." He gave a heartbreaking shrug.

"Don't say that," Jereth said fiercely.

"Why not?" Hugo lifted his chin. "My health is already frail, and with every winter, my cough grows worse."

"I don't know how to cure it, but I do know some herbs that could hide it," said Arthur. "For the span of a short visit, at least."

"Perhaps, when the princess is old enough, you can explain that you have no interest in women, and she'll be good enough to call it off," said Jereth.

"May he be so fortunate," Emry said, with a pointed look at Arthur.

"So," Hugo said with a bright smile. "When do we go to court?"

Gawain eyed him critically. "After you get a haircut. And a new suit."

Chapter 38

Morgana tightened her grip on the dagger and steeled her nerve. For the past week, she had felt Bellicent's gentle pressure inside her bones, and she knew she wasn't imagining it.

The sorceress was trying to find a way in.

Morgana had thought that if she ignored it, Bellicent might stop, but instead, the woman had grown even more emboldened. Morgana found herself nodding off when she wasn't tired, and felt her thoughts gliding away from certain topics, as though being steered by someone else. She didn't trust the sorceress.

And without magic, there was only one way to stand up for herself. With violence.

They had stopped in another village, at an inn this time. Bellicent was tucking a loaf of bread into her pack, paying Morgana no attention.

Now, she thought.

Before she could talk herself out of it, Morgana darted forward, plunging her dagger into Bellicent's borrowed body. The blade struck the girl square in the chest, and a gruesome rosette bloomed across the pale stretch of her tunic.

The fog cleared from the girl's eyes, and she crumpled to the ground, dead. She did not turn back to ice, but simply remained a corpse.

Morgana stared down at the girl with a sense of victory. She had done it. And it had been so easy.

A table creaked, and Morgana turned in time to see a man rise up jerkily from his seat, his eyes a swirl of pale fog, his face twisted into a rictus grin. "Shouldn't have done that," he growled, his voice threaded with Bellicent's familiar tones.

"I'll kill your body again," Morgana threatened.

"I don't think you will." The man's fingers twitched.

Morgana's hand raised, and she found herself pressing the blood-stained dagger to her own heart.

She wasn't doing this.

"Stop it!" she cried.

"You swore to help me," Bellicent snarled. Her new body stalked forward and caught Morgana around the throat. "You swore by your blade that you will break my enchantment. And I swore by mine to protect you until I am set free."

Bellicent's new body let go of Morgana's throat. It unsheathed its dagger and cut its own throat, crumpling to the floor.

Morgana stared down at it, splattered with the man's blood. She was no stranger to killing, but it was a gruesome sight all the same.

Be careful what you promise, Bellicent's voice sang inside Morgana's head.

Morgana's arm lifted. She tried to fight it, but she couldn't. She merely watched, as if from afar, as she flung her dagger into the hearth.

"No," Morgana cried. She made it two steps before her feet stuck to the floor.

A young woman rose up from the table, rosy-cheeked and wide-hipped, with her hair in golden ringlets. A shepherdess, perhaps. Her eyes swirled with fog, and Morgana swallowed back bile.

"Leave it," crooned Bellicent's new body. "You need no weapons while I protect you."

"*Control* me, you mean," Morgana spat.

"It is nothing you didn't agree to. You accepted my protection."

In Morgana's head, the sorceress laughed. *We made a deal. Either break my enchantment, or I'll protect you like this forever.*

Chapter 39

Lance stifled a yawn, wondering how much longer Sir Kay would require his company at the tavern.

The tournament began in six short hours, and what had started as a single drink with an old friend had soon become a series of drinks, with Sir Kay loudly holding court from the table late into the night.

Sir Grummore had long since dismissed his own squire, but every time Lance caught Sir Kay's eye to do the same, the knight shook his head. There was a stiffness in the way Sir Kay sat, and Lance knew that the knight would insist on having ointment massaged into his muscles to ease them before he went to sleep.

It had been a grueling half day's ride to the tournament, through rain and mud, and one of the horses had thrown a shoe. They'd arrived so late that the best rooms at the best inns were already taken. And Sir Kay had blamed Lance for not checking the horses, even though he had, twice. It was simply bad luck. Thankfully, Sir Kay's sour mood had improved with drink, and with the company of some old friends. "What do you hear of tomorrow's tournament?" he asked Grummore.

"Difficult roster, to be sure," said Grummore. "Word is, the knight to beat in the joust is Sir Tor."

Kay frowned. "Tor? I've never heard of him."

"Them," corrected Grummore.

Kay groaned. "Knights should be men," he complained. "That's how it's always been."

Lance held back a sigh at his uncle's closed-mindedness.

"What?" Kay growled, sensing that there was much he wasn't saying.

And Lance was so tired that he didn't think before he blurted, "Actually, the only requirement is a noble bloodline. If the criteria was simply being male, there'd be a line out the door of lads eager to trade their posts as guards and blacksmiths' apprentices."

Grummore let out a hearty laugh and clapped Lance on the back. "The squire speaks true."

"We did have a female knight, though that was long before our time," said Sir Alomere, pouring himself another drink from the near-empty pitcher.

"A female knight?" Lance said, surprised. "They never taught us about that as pages."

"She transitioned after her training," said Alomere. "Caused quite a stir at court. My father squired with her."

"Back in the dark ages," said Grummore with a wink.

Alomere laughed and swatted at him. "Mind your chivalry, sir, or I'll mind it for you."

"Is that a promise, sir?"

"I'll see you in the jousting ring," Alomere said with mock affront, tossing back his drink. "Well, I'm off. Got a lovely lass waiting for me in naught but her naughties, if I'm lucky."

"And he paid her handsomely for it," teased Grummore, letting out a yawn. "I'm also for bed. We're none of us as young as we used to be."

"Speak for yourself," protested Sir Kay.

"Careful, Kay, those gray hairs betray you."

Kay glowered.

Sir Grummore sauntered off, and Lance gave Sir Kay a hopeful expression.

"I'll expect you in the tents an hour before dawn. And before you retire, stop by my room with that liniment for my muscles."

● ● ●

The stands were cheering, and it wasn't for Sir Kay.

"Sir Tor! Sir Tor!" they cried, clapping their hands and stomping their feet in excitement. Lance could see that it set Sir Kay's teeth on edge.

It was the final match of the tournament, and so far, Sir Tor had jousted a perfect competition. And they weren't just undefeated in the ring—not a single knight had managed to score a point against them. It had been a long time since anyone had jousted a perfect tournament.

And now, they were up against Sir Kay, the defending champion. It promised to be the match of the weekend.

Lance handed Sir Kay his weapon, double-checked all the buckles on his saddle, and gave Cerberus, the knight's white destrier, a double pat on the flank.

"All set," Lance reported.

Sir Kay glowered and didn't respond. Lance knew all the cheering and the face paint in Sir Tor's colors were getting to Sir Kay. His mood was tense as the trumpets blared, signaling the start of the match.

Lance watched from behind the wooden gate, his heart hammering with nerves. He had a perfect view of the field, one of the few perks of being a squire.

Sir Kay rode into the ring, lowering his lance and notching it into the cradle at just the right moment. Lance could barely breathe as Sir Tor urged their black destrier forward to meet him.

The young knight leaned forward in the saddle, in a suit of modern, form-fitting armor. Their lance was raised, their intent clear. Lance had never seen anyone so hungry for victory.

Sir Kay rode with his usual arrogant assurance, as though he couldn't imagine meeting a worthy opponent. The blow, when Sir Tor struck, was catastrophic.

Lance gripped the wooden gate so hard he nearly ripped it from its hinges. He watched in disbelief as Sir Kay was knocked almost horizontal by the force of the other knight's hit. Somehow, perhaps by sheer luck, Sir Kay remained on his steed. His lance went flying, the tip still intact as it landed in the dirt.

The spectators gasped, and the crowd went still.

"Two points to Sir Tor," called the referee, holding up the flags, "and none to Sir Kay."

The crowd cheered, as Tor's perfect tournament was just one point away.

Sir Kay rode out of the ring, and Lance noted with concern how the knight slouched forward in his saddle, barely able to keep his seat, and how loosely he held the reins.

"The healing salve," Sir Kay demanded, his voice tight with pain. "Hurry."

"A moment," Lance promised, as he held open the gate, scrambling inside to retrieve Sir Kay's unbroken lance.

As he did, he looked up, and caught Sir Tor's eye. The knight had removed their helmet and was having a drink of water. They were very attractive, Lance noticed, with long, fair hair that was braided back at the sides and worn in a topknot, and charcoal smudged around their eyes.

Tor's mouth tipped up in a grin. The knight raised their wooden cup, saluting Lance. Lance nodded back, and then hurried across the field to tend to his knight.

"The salve, squire," Sir Kay snarled.

"You're not supposed to—" Lance began, but Sir Kay fixed him with such a fierce look that his protests fell away.

"Hold your tongue, squire," the knight said. "Do as you're told or find another knight to serve."

Lance sighed and reached into the bag, handing Sir Kay the jar, even though it was against the rules. Magical interference was prohibited during a match. It was an unfair advantage, if not an outright cheat.

"This is all we have?" the knight demanded, taking in the small amount of salve at the bottom of the jar.

"Unfortunately," Lance mumbled.

Sir Kay unbuckled his sleeved armor from his breastplate, and smeared the meager portion of salve onto his shoulder with a grimace.

His shoulder blade stuck out oddly, and his arm seemed to drag. And Lance knew the salve would do little to mend it, even if there had been a full jar. He watched in disbelief as Sir Kay gritted his teeth and lifted his dislocated arm over his head, reaching for his opposite shoulder until there was a sickening pop.

The knight let out a sigh of relief. "My lance, squire," he said.

"You can't ride like that," Lance protested.

"I won't forfeit. I must finish."

"You'll only make that injury worse," Lance argued. "You need a sling, not a weapon."

"Sir Tor will not beat me and joust a perfect tournament," the old knight ground out. "Tie the lance to my arm, squire."

Sir Kay couldn't be serious. But Lance saw that he was. And he knew better than to argue with the knight when he was in such a state. So he got out a length of leather cord and did so, in tense silence.

All this was against the rules. The healing salve, to say nothing of the weapon tied to Kay's arm.

Sir Tor saluted from their end of the field, motioning for a time-out. The knight rode over, unlatching their visor. Up close, Sir Tor was freckled and tan, and not yet thirty. Tor regarded Kay with a practiced eye.

"You're injured," the younger knight accused.

Kay grimaced. "Hardly. It's just a scratch."

"There is no dishonor in forfeiting due to injury," Tor said gently.

"That cannot be the last time I ride," insisted Sir Kay. "I must finish."

Tor thought about this and nodded. "We'll ride one final skirmish. You'll hold your weapon high and take a hit. I'll be as light as I can with the damage. Your breastplate, if I can manage it, instead of the shoulder."

It was an elegant solution. To take a hit without aiming one's weapon in return was a sign of respect and defeat, like tipping over one's king in an unwinnable game of chess. The crowd would see Sir Kay cede his title as tournament champion to Sir Tor, rather than hear of his forfeit and watch him slink away in pain, the match unfinished.

Resentment flashed across Sir Kay's face, but there was nothing the knight could do. Lance stared admiringly at his knight's opponent, thinking that, if he did manage to earn his knighthood, he wished to be like Tor, rather than Kay. To act with honor, instead of arrogance.

"Do we have an accord?" Sir Tor asked.

Sir Kay looked as if he wanted to refuse. "Fine," he ground out.

Sir Tor smiled.

That night at the inn, Sir Kay stomped upstairs without so much as a second look in Lance's direction.

Humiliating, he had called it. A false defeat.

But it wasn't, and Lance had said as much. He wished he hadn't.

He raised a hand to his cheek and the bruise that lay there, wishing Sir Kay hadn't used all the healing salve. With the knight's dominant arm bound in a sling, Lance hadn't expected the hit.

"How did you come by that injury, squire?" called a merry voice. Sir Tor. The knight sat alone at a table, with a goblet of wine and a leatherbound journal open in front of them, along with a quill and ink. They waved for Lance to join them.

"I was clumsy in my training," Lance lied.

"I saw you training," said Sir Tor, taking a sip of wine. "Out in the woods, earlier. You were not clumsy in the least."

Lance bowed his head at the praise. "Thank you," he mumbled. "I should congratulate you on your victory. I've never seen anyone joust a perfect tournament."

The knight waved a hand, as though it was nothing, but their lips curved into a smile. "Now everyone expects me to do it again. I fear I'll perish from the pressure."

"I suppose that's the problem with chasing your dreams," Lance said. "Whenever you get close, it turns out the target has been moved farther afield."

Sir Tor laughed. "What wise words, from a lad who squires for his father."

"My uncle," Lance corrected crisply.

Sir Tor frowned. "Well, your uncle hasn't shown you how to properly grip the lance. When I saw you earlier, you were choked up too high on the handle."

Lance made a face. "I was?"

"I suspect he has not taught you how to joust," said Sir Tor. "Or else you would not make such a mistake."

"He hasn't," Lance admitted.

"You don't get along with him," Sir Tor said.

"He didn't wish to have me as a squire."

"That's no excuse to treat you poorly."

"I have no other choice, if I wish to become a knight," said Lance. "And I've worked too hard for this to toss it away."

"You won't be much of a knight, if you spend your time sharpening weapons, instead of learning how to wield them."

Lance bowed his head and said nothing, hating that Sir Tor was right.

"My squire, Galahad, is leaving me at the month's end, to become a full-fledged knight," Sir Tor went on. "I would take you as his replacement. I'm not an easy master, but I would be fair. And I would train you, properly."

Lance hesitated. Part of him wished desperately to take Sir Tor up on the offer. Tor was a champion, and a knight with honor, and Lance would be lucky to learn from them.

But Sir Tor wasn't pledged to Camelot.

Becoming Tor's squire would mean forsaking the castle—Arthur, Percival, everyone he cared about—and pledging his sword to a different king.

"I'm grateful for the offer," said Lance, "but I can't. My best friend is the crown prince of Camelot. My sword belongs in his service, not Cameliard's."

Sir Tor nodded. "I am indifferent to whom I serve, and to what kingdom. I have found kings are all the same."

"Then you should pledge to Camelot," Lance suggested. "When I was a guard, Prince Arthur trained alongside me. Not with the nobles and the knights, but with the commoners running laps in the yard. If you fight for a better world, you should fight for Arthur."

"When he becomes king, I will consider it. As might some others I know, who yearn for such things."

"You should come for the wedding festivities," said Lance. "See what kind of a newer world Camelot is hoping to build."

"Perhaps I shall," said Sir Tor.

The ride home from the tournament was tense and silent. Sir Kay fumed quietly, riding with one arm in a sling, wearing neither mail nor armor.

It was strange to see him dressed so plain, Lance thought. He said little, thinking on Sir Tor, and how much it meant that the knight had offered to take him on as squire. It had been a long time since Lance had felt wanted by those he wished to impress.

"What's wrong with you?" Sir Kay grunted as they rode toward London in the cooling evening. "I thought you'd be thrilled, now that I won't be able to compete again until the spring."

Lance was, but he wasn't about to show it. "What will my duties be, while you're recovering?"

"We'll have to see," said Sir Kay. "Perhaps I'll no longer have need of a squire."

"That isn't fair," Lance burst out, before he could stop himself. "I've done everything you've ever asked."

"You let us run out of healing salve!" Sir Kay shouted.

"*I* let us run out of salve?" Lance repeated incredulously. "Master Ambrosius has refused to give you more. Emmett took pity on me weeks ago, and the last jar was my own, left over from a rolled ankle."

Sir Kay muttered something that Lance didn't quite catch.

"Do you know what you could do?" Lance said, summoning his nerve. "Instead of threatening to dismiss me just because you can't compete at tournaments? You could offer to train me during your recovery. To show me how to hold a lance, and tilt at moving targets, and strategize for a melee."

Sir Kay laughed. "Why on earth would I do that?"

"Because I'm owed the training," Lance insisted. "I haven't polished your armor and mended your chainmail and served you at tournaments for no gain of my own. I'm meant to learn, yet you refuse to teach. You could be a great mentor, if you would only stand aside and give others a chance."

"You're tougher than I thought," Kay admitted. "For a soft lad who prefers boys."

"There's nothing soft about it," said Lance. "Knowing what you want is a strength. And living your truest life takes courage. Boys like me are the strongest of all. And I would prove it to you, on the tilting field."

"You want to train?" said Sir Kay. "Fine. I'll train you."

"You won't be disappointed." Lance pressed back a grin as he spurred his horse to go faster. Sir Kay did the same, refusing to be outdone. "We can begin tomorrow, after breakfast."

"We'll begin tomorrow at dawn, squire," said Sir Kay, daring Lance to argue.

Chapter 40

"You're sure about this?" Emry asked Arthur as the château's tallest towers came into view the next morning.

They were walking across the Seine, over one of the stone bridges that was lined with shops and narrow, crooked houses.

"I'm sure I don't have a choice," said Arthur. "My father won't do anything about the duke until his hand is forced. If I run away, I'm as bad as him." He gave her a shaky smile. "Besides, I have you. And Excalibur. All the duke has is Maddoc."

"And an army. And a penchant for poison," Emry pointed out.

"Then perhaps we should stop by the apothecary, to confirm he hasn't made any recent purchases," Arthur said hopefully.

"Oh my god." Emry rolled her eyes. "Are you going to annoy me about this until I take you?"

"Or until the duke tips poison into my wine again, whichever comes first," he said with a sigh.

"Fine," Emry said, "we can stop. But only because I feel sorry for you, and your delicate emotional state."

"I thought it was your foot under the table, not Hugo's! Otherwise I never would have let him go on as long as he did!"

A cart clattered past, sending her and Arthur to the side of the road. His arm bumped against hers, and he didn't take it away.

Their eyes met, and Emry felt her breath catch.

"Well," Arthur said, clearing his throat and straightening his jacket. "How far is the apothecary?"

"It's just up here," Emry promised.

When the building came into view, Arthur was practically vibrating with excitement. Emry pushed open the door.

"Pernelle?" she called.

"Emmyyyy!" screeched Nicolas, who was sitting on the floor, banging a mortar and pestle together. He tossed them aside and clamped himself firmly to her legs.

Emry sighed, peering down at the clinging toddler. "What are you doing here?"

"Sorry!" Pernelle climbed down from the highest rung of the ladder. "His nurse insists her morbid sore throat has become putrid."

"Has she tried elderberry?" Arthur asked.

"I prescribed marshmallow root," said Pernelle, drumming her fingers against the counter in thought. "But you might be right about elderberry."

Somehow, without noticing she'd done it, Emry had picked up the toddler and was bouncing him on her hip. He let out a squeal of pleasure, and then yanked her hair. Hard.

"I will turn you into a toad," she threatened.

"Ribbit!" the boy said happily, reaching for her hair again.

Emry set him on the ground. "I regret everything."

"Don't tell me you've run out of coffee already," said Pernelle.

"You found *coffee*?" Arthur looked scandalized. "And you didn't tell me?"

"I'm withholding it until you're nicer to me," Emry retorted.

"Is that why you snuck down to the kitchens this morning?" Arthur accused. "To have a cup where I wouldn't see?"

Emry shrugged, hating that he'd guessed. "Oh, sorry, Pernelle, this is Arthur."

Pernelle sank into an elegant curtsey. "Enchantée, Monseigneur," she said. "It's not often I have royalty in my shop."

Just then, Nicolas gave an insistent and rather painful tug on Emry's cloak, nearly tripping her.

"Stop that!" she complained. "No!"

"No no no!" The toddler clapped his hands, delighted, and reached to do it again.

"Don't even think about it," Emry warned, stepping out of the way and glaring.

"Horses and babies," Arthur said smugly. "Good to know."

Nicolas sat down heavily and began to cry. Pernelle muttered a curse.

"If you're looking for some temporary childcare," said Arthur, "perhaps I can be of service."

"Ha!" Emry said.

"Go on," said Pernelle.

"My youngest cousin needs to learn some responsibility," Arthur went on. "And earn a bit of coin to settle an unpaid account. I could send him by to assist you. I make no promises that he will be anything other than a burden."

That actually wasn't a terrible idea.

"I'll expect him tomorrow, first thing," said Pernelle.

Emry smothered a grin as she pictured the look on Jereth's face when he discovered Arthur had signed him up for babysitting.

"Now, don't let me interrupt your business." Arthur waved for them to go talk, and crouched down, speaking in gentle French to the sulking toddler. "Tu te comporteras très bien pour ta maman, oui?"

Pernelle bit back a smile.

"I was hoping for the formula for your ladder-moving varnish," Emry said. "And I wanted to ask if anyone has come in to purchase any poisons lately."

"Only the Vicomtesse de Tourcy, but I sold them to her gladly," Pernelle said. "Her husband is vile."

Emry tried not to laugh.

"How is your practice going with the runes?" Pernelle went on. "I was planning to stop in and check, but then you and your young man came in."

"He's not my young man," Emry protested.

"What a pity." Pernelle gave a wicked grin. "You argue as though you make very passionate lovers."

"He's the crown prince," Emry hissed.

"He is sitting on the floor of my apothecary with my child on his lap, teaching him how to hold a pestle," said Pernelle.

Emry twisted around to stare, and sure enough, he was. It was infuriating how Arthur could just do things like that. How gentle he was with animals, and now, apparently, babies.

"Here's the formula for the varnish," said Pernelle, holding out a thickly rolled piece of parchment.

"Thank you." Emry hugged the scroll to her chest.

"I'll be curious to know how it works out," said Pernelle.

"The varnish?"

Pernelle gave her a knowing look. "That too."

"Slow down," Emry complained as Arthur hurried through the castle courtyard. "I can't breathe in this corset."

Arthur was all too aware of the situation, and was desperately pretending he wasn't. "I can't, or we'll miss the king's procession."

He gasped and coughed, out of breath himself.

"I blame you for spending so long at the apothecary," Emry accused. She was wearing her new cloak and had Pernelle's parcel of apothecary supplies hanging from a ribbon around her wrist, looking nothing like a court lady. Certainly nothing like any other lady who was about to stand before the king.

But Arthur wouldn't have had it any other way. He reached over and took her hand, pulling her along behind him briskly. At the steps of the palace, Arthur skidded to a stop, straightening his jacket.

Emry bent over, hands on her knees, glaring.

"The King of France waits for no wizard," he said, offering her his arm.

Arthur was all too aware of the curious stares as he and Emry stood in the line of courtiers. He could see his uncle at the far end, holding a yawning Maddoc up by his collar.

Emry shot Arthur a nervous smile as the king drew near. Arthur gave her an encouraging nod, even though he wished she'd worn anything else. The neckline of her dress was far too low for his liking, and then there was the way Gawain's maid had arranged her hair, over just the one shoulder, showing off the bare curve of her neck . . .

"You have been avoiding me," accused King Louis, stopping as he proceeded to his throne.

"Forgive me if it seemed that way, Your Majesty," said Arthur, with a brief bow. "I took ill over the weekend and convalesced at my cousin's house."

"I hope it was nothing serious," said the king.

"A touch of food poisoning," said Arthur. He could feel the king's eyes on Emry, and the man's curiosity. "Er, I don't believe you've met my apprentice court wizard."

Emry sank into a curtsey. "Enchantée," she murmured.

The king licked his lips, looking for all the world as though he had expected vegetables, but instead had been served cake. "So, this is the famous wizard Merlin," he said. "Forgive me, mademoiselle, you are not at all what I expected."

"I've heard that before, Your Majesty," said Emry. "I wanted to thank you for the assistance of your court wizard. Maître Flamel has helped me greatly with my matter of magic."

"Has he?" the king said, his eyes fixed on Emry's bodice. Arthur felt Excalibur pulse at his side, as though letting him know that it felt equally indignant. "Since you no longer require his services, perhaps you might enjoy watching a friendly game of tennis this afternoon?"

"That would be lovely, Your Majesty," Emry murmured.

"Who will you be playing?" Arthur asked.

The king smiled wide. "The Duke of Cornwall."

Arthur pushed open the door to his guest room at the castle and blinked in surprise. He'd expected the room to be empty, but it was quite the opposite. Lucan was in his shirtsleeves, his cravat untied, playing cards with Brannor and a French guard he didn't know. They had a bottle of wine and a bowl of nuts between them, and Brannor's boots were propped on the hearth.

"Am I interrupting?" Arthur asked sarcastically.

"Your Highness!" Lucan said, scrambling to his feet in horror. "We didn't know when to expect your return."

The French guard stood and bowed, then hastily dashed for the hallway before Arthur could get a good look at him.

"I sent word I was staying the weekend at Gawain's," Arthur said, "not the week."

"And without so much as a spare tunic." Lucan shuddered.

"Fortunately, Emry magicked some of Gawain's things to fit me," Arthur said.

Emry, who was still in the hall, scowled at him and shook her head.

"Er, where's Dakin?" Arthur asked.

"Disappeared again, has he?" Brannor sighed. "Thought he was with you."

"Definitely not." Arthur shuddered at the thought. "Well then, you'd better find him. Immediately. Both of you."

"Yes, Your Highness," Brannor said, sweeping the cards back into his pocket.

Once they'd left, Arthur sank down into a chair with a sigh. "You can stop lurking in the hallway now," he called.

"I really need an invisibility spell," Emry muttered, closing the door behind her and glancing around the room. "Oh. Um. This is cozy."

Arthur laughed. Truly, they'd stayed in nicer rooms at travelers' inns. The stone walls were painted with fading designs rather than hung with tapestries, there was a basin and chamber pot instead of an en suite bath, and the window was a slit narrow enough to fend off a siege of arrows.

It seemed the grandeur had been spent on public spaces, and on the king's personal apartments, and not on temporary guest rooms. Either that, or the king had done it on purpose, to see if Arthur would complain.

"Sorry for dragging you up here," said Arthur. "I just thought we should figure out what to do about the duke. And it was either here or the dungeons."

Emry waved a hand at the door. "Muffling spell," she said, kicking her feet up on the hearth as Brannor had done.

"Good thinking." Arthur joined her at the table, fiddling nervously with the bowl of nuts.

"I'm guessing it's bad news about the tennis match," she said.

"Not necessarily." A thoughtful expression crossed Arthur's face. "If the duke is smart, he'll try and lose the match. So I think we should help him win."

Emry grinned. "King Louis would hate that."

"It would certainly strain things between them," said Arthur.

"But that doesn't solve our problem with Maddoc," Emry pointed out.

"No, it doesn't." Arthur drummed his fingers on the table, thinking. And then he smirked. "I may have an idea."

Chapter 41

Arthur pushed through the men's tennis gallery until he was standing next to Maddoc. The boy wore a sour expression as he peered down at the court. His hair was slicked back with a little too much wax, which made him look like a petulant weasel.

"Looking forward to the match?" Arthur asked.

Maddoc sneered. "Like you care."

Arthur frowned, the picture of innocence. "Why wouldn't I? We're family."

"My father says you're a bastard." Maddoc waited eagerly for the blow to land, but Arthur merely shrugged.

"I'm sure he meant it in the modern sense, and not the biblical."

"He also says you prefer boys."

"I don't prefer anyone," Arthur returned. "But there's nothing wrong with being either of those things. My best friend is both, and he's the best man I know."

"He's probably only friends with you to get things. That's why people try to be friends with me." Maddoc sulked, leaning forward until his chin rested on his hands. "I hate it."

"What if your father sent you away to school?" Arthur suggested. "Maybe somewhere in Cameliard? You'd be the same as anyone else."

Maddoc straightened, eyes flashing. "I don't want to be the same as everyone else!" he returned. "Do you?"

"On my better days." Arthur leaned over the railing. "It's going to be a very exciting game. The king is skilled at tennis."

"So is my father."

"Then you should cheer when your father scores a point," said Arthur.

"Cheer?" Maddoc frowned.

"Don't you cheer when he wins at sword fighting?"

"He always wins at sword fighting. Except when we came to Camelot, and Sir Kay caught him on an off day."

"I believe a 'huzzah' is customary," said Arthur, with a studied shrug. "Look, they're about to begin."

Arthur had never watched a tennis match with such scrutiny. He felt he could barely breathe from nerves as the Duke of Cornwall swaggered onto the court, his sizable gut compressed into a tight white sporting jacket that strained at the seams and was too long in the arms. Borrowed, Arthur realized. The duke had not expected to be challenged in sport.

The king, in just his tunic and trousers, bounced on the balls of his feet in anticipation.

An attendant brought their ball on a golden tray, and the match began.

It was immediately clear that the duke wanted to show his skill. He grunted with each forceful swing of his racquet. Louis darted nimbly across the court to return his hits, but even Arthur could see that the duke was not going easy.

The first point seemed never-ending. And then the duke swung again, the ball hitting so high on the wall that it sailed over the top of the gallery.

"Out of bounds!" came the cry.

"Aghhh!" cried the duke, throwing down his racquet.

So that was how he intended to lose. By hitting out-of-bounds enough that the king won by default. Clever.

Arthur caught Emry's eye in the women's gallery, and she gave him a thumbs-up. He nodded in return. Their plan was on.

The duke continued to use brute force with every hit. He was sweating, and King Louis wasn't faring much better. The galleries watched with interest.

"Why isn't he winning?" Maddoc whined at Arthur's side.

"He's tiring the king out, of course," Arthur whispered conspiratorially. "It's a brilliant strategy."

"Oh." Maddoc thought about it. "I guess."

The duke swung his racquet again, and Arthur sensed Emry's magic build and release. The ball flew at the wall with alarming speed, dropping low at the last moment. It bounced at an angle and shot right at King Louis's face.

The ball connected with a sickening thwack. There was an audible crack as the king's nose broke, and a gush of blood. The duke dropped his racquet, wringing his hands.

And then, in the shocked silence, Maddoc loosed a loud and triumphant, "Huzzah!"

The entire court stared at him in horror.

"How dare you!" thundered the king. "Someone get them both out of my sight immediately!" He turned to his attendants, angrily barking orders.

Arthur suppressed a grin.

Guards stepped forward, seizing Maddoc roughly by the shoulders.

"What are you doing to me?" Maddoc complained. "Let go! Arthur! Help me!"

Arthur shrugged.

"Tu as applaudi pour la mauvaise chose," he said, pitching his voice so everyone could hear him.

"What does that mean?" Maddoc whined.

Arthur raised an eyebrow. "You never cheer the misfortune of the king."

Arthur leaned back against a balustrade in the front of the castle, watching with satisfaction as the duke and his son were packed off into a carriage, still protesting that this whole thing was an outrage. At his side, Emry lounged as well, her new cloak fastened around her shoulders, toying idly with her wand.

"I keep reliving that moment when Maddoc cheered," she said. "Truly a masterpiece."

Arthur grinned. "We make a good team."

"Huzzah," she agreed, and his shoulders shook with laughter.

The duke stomped around the carriage, making sure all his luggage was accounted for and properly secured. And then he spotted Arthur and went rigid with anger.

"You," the duke barked. "What are you doing here?"

"Taking a turn about the gardens with my apprentice court wizard," said Arthur, gesturing toward Emry.

Emry dropped into a mocking curtsey. "Did you enjoy your stay in France, Your Grace?" she asked prettily.

Arthur swallowed a laugh.

"I did not," the duke bit off. Anger radiated off him. "You don't fool me. You did this."

"Packed your luggage with insufficient straps?" Arthur frowned.

The duke went purple. "You magicked the ball," he accused Emry.

"Me?" She tilted her head to the side, as though she had been asked a difficult question. "From all the way in the ladies' balcony? I'm only an apprentice. I doubt I could manage an illusion from that distance, much less the real thing."

He jabbed a finger toward her. "I know you are far more powerful than you let on."

"That can be said of most women, Your Grace," Emry replied.

Arthur pressed back a grin.

The duke whirled on Arthur. "And you. You told my son to cheer," he hissed.

Arthur gave a studied shrug. "If you scored a point. Not if you blinded the King of France."

"Make no mistake, I will repay you for this," threatened the duke.

"What's it to be?" asked Arthur, sounding bored. "Poison in my wine again? It was so effective the last time, don't you think?"

The duke seethed. "You don't want to find out what happens to those who stand in my way."

"Your Highness," corrected Arthur. "I believe you meant to say, 'You don't want to find out what happens to those who stand in my way, Your Highness.' In fact, you have failed to address me properly for the entirety of this conversation. But you are family. So of course I will overlook it. You may thank me, for my generosity."

The duke's glare turned dark and terrifying. "Then I thank you, Your Highness," he said through clenched teeth.

"I wonder," Emry mused, "if magic can turn a poison harmless, it must also be able to turn a harmless drink to poison. What do you think, Your Highness?"

"What a fascinating theory, wizard," Arthur replied. "Someone should test it." He turned back to his uncle. "I believe we're done here."

"We are," said the duke with an oily smile, climbing into the carriage. The driver gave a slap of the reins, and the carriage clattered toward the castle gates. The duke leaned out at the last moment and called, "I look forward to your wedding."

Chapter 42

Arthur bowed before King Louis in his throne room the next morning, and at his side, Prince Hugo did the same.

"My court seems to attract more foreign visitors by the day," said the king.

"I don't believe you've met my dear friend Prince Hugo, from Flanders," Arthur said smoothly. "A schoolmate of my younger cousin's. He has recently come to Paris to consider its great universities."

Hugo bowed, and King Louis examined him. Gawain had done a good job, Arthur thought. The boy's pale blond hair was combed back, and he wore a well-cut velvet coat with gold buttons. There was color in his cheeks, and a family ring glinted on his hand. His boots were new, their gold buckles shining in the candlelight.

"The Flemish royal family is large," said the king. "You are which son? The second?"

"The fourth, Your Majesty. After me is Pietr, but he's only three."

"And what is it you have come here to study?"

Hugo gave a beautiful smile. "Music, of course. I'm told I have some skill composing arrangements."

"Hugo . . . your name is familiar. It will come to me . . ."

The chancellor leaned forward and whispered something.

"Ah, that's right. You're the sickly one."

Hugo gave a very theatrical grimace. "Is that what's being said? Good lord, it was pneumonia, nothing more. I was riding through the blue forest and got caught in a downpour. But my mother overreacted. She lost her sister to it, you know." Hugo paused, the perfect actor.

"When Prince Arthur told me your daughter's betrothal had fallen through, I thought I might present my suit."

"Your suit?"

"For Princess Anne's hand in marriage, when she comes of age. I hear she is very beautiful, and we both share a great love of horses." He gave that magical smile again. "If you were agreeable, I know my father would be. My older brothers are, of course, already promised. And my father has been so preoccupied finding matches for my sisters that he's quite forgotten about me. I doubt he even remembered to send word I would be in Paris, so I might be received at court."

The king looked to his chancellor, who shook his head.

"He did not," said King Louis.

"Then it is good I have taken some initiative," Hugo went on. "We do share a border, so beyond the duchy of Brabant, there is no greater alliance I could make to help strengthen my family's kingdom. You are, I believe, unhappy with the new duke's Catholic leanings, considering the religious unrest here in France. Or, have you moved your men away from the border?"

"They are still there," said Louis. "As they have been for years."

"My father worries he'll soon have to dispatch men to do the same," said Hugo. "He says there is no need for our people to declare alliance to anything other than their kingdom and king."

"Quite right he is," said Louis. He frowned. "You're aware my daughter is but seven."

"And I am seventeen," Hugo said, "and in no hurry to be married. My parents are fifteen years apart, and the difference suits them. There are eight of us, you know."

King Louis smiled at Hugo's implication. "I will consider it, under one condition," he said. "You will play tennis with me tomorrow."

"I would be honored," said Hugo. "Although I must warn you, I am still a little winded from my pneumonia, and fear I will not be much of an athletic opponent."

The king grinned. "What a pity."

He moved on, and Hugo turned back to Arthur, giving him a big thumbs-up.

Arthur unbuckled Excalibur and placed it in the chamber pot, to the utter shock of the king's guards, who had not been expecting him.

"Please inform His Majesty that I would like to join him for lunch," Arthur said, his expression daring the men to disagree.

They exchanged a look and disappeared into the king's chambers.

Arthur waited, trying to smooth his nerves.

When the men returned, they didn't look pleased. "Entrez," one of them ground out.

"Merci," Arthur said serenely, pushing past.

"You have some nerve," growled the king. His nose was still broken, and he sported two black eyes from it, which did him no favors.

"I did leave Excalibur in your chamber pot," Arthur replied with a brief bow. "I saw no other opportunity to speak with you alone, and there are matters I wished to discuss privately."

"Then speak, by all means," said King Louis.

Arthur glanced around. The long table held only the one chair. "A moment," he apologized, spotting a small chair in the corner, by the door to the rest of the king's apartments, no doubt meant to be occupied by a guard. He dragged it over and set it at the table across from King Louis.

"The Duke of Cornwall slipped poison in my wine at a sword-fighting contest," said Arthur. "He is not a man who likes to lose. Nor does he easily forgive those who have embarrassed him."

"So I've learned," said King Louis, taking a sip of wine. "And I believe I've learned something else."

"Which is?"

"You came here hoping for an alliance," said the king with a shrewd expression.

"I did," Arthur agreed. "But I don't ask for your kingdom's resources. It's peace I'm after, not war. I hope that a formal friendship between our kingdoms will be enough to dissuade men such as the Duke of Cornwall from any future actions."

King Louis nodded, regarding Arthur sharply. "Does this proposal come from Camelot's king, or merely its prince?"

"I—" Arthur winced. "My father will be agreeable to whatever I negotiate."

"I remember the months right before my father died," said King Louis thoughtfully. "We all knew it was coming, and I found myself carrying more responsibility than I wished, as a man of four and twenty."

"Did you, Your Majesty?" said Arthur blandly, giving nothing away.

"I said such things then as you do now." King Louis's expression grew even more shrewd. "As to an alliance, unfortunately, it is out of the question."

"Ah." Arthur drew in a shaky breath. He hadn't truly thought it would work.

"However," Louis went on, "I will certainly think twice before allying myself with any who intend to move against you."

Arthur couldn't believe it. "You will?" he said.

"There is nothing my kingdom will gain from getting pulled into a battle with wizards and magic swords and doorways to other worlds," said the king. "We have enough problems on our own continent, with those who are pledged to one church, and those who prefer another."

"I understand," said Arthur. "I'm sorry to have taken so much of your time."

"It was most amusing," said the king. "I did not think you would last so long in the company of my half brother."

"You should keep an eye on him," Arthur warned. "He stirs trouble for mere amusement."

"And you should be wary of your uncle. He has aspirations far beyond his lands, and he will stop at nothing to attain them."

Arthur clenched his jaw. "I'm aware."

The king offered Arthur a small smile. "When do you leave?"

"As soon as I can make the arrangements," said Arthur.

"Then allow me to lend you a carriage for the return journey."

Arthur was about to protest that it wasn't necessary. But then he stopped himself. This wasn't a moment to be the boy who had let King Louis mock him so thoroughly upon his arrival. King Louis's overture of friendship was a valuable gift indeed.

He rose from his chair and bowed. "Thank you, Your Majesty. That would be most appreciated."

"We wouldn't want you to miss your wedding," he said pointedly.

"No, we wouldn't," Arthur agreed, smothering a sigh.

Chapter 43

"I hear you're leaving, girl," said Flamel when Emry pushed open the door of his lab.

Emry nodded. "Prince Arthur sees no reason to remain here any longer, now that my magic is under control."

"A shame," Flamel ground out. "It was useful having an apprentice."

"He enjoyed bossing you around," said the gargoyle. "And complaining about you after you left."

Emry pressed back a smile. "I am very annoying," she agreed. "Most wizards are."

Flamel glowered. And then a thoughtful expression came over his face. "I shall send you off with a present," he declared. "The gargoyle will go to England with you."

"That's quite all right," Emry hedged.

The gargoyle gave an indignant squawk. "You can't just send me to England!"

"Oh yes I can," said Flamel, grinning. "Unless, of course, you'd rather I kill you?"

"Er, about that," said the gargoyle. "I've changed my mind. I believe Camelot will suit me nicely."

"Excellent. I'll have you packed into a crate this afternoon," Flamel said, looking incredibly pleased with himself.

"I wish I'd never come to say goodbye," Emry muttered.

"But you did," called the gargoyle. "And now you're stuck with me."

○ ○ ○

Emry's heart felt heavy as she stepped inside Pernelle's apothecary.

"May I help you?" Jereth asked glumly from behind the counter. He wore a leather apron over his tunic, and a miserable expression. Spread out in front of him were a mess of mathematical scrolls.

Nicolas sat at his feet, smudging paint over his clothing and a sheet of parchment with his fingers.

"Emmyyyy!" he cried.

Emry gave him a small smile. "I'm looking for Pernelle."

"She's in the back. Oh, and tell her I've sold the last of the arrowroot."

Emry pushed aside the curtain.

"What now, Jereth?" Pernelle snapped, and then she looked up from her glass alembic, placing her goggles on top of her head. "Oh! Never mind."

"Jereth's helping you with the shop?" Emry asked.

Pernelle shrugged. "I could use someone in the front. He actually isn't bad with accounts and ledgers."

"He says he's sold the last of the arrowroot."

Pernelle's eyes lit up. "Wonderful. It was starting to go limp."

"What are you working on back here?" Emry asked.

"Oh, nothing," Pernelle said guiltily.

She had her husband's formula for the prima materia in front of her, and had made several corrections in red ink.

"He thought he was working the materials at the wrong temperature," Emry offered.

"He most certainly was," said Pernelle. "He needs a coal fire, not a burner."

"If there's anyone who can figure out the elixir of life, it's you," Emry said admiringly.

Pernelle grinned. "That's probably true, but I might let my husband believe the idea is his, so he doesn't get into a mood."

Emry laughed.

"I'll bring the correct equipment to the lab tomorrow," Pernelle promised. "We'll need your help regulating the pressure."

Emry winced. "I can't. I'm headed back to Camelot. I only came to say goodbye."

"I wondered when that was going to happen." Pernelle gave Emry a sad smile. "I'm going to miss you."

"And I'm going to miss you," Emry said, throwing her arms around the woman.

"But I suppose I can't hold it against you, leaving to be with your prince." Pernelle flashed a wicked grin.

"He's not my prince," Emry protested.

"Of course he is. It's only that the two of you are so clever that you can't see what's right in front of you."

Chapter 44

Emry watched Arthur stand at the prow of their ship as they sailed across the channel. He looked different. Like a man who knew how to give orders. Like a king who expected them to be obeyed.

Something in him had changed while they were away, and Emry realized that something within her had changed, too. And it wasn't what she'd thought.

She was no longer afraid of embracing her power, and her ambitions, despite Master Ambrosius's warnings. And she no longer minded that some saw her as a lady, while others viewed her merely as a castle apprentice. She didn't fit the idea of what anyone thought she should be, and that wasn't necessarily a bad thing. She'd been carving out her own path her entire life—now she just had to dig a little deeper, and a little wider.

Arthur flashed her a wide smile, motioning for her to stand at his side. His hair whipped around his face, and when she joined him at the rail, she felt the spray of salt and sea moisten her cheeks.

Belowdecks, Dakin and Brannor were playing cards, and Lucan was hanging over the side of the boat, looking ill.

Next to him, in their pile of luggage, the gargoyle was very helpfully telling him to breathe deeply and imagine a happy green blob, and Lucan looked as if he wanted to strangle it.

Everything had changed, and yet nothing was different.

"It's going to feel strange, being back," said Emry.

"You're not the one who's getting married." Arthur sighed.

"No, but I do owe Lionel Griflet a walk through the gardens, so both of us have equally grim things to look forward to."

Arthur laughed. His hair ruffled in the wind, and Emry could barely resist the urge to run her fingers through it.

They stared out for a while at the water, and the empty horizon.

"I can't believe that worked," Emry said. "Flamel. Prince Hugo. All of it."

"I know," Arthur said, his dark eyes serious. "For a while, I wasn't sure I'd be able to keep pretending."

"Pretending?"

"To be the man I need to be in order to helm a kingdom that isn't quite ready to change."

"Are you still pretending?" Emry asked.

Arthur gave her a small smile. "Always," he said. "I'll always be that boy in the library."

"You haven't been that boy for a long time," Emry told him.

Over the past few months, he had grown into a future king. Perhaps not a king like his father or Louis or Yurien, but a man of quiet authority and good intentions.

"I feel as though I sail to my doom," Arthur confessed.

"You still have a choice," Emry pressed. "Guinevere's reputation isn't your responsibility."

"I made a promise," Arthur insisted. "I won't see her ruined. The price of her mistake shouldn't be her kingdom's safety."

"It shouldn't be your happiness, either," Emry said gently, wishing Arthur would realize that.

"There's no version of a royal marriage that could ever make me happy," Arthur said.

He gave her a long look, and she bit her lip, turning away. He placed his hand over hers, and they stayed like that for a long time, staring out across the channel, together.

◐ ◐ ◐

Arthur sighed when the dark silhouette of Castle Camelot came into view. It didn't feel real that he was returning home, with his wedding less than a week away.

Beside him, Emry beamed. "Coffee," she said happily. "And a hot bath, and my own bed."

"And your turn about the gardens with Master Griflet," Arthur pointed out.

Emry stuck her tongue out at him. "Be nice, or I'll give you the gargoyle as a wedding present," she threatened.

Arthur went pale. He'd had enough of the thing after the first afternoon with it trussed to the roof of their carriage.

"I can hear you," the gargoyle called. "Is that your castle up ahead? It's rather small."

Arthur sighed, and Emry stifled a giggle.

"Perhaps the King of France meant to give the thing to your father, as a gesture of friendship?" she suggested, raising her voice.

"You wouldn't dare," the gargoyle called back.

"Oh yes we would," said Arthur, "so you had better behave yourself." He shot Emry a wink, and she rolled her eyes.

"Make way!" Brannor called. "For His Royal Highness Arthur Pendragon, crown prince of Camelot."

"And a fearsome gargoyle," called the gargoyle.

Emry let out a laugh, but Arthur sat up straighter on his saddle, tugging the wrinkles from his jacket.

"Let me," Emry said, flapping a hand in his direction.

"Thank you, laundry wizard," he replied.

As the trumpets sounded their fanfare, Arthur took a deep breath and tried to roll the tension from his shoulders.

The king burst through the castle doors, followed by his attendants. The inner courtyard began to fill, and Arthur noticed that all the younger court ladies had abandoned their tight bodices in favor of loose, flowing dresses with trailing sleeves.

"This is all you," Emry said, cutting her horse toward the stables.

Arthur watched her go, wishing he could follow. And then he pasted on his most princely grin and slid from his horse.

"Father," he said with a bow. "You look well."

"As do you," said the king. "Go, greet your fiancée. We shall speak later."

Arthur looked through the crowd for Guinevere. He spotted her standing far too close to that loathsome Merlin lad. She was wearing one of those voluminous dresses that seemed to be the current fashion, and she was twisting her hands nervously.

"Princess," Arthur said, favoring her with a short bow.

"Your Highness," she murmured, and then dropped her voice to the barest whisper. "We have much to discuss."

Arthur frowned. "Is everything all right?" he asked.

"Perfectly," Guin said. "I'll be waiting in the library."

"I'll join you when I can," Arthur promised.

"That was a clever bit of diplomacy," said Lord Agravaine, pacing the length of the rug in his study, "with the young prince of Flanders."

"I'm glad you think so," said Arthur.

He had spent the past half hour getting the king's advisor up to speed on all the important matters that had transpired in France.

"It sounds as if you did well," said Lord Agravaine. "As did Miss Merlin."

Arthur bowed his head at the praise. "I'll let her know. And what of my father? How fares his health?"

"He has given up wine, at the urgent behest of the royal physician, and is much improved."

"That's wonderful," Arthur said with relief. He hadn't realized how nervous he'd been about his father's health, until his chest had clenched with fear at what Lord Agravaine would say.

"The wedding will be a great celebration," the advisor went on. "And an important showing of the unity between Camelot and Cameliard."

"Yes, of course," Arthur said blandly.

Lord Agravaine regarded him carefully. "Your princess strays, but I believe you already know that."

"I do," said Arthur.

"Good. Because youthful indiscretion is no reason to abandon such an important union." Lord Agravaine offered a shrewd smile. "Your father wishes to speak with you."

"Then I will go to him directly," Arthur promised, stepping from Lord Agravaine's study with considerable relief.

Guinevere's secret hadn't been found out. That's what was important.

His father's guards stood aside with a crisp bow, and Arthur took a moment to brush some invisible lint from his jacket as he tried to summon his nerves.

"Get in here, already," his father called. "You're dawdling."

He was dawdling, but he didn't wish to admit it. "I believed I had lost a button," Arthur said, stepping into the warm, wood-paneled room. An enormous fire blazed in the grate, and Arthur immediately felt his armpits go damp.

"How is King Louis?" asked Uther.

"As you would imagine," Arthur said noncommittally. "I have filled in Lord Agravaine on the entire journey. You may hear the particulars from him, if you wish."

"Unimportant," grunted the king.

"I will say, King Louis was very grateful that I saved his life."

King Uther looked taken aback. "You did?"

"While hunting," said Arthur. "But it was Merlin who made sure the Duke of Cornwall broke King Louis's nose."

King Uther choked. "The duke was there?"

"And his son," said Arthur. "Not to worry, we took care of it. Princess Anne is now engaged to Cousin Jereth's boyfriend. I believe you'll find the King of Flanders to be most grateful, should you ever need to call on him. And the French court has gifted us a talking gargoyle."

"You speak nonsense," King Uther complained, reaching for a golden goblet on his desk, which was filled to the brim. He drank greedily, as if the wine were merely water.

"Father," Arthur said in warning, and then realized too late what he had done.

"It's grape juice," said the king, wiping his mouth with the back of his hand. "I wondered at your presumptions. And then Bruwin confessed that he had told you, and all made sense."

Arthur winced, hating that he had been betrayed by that farce of a royal physician, of all people.

"You thought me to be feeble. Infirm," the king went on. "An old fool with one foot in the grave."

"No," Arthur said, horrified. "I—"

The king advanced on Arthur, jabbing a finger into his chest. "Take heed, boy, I am not."

"I never." Arthur scrambled for words, shaking his head. "I never . . ."

"I hope you enjoyed your freedom, because that ends now. You will stay away from that meddling Merlin girl. You will marry Princess Guinevere and ensure that she produces an heir. Immediately."

"Of course, Father," Arthur murmured.

"I am having Bruwin send a virility tonic to your chambers daily. He has instructions to watch you drink it."

"That isn't necessary," Arthur protested, trying not to think what vile nonsense the court physician might put in such a concoction.

"Oh, it very much is," King Uther warned. "Step one foot out of line before Guinevere is your bride, and I'll give instructions for Bruwin to watch on your wedding night and make certain you carry out my orders. Now leave."

Chapter 45

Arthur burst from his father's chambers, wondering if it was too late to return to Paris and stay there. And then he remembered he'd promised to meet Guinevere in the library. Great, just great. She was the last person he wanted to see right now.

When he pushed open the door, he was surprised to find Emmett there as well, leaning back in a chair and looking bored. Scratch that, *Emmett* was the last person he wished to see right now. Arthur's hands balled into fists, itching to swing a punch at that smug wizard.

"Well? What's so important?"

"We figured it out." Guinevere broke into a grin. "Actually, Emmett did."

"Figured what out?" Arthur asked.

"A plan that guarantees we won't have to go through with the wedding, and there will be no hard feelings between our kingdoms."

That was the last thing Arthur had been expecting. He blinked at her in disbelief. "I'm listening," he said, taking a seat.

Across the table, Guin looked over at that insufferable wizard and blushed. And then Emmett took her hand.

"We can't be married if I'm already married to someone else," said Guin.

"But you're not," Arthur said.

"We will be." Emmett broke into a wide grin. "If you give us your blessing, we'll elope."

Elope. Arthur nearly choked at the thought. But the idea wasn't half bad. "When?" he asked.

"The day before the wedding," said Guin. "I can pretend to take to my room with nerves and ask not to be disturbed."

"We'd go to Brocelande," Emmett put in. "The priest has known me my entire life, and he won't hesitate to perform the ceremony. Plus, he won't ask questions. And there would be witnesses."

"We'd be back the next day," Guin said. "It's a foolproof plan."

"It does have its merits," Arthur said, thinking it over. "It's just, I'm sorry—the two of you truly wish to be married? In haste? To each other?"

Arthur couldn't quite wrap his head around it. Guin blushed, looking down at her lap. Emmett put a hand on her shoulder. She smiled at the wizard, her real smile, not the perfect one she so often wore at court.

"We do," Guin said.

"Very much," said Emmett.

Ah, Arthur thought, looking back and forth between them. How had he missed it? They were so obviously in love.

"The plan can go back to what it was," Guin went on, "with just a few alterations. I'll refuse your hand in marriage on the grounds of already being married to another. You'll act as if this is happy news and insist that naturally a peace treaty should exist between our kingdoms, since I've married a member of your court."

"I'm only an apprentice," Emmett protested.

"Still counts," said Guin, lifting her chin. "Isn't that right?"

"It is," Arthur said. She looked so fierce that Arthur didn't dare to contradict her.

Emmett nodded slightly, in thanks.

"This might actually work," Arthur murmured. "But what about, er . . ."

He gestured uselessly in Guinevere's direction.

"The baby?" Guin said, resting her hand on her stomach. "Emmett had the most wonderful idea."

"Did he?" Arthur arched an eyebrow at the young wizard. "Very well, wizard, let's hear it."

Emmett fidgeted. "Well, er, you know how time moves more slowly on Avalon?" he said. "I thought, after the wedding, Guin and I should spend some time there, and make things seem a bit less of a scandal."

"That is clever," Arthur said approvingly. With the way time was distorted on Avalon, if they spent three weeks on the island, it would be three months everywhere else. Their secret wedding would be a scandal, but their child wouldn't be.

"The Lady of the Lake did say that I should heed the passage of time in all of its variations," Emmett admitted. "And that she might be able to help. I didn't know what she was talking about at the time, but this has to be it."

Arthur nodded, his mind made up. "Then you have my approval. And my blessing."

"Thank you," Emmett said quietly. He looked at Guin again, his face lit with joy. "I can't believe it."

"Last chance to back out," she told him, her expression teasing.

"Never," Emmett said fiercely. "You're stuck with me, Princess." He raised her hand to his lips, and Guin blushed.

Arthur watched the two of them, feeling overwhelmed. He had been so furious with Emmett and Guinevere when he'd thought things between them were only casual. But seeing them like this, and seeing how deeply they felt for each other, his anger dissipated. He slumped down in his chair, his mind spinning to make sense of this surprising change in circumstance.

He'd really thought he was going to have to marry Guin and raise her baby as his own. He'd assumed it would be expected of him, and now that it wasn't, he was shocked by his good fortune.

"I'd tell the two of you to get a room," Arthur said, "but I believe you already have adjoining ones."

Guinevere turned pink.

"We do," Emmett admitted.

Guinevere beamed at him. "Although, we were hopeless long before we found that passage," she said, and then she turned to Arthur. "It was noble of you to agree to marry me, so I wouldn't be ruined. But I'm going to marry for love and live my life on my own terms. And I only hope you'll do the same."

"Fall in love?" Arthur asked.

Guin shook her head. "Know what to do about it."

Arthur knocked on Lance's door, impatient to share the news of Guinevere and Emmett's impending elopement. But there was no answer. Which was strange, since, from the sound of things, Lance was definitely inside.

"I know you're in there," Arthur called, pushing open the door.

His cheeks went red. "Sorry!"

Lance fumbled to pull up his trousers. Percival, who had no trousers in sight, reached for a pillow, holding it strategically.

"Welcome back, Your Highness," said Percival, looking panicked.

"For god's sake, don't even think of bowing," said Arthur. "You'll injure yourself."

"Thank you, Your Highness," Percival said tightly.

"I'll see you at supper," Arthur said, pausing in the doorway. "Both of you, I assume."

"Yep." Lance said.

"Well, carry on," Arthur said, biting back a smile.

"Meet us in the dungeons after supper," called Lance. "We have something to show you."

◖ ◖ ◖

Arthur's bootsteps echoed through the stone stairwell as he made his way to the dungeons. Dimly, he could hear voices. Lots of voices.

What on earth was going on?

Tristan stood guard at the door, and tipped him a wink, before banging his halberd against the floor.

The voices stopped.

"You can go on through," Tristan said, as though Arthur was a guest at a party.

Arthur's brows knit together in confusion, but he ducked through the low-hanging doorway, into a large candlelit chamber. A dozen familiar faces stared back at him, standing in two even lines, like the guard did at training. At the front stood Lance and Percival, swords at their waist, and practice padding over their tunics.

"What's this?" Arthur asked with a frown.

"These are your knights," said Lance. He gestured toward the torture device that took up half the space. "Of the round table."

"The name needs work," said Percival.

"Actually, it has a nice ring to it," said Arthur. He frowned. "Why are my knights in the dungeon? And why are half of them members of the castle guard?"

Emmett stepped forward, and Arthur's eyebrows rose in surprise to see the young wizard was part of this. "We've assembled a group of men who wish to defend Camelot from attack," Emmett explained, "despite assurances that such preparations are unnecessary."

"We?" Arthur asked. "Just whose idea was this?"

"It was mine and Tristan's," said Emmett. "I roped in Lance, and spoke with some friends, and, well, this is the group."

Lance cleared his throat. "Knights," he prompted.

"Hail, Prince Arthur," said the knights, in unison, raising their fists to their hearts. "We pledge our blades and our lives in defense of Camelot."

Arthur stared at them, overwhelmed. It wasn't just members of the castle guard. There was also a surprising handful of nobles, including the vexing Lionel Griflet and his younger brother. And Sir Dinadin's bumbling squire.

For so long, Arthur had felt he was alone in protecting Camelot, but he'd been wrong. He had overlooked many potential allies right here in this castle.

"I accept your pledge," said Arthur, drawing Excalibur from his sheath, "and I dub you all Knights of the Round Table for your courage, honor, and devotion to this kingdom."

"We should have a toast," called Lionel.

"We should have a training session first," retorted Percival.

"I agree with Perce," said Lance. "Train now and earn your drink."

"Yes, sir," called the group, strapping on padding and removing a stash of swords from behind the torture wheel.

Arthur shrugged off his jacket and began to roll up his sleeves.

"What are you doing?" Lance asked.

Arthur grinned. "Earning my drink?"

An hour later, Arthur lowered his blade, his forehead damp with sweat. The others looked equally exhausted. Lance and Perce had pushed them hard, and Arthur was impressed by how eagerly they had taken the corrections and applied themselves to the training.

"I believe it's time for that toast," said Lionel.

And then Arthur heard footsteps on the stairs.

"Quiet," Lance warned, raising a hand for silence.

"Er, halt!" Tristan said, scrambling back to his guard post. "Who goes there? The dungeons are off-limits."

"Don't be ridiculous," a girl's voice said. Emry pushed past him and folded her arms across her chest, taking in the scene. "What the hell? Why is everyone in the dungeons without me?"

"Emry!" Arthur said, at the same moment as Lionel bowed and said, "Miss Merlin."

"Someone better tell me what's going on, or I'm giving all of you a third nostril," she threatened, pulling her wand from her sleeve. "I can't promise it will be on your face."

A couple of the lads paled.

"Have your drinks," Arthur said, reaching for his jacket. "I've got this."

Arthur motioned for Emry to follow him, and they walked farther into the dungeons. She shivered, and he didn't think it was from the cold.

"I hate it down here," she muttered under her breath, staring uneasily at the empty prisoners' cells.

"Don't tell me the great and powerful Merlin is afraid of a basement?" Arthur teased.

"It's a perfectly valid trauma response," she snapped. "And no, I'm not afraid. Certainly not of a secret boys' clubhouse where my brother and Lionel Griflet drink wine in sweaty tunics."

Arthur snorted.

"It's not a boys' clubhouse," he said happily. "The Lady of the Lake was right. By going to France, I found allies. Only they were right here, in this castle." He explained about the Knights of the Round Table, and Emry grinned.

"Nimue really does speak in riddles," she said. "Also, hold on, my *brother* is responsible for this?"

"In large part, it seems. I may have misjudged his character."

"Believe me, you haven't," Emry said. "He does this sometimes. Redeems himself. It's very annoying."

Arthur laughed. "It really is. Speaking of your brother, there's something I need to tell you."

"Oh god." Emry made a face. "What has he done now?"

"Something else surprising," said Arthur. "He's asked Guinevere to elope."

Emry's eyes went wide with shock. "He has?"

"And she's said yes," Arthur went on, unable to hold back his grin. "So I believe we shall be turning each other down after all—"

"—since you can't marry someone who's already married," Emry finished.

"Exactly," Arthur said as Emry threw her arms around him.

"I don't know who I'm happier for," she said. "The two of them for finding love, or you for being spared a marriage without it."

They pulled apart, and Arthur flashed his best grin. "Probably me," he said. "You like me best."

"You'll never prove it."

Arthur leaned forward, until his lips were inches from hers. "You sure about that, wizard?"

Something invisible shot past them and cracked into the wall at the end of the corridor, and they sprang apart.

"Emmett!" Emry warned.

"Oh, sorry, I didn't realize anyone was here. In the dark. Alone," her brother replied, tapping his wand against his palm in what he clearly meant as a threat.

"I hear congratulations are in order," Emry said.

Emmett looked smug. "In more ways than one."

Arthur shook his head and sighed.

"You are *such* an arse," Emry complained. "Also, what on earth was that spell?"

Emmett shrugged. "Combat."

"Are you serious? Master Ambrosius taught you how to fight?"

"Course not. I found it in a library book," said Emmett, shuddering at the memory.

"That's right," Arthur put in blandly, "I keep forgetting you know how to read."

Emmett shot him a glare.

But Emry pulled out her wand, her eyes bright with excitement. "Don't just stand there," she snapped. "Show me."

Chapter 46

"Go again," said Sir Kay. "And *try* not to couch your weapon until your horse is up to speed."

"It feels wrong to adjust my grip mid-charge." Lance reached for the hollow-tipped practice weapon that Sir Kay clumsily handed up to him, since his right arm was still bound tightly in a sling.

"That's why most knights don't do it," Sir Kay explained. "But you'll have better aim if you wait until you're closer to your target."

Lance thought about this. "Makes sense."

Sir Kay shook his head. "I can't believe I'm teaching you all of my secrets."

"You won't regret it," Lance promised.

The previous afternoon, Lance had taken Sir Kay to the wizard's workshop in hopes that Emry might be able to help speed along his recovery. She'd said nothing as she'd examined the old injury, then had spoken with Master Ambrosius in a low voice before returning, her expression grim.

"I don't know how to half heal something that's already started to mend," she'd said. "And I don't want to make it worse."

Lance had worried that Sir Kay would lose his temper over the disappointment, but he'd been remarkably accepting. It was almost like the knight was relieved to have an excuse to take it easy, something he would never admit.

Not that *Lance* was taking it easy. Sir Kay had him on the training field every morning at dawn, and he couldn't remember the last time he'd worked so hard or learned so much. Even the other squires asked him questions at supper, eager for anything they might learn second-hand.

Lance pressed back a grin as he rode onto the tilting field. Even though his every instinct warned otherwise, he waited until the destrier had reached full speed before tucking in his elbow and bracing the lance. His eyes narrowed, and his heart pounded as he approached the practice dummy.

He stood in his stirrups, aiming the weapon, until *crash!* The tip splintered neatly against the dummy's breastplate.

It had worked! He let out a whoop, wheeling his horse around.

"Better!" called Sir Kay. "Now do it again."

Lance went again, and again, until he was dripping with sweat, and so exhausted that his arm trembled when he reached for his weapon. But now he hit the target every time.

"One last adjustment, before you wash up for supper," said Sir Kay. "This time, you're to hit the target blindfolded."

Lance stared at him in disbelief. "Blindfolded?"

"Afraid you'll miss, squire?" the knight asked coolly.

"Hardly," Lance protested, even though everything in him was screaming that the task was impossible. He had to ask, "Why blind-folded?"

The knight grinned. "To make certain you'll keep your focus no matter what happens," he said. "What if your visor tilts on your ap-proach and you can't see? What if dust blows into your eyes? A good knight can aim true without seeing his target."

"Next thing you'll want is for me to try it with a moving target," Lance grumbled half-heartedly.

"Sir Dinadin's squire will be joining us tomorrow. Do try not to permanently injure the lad."

Lance couldn't tell if the knight was joking. But he knew better than to ask. *Poor Dryan*, he thought, although learning how to take a hit was nearly as useful as learning how to give one.

Sir Kay patted his pockets and sighed. "I could have sworn I brought a blindfold."

"Does that mean I don't have to do it?" Lance asked hopefully.

Sir Kay shot him a look. "Remove your sock, squire."

"You can't be serious," Lance protested. "I've been training all day!"

"I have something you can use," called a familiar voice.

Percival sprinted across the tilting field, his short crimson cape rippling in the wind. In the golden glow of early evening, the guard seemed even more handsome than Lance had thought possible.

"Watching me train, were you?" Lance asked, teasing.

Perce shrugged, almost bashful. "I was headed to change out with Tristan at the guard tower and saw you jousting. You're very good."

"He's improving," Sir Kay allowed. "But it's a long road from squire to tournament champion."

Lance went pink at the praise.

Percival unwound a gray woolen scarf he'd tucked down the neck of his guard's uniform. "Will this work for a blindfold?"

Sir Kay nodded. "It will suit."

Perce offered it to Lance.

"Are you giving me a favor to wear?" A corner of Lance's mouth hitched up in a grin.

Perce bit his lip. "I guess I am."

Lance reached for the scarf. It smelled of Percival. Of sharp steel and pine needles, and something softer, almost like cinnamon.

He tied the scarf around his eyes, and somehow, he wasn't nervous anymore. Not about hitting his impossible target, or disappointing Sir Kay, or struggling to find a balance between everything he wanted for his future.

"I'll need a lance," he said, holding out his hand.

"Percival, is it?" asked Sir Kay. "Make yourself useful, then, if you're going to stand here mooning at my squire."

"Yes, sir!" Percival sang out.

Lance grinned.

"That's what I've got so far," Emry said modestly, bringing her hands together, the purple flames vanishing.

Master Ambrosius stared at her in shock. "But how are you controlling it?" he asked. "You didn't use a wand, or speak the spells aloud."

"It's not spells, it's runes." She beamed, pleased. "I'm just glad it wasn't leeches. Or snake venom. Or hypnotism."

"Why on earth would it be hypnotism?" Emmett asked.

"You know, I asked Maître Flamel the same question, and he didn't have an answer," said Emry. "At least now I'm not a magical menace."

"You definitely still are," said Emmett. "Right, Master Ambrosius?"

"You're both impossible in your own ways," said the old wizard, shaking his head. "Now run along, boy, and fetch me these herbs from the garden."

He held out a slip of parchment, and Emmett sighed. "Just me?" he asked.

"I wish to have a word with your sister."

Emry felt her chest clench. This didn't bode well.

After Emmett had gone, Master Ambrosius went to stand in front of the hearth, staring into the flames.

"Anwen's magic. For months, you've had the kind of power that some have given their lives searching for." He shook his head. "And I frightened you into silence."

Emry bit her lip. "I'm sorry. I should have told you."

"Actually." The old wizard held up a hand. "You were right to keep this from me."

"I was?" Emry didn't think she'd heard him correctly. She'd been expecting to be scolded for keeping secrets. Not—whatever this was.

"I don't believe I would have been much help to you. In fact, I may have been quite the opposite."

"You mean you would have told King Uther," said Emry.

"Perhaps," he said honestly. "There are prejudices about Anwen's magic, and I'm not sure I could have gotten past mine."

"Because of Morgana, Nimue, and Bellicent," Emry said.

"I am an old man," said Master Ambrosius, with a sad smile. "In my time, I have seen the world embrace many things that it shunned in my youth. But that is no excuse to be set in one's beliefs when the evidence in front of you disproves them."

"Maître Flamel was nervous, too, at first," Emry said. "It was only after the gargoyle assured him the magic was harmless, and I wasn't under the influence of the High Sorceress of Anwen, that he got over his own fear."

"Forgive me," Master Ambrosius frowned. "It seemed like you were saying Maître Flamel has a talking gargoyle?"

"No, he doesn't—" Emry said.

"Well, that's a relief," said the old wizard.

"Because he gave it to me."

Emry removed her cloak from the table, and Master Ambrosius stared at the creature, his mouth hanging open.

"Good lord, you're old for a human," the gargoyle said, peering back at him. "You're not about to die, are you? It sounds very depressing to watch, so I would appreciate some advance warning."

Master Ambrosius gave Emry an accusing look.

"You, er, get used to it?" she said.

◐ ◐ ◐

"You should have told me!" Emry scolded, pushing past Guin into the princess's sitting room.

"I couldn't," Guin insisted. "You would have been so angry with me. And you would have told your brother."

"Probably," Emry said with a sigh.

"And you're one of the few friends I have in this castle," Guin said. "I didn't want to ruin it." She offered a tentative smile.

"Now we're going to be sisters," Emry said, shaking her head in disbelief. "I can't believe you actually want to marry my brother."

"Why not? He's wonderful," Guin said dreamily. "The things he loves about me have nothing to do with my title or my position. He's not intimidated by me. And as a woman with power, that's no small thing."

Emry hated that Guin had a point. "It really isn't," she agreed.

"Sometimes it's lonely, being a princess." Guin trailed off with a sigh. "I felt like the only person in the world who would truly understand me was another royal. But it turns out, all it took was a wizard."

Emry shifted uncomfortably, reminded of the time she'd had a similar thought about herself and Arthur.

"You should have seen him when he found out about the baby." Guin beamed. "I thought he'd run. But he was so excited."

"He's always wanted to be a father," Emry said. "To get everything right that ours got wrong." She handed Guinevere the bundle she'd been carrying—her old purple cloak. "You should take this. For getting past the guards unnoticed when you leave. They'll just assume you're me."

"Thank you," Guin said, wrapping it around her shoulders with a giggle. "I hadn't even thought about that." She raised the hood. "How do I look?"

"Like a Merlin." Emry grinned.

Guin dove forward and embraced her.

"I'll cover for you as much as I can," Emry promised. "And I'll send word to my friend Marion, at the theater in Brocelande. She'll help if you need anything." Emry bit her lip. "Maybe I should go with you."

"We'll be fine," Guin promised. "Besides, I'm sure Arthur needs you here."

"Now that he's reunited with Lance?"

Guin giggled. "The two of them are ridiculous. Did you see Arthur at supper? He nearly took a seat at the squires' table."

"He did spend a long time hovering."

"I didn't realize you were paying such close attention."

"I wasn't!" Emry protested. "I was . . . spying on Lance and Percival."

"My mistake," Guin said, with a private grin.

Chapter 47

Morgana shivered as she stepped into the cave.

Not from the cold, or the fear of what might be waiting for her. She shivered from all the magic. She could taste it on her tongue and feel its icy press from all sides.

There might be more magic in this cave than there was in the whole of England. And yet she couldn't have any of it. The frustration dug at her, scraping at old scars to reveal the tender wounds beneath.

"Hurry up," Bellicent snapped.

Against her will, Morgana's legs quickened their pace. There was no turning back now. Not that she could, if she even knew how.

She wasn't fool enough to sacrifice herself for a world that had forsaken her, so she followed Bellicent deeper into the cave, and deeper into the magic. She could see it in the air like dust motes, like snow, and her heart raced with every breath.

Finally, they came to a rough-hewn cavern made of pure white stone. And there, laid on a block of stone, was a woman's body. Her hair was silver-white, her skin a rich brown, her eyes closed as if in sleep.

"Free me, as you promised," Bellicent demanded.

"How?" Morgana asked.

"Your blood can break these runes. You must paint over them, to remove their power."

Morgana knew this trick. She had played the very same one on Merlin's daughter. And she would not be fooled by it.

She glanced around, and that was when she noticed the second body in the cave. Willyt Merlin lay on the ground, his chin nearly touching his chest. He hadn't aged a day since Morgana had last seen him. His dark brown hair hung in his face, and his pointed beard was just as out of fashion now as it had been when she had called him her mentor.

He was even wearing the same blue cloak embroidered with celestial symbols that Morgana remembered was his favorite, though it looked a bit shabby and worn.

Which meant that he had either caused this curse or gotten caught in it shortly after he'd arrived. And based on the anger Bellicent had displayed when she'd mentioned Merlin, she suspected he was responsible.

"Could we not use his blood? His power?" Morgana asked, gesturing toward Merlin. "If the whom is of no matter."

Bellicent's borrowed body grinned. "You think you're clever," she said. "But you forget one thing."

"What?"

I control you.

Morgana struggled as Bellicent took over her body, as she felt herself pushed down, made smaller, forced further away.

Bellicent's borrowed form held out her knife, and though she tried not to, Morgana's hand took it. She sliced her own palm, letting the blood drip.

No! she tried to scream. *I don't want this!*

It doesn't matter what you want, only what you promised, Bellicent crooned inside her head.

Morgana watched, a prisoner in her own body, as her hands and her blood painted over the runes that held together the curse. Her magic, so long out of reach, rose to the surface. Before she could savor the sensation, or reclaim it, the magic bled out of her, sucked away by the stones.

She felt the binding runes unravel. It was as if the entire world was coming unstuck, strings that held it in place snapping, limbs stretching. The ice began to melt, running in rivulets down the sides of the snowy cave.

And then, to Morgana's horror, Bellicent's body—her true body— twitched.

Chapter 48

Perhaps she wasn't coming.

Emmett craned his neck, trying to see past the carts and stalls. It was just after dawn, and he stood impatiently outside the coaching inn near Blackfriars where they'd planned to meet.

Sard, he was nervous. He didn't think he'd ever been so nervous. It wasn't every day you ran away to marry a princess.

A wizard and a royal. It sounded ridiculous, like something out of his gran's stories.

"Were ye wantin' cushions, or just the seats?" the coachman asked.

"Cushions as well," Emmett confirmed, plucking the coins from his pouch.

"Wagon leaves in ten minutes," the coachman warned. "And no refunds."

"Got it," Emmett said tersely.

He watched an elderly woman clutching a chicken board the wagon, the next few minutes crawling by in an agony. And then he caught sight of a girl in a familiar hooded cloak hurrying toward the inn.

His stomach sank. He'd know that purple cloak anywhere.

"Emry?" he called. "What happened?"

She reached up to lower her hood. It wasn't Emry. Guinevere beamed at him. "I had to get past the gate guards somehow," she said. "Your sister lent me her cloak."

"Clever," Emmett said. "Are you sure about this?"

"Definitely." Guinevere regarded the covered wooden wagon and horses with fascination.

"I've never been on a wagon before," she said.

"I'm sorry it isn't a carriage," said Emmett.

"Don't be," said Guin, squeezing his hand. "Help me up?"

Emmett climbed aboard and extended a hand.

The woman with a chicken on her lap watched them with a smile. "Such a lovely couple," she said, beaming at them. The chicken clucked loudly.

"Thank you. And that's such a lovely, er, chicken," Guinevere replied.

The wagon deposited Emmett and Guinevere outside the Prancing Stag just after midday.

Guinevere glanced around the lively market square and picturesque town, taking in the sights. It was charming, like something out of a storybook, and not nearly as dirty and crowded as London.

A group of young children ran past them, playing with a wooden hoop, and laughing gleefully. The girls wore pigtails tied with ribbons, and the boys had wooden play swords belted to their waists. Guin smiled, watching them run shouting up a steep lane.

Emmett stopped at a few places in the market to buy bread and honey and cheese, and Guin hung back shyly, watching as he chatted easily with the merchants. They all knew him by name, Guin noticed, as if he were a noble. And Emmett met them with his grin and quick laugh, asking after their families, or complimenting their wares.

"It's a small town," he said apologetically, tucking the loaf of fresh bread into his bag. "Everyone knows each other."

"They definitely seem to know you," Guin said.

"It's because of my father," Emmett said.

"The only reason anyone knows me is because of my father as well," Guin said, taking his arm.

Emmett laughed. "Then you know the feeling."

At the top of a hill stood a brick manor house, six windows wide and two stories tall, and crowned with at least a dozen chimneys.

"Is that it?" Guinevere asked.

"Is what it?" Emmett frowned.

"Your home," Guin said, gesturing toward the manor.

Emmett's cheeks burned. "Er, no. That's the Earl of Brocelande's manor," he said. "My home's, well . . . not so much as that."

Emmett led her through the market and past the merchants' shops. As they walked along a dirt road flanked either side by primordial oaks, he pointed out a low wooden fence. "Here's where our land begins," he said shyly.

Guin peered at the flocks of sheep and neat rows of vegetables and one-room cottages in fascination. After a short walk, they reached a stone wall covered in ivy, with an iron gate that had been painted a cheerful cornflower blue.

Beyond the gate sat the sweetest cottage she had ever seen, with a thatched roof and two tall brick chimneys on either side. The cottage was two stories tall and made of half-timbering, with cream-colored walls and flowerpots in the windows. A stone well sat in the front yard, surrounded by sprays of wildflowers and neat rows of flourishing herbs. Past the house was a forest, deep and green and closely packed, with trees that looked as though they hadn't been disturbed for centuries. A wooden swing hung from the nearest one, warped and cracked with disuse.

It was the most tranquil place Guin had been in a long time.

"This is home," Emmett said anxiously.

"It's wonderful," Guin said.

"Don't worry," Emmett said, pausing at the gate. "My gran is going to love you."

Guin's eyes went wide. Somehow, she'd forgotten that part. But too late.

Emmett steered her toward the front door, beaming.

A small, thin old woman opened the door. Her long white hair was wrapped around her head in a braid, and her face was very lined, and she wore a bright purple shawl across her shoulders as regally as any queen. "Your father stood there with the exact same expression, nineteen years ago," Gran said, chuckling. "Lucky for you, it isn't twins."

"How do you know?" Guin asked curiously.

Gran winked. "Tea leaves."

"All done," Marion said, giving Guin's hair one last pat into place. "Do you want to take a look?"

Guin nodded, keeping her eyes closed as Marion steered her over to the mirror.

They were backstage in the Brocelande theater, and Guin had never felt more excited. For the first time in her life, she wasn't being attended to by maids because she was a princess. She was having her hair and makeup done by a friend, as a bride.

"Okay," Marion said.

Guin opened her eyes. Her hair was swept back into an elaborate braid pinned full of wildflowers, her eyelids shimmered with pearlescent pigment, and her lips shone with fresh salve.

"It's wonderful," she said enthusiastically.

And then she stared down at her dress with a sigh. She hadn't had time to pack anything. And even if she had, she wouldn't have wanted to raise suspicions. She supposed it wouldn't be so bad wearing the loose burgundy gown she'd worn in the wagon. But still.

"There's one last thing," Marion said, her eyes sparkling with mischief. "I had to guess at your measurements, but I stayed up half the night working on it."

Marion reached over to the costume rack and pulled out a cream-colored gown with a flowing overskirt. The sleeves were woven with green ribbons, and delicate leaves were embroidered at the neckline.

Guin's eyes filled with tears at the sight of it.

"I know it's a bit worn and out of fashion, but we had it from when the troupe did *The Faerie King*," Marion said. "So I thought—"

Guin threw her arms around the other girl. "It's beautiful."

Chapter 49

"Do you know something about this?" demanded Lord Agravaine, bursting unannounced into Arthur's apartments.

Arthur looked up from his book to find the king's advisor glowering at him. He was certain he had guards at his door for precisely this reason. "Brannor," he called, annoyed.

"He said he'd dismiss me if I didn't stand aside," said the old guard.

"It's fine," Arthur said wearily. He gestured for Lord Agravaine to take a seat, but the man shook his head, remaining standing.

"Well? Answer me," demanded the king's advisor.

Arthur thought quickly. "Did you honestly burst in here just because Gawain asked my court wizard to be his wedding date?"

"He did what?" Lord Agravaine looked taken aback. "No. Of course not."

"Well?" said Arthur, smoothing the wrinkles from his jacket. "Then, what is the problem?"

"Princess Guinevere is missing."

"Really?" He frowned, trying very hard to look as though he knew nothing about it. "Is she not in her chambers?"

"Her maid said the princess was gone when she came in this morning, and some of her toiletries were missing," explained Lord Agravaine.

"Her toiletries?" Arthur raised an eyebrow. "She probably gave them away to a courtier. You know how Guin is—she's already given away half her wardrobe." Arthur shrugged. "If nothing of import is missing except the princess herself, I'm sure she'll turn up in no time."

Lord Agravaine shot him a sharp, probing look. "I sense a scheme, Your Highness."

"If there is one, it's nothing to do with me," Arthur insisted. "You may confirm with Bruwin that I have been dutifully consuming his vile tonics."

Lord Agravaine studied him with narrowed eyes, attempting to parse out the truth. Finally, the advisor sighed. "Your wedding guests are starting to arrive," he said. "Guinevere is expected at the feast this evening. If she doesn't turn up by then, we'll proceed with the alternate arrangement for tomorrow's ceremony."

Arthur frowned. "The alternate arrangement?"

"A royal marriage can take place by proxy. We will simply find another girl to stand in her place and accept on her behalf."

Arthur felt a chill run up his spine. He hadn't known such a thing was possible. "Surely that isn't necessary," he protested.

"Your father's instructions were explicit," said Lord Agravaine. "You are to be married. Legally, neither your presence nor your consent is required. The ceremony is for show. The true contract is signed between your father and the King of Cameliard."

Arthur's chest filled with panic at the thought. If something went wrong and Emmett couldn't find a priest who would marry them . . .

Or worse, if Guin decided she couldn't go through with marrying that obnoxious wizard after all . . .

Or if Emmett balked at the responsibility and backed out . . .

He had been so certain that this plan would work, but now, all he could see were the flaws, and all the ways it might still fail. Guin had to get back in time. If she didn't, they would find themselves married to each other, whether they wished it or not.

"I have every faith Guinevere will turn up," Arthur said, his throat dry.

"Unfortunately, I do not," said Lord Agravaine. "So we shall see which of us is right."

"Are you sure these aren't too loose?" Arthur asked, grimacing at the fit of his trousers. They sagged in the crotch and ballooned out until the knee, and hung curiously low on the hips. He felt ridiculous.

"Not at all, Your Highness," said Lucan, holding out the matching jacket, which featured mutton sleeves. "The royal tailor assured me this is the height of current court fashion."

"I'm sure it is." Arthur pressed back a sigh.

Somehow, clever Guinevere had convinced all of Castle Camelot to dress in flowing, oversize clothing. Not that he could blame her. But still. He hadn't expected the trend to extend to men's fashions as well.

"If Your Highness would prefer—" Lucan began.

"One of the slim-cut brocade suits will do nicely," Arthur said in relief, unfastening the diabolically baggy trousers.

Wedding guests had been arriving all afternoon, and even though the ceremony wasn't to take place until tomorrow evening, Arthur's nerves were in knots. He'd been so confident that he and Guinevere could pull off their scheme, but now he wasn't so sure.

Every time he stepped into the hall, he was assaulted by the smell of floral garlands, or bowed to by some manservant he had never seen before. The castle staff seemed to have tripled, along with the number of courtiers.

And he hated it.

He hated that he was going to have to go out there and pretend—and that, in the end, it might all turn out to be real. He'd foolishly believed he had a choice in this—that he wasn't entirely at his father's mercy. He'd thought that if he tried hard enough, and was clever enough, he could regain control over his future.

But now he wasn't so sure. Tents had already been erected on the lawn, the mews were overflowing with carriages, and Arthur was fairly certain that they were actually selling commemorative mugs in the markets.

He dressed quickly in one of the suits he had worn at French court, and had Lucan fetch his best circlet, and tried to settle his nerves as he made his way to the Great Hall, Excalibur pulsing at his side.

The feast that night was meant to be lavish, and to give all the newly arrived guests an eyeful of King Uther's court before the wedding. Still, his father had definitely gone overboard with the additional staff. At least a dozen attendants Arthur passed in the hall were in old, ill-fitting livery that looked as if it had been dragged out of storage without pressing.

"There you are, cousin," Gawain said, catching up with him outside the Great Hall. "Still trying to serve a cutting-edge look?"

Arthur hated how, somehow, his cousin managed to make a nearly identical suit look twice as good.

"More like avoiding the current court fashions," Arthur said.

"Hideous," Gawain pronounced. "You'd think half the girls at court were secretly with child. Or perhaps just the ones who dictate fashion."

Arthur's eyes went wide, and Gawain lifted a brow.

"Let me guess, keep my voice down?" he surmised. "Who's gone and sarded your fiancée? Because I know it wasn't you."

Arthur pulled him into a corner. "Does your father know?"

"I don't believe so," said Gawain. "And he certainly won't learn of it from me."

"Thank you," Arthur said with feeling.

"My congratulations on your upcoming wedding," a rail-thin ginger-haired man called, his cane tapping against the stone floor as he approached.

"Lord Griflet," said Arthur, pasting on a grin. "How have you been?"

"Tolerably well," said the viscount. "Now, what do you know about this girl my son has his eye on? Not of noble birth I'm told, but of particular royal favor?"

Arthur choked.

"I wish to inspect her," the viscount went on. "I believe she is called Miss Merlin?"

"You must be mistaken," said Gawain, cutting in. "You speak of my wedding date."

"Your date, Lord Gawain?" the viscount frowned.

"Perhaps date is the wrong word," Gawain mused, "as we have spent this past month together in France."

The viscount turned red and mumbled his excuses. Arthur pressed back a grin as the man hastened away.

"That was fun," said Gawain.

"Careful," Arthur warned. "Or you'll cause a scandal."

"You mean prevent King Uther from arranging their marriage?" Gawain said lightly. "A worthy scandal indeed."

Arthur hated that he didn't disagree. "I suppose we should head inside," he said. "Could you, er . . . ?"

"Come with you, to deflect well-wishers?" Gawain finished. He sighed. "If I must."

They stepped inside, and Arthur wished he could turn back around. Everyone's eyes were on him, and everyone's whispers were about the lack of Princess Guinevere at his side.

"There you are, Your Highness," said an oily voice.

Arthur turned to find the Duke of Cornwall approaching them.

"I do so look forward to tomorrow," said the duke. "Now, where is your ravishing bride?"

"Taken ill with a headache, I'm afraid," said Arthur.

"And your little witch couldn't cure it?"

"You take quite an interest in my court wizard, uncle."

"As do you," said the duke.

Arthur bristled at the accusation.

"How is Maddoc taking the news of Princess Anne's engagement?" Gawain asked, joining their conversation. The duke paled.

Arthur had never been so grateful for his cousin's presence. "Do you not know?" he pressed with a grin. "Just days after you left French court, King Louis accepted a proposal from one of the young Flemish princes."

The duke turned red and hastened away.

"Finally," Arthur said with a sigh. "A moment to breathe."

"I believe I have done my part," said Gawain, abandoning him to the crush of well-wishers.

"Your Highness," said Prince Gottegrim, signaling for his attention. Arthur bowed, his heart hammering nervously as he faced Guinevere's older brother.

"Is my sister around? She's been scarce ever since we arrived, and it's not like her. The queen worries."

"Nerves and a headache," Arthur lied. "Nothing more."

"I shall pray for her swift recovery," said Prince Gott. "I should hate for her to miss her own wedding."

"You speak of marriage by proxy," said Arthur, surprised. "I've only just learned about it."

Prince Gottegrim sighed. "My father's threatened me with it for years. Every time I mention joining the clergy, he says he'll marry me off in my absence, and they'll have to turn me away before I can take my holy orders."

"Are all fathers difficult, or just the ones who are kings?" Arthur asked.

Prince Gott grimaced. "I wish I knew. Although, this alliance between our kingdoms is one I approve of. Marriage will suit my impulsive sister. As will motherhood."

Arthur choked, before realizing he was only speaking of their wedding night.

Oh god. Their wedding night. The thought of it made Arthur feel ill. "I'm sorry, you'll have to excuse me," he said, pushing away through the crowd. He hadn't realized how difficult it would be to play this part without Guinevere at his side. Everything felt like it was coming undone. All his plans unraveled with a single pull of the king's golden thread.

And the flimsy excuse of Guinevere's headache was only causing gossip. He could feel it circulating through the Great Hall, and it seemed to him even the staff were gossiping, the way they kept furtively scanning the crowd and whispering in corners.

Wonderful. What a time to be made to look a fool.

He stared glumly out at the crowd, with twice as many tables as usual squeezed into the space. He recognized the princesses of the Isles in matching pink dresses, and Cameliard's royal family, with Prince Gottegrim squirming under the princesses' attentions.

In the corner, a vielle player plucked a somber melody that would have no one in high spirits.

"A toast," King Uther said, holding his wineglass high. So much for grape juice, Arthur noticed, taking in the redness in his father's cheeks, and the glassy sheen in his eyes.

"To the happy union of Camelot and Cameliard," he said.

Arthur almost groaned at how impersonal his father's words were.

"And to the bride and groom," his father went on, "whose wedding will take place tomorrow."

It was the worst toast he had ever heard. Because it wasn't a toast, it was a threat.

His hand trembled as he raised his glass, and when his father's eyes met his in satisfaction, Arthur went hollow with defeat. He had tried so hard to make everything right, and yet his father insisted on orchestrating his misery at every turn. He excused himself in the middle of the meal and slipped into the corridor, letting the tension fall from his shoulders.

"You're leaving the feast?"

Arthur turned to find Dakin following him.

"I'm just going to the library," he said wearily. "You don't have to come. Tell everyone I'm around somewhere, would you?"

"Of course," Dakin said with a grin. "Have a good night."

"Er, you too," Arthur said, confused by the guard's good mood.

And then he hurried to the library before he could be stopped by anyone else.

Chapter 50

"Come on, you have to tell me where we're going," Arthur protested as Lance steered him out of the castle.

But Lance shook his head and refused, giving him an enormous grin. It seemed he meant to drag Arthur clear across London, too.

Of course Lance had known to look for him in the library. His friend had tossed him a shabby cloak, told him to put it on and get rid of his circlet.

And even though celebrating was the last thing Arthur felt like doing, he welcomed the distraction—whatever it was.

Finally, they reached the Crooked Spire. Arthur eyed the marble slab that sat in the narrow courtyard dividing the disreputable tavern from the gates of St. Paul's, trying to push away the memories. Both of pulling the sword from this stone, and of nearly dying in the caverns beneath.

"Well," Lance said, "have you guessed yet?"

He threw open the door to the tavern, and Arthur spotted Emry, Percival, Gawain, and Tristan sitting in one of the cozy booths in the back.

Arthur frowned. "What is this?"

"What else would it be?" Lance said. "It's your bachelor party!"

"Surprise!" Emry raised her mug of ale, toasting Arthur's arrival, and the others quickly did the same.

"How did you get invited to this, wizard?" Arthur grumbled as Emry slid him a mug of ale.

"It's a bachelor party," Emry explained.

"Right," Arthur said politely. "Er, same question."

"Oh my god, must I spell it out? It's a party for you and your unmarried friends."

"I don't think that's quite the definition," he said.

"Well, it should be," Emry insisted. "Besides, I wasn't going to stay behind at the castle and let you boys have all the fun."

"She threatened to give me a tail," Lance put in.

"I wouldn't have minded, really, if she did," Percival murmured, blushing into his drink.

"So we've changed our minds about the tail?" Emry said brightly.

Arthur spluttered into his ale.

"You do know this place is terrible, don't you?" Gawain asked, wrinkling his nose at the shabby tavern.

"That's why we like it," said Lance.

"It has character," Arthur insisted, gesturing toward the fat candles that had dripped puddles of wax onto their table.

And somehow, he realized, the tension had slid from his shoulders, and he was actually enjoying himself, and not worrying his way into a panic.

He sipped his ale and looked around the table at the collection of friends who had shown up for him. Funny how it kept growing.

If he was stuck marrying Guinevere tomorrow, at least he could spend tonight among the people he cared about the most.

"Drink up," Tristan insisted. "Because Lance said we have to get you absolutely wrecked before we escort you to Madame Becou's."

When the group finally stumbled into Madame Becou's, Emry was thinking that perhaps her place in this bachelor party was a tad awkward.

The moment they arrived at the brothel, twin blonde girls dressed as seductive shepherdesses, complete with beribboned staffs, dragged Arthur into a corner, despite his blushing protests.

Gawain disappeared upstairs with a ginger-haired girl in a copper gown. He came down a few minutes later, a sketchpad under one arm, to procure a bottle of wine and two goblets.

"Jealous, wizard?" he murmured.

"Hardly."

"I could grab a third goblet," he proposed, "but you'd have to pose for me."

"Not happening." Emry folded her arms across her chest. "I only agreed to be your wedding date so I wouldn't have to face Lionel, not because I actually care for you."

"A pity." Gawain leaned down and gave her a kiss on the cheek. "It wounds me that you're not jealous." He glanced over at Arthur. "If you were wondering, the prince certainly is."

"There's nothing for him to be jealous of," Emry protested.

"And yet, his heart tells him otherwise." Gawain lifted an empty wine goblet in salute.

Jealous indeed. Arthur was entirely preoccupied with the seductive shepherdesses, and anyway, it wasn't as if the wedding would go forward tomorrow. Lance had merely used it as an excuse for them all to go out together.

Emry spotted Tristan alone, watching the musicians, and she joined him at his table.

"Cards?" he asked hopefully.

"All right."

Tristan dealt, but Emry paid little attention, instead watching Lancelot and Percival tiptoe up the stairs, Lance's arm slung around Perce's shoulders in a way that wasn't just romantic, but necessary. Bless Percival, she'd never seen anyone so terrible at holding their drink. It was endearing.

"Guess you're the last of the guards standing," said Emry.

"Somehow, I always am." Tristan sighed and picked up another card, sliding it into his hand.

Finally, he revealed his cards, a pair of jacks.

Emry laid down her own hand, and Tristan's jaw fell open. "You changed them," he accused.

"Only the pictures, not the cards themselves," Emry said, laughing. "We are in a brothel."

"And I wish to see no one naked, certainly not the king!" Tristan shuddered, pushing her winnings across the table and dealing another hand.

"You're awfully melancholy tonight," said Madeline, coming over to pour Emry another glass of wine, and to take a sip of it herself. "This sadness of yours . . ."

"Yes?"

"I can make you forget, if you wish." The girl ran a finger across Emry's cheek, making pleasure bloom in her stomach.

The girl's soft skin felt wonderful to the touch, and she smelled of rosemary, a sharp woodsy aroma that reminded Emry of home.

Home. She hoped Emmett and Guinevere were all right.

"You may find me, if you choose to," Madeline said, sensing her distraction. She curtseyed and left.

Emry sighed. Arthur was still being mauled by the twin shepherdesses, whose ribbons had been used in ways that were anything but innocent.

"I think I might head back," said Tristan. "I'm on the gates at dawn."

"I'll come with you."

"Actually," Tristan said, "you should stay. Someone needs to save the prince."

"Save him?"

"From those girls who are trussing him up like a Christmas goose," said Tristan.

Emry laughed. And then she bid farewell to her friend. She smoothed her skirts, feigning interest in the music and sipping her drink until Madame Becou appeared at her side.

"The bathhouse is empty, if you would like," she suggested, handing Emry a stack of linen towels.

Emry offered her a smile. "Thanks," she said, glad for the escape.

The bathhouse was underground, an ancient Roman ruin. Steam rose from the dark water, curling toward the arched stone ceilings. The pool looked so inviting that before Emry knew it, she'd whispered a spell to unlace her dress and was pulling her linen shift over her head.

Oh, the pool was gloriously warm. She floated on her back, and stared up at the ceiling, hating that she was missing her brother's wedding, and regretting that she had agreed to celebrate Arthur's pretend marriage as one of the lads.

Sometimes, liking everyone, no matter their gender, was such an inconvenience. The boys acted as though they could say the crassest things, like she didn't count as a girl. And girls were shocked by small, insignificant differences that she hadn't even realized she had.

But what she'd felt for Kira was nothing like the way she felt about Arthur. That had been a giddy, silly crush, though at the time it had felt like so much more. She cared for the prince more than she wished to admit. More than she could stand, some days.

Emry closed her eyes, and tilted her head back under the water, wishing she could melt into it and disappear. She didn't hear the footsteps until it was too late.

"Aghhh!" she cried, splashing about.

"Sorry," Arthur said sheepishly. "Didn't realize anyone else was down here."

He was still trussed in ribbons, and Emry let out a snort. "You look like a maypole."

"I feel like one." He grimaced. "Could you untie me?"

Emry waved a hand, and the ribbons floated to his feet like confetti.

"Pity," he said with half a smile. "I was told that when you untie them, the pain turns to pleasure."

"Were you in pain, Your Highness?" Emry teased.

Arthur sighed. "More than you know."

He slid down to the ground, his back against one of the stone columns, and put his head in his hands. He looked so despairing that Emry wondered how much of a front he had been putting on for the evening.

Emry swam over to the side of the pool, propping her chin on the ledge. Something was weighing on him, and clearly it was important.

"Whatever it is, it's going to be okay," she said.

"No." Arthur's voice went hoarse. "It isn't."

"You're worried about them, too, aren't you?" Emry said softly. "In case they don't go through with it."

"What do you know about marriage by proxy?"

"I've never heard of it," said Emry. "Why?"

"My father had a backup plan, and I've learned of it too late." Arthur laughed bitterly. "It turns out neither of us needs to be present at our own wedding ceremony. It is merely a stage play, where anyone can accept on our behalf. The true union is a contract our fathers will sign."

"What?" Emry's eyes went wide. "That's absurd! So that means . . ." She trailed off, her mind spinning to make sense of it.

Arthur shook his head. "There's a very real chance I could wind up married to Guinevere tomorrow."

Emry's heart broke for him. "Oh, Arthur," she said.

"There's nowhere I can run, and nothing I can do to change it," he said. "I just have to sit here and wait. My future belongs to Camelot. It was never mine."

"If you can't change the future, then nothing you do tonight matters," she said boldly. "So, we should spend it together."

Arthur looked up at her questioningly. "Truly?" he asked. "Even knowing about Guinevere?"

She had resisted what was between them for too long, and now that it might really be over, all the reasons she'd given herself that had once seemed unmovable felt easily swept away. "Yes," Emry said. "I'm sick of letting circumstances come between us. If tonight is all we have, then I don't want to waste it."

"Neither do I." Arthur stared at her, his hair hanging in his face, a tentative smile rising to his lips. "Are you wearing anything?"

"No," Emry said stiffly.

"Then I shall dress to match. Turn around, wizard."

"Oh my god," she complained, "I have seen you naked before."

"Ancient history," Arthur promised. "I'm far more attractive now. I don't want you to faint at the sight of my bare chest."

Emry had never realized how noisy it was to listen to a boy undress.

"Sorry," he said, after a particularly loud grunt, and a sideways scuffle in which it sounded as though he might have been defeated by his own trousers. "I fear I'm not entirely sober."

"It's your bachelor party," she said. "Sober definitely isn't the point."

"And if it wasn't for you and Lance and the guys, I'd have spent it reading," Arthur concluded with a splash.

Emry turned around, and there he was, waist deep in the fragrant, steaming waters. He was right, the sight of his bare torso really was phenomenal. As was the promise of the rest of him.

"Sard, this feels good," he said, wringing some tension from his neck. "I can almost forget that . . ." He trailed off with a sigh.

"Tomorrow there's a very real chance you might have to walk down the aisle and marry an archery target dressed as a bride?" Emry finished.

Arthur bit back a laugh. "A practice dummy from the weapons room," he suggested.

"A suit of armor wearing a wig," Emry returned.

"Just a horse. Like, everyone's pretending it isn't, but it's literally just a horse," Arthur said, wiping tears of laughter from his eyes.

They were both laughing uncontrollably. And then, suddenly, they weren't. Because there was nothing funny about the situation.

"The truth is, I don't care about tomorrow," Arthur said. "I care about what comes after. About the rest of my life. And I hate that I can't choose any of it."

"Your father chose his bride. He could have at least allowed you the same courtesy."

Arthur didn't say anything for a moment. The steam curled around them, and the rest of the world dropped away, until it was just them, just these dark waters and this cave, and the way they were drawn to each other, even when everything tried to push them away.

"If it was up to me, and there was nothing to keep us apart, I would choose you, every day, for a lifetime," Arthur admitted, his warm brown eyes intent.

"So would I," said Emry.

Arthur leaned forward until his lips were inches from hers. There were beads of water in his eyelashes, and his dark hair hung in his eyes, and when his mouth found hers, for a rare moment, everything was perfect.

Chapter 51

Guinevere sat at a table at the Prancing Stag with a wilting garland of flowers in her hair. She was exhausted from all the dancing and the well-wishes, but happier than she'd ever been. She couldn't remember the last time she'd laughed as hard as she did when the boys from the theater troupe had flung handfuls of sparkling powder into the air as they ran down the church steps.

"It's special effects," Emmett had leaned close to whisper, as the air glittered and shimmered around them.

There had been toasts, so many that she'd lost count. Toasts that had made her laugh, and toasts that had made her blush, and none of them were to a union between kingdoms, or a valuable political alliance.

Now Guin sat contentedly with Marion at her side, watching as Emmett and his friends played some convoluted drinking game where they had to drink and then flip their mugs of ale. Shouts of encouragement went up while the boys played, and somehow, Emmett came out victorious in every round.

"He's cheating, by the way," Marion whispered.

Guin shrugged. "If he's clever enough not to get caught, then I don't mind in the slightest."

Marion laughed. "I like you, even if you are a princess," she said with a grin. "Do princesses play darts?"

"What's darts?" Guin asked.

"A game where you throw miniature arrows at a target." She motioned toward the far wall of the tavern.

"They're so cute and little," Guin cooed. "Yes, I absolutely need you to teach me this game."

Marion and Guin were on their second round of darts when the door to the tavern opened, and patrons started exclaiming, "It's raining!"

"Raining?" Guin said in despair. She looked to Emmett, who seemed equally horrified.

He pulled aside the publican, who shook his head, his expression grim.

"Well?" Guin said when he returned.

"The roads will be mud within the hour. No coachman will risk it before morning."

"Morning?" Guin paled. "Will we make it back in time?"

Emmett chewed his lip. "I don't know."

Emry woke in an unfamiliar bed, with someone's arms wrapped around her. No, not someone's.

Arthur's.

Her heart pounded in distress as the previous night came back to her in excruciating detail.

I would choose you, every day, for a lifetime.

So would I.

Did you just admit that you love me, wizard?

Only if you did, Your Highness.

She had tried so hard to deny her feelings, to keep them in, to get rid of them. And now that she had confessed the truth, she didn't know what to do.

It only made things worse that Arthur felt the same. That she had never been a second choice to him, but a first choice he knew he could never make for himself.

Last night could have been so many things. But somehow, Emry suspected it had been goodbye.

A magnificent, heartbreaking goodbye.

She rolled over carefully, staring at her sleeping prince. His brow was creased with worry, and his eyelashes fanned across his cheeks, and all she wanted to do was hold him close, and press her lips to his once again, and pretend away the world.

· Except she couldn't. Because it was the day of the royal wedding, and the groom was asleep in her bed, and the secretly pregnant bride was either married to her brother, or about to be married to Arthur without her knowledge or consent. If her heart hurt less, she might laugh at the absurdity. Instead, a tear trickled down her cheek. She wiped it away, swallowing thickly.

She had to get out of here.

Arthur couldn't see her crying. Not over him. Not over the future they were never meant to have, and the love she had tried so hard to ignore.

Quietly, she crept from the bed and down to the cool cavern of the bathhouse. The stone arches reminded her of the dungeons back at Castle Camelot, and the last time Arthur had held her in his arms, not out of heartbreak, but out of joy.

"*αόρατος πέτρα*," she commanded, feeling the weight of the invisible stone in her palm. She hurled it at the wall.

It was the spell Emmett had taught her, and it felt surprisingly good to throw something. Even an invisible something. She did it again and again, blinking back tears, until her arm was shaking, and her breath was coming in gasps. Miserably, she sank to her knees in the bathhouse, feeling hollow.

She was an apprentice court wizard at Castle Camelot. It was everything she had worked for, and everything she had dreamed of back home in her small town. Yet, somehow, it wasn't enough.

◗ ◗ ◗

Arthur woke with a groan, momentarily unsure where he was. His head was pounding, and his mouth tasted terrible. The light streaming through the window was too bright, and the noise from the city too loud.

He sat up in alarm, realizing he'd spent the night at Madame Becou's. Next to him, the bed was empty, though a strand of dark hair lay across the pillow.

Perhaps she hadn't really left, he thought hopefully. Perhaps she had gone down to the kitchens, or whatever passed for kitchens in this place, and would return any minute. He'd pretend to be asleep, he decided, so she could nudge him awake with a kiss. They would drink coffee or, more likely, tea in bed, in a glorious state of undress.

He sat up, stretching. And then he saw that her clothes were gone, and her cloak, too. Ah. So there would be no mug of coffee, no bare shoulder for him to kiss, no morning together.

It was just a fantasy, and an impossible one. It didn't matter that he had a glowing sword, or she a magic wand. This wasn't a world in which they could choose each other. No matter how desperately he wished otherwise.

In the distance, church bells rang, signaling the hour, and Arthur's eyes widened in surprise. Nine o'clock.

He hadn't realized it was so late.

And—sard—it was his wedding day. The cold shock of it washed over him as he remembered his father's alternate arrangements. If he didn't get back soon, no doubt Lord Agravaine would find someone else to walk down the aisle in his place. Or maybe just another horse.

He tugged on his boots, pressing back a pounding headache, and tore through the city. It was already decorated for the festivities, with garlands and ribbons. Everyone was smiling, and dressed in bright colors beneath their cloaks, anticipating the ringing church bells, the toasts and dancing in the squares, the celebration of their prince marrying a worthy princess.

He wondered idly if there would still be such a celebration if they knew both parties were unwilling.

A market had sprung up outside the castle gates, selling beer and meat pies and commemorative souvenirs. Arthur stopped and bought a meat pie, hoping the warm, flaky pastry might alleviate his pounding headache. But the man waved away his proffered coin.

"After all, it is your wedding day," he said.

Arthur choked on his pie. "I think you've made a mistake."

The baker laughed. "I know who comes and goes from the castle. Been out here thrice a week for these past six years."

Arthur finished his pie and thanked the baker, hating that he wasn't quite as anonymous as he'd thought.

Tristan was at the gate, and he grinned as he saw Arthur arrive. "Made it back in one piece, then?" he asked, raising his visor with a wink. "Emry returned hours ago."

"She let me sleep," Arthur said, running a hand through his disheveled hair.

"I hope that's not all she let you do," said Tristan, his cheeks coloring red.

Arthur chose to ignore that. "Has anyone else returned?"

Tristan looked theatrically back and forth, even though he was the only guard at the gate.

"You mean Guinevere?" he whispered. "Sorry, Morian's supposed to be here as well, but he's abandoned me again. I swear Dakin's dared him to do it."

"How do you know about—" Arthur began.

"I was the one who let her through in Emry's cloak," Tristan said. "About twenty minutes after Emmett, who looked like he was about to throw up from nerves. Kind of the way you look now." Tristan made a face. "Sorry, am I rambling?"

"A little bit," Arthur said exhaustedly. "Just—keep an eye out, would you? And send word when she arrives."

"Will do," promised the young guard.

"She'll get here," Arthur said, half to himself, as he made his way through the crowded castle. "She has to."

The corridors were a confusion of guests and staff, and there seemed to be some commotion outside the royal wing.

"Let me pass," Arthur protested, as two manservants stood frozen in place, blocking the corridor and gaping at him as if they had never seen royalty before.

Finally, Arthur spotted Brannor, whose expression was grim. "What's going on?" he demanded.

"Oh, thank goodness," Brannor said, with considerable relief. He stuck his head into Arthur's apartments as he proclaimed, "His Highness is unharmed."

"Of course I'm unharmed." Arthur rolled his eyes. "Lance took me out for a bachelor party. He even brought along guards. I didn't mean to stay the night at the brothel, but you know how things go." Arthur gave his guard a sheepish grin. "Now stand aside, I'm desperate for a bath."

"I can't," Brannor said, looking panicked. "You can't—"

Arthur pushed past him, and wished he hadn't.

Lord Agravaine was in his bedchamber, and so was Master Ambrosius. And so was the dead body of the court physician.

Arthur stared down at Bruwin's body. It was bloated and pale, his lips and fingernails black. "What happened?"

"A snakebite, Your Highness," said Lord Agravaine. "Your valet found him this morning."

"Lucan is recovering from the shock in my infirmary," said Master Ambrosius. "He sustained a mild concussion when he fainted."

"Sounds like Luc," Arthur said. He frowned. "I don't understand, who would kill the court physician?"

"I believe they were aiming for a different target, Your Highness," Lord Agravaine said.

"Of course they were," Arthur said, hating that he hadn't put it together sooner. No doubt Bruwin had come to his room the way he had every night for a week, to administer that hateful virility tonic. Except Arthur hadn't been in his room. And a gruesome death meant for him had found the hapless physician instead.

"Did you recover the snake?" Arthur asked. "So we might determine its origins? And perhaps how it found its way into my rooms?"

"I did," said Master Ambrosius. "It is an asp viper, a species not native to England."

"No, it's native to France," Arthur said wryly. "The Duke of Cornwall will be beside himself to learn that he has failed to poison me once again." He crossed to the window and looked out at the commotion of everyone setting up for the royal wedding. "Is there a reason Bruwin's body is still in my apartments?" he asked mildly.

Lord Agravaine sighed. "We did not wish to raise alarm by moving him through the hallways."

"Then use the tunnels." Arthur pushed a tapestry aside and clicked a piece of the paneling. It swung back to reveal a dark passage. "They run the length of the castle from here. Surely a few trusted guards can manage."

Lord Agravaine stared. "I was not aware the tunnels extended to your apartments."

"I'd appreciate if you forgot that they do," Arthur said meaningfully.

Lord Agravaine nodded. "I'll have some guards handle this immediately."

"In the meantime, can someone revive my valet?" Arthur asked. "I guess I have a wedding to attend."

Chapter 52

In a world frozen between one breath and the next, in a cave filled with magic, Bellicent slowly sat up and looked around. The sorceress examined her wrists, her legs, the silvery ends of her hair, all with an expression of ecstasy.

Morgana watched with growing dread. A nagging sensation pulled at her, whispering that she had made a terrible mistake and done exactly what she shouldn't. Suddenly, she realized why the sorceress looked familiar. "I *know* you," she said.

"You know my sister," replied Bellicent.

"The Lady of the Lake." No wonder Avalon and its magic had always drawn her attention.

"Is that what Nimue is calling herself these days? How quaint." Bellicent stepped elegantly from the cool slab, snapping her fingers. A soft, ivory, fur-lined cloak appeared around her shoulders, far finer than the matted, rough-stitched cloak Morgana was wearing.

She stared at it in admiration, hoping the sorceress would transform her garments as well.

"Let's go," Bellicent said instead, as if commanding a servant.

"Go where?"

"You'll open a doorway, and we'll go to your world."

"That wasn't our bargain," Morgana protested.

Bellicent's lips curved into a smile. "Oh yes it was. You promised to set me free. Awake is not enough. I desire to be free of this cursed world."

Morgana winced, hating that what Bellicent asked was beyond her magic. She had hoped the sorceress would be able to open the doorway once she'd regained her body. But she saw now that if Bellicent could, she would have done so long ago. She drew a ragged breath, her heart pounding as she admitted, "I wasn't the one who opened the doorway. I merely stepped through."

"So you lied to me!" Bellicent snarled.

"And you lied to me! I agreed to your protection, not your control!"

"They are the same," Bellicent crooned. "How better to protect someone than to control what they do, and see, and think?"

Morgana hated that Bellicent wasn't wrong. Sometimes, lies were a kindness, and the truth did more harm than any deception. "I know how we can get back to my world, but I must go with you."

Bellicent searched her face, as if trying to find any hint of a trick, and Morgana barely dared to breathe.

"Agreed," the sorceress finally said. "But how?"

"He can do it," Morgana said quickly, pointing at Merlin's still sleeping form. "His daughter let me into your world, trying to rescue him."

"So, there are sorceresses worth their magic on Earth," said Bellicent. Morgana seethed at the insult as the sorceress scowled. "But it will never work. He would rather die than help me reach your world. He's made that quite clear."

Morgana smiled. "But he would help me. His sweet former student, who came here to rescue him and got stranded doing such a noble deed."

Bellicent's laughter rang through the cave. "Is that so?"

"He'll open a doorway for us. I'll make sure of it."

"You'd better," Bellicent snapped. "And when he does, you may return to your world—so long as I come with you. Agreed?"

"Agreed," Morgana said, relieved.

"You are of no use to me if you fail," warned the sorceress. "I will not help you survive this place should the wizard leave you behind, or not have the power you promise."

Morgana swallowed nervously. She did not want to die here, in this frozen world. She would have to convince Merlin to bring her home with him.

Bellicent stalked out of the cavern. Her movements were no longer unsteady, as they had been in her borrowed bodies, but terrifyingly graceful.

I am still watching, she whispered in Morgana's head.

Morgana shivered at the sensation. She'd thought all this would be over once she awakened Bellicent, but it wasn't. It wouldn't be truly over until she was safe in her own world, reunited with both her family and her magic.

She found the runes etched on the floor of the cave, by Merlin's sleeping body. There was blood crusted under his fingernails, and she knew that he had been the one to set the curse. To turn this rare world of magic into a cold, frozen tomb, rather than give the sorceress access to Earth. He had trapped Bellicent, and then he had trapped himself, so the sorceress had no way to escape. And she had undone it all.

Morgana's hand was still bleeding, and she pressed it to the runes, wiping away their power.

It didn't take long before the wizard came awake. He groaned, struggling to sit up. She had always thought of him as an old man, but he was barely forty. In her youth, that had seemed much older.

"Master Merlin?"

He frowned, taking her in. It had been eight years, she realized, yet her former tutor hadn't aged a day, while she had lived every one of them.

"Morgana? Is that you?"

"Of course it's me," she snapped. "Is it so hard to recognize your old student now that I'm no longer a girl of seventeen?"

"Hardly." Merlin frowned. "Though I admit I'm surprised. What are you doing here?"

"Rescuing you."

Merlin paled. "You never should have come!" He struggled to his feet. "You need to leave before Bellicent realizes that you're here." He took in the empty space where the sorceress had once lain in her enchanted sleep and dropped to his knees. "No," he whispered. "No, it can't—she can't—" He looked up, his eyes dark with fear. "What have you done?"

"Me?" Morgana felt like she was seventeen again, following Camelot's most powerful wizard through the woods, eager to taste every crumb of magic he offered, and quick to apologize when scolded. "I've done nothing! The cave was like this when I found you. Someone else must have gotten here first."

Merlin looked unconvinced.

"Please, Will, you have to open the doorway," she said quietly. "I came here to help, knowing you were my only way back."

"I can't." Merlin shook his head. "It's too dangerous."

"You have to," Morgana insisted. "I have a child. I need to get back to him. And you have children as well. Whatever you're afraid of— whoever you're afraid of—is it worth both of us making that sacrifice?"

Merlin sighed, and Morgana grinned in triumph at how easily she had manipulated him. "Quickly," he said. "Before she finds us."

"Before who finds us?" Morgana asked innocently.

"The sorceress known as Bellicent. I trapped her with an enchantment, but someone must have broken it."

"If you trapped her," Morgana asked, following breathlessly at his heels, "then who trapped you?"

Merlin twisted around, his expression incalculably sad as he said, "It was the only way to make the enchantment hold. I could not spare myself. And I doubt she will fall for the same cleverly worded bargain again."

When they reached the forest, Merlin picked up a thick wooden stick and used it for walking, like a staff. Morgana pressed back memories of how he had done the same when he was her teacher. When she was just a young girl of seventeen, hungry for power and unsure how to attain it.

They walked in silence, and Morgana was grateful for it.

"How long has it been?" Merlin finally asked.

"Eight years since you disappeared."

He winced. "It seems like eight days. Then my twins are grown."

"My son is nearly nine," Morgana said. "He shows signs of magic, but he can't yet control it."

"He should do the training exercises," Merlin said. "Do you remember them?"

"I am no fool," Morgana snapped, and then realized her mistake. "I mean, of course I remember them." She had forgotten herself for a moment. Merlin did not know what she had become, or all that had happened. After he had gone through the stones, she had tried to follow. She hadn't known the door would close behind him, or that she wouldn't be able to open it herself.

"Who is this sorceress you're so afraid of?" Morgana asked.

"Bellicent is no mere sorceress," said Merlin. "In a time of monsters and magic, she was worshipped as a goddess. She is the reason the doorways exist, and the reason Avalon stands sentry between our worlds, guarding us from her return. She desires power. Control. Not just over kingdoms, but over the minds of their people."

"And you trapped her?" she asked incredulously.

"It wasn't easy," said Merlin. "She tried to trap me first, in a bargain. But I twisted the terms and was able to curse us both to an eternal sleep in that cave."

"Then your magic works here?" she asked, eager to know the secret.

"Some. My father was of this world, and I inherited the gift. As did my children." His voice was light as he asked, "How did you get here, by the way?"

Morgana thought fast. "Your son wished to find you," she lied. "I was willing to go through the stones. After all, it's my fault you got stuck here. And I have had to live with it all this time." She blinked at him in despair, as though she had been carrying around guilt, and not a burning resentment for what he had done, helping Uther by erasing Igraine's memory.

"It isn't your fault," Merlin said. "Neither of us knew what would happen. So, you know my son? How is he?"

She had never met the boy, but she could recognize a father's pride, so she lied, "He fares well. He is a powerful wizard in Camelot's royal court."

Merlin nodded, pleased. "And my daughter?"

"Also well," said Morgana, tiring of this mindless chatter. It would be over soon enough. And then she would be home, with her magic.

Finally, as the sun began to sink through the trees, they reached a stone arch, a different one than she had come through.

"Go on, open it," Morgana urged greedily.

"I will," Merlin said. "After you tell me the truth."

Morgana's blood ran cold. "I don't know what you mean."

"My son could never open a doorway to Anwen." Merlin arched an eyebrow. "You set the sorceress free."

Morgana lifted her chin at the accusation.

"Why?" he pressed. "What did she promise you? Is it magic? Power? You have always had too much ambition."

Tell him nothing, Bellicent urged in her head.

"She didn't promise me anything!" Morgana insisted. "She saved my life and forced me to repay the debt by releasing her. Now open the portal, so we can escape this cursed place before she follows us!"

"I don't know if I can trust you," the wizard said gravely.

Morgana made her eyes wide and pleading. "Then believe me when I tell you I'm done with Anwen and its magic. The sorceress owes me nothing more, and there is nothing I can give her. I wish only to go home to my son."

He nodded. "You always wanted too much," he told her. "I'm glad to hear you have settled for a normal life."

Morgana wondered how he did not see it. The half-truths, the deception, the anger coiled within her. The power she held. He underestimated her, the way he had always done. She could barely resist bragging that her life was anything but normal, and she had certainly not settled. She was a queen. A sorceress. She had stolen an enchantment that cheated death, killed Uther's son, and stepped through a doorway to another world. She ached with the need to force Merlin to his knees, to wrap an invisible hand around his throat, to make him fear her, instead of scolding her like she was still a naive girl. Her hands trembled at her sides, and she gritted her teeth. *Just hold on*, she told herself. *He is about to give you what you desire.*

She sensed movement in the forest, and turned to see a flash of a white fur hood. The sorceress had found them. Or perhaps she had been waiting here.

You have done well, Bellicent crooned inside her head.

Merlin pulled a knife from his boot and slashed his palm. Morgana grinned eagerly as her former tutor pressed his hand to the stones. *"άνοιξε την πόρτα!"*

The stone doorway trembled. A shimmer of light appeared and grew stronger.

Merlin gritted his teeth, widening his stance, his body trembling with the effort.

On the other side of the doorway, a faint outline of a forest appeared.

The forest grew sharper and more realistic, until the shimmering stopped, and the world beyond stood still and waiting.

"Where—?" Morgana started to ask.

"Avalon," Merlin said. "Come on."

Smiling wide, Morgana followed him through the stones.

Chapter 53

Arthur stood at the threshold of the royal chapel, feeling as if he marched to his doom.

He could barely put one foot in front of the other as the beaming courtiers, nobles, and royal guests watched from the crowded pews.

The November afternoon was bright and clear, but you'd never know it from the grim, meager light that filtered through the chapel's stained glass windows, casting everything in a murky gloom.

His coat was too stiff, made of heavy red wool with golden braid at the shoulders, and his hair was slicked back with thick, sweet-smelling wax beneath his best circlet. The Pendragon crest was placed above his heart.

A heart that was beating frantically.

Please, Guinevere, he thought. *Don't mess this up.*

He could barely breathe as he approached the alcove where his father and the royal family of Cameliard sat on gilded chairs, because apparently they couldn't deign to sit in the pews. His expression went hard as he bowed to them, and then approached the altar. The wait seemed unbearable. Finally, the chapel door opened, and everyone rose for the bride.

A heavily veiled woman in a wedding gown took a few tentative steps down the aisle. Could it be?

No, Arthur's heart broke as he realized the girl was too tall and too thin to be Guinevere.

She hadn't made it back after all.

And this girl, this stranger, was going to say yes. Arthur felt as if he might faint.

He wanted desperately to turn and run. Out of the chapel and onto the castle lawn, through the courtyard and gates and into the city, and back to that small bedroom at Madame Becou's where he'd spent the night with the woman he actually loved.

But Emry wasn't at Madame Becou's. He could see her at Gawain's side, in a gown of gray silk, watching the girl walk down the aisle with an expression of sadness that broke his heart.

So, this was it. The moment his future became monstrously unfair, something he didn't know how he would bear for a single night, much less a lifetime.

Arthur's eyes met Emry's, and her chin trembled slightly. His brave wizard. He hoped she would be happy, because he needed one of them to be happy.

Fake Guinevere came to stand at his side, playing her part well. She curtseyed to him, this stranger, and Arthur bowed in return, his throat tight as they turned to face the archbishop.

"We are gathered here," the archbishop began, "to bear witness to a historic joining."

Sard, Arthur thought with a groan, the man wasn't even doing it in Latin. But of course not. The ceremony wasn't a religious one of marriage, but a political alliance dressed up in a gown. One that needed witnesses who understood what was being said.

This couldn't be his wedding. This farce of a ceremony, with a complete stranger under a veil, and this horrible, clenched feeling in his chest as though he was standing on the edge of something terrible, knowing his father wanted nothing more than to push him over.

He swallowed nervously, looking anywhere except at the girl playing the role of his bride, or his heartbroken wizard. Strangely, the

Duke of Cornwall didn't seem to be in attendance.

Arthur gave one last desperate glance at his father, wishing he would put a stop to this. That someone would, before it was too late.

And then it was too late.

"Does Guinevere, Princess of Cameliard, accept the hand of Arthur, Prince of Camelot?"

The girl curtseyed and murmured, "She does."

Arthur felt as though he was going to faint.

"And does Arthur, prince of Camelot, accept the hand of—"

"*Stop!*" a girl called from the back of the chapel. "Stop the wedding!"

The crowd murmured in curiosity, turning as one to see who had caused the disruption.

Arthur's heart leapt as Guinevere hurried forward. Behind her was Emmett. Arthur had never been so pleased to see the obnoxious young wizard in his life.

Guin tossed Arthur a smile. "Am I late?" she asked, her tone light.

"Just a bit," he replied. "They had to start without you."

"Then they may stop, now that I'm here." Guin gestured toward the girl standing across from Arthur. "Shoo. Go away."

If Arthur hadn't been so nervous, he might have laughed.

"I am Princess Guinevere of Cameliard," Guin announced, "and I do not accept Prince Arthur of Camelot as my husband."

Arthur had never admired Princess Guinevere more. She stood there in a wrinkled velvet gown, her hair in braids that looked as if they had been slept in, late to her own wedding, and having none of it.

A wave of confusion washed over the crowd, followed by furious whispers.

"What do you mean you don't accept?" demanded the archbishop.

"I can't marry him, because I'm married to someone else," said Guin.

Arthur's shoulders sagged with relief. So, they had gone through with it.

"Lies!" exclaimed King Leodegrance, rising from his seat. "My daughter is an unmarried virgin! I swear to it."

At his side, his wife nodded emphatically, looking panicked. "She is an innocent maiden!"

Guinevere actually cackled. "I have our marriage certificate right here." She handed a scroll to the archbishop. "I believe you'll find everything in order."

The archbishop frowned down at the piece of parchment. Arthur half expected the man's fingers to come away wet from the fresh ink. "The marriage is legal. But who on earth is Emmett Merlin?"

"That would be me, your archbishopness," said Emmett, stepping forward. Arthur took in Emmett's rumpled appearance, and realized he'd never seen the young wizard so disheveled. Guinevere didn't look much better. It was clear they had arrived in a hurry.

"You married a commoner?!" King Leodegrance roared.

"Not a commoner, a wizard!" Guinevere beamed.

"An apprentice wizard," Emmett corrected.

"I never expected such treachery within my court!" growled Uther.

"What treachery?" Arthur asked. "They married for love, and they did so with my blessing."

"Your blessing?" Uther echoed in disbelief. "You knew about this?"

"You weren't the only one with a backup plan," said Arthur. "And as a friend of the bride and the groom, may I just say, I wish the two of you all the happiness in the world. And I hope everyone here will join me in doing the same." He slung an arm around both Emmett and Guinevere, and all three turned to face the crowd.

The audience stared back at them in stunned silence.

And then Emry stood and called out, "Huzzah!"

"Huzzah!" Gawain echoed, applauding.

"Huzzah!" Lance called.

"To the bride and groom!" shouted the young lords with whom Emmett was so friendly.

"To the bride and groom," more members of the audience repeated, tentatively beginning to clap.

Guinevere turned to Emmett and threw her arms around him, giving him a kiss.

Arthur stood there beaming. And then he turned to the archbishop. "I'll take it from here," he told the man.

Arthur cleared his throat and faced the shocked crowd. "As my father reminded us so eloquently at last night's feast, we have gathered to witness a union between two kingdoms, not just two individuals. I hope Cameliard will still ally with Camelot, though we only offer you friendship in return."

"Of course we will," Guinevere said, lifting her chin. "Right, Father?"

King Leodegrance spluttered. "I—I suppose if the treaty is still on the table, then yes, Cameliard will sign it."

"Wonderful," said Arthur. "Then tonight we will celebrate something far more meaningful than a forced marriage. We will celebrate peace and the power of diplomacy. This will mark the beginning of a golden age, not just for Camelot, but for all of our kingdoms."

Outside the chapel, there was the ring of steel clashing against steel, followed by a lot of shouting.

Arthur tensed, gripping the hilt of his sword.

"What's going on?" King Leodegrance asked of King Uther.

"Whatever it is, it doesn't sound good," said Guin, her eyes wide with fear.

Arthur withdrew Excalibur, filling the chapel with a bright glow. The guards reached for their own swords, and the audience murmured with fright. Through the stained glass windows, it was impossible to see what was happening outside on the castle lawn, or to know what was occurring inside the castle.

The chapel doors burst open, and Percival and Tristan staggered inside. Perce's tunic was slashed, and a bright spray of blood arced across Tristan's cheek. They dragged Dakin between them, his bruised face looking like it had clashed with more than one fist.

"What's happening out there?" King Uther demanded.

Tristan shouted, "The castle is under attack!"

Chapter 54

"Under attack?" Arthur repeated, hoping he had misheard. "But that's impossible!"

The castle walls were enchanted to be impenetrable to attack. There was no way an army could get through.

"Tell them," Percival said, glaring at Dakin.

Dakin grinned, although with his injuries, it was more of a grimace. "I've been helping the Duke of Cornwall smuggle his soldiers into the castle for days."

A shocked murmur rippled through the crowd of wedding guests.

"They're masquerading as servants!" Tristan put in. "And there are dozens of 'em!"

A shiver ran down Arthur's spine. An army that didn't look like an army. One that had been passing unseen among them for days. It was terrible and clever. And it certainly explained the uptick in castle staff. He'd assumed it was for the wedding, but the duke had merely used the festivities as a cover.

"You dare to betray your king?" Uther demanded, furious.

"Gladly," spat Dakin. "And I would do it a thousand times over, to see a great man like Gorlais rule Camelot, instead of a dying old drunk!"

Arthur winced. The crowd gasped and whispered, throwing sidelong glances at the king. After all, Dakin wore the unmistakable livery of a royal guard.

"I—you—" the king spluttered, at a loss for words. His face was a deep and angry shade of red, and his hands were fisted at his sides, and Arthur knew that if his father had had a weapon, he would have drawn it.

Royal guards were sworn to serve and protect, not just the royal family's lives, but also their secrets. Which made Dakin's betrayal so much worse.

"He doesn't even deny it!" Dakin crowed, playing to the crowd. "Is this sickly old man truly who you want ruling Camelot? Or perhaps you're eager to bow to his pathetic bastard son?"

The traitorous guard gasped and doubled over, a bloody welt appearing at his temple. He sagged forward in Percival's and Tristan's grips, his eyes fluttering shut.

"Sorry!" Emry called, not sounding sorry in the slightest. "I got tired of waiting for someone else to knock him unconscious." She tapped her wand against her palm, looking smug.

Arthur barked a laugh. "Thank you, wizard."

"Lock up that traitorous, lying guard immediately," King Uther commanded. "Where's Captain Lam?"

Percival shook his head, his expression grave. "The Duke's men dispatched him first, so the guard would have no orders."

"Your orders are to defend the castle, and to get me to safety," the king snapped. "I'm unarmed, uninformed of our strategy and numbers, and unprepared for a fight."

"What about the rest of us?" called King Leodegrance. "Are we to be invited here as guests, only to be led to slaughter?"

Others loudly voiced their concern.

"My friends!" said Uther, trying to quell the panic. "You are all guests in my castle, and I give you my word that I will personally ensure your safety."

"How?" someone called.

The king blanched and looked to Lord Agravaine. The advisor had finally lost his unflappable calm and seemed just as horrified and lost as everyone else. He shook his head, rendered speechless.

"Don't worry," Tristan promised. "We have a plan!"

"Are we going to waste precious time listening to these lowly guards?" Lord Dagonet complained, and the crowd loudly agreed.

"They're not lowly guards," Arthur called out. "They're the leaders of my personal order of castle protectors!"

Tristan beamed. And then Master Ambrosius cried out and fell to his knees. He looked to be under considerable strain.

"I have the chapel warded from attack," the old wizard said, his body trembling, and his jaw tight. "But I can only manage it for a few more minutes."

"Then we must plan quickly," said Arthur. "What of the castle exits?"

"One hundred of the duke's men wait outside the gates," said Percival. "Any escape is effectively blocked."

"So, we're trapped," Arthur said thoughtfully, "but they're outnumbered."

"Technically yes, but the duke's men are trained soldiers," Lance put in. "Fighting against guards and staff, who are woefully unprepared for an attack. Especially from someone in Pendragon livery."

Arthur thought fast. "Tristan, do you know how to navigate the tunnels from here?"

"Backward and forward," the guard said proudly.

"Take everyone you can to the royal safe room," said Arthur. "There's only one way in from the castle, so a single guard can hold the tunnel. Inside, a door leads to a private dock. Light the lantern to signal the wherry boats for passage. Women and children out first—along with our guests from other kingdoms."

Tristan nodded and gave an eager salute. "You heard him. Everyone who's coming, follow me."

"Everyone else, prepare to defend the castle," said Arthur.

"But we don't have weapons!" Lionel cried.

Curse this ceremony for taking place in a chapel, Arthur thought. Out of respect, many guests hadn't dared to wear a blade.

"There are spare swords in the guards' barracks," said Percival.

"And the armory," said Lance. "Chainmail and armor, too."

"Good." Arthur nodded his approval. "Lance, see that any who wish to fight are armed and given orders. Not just the men."

"Not just the men!" King Leodegrance spluttered. "You can't mean that!"

"Welcome to Camelot," Arthur said crisply. He turned to his father. "Does that plan meet with your approval?"

"It will do," muttered the king.

"Father, do you wish to command the castle's defenses from the safe room, or will you require someone to lend you their sword?" Arthur asked.

It was a neatly phrased question, one that revealed far more than it asked, and they both knew it.

"I shall see that our honored guests have a safe exit from my castle, as I promised," said Uther. "As will you."

"Absolutely not. I'm fighting alongside my wizard," Arthur said coolly.

"That's exactly what the duke wants! To dispatch my only heir!"

"I'd like to see him try." Arthur's jaw tightened, and he gripped his blade with renewed purpose.

He glanced toward the old wizard, who was keeping them all safe, for the moment. The man was ashen, his skin slick with sweat, his expression pinched with pain. Arthur knelt at the old wizard's side. "Tell me when it's too much," he said softly.

"I believe you will know, Your Highness."

Arthur swallowed thickly, understanding all too well what the man was implying.

Emry crouched beside him, trembling and holding back tears. "Master Ambrosius?" she said, her voice thin and nervous. "I'm here. I can help."

"Save your magic, child," croaked the old wizard. "This is my duty. And soon, it will be yours."

"No," she whispered, heartbroken.

"I am—honored—to have you as my successor," the old wizard gasped as Emry sobbed.

Arthur pushed to his feet, giving them time together. Giving Emry the chance to say goodbye.

"We must empty the chapel!" he called, his voice ringing with command. "Make haste!"

Tristan fumbled on the wall, and a portion swung open, revealing the dark entrance to a tunnel.

"φως," said Emmett, illuminating the tip of his wand and touching it to a display of candles, which all lit at once. "It'll be dark, so grab prayer candles! Quickly!"

Arthur watched as hasty goodbyes were uttered and his wedding guests hurried into the tunnel. His father gestured for him to come closer, and he did.

"This is no fair fight," said King Uther quietly, so he might not be overheard. "It's an underhanded siege. You must come and save our bloodline."

"I would rather save Camelot," Arthur said. "Go then. Before the ward comes down." He held open the door to the passage, waiting for his father to step through.

The king did, angrily. Without so much of a word of encouragement for those who stayed behind.

Arthur watched as Guinevere pressed a desperate kiss to Emmett's lips. When they pulled apart, she caught Arthur's eye, flashing him an encouraging smile. "Give them hell," she said, "for ruining my wedding celebration."

Despite everything that was happening, and the grimness of their situation, Arthur nearly laughed aloud. "You have my word, Mrs. Merlin."

Guin blushed at the name. She was the last to step into the tunnel. Emmett closed the panel behind her, his face pale, as though worried he might never see her again.

"They'll be all right," Arthur promised him.

"Will we?" the young wizard replied.

Arthur didn't know.

"I thank all of you for your bravery," he said to the crowd. "We fight not just for Camelot, but for a better world. There is no time for all I wish to say, so I hope that is enough."

He surveyed the chapel, taking stock of who had stayed behind. His brave Knights of the Round Table, including even the annoying Lionel Griflet, all stood in their courtiers' finest, looking grim yet determined.

Gawain and Emry had stayed, of course. And many of his father's knights and their squires. Along with Guinevere's two court ladies, who stood trembling with nerves, and tightly holding hands.

There was a knight Arthur didn't recognize, tall and blond and attractive, dressed in a velvet tunic and matching trousers that were neither gown nor suit.

"Sir Tor," said Lance. "You came!"

"I did," said the knight, who turned to Arthur, drawing their blade. "My sword is in your service, young prince."

"As is mine," said Prince Gottegrim, rising from where he knelt in prayer before the altar.

"I didn't realize you'd stayed behind," said Arthur.

"We agreed to a treaty of aid and alliance, did we not?" he said.

"We did." Arthur tightened his grip on his sword and tried to steady his nerves. "Knights, see to the duke's men who block the castle gate."

"Yes, Your Highness," they said in unison.

"Anyone armed, head to the castle under Percival's command," Arthur went on. "Anyone who needs a weapon, go with Lancelot to the armory, and follow his orders."

"I could use a wizard," Lance said. "With so many unarmed."

"I'll go." Emmett stepped forward, wand out.

Emry came to stand at Arthur's side, and he looked to her with a grim nod. She nodded back. Her eyes were hollow, and she was trembling, but trying to put on a brave front.

"All right?" he asked softly.

She swallowed, her eyes on the old man, whose shoulders hunched in agony. "Not really."

She mumbled a spell, and her gown changed into a boy's jacket and trousers. And then she placed a hand on Arthur's shoulder.

"A red coat is a terrible thing to wear into battle," she said.

He looked down, and found he was no longer dressed in his flashy wedding suit, but in a worn cloak over a simple tunic and trousers.

"Good thinking," he said in admiration. Dressed like this, he wouldn't make quite such an obvious target.

He removed his circlet and tossed it aside, just as Master Ambrosius collapsed to the ground, his eyes wide and unblinking.

Chapter 55

The castle was in chaos.

Emry tried not to look at the dozens of slumped bodies as she raced through the hallways. And she tried not to think about Master Ambrosius, and how the old man had sacrificed his life to give them all a chance to fight and escape.

Her heart squeezed with despair, but she couldn't let the sadness overwhelm her, because there wasn't time to mourn. Not yet.

So, she pushed it away, blinked back her tears, and hoped the Lady of the Lake had been right about Arthur becoming a great king, because she didn't think she could bear to lose anyone else today.

At her side, the prince quickened his stride, his jaw tight, his sword raised.

In his hand, Excalibur pulsed with light, as though the sword matched the pounding of his heart. The duke's men were everywhere, dressed as grooms and footmen and valets, and they didn't hesitate.

Swords clashed, and young, inexperienced guards who had only ever stood outside doorways crossed blades with trained soldiers. Some of the maids had grabbed fireplace pokers, and footmen fought with spears they'd grabbed off suits of armor.

Emry's eyes went wide as she saw Guinevere's maid, Dorota, wielding a candelabra against a man twice her size. She gasped when the soldier dispatched the maid, and the girl crumpled to the floor, his sword buried in her stomach.

But all that was nothing compared to what they found in the Great Hall.

Percival and a dozen guards, nobles, and squires fought, heavily outnumbered against the duke's men.

Platters of spilled food littered the floor around them, along with the bodies of the castle staff who had been setting up the feast.

The stone floor, normally polished to a heavy shine, was dark with blood.

Emry stared at the scene, feeling ill. Those poor people, who had been going about their jobs, expecting a night of celebration.

And now, their friends fought for their lives against the men who had done this.

Extergio, she thought, the cleaning spell gliding across the floor and removing the sticky pools of blood.

Arthur joined the fray, his sword raised, but Emry hung back, pressing herself against the wall between two suits of armor, trying to figure out how she could be useful.

She felt as if she were back in the forest, back in France, terrified that she didn't know what to do. Fire might miss and hit one of their friends, and she couldn't burn down the Great Hall. Lightning wouldn't work, either.

She pricked her finger on the dagger she wore at her side.

Isaz, she thought, mentally tracing the rune. Shards of ice appeared above her palms, and she threw two into the fray before realizing it was useless. She would only draw the fight to her, and she didn't want to test her magic against the deadly precision of a trained soldier's blade.

Was there nothing she could do? She stared at the fight in despair, at Arthur, his glowing sword coming up in an arc, the light bouncing off the suits of armor that lined the walls.

The armor. Emry's eyes went wide as an idea struck. She reached for her dagger, pricking her finger again and letting Anwen's magic loose.

She wasn't sure if she could manage—if it would even work—but she had to try. Those were her friends out there. She tried not to think of Master Ambrosius, and the way he had looked as he'd collapsed, as though he had known the price. He'd given all he had, and she would do the same, if it meant saving Arthur and Emmett, and everyone she cared about.

She swallowed thickly, determined not to lose anyone else. Purple flames crackled to life in her palms.

Logr, she thought, bringing her left hand into the pattern for the rune, and *Elhaz*. She swung her right hand into the other pattern and hoped.

It was Master Ambrosius's tandem spell, done with Anwen's magic. She didn't know if it would work, if it was even possible, or if she had wasted precious time that they didn't have.

Please, she thought.

Abruptly, the fire above her palms turned silver, dripping from her hands like honey. She flung it at the suits of armor, barely daring to breathe as she waited. For a moment, nothing happened, and then two dozen suits of armor shimmered, absorbing the magic.

They raised their weapons and stepped forward, clanging as they ran to join the battle.

Emry stared, hardly daring to believe what she had done. She hadn't just controlled Anwen's magic, she had used it to create an impossible enchantment. She expected to feel drained from the undertaking, the way she always did when she used too much of her magic, but she didn't feel a thing. Because she hadn't used her own magic. She had used Anwen's magic.

The suits of armor swung their axes and halberds, seeming to magically know who was an enemy and who was not. Silently and relentlessly, they made quick work of dispatching the duke's men. And then they straightened, turned in unison, and saluted her with their weapons.

Arthur, Percival, and the others stared in disbelief, first at the suits of armor, and then at Emry.

"You're under the prince's command, not mine," she told them.

They pivoted to face Arthur, who squared his shoulders, wiped a spray of blood from his cheek with his sleeve, and said, "Right. Well, go and see how many more of the duke's men you can take down."

The suits of armor saluted again, and then marched off.

"What *was* that, wizard?" Arthur asked.

Emry shook her head. "I didn't think it would work."

The spell had been enormous. Yet she felt as if she had barely used any magic at all.

"Good thing it did," Percival said grimly, wiping down his blade. "Anyone injured?"

Emry made quick work of healing a few minor stab wounds, and found herself blinking back dizziness. *How inconvenient*, she thought, wobbling.

Arthur's steady arms caught her. "Breathe. We can't have Camelot's new court wizard fainting on the job."

"Oh god," Emry said, cringing. The loss hit her all at once, and her eyes welled with tears. "He—I—I can't believe he's gone. And that I'm . . ." She trailed off, unable to say it.

That she was no longer his apprentice, but his replacement.

"He knew what he was doing," Arthur said gently. "And he knew he was leaving the castle in good hands."

Emry nodded, wiping her eyes. She was dimly aware of Arthur speaking quietly to Percival, and the guard nodded before leading his men from the Great Hall.

All she could think about was Master Ambrosius giving her a chance to prove herself, despite knowing that she was a woman. The old wizard had taught her so much, and now he was gone, and she had barely gotten to say goodbye.

When she managed to catch hold of her grief, she realized she was alone with Arthur, the floor strewn with corpses, and the castle still under attack.

Arthur pushed aside a tapestry, revealing a tunnel. "We should check on the safe room."

Emry nodded, mumbling a spell to light the tip of her wand.

"Save your magic," he said. "We'll light the way with my sword."

"Okay," Emry agreed, taking a deep, shuddering breath. She extinguished the tip of her wand and followed Arthur through the dark, rough-hewn tunnel, trying to smooth back her nerves.

"Do you think we're winning?" she asked.

"I can't tell." Arthur sighed, scraping a hand through his hair. "I should have killed the duke when I had the chance."

"What would you have done, run him through in the gardens of the Palais de la Cité?" Emry asked.

Arthur raised an eyebrow. "Not the worst idea you've had, wizard."

"A shame we killed all of those bandits on the post road," Emry deadpanned.

Arthur's shoulders rose in a quick burst of amusement. The pair turned a sharp right, the tunnel dipping lower beneath the castle.

"Who goes there?" a boy's voice called.

"Tristan, it's me," Arthur said.

Tristan's pale face came into view. He stood gripping his blade with both hands, the passage around him lined with prayer candles.

"Has anyone tried to come through?" Arthur asked.

Tristan shook his head.

"You're doing great," Arthur told the guard, whose chest puffed with pride.

Emry followed Arthur the rest of the way down the tunnel and into the royal safe room. It was an underground chamber that might once have been used as a very old castle dungeon. The ceiling hung low, and torches burned on the walls, casting everything in a dim light. Emry flicked her hand at them, and the flames grew brighter.

At the far end of the cavern was a rough-hewn arched doorway that opened onto a small wooden dock, and in the center of the space was King Uther, surrounded by a dwindling number of courtiers, his advisors, and the King and Queen of Cameliard.

Everyone turned to stare at them, and Emry was suddenly aware that she was in boy's clothes, clutching her wand, and that, at her side, Arthur wore humble rough-spun cloth, his tunic splattered with blood.

But there was no mistaking him for anything but a prince. And it wasn't just that he was holding Excalibur. It was the set of his shoulders, and the quiet way he commanded the attention of everyone in the chamber with just his presence.

"Well?" his father demanded.

"What of our son?" the Queen of Cameliard asked, her voice quivering.

"He is well," said Arthur. "The battle goes well." He turned to Emry, his eyes shining with admiration as he said, "Thanks in large part to our new court wizard."

Arthur kept Excalibur in hand as he followed his father onto the narrow dock, his heart pounding.

There was rage in the king's eyes, and Arthur braced himself for whatever it was his father so desperately wished to say to him where others wouldn't overhear.

"How dare you?" Uther accused, whirling to face him.

"How dare I what?" Arthur snapped. "Defend this castle with my own sword? Or deputize others to do the same?" When his father didn't answer, Arthur sighed. "Do you wish to have a guard without a captain? Our people are being slaughtered, and we need to protect them!"

King Uther spluttered. "They can protect themselves!"

"They're maids and serving boys, not soldiers," Arthur returned.

"They're expendable," replied the king. "Unlike the guests whose safety I promised, then personally ensured. Camelot needs an heir and loyal nobles and foreign allies far more than *kitchen maids*. You have a lot to learn, boy, before you become king."

Arthur didn't dare to point out that it was actually Tristan, Percival, and Master Ambrosius who had ensured the guests' safety. His father was so utterly convinced that he was always right, and Arthur was tired of fighting over their constant difference of opinion. All he wanted was a measure of peace between them. So, instead of a sarcastic quip, he extended an olive branch.

"Then teach me," Arthur said. "If I have so much to learn, and you disapprove so thoroughly of my choices, explain why I should choose otherwise."

"A king shouldn't have to explain."

"Is it so impossible, to be both a king and a father?"

The king frowned, as though he had never been asked that question. And Arthur wondered if he had ever aired his frustrations quite so openly.

"You would listen, if I did?" King Uther asked, as if he didn't believe it.

"There are some things that can't be learned from books," Arthur said, lifting his chin. "I would learn what I can, while there's still time."

The unspoken question passed between them, of how much time that would be.

"Very well. I suppose it's time I taught you how to live up to the Pendragon name. After all, you are my son."

Arthur gave his father a tentative smile.

And then Lord Agravaine cleared his throat. The king's advisor stood on the sand, looking like the last thing he wanted to do was interrupt.

"What?" snapped the king.

"There is news." The royal advisor stepped aside, and Lance pushed forward.

His suit was splattered with blood, and there was more of it on his sword, but he was thankfully unharmed. "Did you know empty suits of armor are defending the castle?" he marveled.

"They're still going?" Arthur replied. "Emry will be delighted."

"They're amazing," Lance said admiringly.

"You had something to say, squire?" the king demanded.

Lance gave a crisp bow. "The Duke of Cornwall has called for his men to stand down, and is waiting for you in the castle courtyard, Your Majesty."

"To discuss his surrender?" the king asked eagerly.

Lance shook his head. "To come out and fight him yourself."

Of course. It was always going to come to this, Arthur realized. His father had played exactly into Gorlais's hands, almost as if the duke knew what the king would do. Arthur's heart clenched as he wondered how many casualties could have been avoided, had his father met the duke at the chapel doors with the same challenge.

"So, he means to finish this between us," said Uther with a grim nod. "I accept."

"Your Majesty, if I may—" Lord Agravaine broke in.

"You may not!" the king thundered. "He has made me look weak. Now I must prove that I am no coward! I granted Gorlais his power, and it's past time I took it away." Determination burned in the king's gaze, and Arthur knew this expression. It meant the king was beyond arguing with.

"Father, are you sure about this?" Arthur asked uneasily.

"I am," said the king. "He attacked my castle. He threatens my rule. And he wounds my pride!"

"But the duke is an expert swordsman," Arthur protested.

"Which means my victory will be all the more of a triumph," said Uther. The king held out his hand. "Give me your sword."

Arthur didn't think he'd heard his father correctly. "My sword?"

"Excalibur," the king said, his eyes glittering with anticipation. "I require it. Let's see what the duke makes of an unbeatable magic sword."

"But the sword doesn't work for you," Arthur protested, remembering the last time the king had held it, and the feeble light it had given off before going dim.

"It is a magic sword!" King Uther roared. "And it is the best one! Now give it to me!"

Arthur bowed his head and held out his blade.

Chapter 56

Arthur's heart thundered in his chest as his father swaggered forward, holding Excalibur with an arrogant tilt of his shoulders. Someone had retrieved the king's breastplate and bracers, which he wore over his wedding finery, his crown glinting in the fading golden light.

Everyone had stayed their weapons to see what would come of the duke's challenge, though the knights remained at the castle gates, alongside the animated suits of armor.

In the cooling twilight of the castle courtyard, a sizable crowd had gathered, circled around the duke. Gorlais wore mail over his tunic, his hair slicked back, a smug expression on his piggish face.

"So, you have not fled the castle after all," he goaded, raising his voice so the taunt echoed through the courtyard.

"On the contrary," said King Uther. "I ensured the safety of my valued allies, and now I will ensure the safety of my kingdom. Before I do, by my power as the King of Camelot, I hereby strip you of your dukedom."

The duke laughed. "Is that so? I see no king before me, just a dying old man desperate to maintain his rotten legacy."

The king's eyes flashed with anger, and he tightened his grip on his sword. "The only thing rotten in my legacy was giving you power."

The duke raised his blade, slashing it in challenge. And King Uther met that challenge, stalking forward, and settling into a fighter's crouch.

Arthur watched, unable to recall the last time he had seen his father fight, or even train with a weapon.

In the king's grip, Excalibur did not flash or glow. It could have been an ordinary sword, albeit one whose blade looked slightly too sharp, and whose pommel was a bit too intricately decorated. Arthur wondered if it would work. If his father could truly wield it to any advantage.

The duke pressed forward, and the clash of swords rang out through the courtyard.

Arthur winced.

Somehow, he could still sense his sword if he willed it, so he concentrated on the invisible connection between himself and the blade, trying to make it do for his father what it did for him.

"Arthur?" Emry appeared quietly at his side. "You all right?"

"I'm fine," he said tensely.

"No, you're not."

She was right. And he was grateful that she had said it. That she understood his inner anguish, even when he pretended it away.

There was no one else he would rather have by his side, not just in the best moments, but in the awful ones as well.

She had to know that. Surely he had told her that?

He didn't remember. He couldn't think. His heart pounded, and his empty hand itched for his sword. He could barely breathe as he watched his father parry and strike, his forehead slick with sweat.

The duke was the superior swordsman. Anyone could see that. The man drove Uther back, into defense, his expression dark and intense and ruthless.

The duke's blade struck Uther in the shoulder, and the king winced, blood trickling down his sleeve. He gritted his teeth and pressed forward, tipping his blade down, and landing a solid hit to the duke's right leg.

Arthur didn't remember taking Emry's hand, or perhaps she had taken his, but he tried to concentrate on the reassuring pressure of it as his father began to slow.

Both men looked exhausted. King Uther's left arm hung uselessly at his side, and sweat ran down his brow. The duke limped with every step, though he fought through it, his blade lightning fast.

"You tire of this," the duke hissed.

"I tire of you," King Uther replied, his breath coming in gasps.

Another clang, slower this time, with the drag of one blade catching another. But still, the men pressed on.

"This kingdom," Uther said raggedly, "will never be yours." He lunged forward, the tip of his sword grazing the duke's chest.

Gorlais grimaced, stumbling back, a cold fury in his gaze.

And then the duke thrust forward with a grunt. Aiming just beneath the breastplate, he buried his sword deep in the king's stomach, nearly to the hilt.

Uther froze in place, staring down at the blade in disbelief. A trickle of blood ran from the corner of his mouth. He staggered, dropping Excalibur.

"No!" Arthur cried out.

He rushed forward, stumbling as he caught his father's fall. He didn't care that he was unarmed, that he wore no protective mail or plate. Not half an hour ago, the great Uther Pendragon had promised to try and be both a king and a father.

And now it was never going to happen.

Their long-awaited reconciliation was bleeding out into the castle courtyard, and there was nothing Arthur could do to stop it.

"Father," he whispered, as the two of them sank to the ground. "No, please, no."

There was so much blood. Not just a puddle, but a pool.

Tears burned in Arthur's eyes, and his chest felt like it might rip apart from grief.

His father coughed wetly. "Why didn't it work?" he asked, his voice the barest whisper. "This sword was supposed to make me unbeatable."

Arthur swallowed back a sob. "Death is not the same as defeat," he told the fading king.

"My son . . ." King Uther whispered. And then his eyes grew unfocused. "Igraine . . ."

He reached for Arthur with a trembling hand. And then the hand dropped, and he went still, staring up at the purpling sky.

Tears spilled down Arthur's cheeks, and grief clawed at him, ripping apart his entire world, until all that was left was the knowledge of what he had to do.

"Someone lend me a sword," the duke called. "So I may kill a second unworthy king today."

The taunt rang through the courtyard, and Arthur watched in disbelief as one of the duke's men stepped forward, proffering his blade.

"Well, nephew," goaded the duke. "Are you man enough to face me in a sword fight, or are you still afraid?"

Arthur lowered his father's head gently to the bloodstained ground. Somehow he found the strength to reach for the sword that lay at his side. He took up Excalibur with trembling hands, and when he did, the sword glowed so fiercely that he was momentarily dazzled by it.

The duke stumbled back, shielding his eyes.

Arthur's connection to the weapon felt stronger than it ever had before. The pommel pulsed in his grasp, and he could feel the eagerness of the sword, the magic that rushed deep within it, waiting for him to give it purpose.

"I have never been afraid," Arthur said coolly, advancing on the duke.

The duke stumbled, his footing lost. Arthur pressed his advantage, pushing forward as he swung Excalibur in a complicated pass between them.

The duke parried mid-retreat. His blade met Arthur's, yet Arthur could feel the man's back foot sliding in the dirt.

"Am I supposed to be impressed by a glowing sword?" the duke scoffed. "It certainly gave your father no advantage."

"I am not my father."

Arthur's movements became a blur, his advance impossible to counter. The duke had no chance to hold his own.

Arthur came to a stop with the tip of the blade pressed against the duke's heart. "You may beg me for your life, if you wish," he said coldly, applying enough pressure to bring forth a trickle of blood.

He did not truly expect that the duke would do it. But the revulsion in the man's eyes was replaced with unabashed fear. The duke licked his chapped lips. "Please, Your Highness."

"Please what?"

"Have mercy. My quarrel was with your father, not you."

"Yet you've tried to kill me twice. While I was unarmed. And you call me a coward? An unfit bastard? I am the son and heir of Uther Pendragon. You merely married his sister."

The duke blanched.

"You sent your men—your army—to kill innocent people. Un-armed maids and footmen and stable boys," Arthur went on, raising his voice. "You have made a bloodbath out of a celebration. And you ask for my mercy, after this unforgivable demonstration of evil?"

"The people of Camelot will never have you as their king," the duke spat, anger replacing his fear.

"They already do." Arthur didn't hesitate as he drove the blade in to the hilt, running the man straight through the heart.

The duke sank to his knees, dropping his own weapon, his expression a mix of pain and shock.

Arthur stared down at the man who had tried to kill him, who had murdered his father, who had caused so much pain and death in a desperate bid to gain a throne.

When it was through, when the Duke of Cornwall lay crumpled and lifeless in the castle courtyard, Arthur knelt and retrieved his sword.

Excalibur came free as easily as if it had been resting in a simple sheath.

He looked down at his shaking hands. At Excalibur, its magic blade tinged crimson with the blood of his enemy. So, this was what it felt like, he thought dully, to become exactly what you were afraid of.

"Hail, King Arthur," cried a familiar voice.

It was Lance. Brave Lancelot, who dropped to one knee and bowed his head in respect.

Arthur watched in shock as the rest of the courtyard did the same. He stared out at the crowd, at his father's courtiers, and Percival's men, and his friends, and the assembled knights and squires, at the castle staff, and the duke's men who had thrown down their swords, hoping for mercy.

At his subjects, who bowed before their new king.

"Hail, King Arthur," the crowd repeated.

It didn't matter that he wasn't ready. That he had been born a scandal and raised as a spare. That he spent his nights poring over books, and was hopelessly in love with his court wizard.

He held the sword of the one true king in one hand, and the future of Camelot in the other.

And nothing would ever be the same again.

Chapter 57

"Your Highness," Lord Agravaine said, laying a hand on Arthur's shoulder. "It's been a long day. You should rest."

Arthur was about to protest that there was so much more to do. The duke's men were locked in the dungeons. Anyone with medical skill or healing salve had seen to the wounded, and most bloodstains had been removed from the castle. Maddoc had been found hiding in the hedge maze, and plates of food had been distributed from the kitchens.

But that barely scratched the surface of all he had to contend with. The enormity of what had happened was daunting, and the matters that required his attention seemed never-ending.

The good people of Camelot had expected to celebrate a royal wedding: instead they were mourning the loss of their king.

Lord Agravaine was right. There was nothing more they could hope to accomplish that night.

So, instead of exhausting himself beyond the point of reason, Arthur merely nodded at Lord Agravaine's suggestion of sleep. "I will," he promised. "As should you."

The advisor bowed.

"I would ask a favor of you," Arthur went on. "Can you arrange a council meeting for tomorrow morning?"

"Consider it done," said Lord Agravaine.

Arthur gave the man a nod of thanks. "I will want some additions. Lancelot, Percival, Tristan, Gawain, Emry, Emmett, and Guinevere will join us."

Lord Agravaine gave Arthur a long look, and then nodded. "It will be a tight fit in the usual chambers."

"Then we shall meet in the library," Arthur said. "Until more permanent arrangements can be made."

"I shall let everyone know." Lord Agravaine bowed once more.

"Thank you." Arthur offered him a tired smile, and the man nodded back.

Arthur was halfway up the staircase before he realized a retinue of guards were following him. "Can I help you?" he asked, turning.

"We're the king's guards, sir," one of them explained.

"Right," Arthur said politely. And then he realized what they meant. "Oh. Um."

He sighed. And then he squared his shoulders. "Very well. Which of you have been on duty the longest?"

Two weary-looking guards bowed.

"You're dismissed for the night," Arthur said. "Get some rest. And stop by the kitchens on your way, if you've missed your supper. The castle kitchens, not the guards' mess."

The guards exchanged a look of surprise and bowed again. "Yes, sir," they said eagerly.

Once the guards were handled, Arthur closed himself inside his bedroom and slumped back against the door. He felt drained. Numb. As though he barely had the energy to undress and climb into bed.

He tugged open the neck of his tunic, shrugged out of his jacket, and kicked off his boots.

And then he saw the flower petals strewn across his bed and gave a hollow laugh.

It was supposed to be his wedding night. He had forgotten.

He slouched down in the battered chair by the fireplace and put his head in his hands.

A door opened, and Arthur looked up in annoyance. "Yes?" he snapped.

"I see Your Majesty has already undressed," Lucan said, gingerly retrieving the jacket.

"Please don't," Arthur said tiredly.

"But it will crease," Lucan argued.

"I didn't mean the jacket. I meant the—just, not yet."

"As you wish," said the valet.

Emry stood in the doorway of the wizard's workshop, blinking back tears. The tower looked as it always had, with its fragrant bundles of herbs hanging from the ceiling in the morning light.

Yet there was a stillness to the space that made her feel as if she were entering a church, or perhaps a tomb.

"Morning," the gargoyle called. "Where's the old wizard?"

Emry swallowed thickly. "Gone."

"Oh." The gargoyle considered this. "I believe I am depressed," it announced stiffly.

Emry gave it a small smile. "That makes two of us."

And then she heard footsteps on the stairs. It was Emmett, clutching two mugs of coffee. He was dressed in his courtier's finery, and when he handed her a mug, a silver wedding ring glinted on his hand.

"Thanks," she said, taking a sip.

"Figured it was the least I could do, as your apprentice," he said sourly.

Emry let out a surprised laugh, then wished she hadn't. Her heart twisted with guilt that she was able to laugh at a time like this.

Her brother scowled. "It's not funny."

"Sorry," she apologized. "I honestly hadn't realized. Can I call you my assistant? Is that better?"

Emmett's scowl turned to a grimace. "I'd rather you not. Especially since I don't mean to stay."

Emry frowned, motioning for him to join her at the battered wooden table. "What do you mean?"

"Guin and I are bound for Avalon. I doubt we'll return before February. And when we do, well . . ." He trailed off with an embarrassed shrug. "Being the court wizard was always your thing, not mine."

"Then what are you going to do?" Emry asked curiously. When she saw the look of panic on her brother's face, she realized that he didn't know. Emry thought about the way her brother was always trying to overhear news at taverns, and how he and Tristan had organized the knights of the round table, to defend the castle in secret. How it wasn't just a group of commoners, but nobles and squires as well. How all of them seemed to be comfortable around Emmett, and how easily he was able to blend in with the lads of the theater troupe back home, as well as the young courtiers.

"Actually, I have an idea," she said.

Emmett smirked, lowering his mug of coffee. "This is going to be good."

"You should spy for Camelot," she said. "After all, you're a natural at skulking around taverns and getting people to talk to you. Plus, magic is an excellent ability for a spy."

Emmett considered it, and then he grinned. "That actually sounds badass."

"Talk to Lord Agravaine," she said, pleased that her brother actually seemed excited about doing something useful.

After Emmett left, Emry spent the rest of the morning taking inventory of the wizard's supply closet. They would need more healing salve. Tristan had brought the last of it to the royal infirmary. And she'd need to speak with the castle falconer about all the canaries. She had no idea what to do with them, and they were making a racket in their cages.

"I can't do this," she whispered, resting her head on the cool leather surface of Master Ambrosius's desk.

She had dreamed of being Arthur's court wizard, but she hadn't thought it would be like this.

Arthur! She had nearly forgotten.

She ran to the window and leaned out, straining to see the display on the clock tower. "Sard," she muttered. The council meeting started in five minutes. And she was wearing a plain wool kirtle, with a dusty scarf covering her hair.

There was no helping it, she thought despairingly. And then she realized that actually, there was.

She smoothed her hands over her bodice, and the fabric changed from drab wool to black silk embroidered with tiny stars and moons. The sleeves lengthened, and the neckline dipped, and fabric swished as it lowered from her ankles to the tops of her boots. She tore the scarf from her hair, and reached for her wand, tucking it into her sleeve.

"Where are you going?" the gargoyle called petulantly.

"The library," Emry snapped.

"Aren't you a little dressed up for the library?" the creature asked. "Unless, are you going to see your prince? Is that why you've made your dress all swishy?"

"It's none of your business," Emry replied. "And anyway, he's not a prince. He's a king."

Arthur hurried toward the library, smoothing his nerves and the stiff black fabric of his jacket. The last time he had worn it was two years ago, in mourning for his mother.

Lucan had dug it out of the back of his wardrobe, and Arthur's throat had gone tight at the sight of it, and the difficult memories it conjured.

He had known loss before, but he wasn't prepared for this. For everyone to look to him in his grief and mourning, and to have to suddenly take on the responsibilities of the father he'd lost.

His father's guards followed behind him, his own guards now. He couldn't count how many times he had pushed past them into his father's chambers, had been humiliated or scolded in their presence, and yet they gave no indication that they remembered any of it.

He was late. He had been late to everything all morning. There was so much to do, and all of it was new to him. He had a dungeon full of prisoners, and a castle guard with no captain, and an infirmary being staffed by Bruwin's overwhelmed apprentice, who had burst into tears when he'd run out of healing salve and learned it would take Emry weeks to make more.

Arthur had spent half an hour he didn't have showing the lad which herbs and infusions to use instead.

And then he'd realized he had forgotten his circlet, and had doubled back to his rooms, only to wind up late to a meeting with the King of Cameliard, which of course meant he was running late for his first council meeting.

Lord Agravaine, also dressed in black, was waiting for him outside the double doors, with the Pendragon crest pinned above his heart. "Did King Leodegrance sign the peace treaty?" he asked.

Arthur nodded. "He did, although it took some reassurance. Is everyone here?"

"They are," said Lord Agravaine. "Before you go in, I have a few pieces of private business."

Arthur motioned for the man to go ahead.

"I've made your father's funeral arrangements," Lord Agravaine said. "The ceremony will occur in two days."

Arthur nodded, not trusting himself to speak without his voice cracking.

"And then there's the matter of your coronation, and the coronation ball," Lord Agravaine went on, and Arthur felt an overwhelming sense of panic. "I believe we should announce the date well in advance."

"That's fine," Arthur said. "It's—it's all fine."

Lord Agravaine rested a hand on his shoulder, and Arthur knew the man meant it to be encouraging, but all he could think about was how his father had never once wished to encourage him, until those last few minutes . . . sard, he was shaking. And Lord Agravaine could tell.

"Should anyone question the additions to your council, I will stand behind you," Lord Agravaine promised.

Arthur nodded. "Thank you. I know this is going to be rough for a while, and I'll probably get some things wrong, but you have more than earned your place as my seneschal."

Lord Agravaine bowed, and then he opened the doors.

A long table had been moved into the center of the space, its chairs taken by many familiar faces. All of them stood when Arthur entered, and as he joined them, he thought sadly that no one would ever mistake him for a librarian again.

"Thank you all for waiting," Arthur said. He took off his jacket and rolled up his sleeves. "Now, let's get started."

When the council meeting was over, Arthur felt drained, but hopeful. He looked around the room, at everyone who was there to help him run this kingdom, and he thought that, perhaps, his words yesterday about a golden age hadn't been spoken in haste.

And then he caught sight of his wizard. She wore a dress sparkling with stars, and her hair in a messy braid, and she was laughing at something Gawain had said.

Arthur noticed sourly that his cousin looked excellent in black. Emry noticed him staring, and came over to join him.

"So," Arthur said, "how was I?"

Emry rolled her eyes. "Annoyingly good at it. Just as I suspected."

Arthur looked pleased. "Is that a fact, wizard?"

"It was a smart idea to repurpose Castle Cornwall as a training facility," she said.

"And an even better one to send Brannor to run it," put in Lance, joining them.

Arthur shrugged. "I figured he could use some excitement. And I'm pretty sure he'd murder me in my sleep after a few hours listening to Tristan blather on."

Emry laughed. "He really doesn't shut up. Are you sure you want him as a royal guard?"

"As opposed to what? My master of the privy?" Arthur asked with a self-deprecating grin.

Emry choked, and Lance laughed aloud, drawing some curious looks in their direction.

"See, I *knew* you were going to have one," Lance returned. His eyes lit on Emry's dress, and he grinned. "This is lovely."

"I only wore it so you could tell me and Emmett apart," she returned.

"Perhaps he should be my master of the privy," Arthur said thoughtfully.

"I take back everything I said," Emry told him. "You're a terrible king, and I wish to have a refund."

"No refunds. Besides, now that you've accepted the position of court wizard, what am I to do with your brother?"

"Wish him and Guinevere a lovely honeymoon in Avalon?" she suggested.

"That's right." Arthur shook his head in disbelief. "When are they leaving?"

"Tomorrow," Guin said, joining them. "Providing my position on your council will be held until my return."

"It will," Arthur confirmed. "And I'm lending you a carriage, for the journey to Avalon. You really shouldn't be riding in—"

Guin cleared her throat in warning.

"—this unpredictable fall weather?" Emry supplied.

"I was going to say a dress," Arthur muttered, trying to save himself from the misstep. Nobody looked as though they believed it. He wondered if they would let it drop, what with his being the King of Camelot.

"You are such a liar," Guin accused. "You're even turning pink."

"Extremely pink," Emry agreed. "A very fashionable color this season, I'm told."

"Next he's going to run a hand through his hair in anguish," Lance put in.

"Nice try," Arthur said. "I know I'm wearing a circlet."

"Are you, though?" Emry asked, flicking her fingers. Her mouth tipping into a grin as the crown rose to hover above Arthur's head. It rotated slowly, before floating off to find someone to torment.

Gawain, who was deep in conversation with his father, looked horrified as the thing nudged him insistently in the shoulder.

"You're the worst," Arthur accused. "All of you."

"Of course we are," Emry said fondly. "What did you expect?"

That night, there was a commotion outside Arthur's door. He held back a groan, wondering what it was this time.

"Come on, Brannor," a familiar voice complained. "Tell them they're being ridiculous."

Arthur poked his head out, and the coterie of guards snapped to attention. "Is there a problem?" he asked mildly.

The guard with the sausagey mustache, whose name Arthur kept forgetting, gestured toward a scowling wizard.

"Says she doesn't need an invitation, and to let her in."

"Better do as she says," Arthur said gravely. "Or else she might turn your balls into cabbages."

The reaction was a stony, horrified silence. Except for Emry, who grinned as though she rather liked the idea.

"I'd turn them back eventually," she promised, still grinning as she followed Arthur inside.

"Sorry about them," he apologized.

"They better not be permanent," Emry said, "or else I'll have to magic myself invisible to get past."

"Can you do that?" Arthur asked curiously.

"I've never tried," Emry said with a wave of her hand. "But how hard can it be?"

Arthur leaned back against the doors of his wardrobe, wondering why she had come, and thinking that she looked beautiful in the candlelight. "You'll have to show me when you've mastered it."

"Or not show you," Emry corrected.

"Touché," Arthur said. He bit his lip before adding, "I was hoping you'd come."

The line came out more forward than he'd intended, but too late to take it back now.

"Yet you left your guards no instructions to let me in if I did," she teased.

"A mistake that won't happen again, I assure you," Arthur promised. "Actually, I'm glad you're here. There's something I wanted to ask you."

"Yes, I'll come to the pub with you and Lance," she said, rolling her eyes, "But only if you wear a horrible fake mustache and we get to call you Gilbert."

Arthur pressed back a grin at the thought. "That wasn't what I was going to ask," he said, his eyes meeting hers. They stared at each other for a long moment, both weary and overwhelmed and grieving, and a long way from the night in the brothel.

"I know," Emry said. She swallowed nervously, her hands twisting the dark fabric of her skirts. "It's just—can whatever you were going to ask me wait? And in the meantime we can just . . . do our thing?"

"Our thing?"

"You know." Emry sighed, clearly hating that she had to say it. "Kiss and make fun of each other."

Arthur laughed, relieved. "That's fine."

"'That's fine'?" she echoed with an incredulous laugh of her own. "Weren't you going to ask me to marry you?"

Arthur choked. "Of course not! I'm only nineteen! I have no desire to be married."

Emry seemed relieved as well. "Good, because neither do I." She frowned, considering. "Then what were you going to ask me when you got all serious a moment ago?"

Arthur's cheeks went pink. "I was wondering if you'd be my date to the coronation ball."

"That's nearly as bad!"

"Hardly," Arthur argued. "It's one night of dancing, and we'd sit next to each other at supper."

"Why are you asking me now? I thought it wasn't for a while."

Arthur shrugged. Just knowing she'd be by his side on the most nerve-racking day of his life would make it seem less daunting, but he didn't know how to explain that. "Well, I figured if I already have a date, Lord Agravaine can't scheme to invite a bunch of eligible princesses," he said lamely.

"So, it would be a favor," Emry said, grinning. "You're asking for a favor."

"The Lady of the Lake did say that I'd be a great king with you by my side," he reminded her.

"Fine, I'll consider it," Emry said. "but you'll owe me."

"I already made you my court wizard!"

"Your only other option was Emmett," Emry pointed out.

"I took you to France!"

"Actually, I believe the records will show that *I* took *you* to France," Emry said.

"Fine then, I let you come to my bachelor party."

"That doesn't count! You didn't actually get married."

Arthur grinned. "I know."

Chapter 58

Morgana had thought it would be easier a second time, stepping between worlds, but in fact, it was worse. The shock shuddered through her in reverse, as though she was traveling backward through nothingness.

Her vision swam, and she reached for a stone pillar to steady herself. She gasped as her magic rushed back to greet her, and then she smiled, savoring the power that once again waited at her fingertips. She flicked her wrist, smoothing the stains and rips from her clothing. This was who she was, not that broken, starving thing she had been back in Anwen, powerless and desperate enough to agree to a bargain she didn't understand.

She was a queen. A sorceress.

She glanced nervously back at the doorway, worried Bellicent would step through before Merlin could close it.

The wizard looked awful, bracing his hands.

"Close it," she hissed.

"*Anoishe ta porta,*" he muttered, staggering toward the stones, his palm outstretched.

Morgana watched, barely able to breathe, as the glow rippled and faded.

They were safe.

She had made it back to her own world, where her own magic sang sweetly through her veins. And away from that horrible sorceress who spoke through borrowed corpses, crept inside her mind, and made her a prisoner in her own body.

"That certainly was a rough journey," Merlin said grimly.

"I didn't notice," Morgana lied.

Merlin had gone gray, and she hoped he wouldn't faint, because the last thing she wanted was to play nursemaid.

And then she realized—she didn't have to. She didn't need anything from anyone anymore.

"Eight years," Merlin said softly, staring at the forest with wonder. "Or has it been more?"

More? Morgana took in the crisp fallen leaves on the ground and shivered at the chill in the air.

They were definitely in Avalon, and it was evening, the shadows of the trees stretching to impossible lengths. But *when* was it? Not summer anymore, clearly. She didn't know whether she had been gone for a day or a year.

"What have you done?" A familiar figure stepped from the forest, with dark hair and fog-filled eyes.

She hadn't heard the Lady of the Lake coming, but then, she never did.

"My Lady," said Merlin, sinking to one knee.

Nimue held up a lantern, quietly furious. It was uncanny how similar she and Bellicent looked.

"I warned you not to travel through the stones, child of Igraine," the Lady of the Lake said. "Yet you did not listen!"

"I am not a child!" Morgana snapped. "I don't have to listen to you!"

"You should have," said the Lady of the Lake. "Now it is too late, and you have fouled the rightful course of history with your selfish meddling."

Morgana scoffed. "I don't need a lecture. Especially not from *Bellicent's sister.*"

"That's no way to speak to the Lady of the Lake," Merlin scolded.

The Lady held up a hand, asking for his silence. "I am not insulted to be called what I am," she said. "Nor should you be, child of Igraine."

"Stop it!" Morgana hissed. "Stop acting as if nothing I've accomplished matters more than my birth!"

A sudden gust of wind picked up, and the sky seemed to go dark all at once. Nimue's hair whipped back from her face. Her eyes went entirely white, and when she spoke, her voice seemed to echo through the forest. "It is not what you have accomplished that interests me, but what you will do next. You may still fix what you have ruined. It is not over yet." The Lady blinked, and the strange breeze stilled. "There is a boat at the dock," she said. "Take it and go."

"Fine," Morgana snapped. "I don't need you. I don't need either of you!"

"Mor—" Merlin began in protest.

"Let her choose her fate, as you chose yours," said the Lady of the Lake.

Morgana didn't stick around to hear her old tutor's response.

She stumbled into the forest without so much as a glance back at the stones. Avalon's strange magic pressed at her, like the magic had done in the cave, and she gave it a tentative pull. "*Callis*," she demanded, and the very forest itself pulled back to reveal a narrow dirt path.

In Anwen, the forest had nearly beaten her, but here, she could bend its trees to her will with a mere word. The ill-gotten magic throbbed within her, but she did not stop. She reached for more of it, drinking it in greedily. The trees lining her dirt path shuddered and swayed. A root snapped up with a sound unnervingly like a scream.

Morgana grabbed as much magic as she could hold, and then she stumbled into the boat that waited on the dock.

But the boat didn't move.

No.

"Come on!" she snarled, yet the boat remained suddenly still. And somehow, she knew what she had to do. She let go of a handful of the magic she'd taken, and the boat gently pushed off the dock. Then it stopped.

She released more of the magic, and the boat drifted a few more feet into the lake.

Morgana screamed, letting go of everything she had taken.

There is still more, the mist seemed to whisper.

She shook her head, unwilling. She had taken magic from this island before, and the boat had let her pass. She could still feel that magic deep within her, the hard-gotten power she had held close for so long.

She couldn't be without it. She couldn't return home less powerful than when she had gone. But the boat sat still in the lake, waiting, and if she had another choice, she didn't know it.

You have an enchantment that defeats death, she reminded herself. *You are still the most powerful sorceress of this world.*

Except she wasn't. Yurien had taken the enchantment for safekeeping, the way men took everything that sparked their desire and made them feel important. And Merlin's daughter, that wretched girl, could open a doorway between worlds.

A sorceress worth her magic, Bellicent had called her. Morgana sneered at the unpleasant memory.

"Take it," she snapped, grudgingly letting go of the last bit of Avalon's magic.

The boat gave a smug lurch, and shot out into the lake, toward home.

It took another week of hard travel for Morgana to reach the fortress of Dunlothian. And when the royal keep came into view, high on its hilltop, a smile rose to her lips.

Home. She was home.

She would be greeted as a queen.

She would see her son.

She would endure her husband.

What did it matter that her journey through the stones had yielded nothing? Now she could finally put thoughts of Anwen aside. Now she would get her revenge on King Uther. She would kill the man who had coveted her mother, who had flung her away as a helpless child, who had orchestrated her misery out of greed and selfishness.

His kingdom would be hers. Camelot would fall, and everyone would see her for who she truly was. A queen. A sorceress. A woman to be respected and feared.

Her horse was lathered with sweat, but she spurred it on toward the castle.

As she approached the gates, her arms jerked suddenly back on her reins. The horse reared, neighing in protest.

She gasped as someone's will slammed into her own, spreading through, bending it back, until she was falling through the depths of her own mind, helpless and afraid.

She felt her hands let go of the reins. She slid backward in the saddle, scrambling to grab on to anything that would save her, but it was too late.

She tumbled from the horse, unable to brace herself before she hit the ground. Because she wasn't in control. And her throat went dry when she realized who was.

You believed you had escaped me? whispered a familiar voice.

No. It couldn't be. Morgana lay on her back, staring up at the fortress, her vision spotting around the edges. The back of her head was sticky and wet, her ankle throbbed, and she struggled to catch her breath.

Dimly, she heard shouting. Two guards approached, peering down at her.

"It's the queen!" one of them shouted.

"Come quickly! She's injured!"

Morgana rolled weakly onto her side, trying to sit up. This wasn't the triumphant return she had imagined, or even the quiet one she had made peace with.

Even a world away, you can't escape me, Bellicent crooned.

"But you let me go," Morgana whispered. "You didn't follow."

Of course I did. Bellicent's laugh rang hollow. *You said I could come with you. And here I am.*

Acknowledgments

When I was younger, I used to dream of leaving my unremarkable life behind to live in a castle, learn magic, and have thrilling adventures. But those things never happened to girls like me, not even in stories. At least, not in the stories I read.

Then, I realized I could write my own stories. Not just for myself, but for everyone out there who felt the same. (Game. Changer.)

This book series is for us. For the smart, lonely outsiders. For the queer kids who have known for a while and for those still figuring things out. For the girls who were told they were too much and the boys who never felt they were enough. Thank you for joining me on this adventure and for putting up with my jokes. (I hope some of them made you laugh? OH GOD, PLEASE TELL ME YOU LAUGHED AT LEAST ONCE???)

Before you go back to scrolling TikTok or writing this book a glowing online review (which you were totally going to do, right?), I hope you'll stick around for one last page where I thank all the incredible people who have helped bring this book series to life.

First, to my agent, Barbara Poelle, who pulled this story from the slush pile and became its fiercest champion. Thank you for being the advocate this book series needed and for encouraging me to tell the stories I'm most passionate about.

Next, to my editor, Jenny Bak, for seeing straight to the heart of this book and for understanding exactly what it needed to shine. This story is so much stronger because of your input and guidance. Also, I can't thank you enough for the time and care you spent helping this series find its perfect cover.

To the entire fabulous Viking team, for your enthusiasm and expertise, with particular gratitude to Lizzie Goodell, Felicity Vallence, Krista Ahlberg, Alicia Lea, and Tony Sahara.

Thank you to my mother, who has bravely read all of my stories, from handwritten things with misspelled titles to early drafts of my novels. And to Daniel, for traipsing through France with me in the December cold and not complaining when I filled our days with endless visits to obscure medieval castles, museums, and gardens instead of, like, boat tours where they serve champagne.

Thank you to my family, friends, and writing community for always cheering me on and always being there for an adventure, a phone call, or a hug. Special thanks to Amy Spalding and Christine Riccio, my local author friends in the trenches, for always being a text away.

My deepest gratitude to every bookseller and librarian who has kept my titles on their shelves for this long, and to the YA authors whose work is paving the way for more stories of queer joy.

Thank you also to the BookTok community, for discovering and championing this book to so many wonderful, enthusiastic readers.

Lastly, thank you to my readers, both the loyal and the new, for your support. My books truly wouldn't exist without you. Let's meet back here in a year for the thrilling conclusion to this series. Deal? Deal.